The Lion of Macedonia

The Lion of Macedonia

John McLeod

Copyright © 2005 by John McLeod.

ISBN :		Softcover		1-4134-8549-9

All rights reserved. No part of this book may be reproduced or transmitted in any form or by any means, electronic or mechanical, including photocopying, recording, or by any information storage and retrieval system, without permission in writing from the copyright owner.

This book was printed in the United States of America.

To order additional copies of this book, contact:
Xlibris Corporation
1-888-795-4274
www.Xlibris.com
Orders@Xlibris.com
27559

CONTENTS

Chapter One : The Festival of the Mysteries 9

Chapter Two : Three Victories 25

Chapter Three : The Treasury 39

Chapter Four : Quizzing the Persians 53

Chapter Five : Manhood 68

Chapter Six : The Peace of Philocrates 84

Chapter Seven : Ox-Head 96

Chapter Eight : The Gardens of Midas 120

Chapter Nine : Rivals 144

Chapter Ten : Arete 163

Chapter Eleven : End of the Idyll 178

Chapter Twelve : The Valley of the Strymon 193

Chapter Thirteen : Sacred War 210

Chapter Fourteen : The Land of the Agrianes 236

Chapter Fifteen : The Pixadorus Affair 252

Chapter Sixteen : A Wedding at Aegae 265

Chapter Seventeen : Hegemon of the League 292

Chapter Eighteen : Pothos.. 305

Chapter Nineteen : The Lion of Macedonia 331

To Jen: without your constant encouragement and support I'd have given up long ago.

Chapter One

The Festival of the Mysteries

The men of Greece assembled on the plain of Troy, flanking the cortege that carried the body of Achilles. King Agamemnon led the procession, his differences with the hero finally forgotten. Odysseus and Ajax followed close behind, already arguing as to which of them should receive the holy armor of their fallen idol. They fell silent as the body was laid on the pyre and the torchbearers lit the kindling, and then raised their hands in supplication as the king led the lament.

"Noble Achilles, son of Peleus and the divine Thetis; we mourn your loss. We hang our heads in despair, for will we ever breach the walls of this accursed city without you at our side. Never has the world seen such a man as you; will the world ever see your like again?"

Agamemnon watched the flames consume the body. Smoke stung his eyes and dried his throat, and he turned away from the blazing pyre. One by one, the men of Greece followed him back to camp and the endless war.

The Isle of Samothrace floated on the horizon, barely visible against the glare from the sea. The two ships altered course as it came into view, the trading vessel with its human cargo retching bile across its deck, and the sleek new war galley with a phallic prow and yellow awning rigged up at the stern.

King Philip grinned from the shade of the awning as his ship sped past the little coaster, making it roll further as it became caught in the wake of the faster vessel. He called over to the tallest of the three men standing across the deck from him. "So, Parmenion, do you still think we should have traveled with the others?"

The general turned toward him and smiled. "No, you were right. You knew best, as always." He glanced at his companions, who nodded in wry agreement.

Aristander, the king's personal fortune-teller, spoke. "It's just that we thought you might seem aloof if you traveled separately, sir. There are many new faces at court this year and it would be wise to win their respect. Sailing with them would have been a good opportunity."

"That's true." The king shifted position in his chair and beckoned to a slave for more wine; he'd been drinking since they'd left the mainland. "And it's of no consequence. They are still too new and eager to impress to be a threat, so I have plenty of time yet to win them over. Let them be sick as dogs while we travel in comfort."

Parmenion smiled and stood studying the figure sprawled in the collapsible, high-backed chair that served as the king's throne on campaign. Philip stared back at him, a smirk on his lips. He could guess what Parmenion was thinking, what they always thought. How had he managed it? Just two years ago, he had been a shaky pretender to the crown of a split and occupied country. In that time, he had disposed of his rivals, expelled the invaders, and, most importantly, had pacified the hill tribes to create a united Macedonia. Even Parmenion himself, a chieftain of Pelagonia, had surrendered his independence to follow Philip.

The king pulled himself to his feet and ambled over to the ship's side. "You're giving me that look again, Parmenion," he chided, then swirled the wine around his two-handled drinking cup and made a show of hurling it into the sea. "Poseidon! Accept my humble offering!" He spun around, swaying slightly, and grinned at his three companions. They dutifully smiled.

There was an awkward silence in the wake of Philip's drunken outburst. He let his attention drift toward the island, and was content to listen to the flapping of the wind in the sails for a while. Samothrace was closer now, the high peak of Mount Fengari thrusting skyward from its center.

Aristander gestured toward the mountain. "The islanders call it the Mountain of the Moon. They say Poseidon used it as a seat to watch the great siege of Troy."

The discomfiture of his friends had sobered Philip and he was grateful someone had broken the silence at last. He turned to face them.

"There's something troubling you, gentlemen. What is it? Tell me."

The men looked at each other, and then Parmenion spoke for the trio. "Why are we here, Philip? Why do you feel the need to become an initiate of the mysteries? Surely your success so far shows that the gods, why, Zeus himself, must smile upon you." He jerked his head in the direction of the island. "Why do you need the support of these demons?"

The eldest of the three butted in. "Philip, your kingdom is not yet secure. Your enemies line your borders and harbor your surviving brothers. They could use this cult against you." The most senior general in the army, he wore the yellow cloak of the Companion cavalry over his tunic.

Philip directed his answer at the older man. "Antipatros, my friend. The cult of the mysteries is not evil. The reverse, in fact, for is it not associated with Dionysus himself?" He gave each of the three men a long stare. "No, do not worry, my friends. I would never have set foot outside Macedonia unless I'd thought it through first, and certainly not with such a small force."

"You still haven't told us why." Parmenion again gestured toward the island. "What use can the mysteries be to you?"

The king laughed. "Think, Parmenion. Dionysus is already popular with my troops, but even more so with the women of Macedonia. And don't we all have wives and mothers? To embrace his cult will bring approval from all corners, and for that alone this trip is worth it." Out of the corner of his eye, he saw that Antipatros was nodding in agreement. Philip grinned in triumph, enjoying this demonstration of the superiority of his reasoning. This was why he was king, not they.

"And the main reason?" He raised an eyebrow. "Well, who pose my greatest threat? My brothers are either dead or in hiding. As for the Dardanians and the other tribes to the north, I have already beaten them and they live in fear of me now." Philip gripped the ship's rigging and stared at the island. "From now on, my enemies lie to the south." He turned back to face them. "And that means Athens, gentlemen, and the Athenian fleet. My small navy cannot hope to match them, but the gods of Samothrace offer protection from shipwreck." He gave them a sly grin. "And, perhaps, will inflict it on the enemies of their most devoted, or should I say generous, followers."

The three men shot each other bemused glances, and then looked back at the king. Philip had a broad smirk on his face, his eyes dodging from man to man. One after the other they began to laugh.

The island of Samothrace was alive. Thousands had arrived for the Festival of the Mysteries and the streets of the tiny port were choked with people, while an army of tents stood pitched among the wooded slopes above, stretching all the way to the sanctuary farther along the coast.

Philip established his camp in a clearing just outside the town. A prime site, his sailors swiftly evicted the clan of Cypriot fishermen who had already claimed it, and prepared the ground for the giant tent that accompanied the king on campaign. This was an impressive pavilion, consisting of two halves separated by a central hallway. One half was a large chamber, where the king held his councils of war with his generals. Beyond that, watched over and maintained by the king's personal stewards, the second half contained his own sleeping quarters.

Philip settled himself on a convenient tree stump, ordered more wine, and passed the time until his lodgings were ready by teasing his bedraggled courtiers as they trudged up the path from the harbor.

The tent erected, his stewards began moving in the trappings of comfort that the king liked to have with him in the field: a large wooden cot, a Persian rug, a metal bath, and a full-length mirror of burnished copper.

And then it was ready for Philip. He retired to bathe, tended to by his stewards. These men, nobles themselves, dressed him in the robes of an initiate of the mysteries. He was supposed to be fasting in preparation for the ceremony, but he wanted food, so they fed him and gave him more wine.

He emerged as the sun's light began to fade. His courtiers stood waiting for him, also dressed in initiate robes. They, too, had been drinking, but few could match Philip. He greeted them jovially, slurring his words and waving at a large party of sightseers, who had gathered as word spread that the King of Macedonia was on the island. A detail from the Companion cavalry kept them well outside the campsite.

They processed out of the camp and made their way toward the sanctuary, the Macedonian contingent forcing others off the narrow track and into the forests of oak and plane trees that covered the island. All carried a flaming torch, except Philip, who by now could barely stand. Parmenion and Antipatros each supported an arm.

Two bulls had been sacrificed at an altar just inside the entrance to the sanctuary, and their butchered carcasses bubbled in a vast cauldron, stirred at regular intervals by a slave. A second slave fished out the boiled meat and set it down on a slab, where priests cut slivers from the joints and fed them to the initiates as they filed in. This was the first part of the ceremony and symbolized the feasting of the Titans on the body of the baby Dionysus. Next, they would be cleansed of their sins before being reborn into the cult, as Dionysus had been reborn of Zeus.

Philip demanded more meat from the priests.

"I'm hungry," he told their stunned faces. "I've been fasting all day and that morsel you've given me isn't enough." Ox fat was plastered to his beard and he wiped his greasy fingers on his initiate's robes. Parmenion gently tugged on his arm and pulled him toward the Anaktoron, the Hall of the Lords, for purification.

The hall was filled with people, the air heavy with the scent of incense and the sweet smell of fresh sweat. Philip was swiftly sick down the back of the initiate standing in front of him. In his drunken haze he remembered little of the ceremony that followed: ritual washing from huge wooden tubs, the hall resonating with the chant of a thousand voices, his eyes smarting from the smoke of the torches, a priest dabbing sacred water on his chest and forehead. And then there was the argument with another initiate, abruptly ended when the Macedonians drew knives from beneath the folds of their robes. On their way out, they collected the parchments that attested to the fact they had completed the Myesis, their baptism into the cult. Aristander took Philip's for safekeeping.

Then they were outside again, stumbling through the darkness toward another building. The breeze off the sea revived Philip and he breathed in a lungful of the cool night air.

They reached the Hieron, the huge rectangular temple where the Epoptia, a higher initiation ceremony, took place. Against Aristander's advice, Philip had insisted they complete both stages in one go; he had no wish to make a return journey to the island.

A priest barred their way. Standing beneath a flaming torch and flanked by sacred stones, he demanded they confess their sins, that they might receive absolution. Philip stared at the man in bemusement, then sneered in his face.

"Confess—to what? I am a king. Whatever I do, I do because it's necessary for my country. I have nothing to confess to you. Let me pass."

Aristander intervened. It took several minutes of earnest discussion, and the knowledge that the Macedonians were armed, before the priest agreed to allow Philip through. He grudgingly absolved the monarch of whatever sins he may have committed in the name of the throne, and then blanched as he heard confession from first Parmenion, then Antipatros. He waved through the rest of the party, and sent a slave to bring him wine.

The Hieron was still unfinished, its walls and ceiling complete while the inner fixtures waited further funding. Rows of wooden benches lined both of the longest walls in place of the stone seating that would one day accommodate spectators.

At the far end stood the altar, in front of a huge painted statue of Dionysus. The god gazed down on his priests as they performed the rebirthing ceremony on the crowds that milled around them. As each initiate was received into the cult, so he backed away and took his place on one of the benches to consume the sanctified wine the priests had given him. But it was the spectacle taking place in the open space in the middle of the temple that caught Philip's eye.

The floor was filled with dozens of nubile young dancers, many naked, some cavorting with snakes. Musicians walked among them, clashing cymbals and blowing discordant noises from horns and trumpets. A heavy bass drum banged out a beat from somewhere.

Philip had heard of the corybantic dancing that accompanied the ceremony, and his curiosity had played no small part in his decision to sail to Samothrace. He immediately headed toward the front row of benches, ordering his men to clear the scattering of initiates who already occupied these choice seats. He sat himself in the middle of the row, calling to the others to join him.

"I think, sir, that we are supposed to be reborn first," ventured Aristander, indicating the far end of the hall with his finger.

Philip glanced up the room. "You see to that. Leave the bodyguard and take the rest." He flung a grin at Parmenion and added, "Don't worry, Aristander. We'll save you a seat."

The exasperated seer gathered the Macedonian courtiers together and shepherded them toward the altar. Philip settled himself down, catching the anxious look on Parmenion's face as he and Antipatros took their places either side of him.

"No need to worry, Parmenion. I still have the bodyguard for my protection." The bodyguard filled the seats around them. These seven men accompanied the king everywhere. They were chosen for their loyalty and friendship, and only they could wear the purple cloak with yellow edging, the reverse of the cloaks worn by the Companion cavalry.

The dancers were becoming ever more frantic, winding snakes around their bodies ever more intimately. A piglet was released onto the stage and ran squealing as the dancers turned on it, grabbing at its legs, leaping on it. They caught the animal and it disappeared beneath a melee of frenzied women. They tore it limb from limb, young girls triumphantly emerging with a piece of the carcass or a sliver of bloody innards.

Philip gripped Parmenion's arm. "What do you think, Parmenion? Can you believe this?" His voice was thick with lust.

"I have seen this sort of thing before, among the women of the hill tribes. It's part of their worship of Dionysus." His voice betrayed his anxiety. These women achieved their trance-like state by imbibing wine mixed with ergot-infected barley and, under the influence of the fungus, were capable of ripping a man apart if he was fool enough to get in their way. The general took hold of a fold in Philip's robe.

One of the dancers had wandered in front of the Macedonians. She was a tall girl, about eighteen-years-old, and her long, dark hair was draped across her shoulders, limp with sweat. Blood from the pig smeared her body and she held a dead snake in her hands. Her eyes were glazed and her face shone with sweat and excitement. She wound the snake around her wrist and dangled its head below her navel, then thrust her hips, slapping her groin against the snake's head.

"All the gods!" breathed Philip. "Did you see that?" Parmenion said nothing, but shot a look at Antipatros when the older man hissed a word of caution.

The girl continued to gyrate her hips. In her hypnotic state, she was unaware of the group of men watching her from only a few paces away. Grunts and moans began issuing from this priestess of Dionysus, the Bacchae sounds that gave the god his other name.

Philip felt the lust in his loins and started to speak, but his mouth was too dry and it came out as a croak. "I must have her, Parmenion. I must!"

"Yes, my King."

"I will have her. Tonight!" He twisted around and beckoned to one of the bodyguards. "Cleitus, find out who she is and how much she'll cost." The man stood up, an uncertain look on his face. He spotted the Macedonian contingent among the crowd around the altar, and ran to find Aristander.

The girl crashed to the floor, almost at Philip's feet. She arched her back in ecstasy, and then slumped into a quivering ball. A slave ran over and splashed water on her face, then another arrived and they started to help her to her feet. Philip seized the opportunity and stood up.

"Stop!" Antipatros clamped a hand on his wrist. "Stay with your bodyguard. Besides, she's of no use to you in that state."

They persuaded him to return to the camp and wait for Aristander to bring the girl. Parmenion and Antipatros joined Philip in his private quarters and they drank in silence, Philip's head too full of the girl to talk. Parmenion stifled a yawn while Antipatros had his eyes closed, seemingly asleep.

It was two more hours before Aristander arrived. He stepped through the corridor from the outer chamber, but then hovered by the doorway. From the anxious look on his face, he did not have good news.

"Well?" Philip's tone was expressionless. He was tired. He'd been awake for hours and his excitement over the girl had quietly evaporated. He wasn't sorry to see that the seer was alone.

"I have news, sir," said Aristander hesitantly. "Her name is Myrtale. She is a princess of the royal house of Epirus, and the niece and ward of King Arybbas of that country. She is not to be had, sir, except in the wedding bed."

Philip gave Parmenion a weary look and rose from his couch. "Well, I have other wives," he said. "What's one more?" He smiled and lightly shook Antipatros' shoulder; the general woke with a start. "I'll bid good health to you all, gentlemen. I am going to bed." He turned to call in a steward.

"Do you think he means it?" Aristander whispered to Parmenion.

"Means what?" snorted Antipatros blearily.

Philip glanced around. "Of course I mean it, Aristander. They're a backward race and I doubt they'd be of much use in the field, but an alliance with Epirus would secure our right flank in any war with both Thebes and Athens. That alone makes it worth marrying this Epirote princess. And you saw her, boys." He thrust his hips and grinned, despite the stab of pain the movement caused across his temples.

"What!" Aristander was aghast. "Think of the consequences, sir. What if Thebes saw an alliance with Epirus as a threat?"

Parmenion interrupted. "We're all tired," he said, rising and walking to the entrance. "Let's discuss this in the morning."

"Discuss what?" barked Antipatros, as he rose and followed his companions through to the council chamber.

The Macedonians slept late that morning. When he awoke, Philip summoned Aristander, the seer arriving red-eyed and disheveled. The king sat in his private quarters, eating a late breakfast.

"Ah, Aristander," he said, gnawing at a chicken leg. "This girl. What more can you tell me?"

Aristander looked at him incredulously. "Surely you're not serious?" The king flashed him a look and the seer's shoulders crumpled. "Only what I told you last night, sir, and that she is here with her uncle, a man named Leonidas. I don't know anymore than that." He flopped onto a couch without waiting for the king's invitation; Philip ignored the gesture.

"Approach this man, this Leonidas." Philip swigged from his drinking cup and wiped a hand across his beard. "See what authority he has. Does he speak for the Epirote king? Does he speak for the girl? If you think he's worth my time, arrange a meeting." The seer sighed and began to rise from his seat. "And how many times do I have to tell you, Aristander? There is no need to address me formally. My friends call me Philip." The king grinned as the prissy holy man left the tent.

The meeting took place late that afternoon, after a day in which Aristander had seesawed between the two camps. The Epirotes had secured lodging in a house in the port, a cheap, shabby dwelling according to Aristander. Their party consisted only of Leonidas, Myrtale, a bodyguard and two slaves. To everyone's surprise, the girl accompanied her uncle to the meeting.

They were ushered into the king's tent, Myrtale's bodyguard standing alongside Philip's own men at the entrance. Two couches had been arranged at the far end, with a table laden with fruit, wine and sweetmeats placed between them. Philip greeted the Epirotes and took his place in the center of one couch, beckoning to the visitors to take the other. Parmenion and Aristander stood behind their king and a scribe sat on a stool nearby, ready to record details of any agreement.

Leonidas was a small, runty man, with sunburned arms and a bald, shiny head. He reminded Philip of the stallholders in the marketplace at Pella, the Macedonian capital.

Not that he cared. He only had eyes for Myrtale. By daylight, a large nose prevented her being either beautiful or plain, but neither was she ugly. Her hair was jet black, expertly arranged into a bun with a silver hairgrip in the shape of a snake. Unlike the pasty-faced women of Philip's court, her skin was tanned, as though she spent much of her time out of doors. Her eyes were a deep green, and smoldered with a fire that seemed to promise untold passion.

Philip made polite conversation with Leonidas for a few minutes, and then was stunned into silence as Myrtale leaned forward in her seat and said, "We know why we are here, sir."

Philip looked up at his advisers, his mouth gaping open in surprise. They looked down his throat, then at each other. Aristander was the first to speak.

"Perhaps, sir." He was speaking to Philip but directed his gaze toward Leonidas. "The gentleman could inform us as to his authority to speak on behalf of King Arybbas."

Leonidas glanced around at Myrtale; he looked a little flustered. Myrtale stared straight ahead.

"I am a princess of Epirus, sir, and I speak on my own behalf." She had a deep voice, almost like a man's.

Philip sat with a bemused smirk on his face, staring at the girl. She seemed even taller beside her uncle. "The girl has spirit!" he blurted inanely.

Myrtale's eyes sparked. "What do you want, sir?" She stared back at him, her green eyes boring into his. "Well, sir?"

Philip gave her a sly grin. "I think," he said, "that an alliance between Macedonia and Epirus would be beneficial to both our countries." He shot a glance at Leonidas. "Do you not agree, sir?"

The man agreed profusely, grateful that the king had decided not to leave him out of the discussion completely.

Philip spoke to the room. "In that case, this alliance would be best sealed with a marriage between our two houses." He winked at Myrtale before leaning forward and asking Leonidas, "Does the royal house of Epirus possess anyone suitable for such a marriage?"

Leonidas played the game. "Why, yes, sir, there is. My niece, Myrtale, is unwed."

"Can you speak for King Arybbas on that, sir?" Aristander interrupted.

Leonidas nodded. "Yes, I think so. The King bears no hostility toward Macedonia, and I'm sure would welcome an alliance if he were present."

Philip slapped his thigh. "Then it's settled." He turned around to announce to Parmenion, "I shall marry this Myrtale, and our children will unite our two countries in undying friendship."

"And may I be the first to offer my congratulations, sir."

"I have a question, sir." Aristander sounded grave. Philip scowled at him. "Is the lady free to marry? A royal princess of such an age would normally be married by now, or at least betrothed. This is not the case?"

Philip frowned; it was a valid point. It certainly was unusual for a girl of her age to not be married, and an explanation was merited.

Myrtale answered for herself again. "Sir." She spoke directly to Aristander. "My uncle, King Arybbas, has brought me many suitors, but knows better than to try and choose a husband for me." Leonidas nodded sagely.

"I'm free to choose my own man," she continued, "but none have been worthy of anything more than my contempt." She turned to stare into Philip's eyes. "Until now."

Philip smirked gleefully at Aristander. "Now it is settled," he said, and beckoned to the clerk in the corner. "Scribe, come closer and draw up the document of betrothal; this alliance is ready to be made legal." The clerk hurried over.

"But, sir!" cried Aristander. "What about the dowry? We've not discussed the dowry yet."

Leonidas looked nervous. Philip could expect a substantial endowment in return for the privileged position he was offering. "We are a poor country, sir," he began. Myrtale interrupted him once more. Her voice sounded contemptuous.

"Whatever grant your lawyers may negotiate with mine, sir, bear in mind that my lineage is my dowry. I am a princess of the Royal Molossian House of Epirus. Not only am I a descendant of Achilles, the hero of the Trojan War, but also of King Priam, the ruler of that noble city. And that ancestry, sir, will be passed on to any offspring I may produce."

Philip was impressed. The rest of Greece regarded the Macedonians as little more than crude and uncivilized northerners, and it was a prejudice he deeply resented. Proving his people were as good as the cultured Athenians had become an obsession, and Achilles was a truly Greek hero who would make a valuable addition to the pedigree of the Macedonian royal family. Furthermore, and this was his shrewd mind working, a dowry was returnable if a husband divorced his wife, but a dowry such as this could never be returned. It would benefit his descendants forever. He turned and looked at Aristander, interested to know what his opinion would be.

"Yes, I am aware of Princess Myrtale's heritage." The holy man would still not talk directly to a woman. "But many noble ladies can boast of equally renowned forebears, and have the wealth that should accompany such a lineage."

Philip faced forward again to see how Myrtale would reply, enjoying this exchange of wits.

But Myrtale sat in silence; a stern look on her face. Then she stared straight at Philip and spoke slowly. "I am sure, sir, that you would prefer to discuss my dowry in private. I have certain jewels that would be of interest to you." There was silence in the room. Parmenion and Aristander stood with open mouths, while Leonidas fidgeted uncomfortably.

But Philip's face had lit up like a child's. The girl had thrown caution aside and was appealing directly to his baser instincts, and it worked. He was stunned at how outrageous she was. She excited him more than any woman he'd known, and he'd known many. He turned to Parmenion. "I see our guest's cup is empty. Please see that it's refilled, my friend."

Parmenion was well trained. He gestured to a slave and Leonidas' barely touched drinking cup was filled to overflowing. The general walked over to sit next to him. "I hear your country is much like my own Macedonia," he said. "Is that true? Tell me about it."

Philip and Myrtale slipped through the vestibule and into his private quarters. The coupling that followed was fast and frantic, and Philip's stewards would joke about the scratches across his back for many days.

His lust sated, Philip fell asleep. He began to dream.

He saw himself in his palace at Pella. He was tiptoeing down a corridor toward a half-open bedroom door, from which issued the sound of groaning. He pressed his eye to the crack in the door and peered in. A gigantic bed took up almost the entire room, with Myrtale spread-eagled across it and a giant of a man towering over her. Philip recognized Zeus at once. The father of the gods stood by the side of the bed, the girl prone before him. A massive, hissing snake was uncoiling itself from between his legs, aiming unswervingly for her groin. The god seemed to sense Philip's watching eye and jerked his head up to stare at the door, a taunting leer on his face. Philip reeled back and fled, the god's mocking laughter echoing up the corridor behind him.

Myrtale woke with a start and took a moment to realize where she was. Philip was still asleep, but fitfully. His mumbling and trembling arm had woken her. She stared down at him, her fingers stroking his hair like he was a fretful child. She pondered the turn of events that had brought her here.

Tales of this young, handsome king had spread to Epirus. They told how he had fought to unite and strengthen his kingdom, and was now seizing land from beyond his own borders. Myrtale had watched him come ashore the day before, arriving on his own warship, a crowd gathering to watch the event, his men arrogantly clearing a path for him through that crowd. Here was a man in ascendancy, and as handsome as the stories had said. He was a young Zeus, well-muscled, tall and sleek, with tightly curled hair and beard, and a ribbon around his forehead.

So, she had been in the Hieron, dancing with the others in adulation of her god, when she'd seen the king in the front row, obviously enjoying the display. It had taken only moments to work her way over to where he sat. She thought her performance had failed, and then the Macedonian priest had appeared at their lodgings.

Now here she was, in the bed of the King of Macedonia. He seemed a bit of a buffoon but finally, a man with a position worthy of her. She smiled at the ease with which she'd seduced him. It had been a gamble, but put paid to the priest's arguments.

She planned her new life in the royal palace at Pella. She'd heard that it was huge, decorated by the finest artists and with mosaics laid in every room. To be queen of such a palace was all that she desired.

Philip's other wives would be a challenge, but they had only managed to produce one son between them thus far. Philip would choose the mother of his heir as his consort, and Myrtale had no doubt it would be her. The existing child was the king's current successor but, as a priestess of Dionysus, she knew enough about the fruits of the forest to discreetly dispose of any rival to her future sons. And that went for the holy man, too. She had won tonight but he could be a danger.

Myrtale smiled as the sound of Leonidas trying to sing drifted through from the main chamber. She wondered how late it was. Philip began to snore and she pushed his head off her stomach; he would not be welcome in her bed too often if he were going to make that noise. She drifted back to sleep.

She, too, began to dream.

In her dream, also, she was in bed. For her, the heavens parted and Zeus hurled a flaming thunderbolt at her defenseless, open body. It entered her belly, traveling to the farthest extremities of her fingers and toes. Then it erupted from her womb and spread across the face of the world, like an unstoppable tide. A smile curled the corners of her lips.

The two slept on; Philip tense and restless, Myrtale smug and content.

Chapter Two

Three Victories

"Well?" asked the king.

Philip of Acarnania shut the bedroom door before shaking his head. "I think the child will live," said the doctor, "but cannot say as to his competency." The two men walked up the corridor. "Sir, I must tell you that I think your son's been poisoned."

Philip nodded. "I suspected as much." He touched the doctor on the shoulder. "Continue to tend to Arridaeus, Philip. I rely on you to keep him alive and to do what you can to recover his wits. Thank the gods the soothsayers say Queen Myrtale is carrying a son. It looks like I'll need another one now."

Philip called a meeting of his advisers that afternoon, the men assembling in his dayroom.

"Philip," he began, looking at the doctor. "What can you tell us about the poison?"

Philip of Acarnania looked around the room. "Very little. Prince Arridaeus was taken ill immediately after eating, so it must have been a fast acting poison that could be mixed with food without affecting the taste or smell."

"That may not be the case," warned the king. "Arridaeus likes his food and may well have wolfed it down without noticing anything amiss."

"His last meal was mutton," added Antipatros. "That tends to be heavily seasoned anyway."

"Have you been able to find anything out?" Philip directed his question toward the general.

Antipatros shook his head. "I've questioned everyone from the serving maids to the shepherd. None have anything to tell." He smiled grimly. "And I can assure you my men know how to make people talk. If they were involved, they would have confessed by now."

"Maybe it was an accident?" suggested Parmenion. "I know I've eaten things that have laid me low enough times."

"Not to this extent," said Philip of Acarnania. "The boy's mind is gone and he's talking like a simpleton. You wouldn't get that from a piece of rotten meat."

"Can't you see?" Aristander stood up. "This is Queen Myrtale's work. I warned you she's a sorceress, but you wouldn't listen."

Parmenion stifled a mock yawn. "Not that again, Aristander. Just because you don't like the Queen, you accuse her of everything that happens in this palace."

"I'm not the only one," retorted Aristander. "I have it as fact that she's been seen casting spells. Why else would she keep snakes in her bedroom?"

"That's enough, Aristander." Philip couldn't afford to let the meeting descend into petty squabbling. "You have no evidence to accuse the Queen beyond your own dislike of her. Besides, how would she have administered the poison? I can't see her walking into the kitchens without being noticed."

Philip shifted position on his couch. "There is something else to consider. Arridaeus is my only heir, but he's worthless if his mind doesn't recover. I have to have an heir, gentlemen, and Queen Myrtale is with child. Even if she is behind this, and I don't say she is, I'm not going to execute the woman who could be carrying my successor."

He looked about the room. "I know the Queen is unpopular, but I won't do anything to jeopardize my future heir." He smiled. "At least, not until the child is born. Meanwhile, I want this matter brought to a close without any scandal."

He turned to Antipatros. "Pick out one of the kitchen slaves, and have him confess that he was paid to poison the food by an agent of one of my exiled brothers. Then have him crucified before there's any talk of a trial."

The meeting was over. Philip remained on his couch after the others left, drinking wine and mulling the thoughts in his brain. One dominated above all others: Myrtale was a mistake.

He had received a message from King Arybbas within weeks of his return from Samothrace; his niece was with child. Antipatros was dispatched to bring Myrtale to Pella, and a wedding hurriedly arranged.

For a while, it had seemed like that heady night on Samothrace, but his enthusiasm soon waned as his new wife revealed herself. Myrtale's bouts of temper were alarming, and she was objecting to any talk of him taking other wives, an essential diplomatic tool. Now there was gossip she was practicing witchcraft, and the conservative Macedonian court was outraged by her unladylike interest in politics and decision-making. She was proving to be the most ambitious of his wives and would undoubtedly use her position as the mother of the new heir to increase her influence further. And he had little doubt she was behind the plot to kill Arridaeus.

The heat was stifling, as usual. Myrtale pressed her bare arm against one of the stone pillars that lined the terrace in front of the palace, taking comfort in its coolness against her skin. She walked on, trying to find the breeze that her maid assured her drifted across from the hills to the west of the city. There'd been no evidence of it yet.

She reached the garden that abutted the western end of the palace. The nearby city wall cast a deep shadow across the lawn, so she stepped through the gate in search of the shadiest stone bench. Aristander already occupied it.

They stared at each other. The priest eventually got to his feet, as he was obliged to do in her presence.

"Joy to you, madam," he said, giving her the traditional greeting. His voice was toneless and his exaggerated movements showed his contempt for her position.

Myrtale didn't bother to reply. Their mutual dislike was no secret and she saw no reason to pretend to the man. She turned to leave. A thought occurred to her and she looked back.

"I wish to make sacrifice tomorrow. How do I reserve the palace temple?"

"You see me, madam."

"Well, that's what I'm doing, then."

"How many will be in the party, may I ask?"

"Ten. Maybe more."

Aristander raised an eyebrow. "The temple is not that large, madam, but I daresay there won't be a problem if you use the outside altar. Do you wish me to perform the ceremony?" He smiled smugly.

"No, I shall be conducting the sacrifice myself." Myrtale watched his jaw drop and sneered. "I am a priestess of Dionysus. I think that means I outrank you."

A look of rage swept Aristander's face. "Never! I will never allow you to despoil the temple with your heathen practices. A priestess? Pah! A witch, more like. Why Dionysus tolerates your cult, I do not know, but I will never allow it inside my temple."

"Your temple?" Myrtale grinned. She felt like laughing at the holy man's outburst. "I thought this palace belonged to the King. And who is the King's principal wife?"

Aristander glowered at her. "And how did that happen, madam? How did a minor princess from an impoverished country like Epirus find her way into the bed of the King of Macedonia? It can only be witchcraft, madam. You enchanted the King into marriage, and now he suffers for it; his son suffers for it; the whole of Macedonia suffers for it. Go home, madam. You're not wanted here."

It was Myrtale's turn to be outraged, but she was more controlled, more devious. She knew how to infuriate the priest further.

"I've seen you with your yellow powder and chicken blood, Aristander. The King may believe your divination, but you use nothing more than cheap tricks that would shame a quack in some sideshow at a festival. I've been initiated into the true arts by

Dionysus himself." She smiled sweetly. "Would you like me to teach you his secrets?"

There was a long silence, and then she was stunned by his reply.

"Yes."

She stared at the priest. He must know she was taunting him. "You would?"

"Yes, madam." Aristander's cheeks had turned a bright red and his eyes were lowered.

It seemed she had underestimated the priest. He must truly care about his profession to let the prospect of learning real magic spur him into humiliating himself like this. She considered the possibilities. Aristander was close to the king, and that could be useful.

"Very well," she said. "Attend the sacrifice tomorrow, and I will show you how to keep an animal's heart beating long after it's dead."

Three victories. First, a runner arrived with the news that the king's horse had won the great equestrian event at the Olympian games. Then within the hour, a messenger from Parmenion reported that his force had found and defeated the Illyrian army. Now another messenger had arrived, carrying the best news of all. Queen Myrtale had given birth to a healthy baby boy. She had named him Alexander.

The news spread quickly through the camp. Wherever Philip appeared, his soldiers gathered to cheer and congratulate him. A delegation from the senior regiment presented him with a gold statuette of Zeus, pillaged the day before from a burning Thracian hill fort. Not to be outdone, the gentlemen of the Companion cavalry put on a display of horsemanship skills, weaving and bobbing across the plain to the jeers of the infantry. A roar of delight swept through their ranks when two of the young nobles collided and were sent sprawling in the dust. Afterwards, Philip attended a ceremony at a nearby temple, sacrificing a lamb in gratitude to the gods for the safe delivery of his son. The fortune-tellers huddled around the entrails, shoving each other aside and muttering dark threats as they sifted through the bloody mess. Then they happily announced that Zeus was pleased. The three victories together, they agreed, showed that the child was blessed and would be invincible.

It was evening, and the camp had settled down for the night. The troops gathered around campfires to eat and to clean equipment by the light of flickering torches. The main topic of conversation was whether they would still need to fight. Now that Parmenion had intercepted and defeated the Illyrian tribes before they could join forces with the Thracian army, nobody believed that Thrace would attempt to face them alone. A few grumbled that it meant they had lost the chance of any real booty.

Philip worked his way through a goblet-sized drinking cup of red wine. He lay sprawled across a couch in the council chamber of the royal pavilion, playing host to the senior troop of the Companions. They'd been drinking for hours. The banter and horseplay had subsided and now they were lost in their own thoughts as a bard recounted the story of the labors of Hercules. Outside, a clear, moonlit sky bathed the camp in a mixture of soft, milky light and starkly black shadows, and a delicate breeze wafted cooking smells and an occasional raised voice through the open tent-flaps.

Philip stared at his drinking cup, his mind elsewhere. He had prayed that Myrtale would give birth to a healthy male child, a replacement for the drooling idiot that Arridaeus had become. Now he had a strong son again, but at a cost.

For weeks now, he'd been troubled with strange dreams. In the most vivid of them, he'd seen Myrtale's belly scarred and sealed with the impression of a lion. Several of the soothsayers had interpreted the dream as being a warning to Philip that he should be cautious of his new wife, and then Aristander had unexpectedly proclaimed it to be good news. The queen's son, he said, would be as strong and courageous as a lion. Philip accepted the explanation, but one thing he'd already decided: he would need to get the boy away from his mother.

Vaguely, he became aware that the council chamber had fallen silent. Snapping out of his contemplation, he focused his eyes. The recital was over and the bard stood waiting for his approval, while the audience fidgeted uncomfortably in the silence. He raised his drinking cup and nodded. The poet bowed and withdrew from the king's presence, to the accompaniment of a slight ripple of applause.

Philip passed the cup to a slave and stood. "Friends," he said, addressing the assembled noblemen of the Companion cavalry. "Today has been a great day for Macedonia. Our soldiers have been victorious in battle and the royal horse has won the bell and prize at the games, and now the Queen has been delivered of a prince. The seers say that the gods must surely favor this child, and I must do the same. I therefore nominate my son, Alexander, as my successor and heir to the throne of Macedonia." He glanced around the tent, searching for any trace of dissent.

The Companions, the highborn of Macedonia, raucously voiced their approval. However, Philip knew their shouts meant little. It would be many years before the boy would be old enough to succeed, and then only if Philip managed to survive that long. Even then, Alexander would need to have the backing of the army, and that could never be guaranteed. No, behind their cheering and roars of congratulation, he knew that few of those present expected the king's new son would inherit his father's throne. And it was almost certain that one or two would have their own ideas on the matter.

Philip called for more wine and urged that the festivities continue on into the night, finally retiring as the first red glow of dawn illuminated the eastern sky. He summoned his current favorite, but had fallen into a drunken slumber by the time the youth arrived. His snoring was clearly audible to the bodyguard stationed outside his sleeping quarters.

Eager to see his new son, Philip told Parmenion to negotiate the Thracian surrender and took a small escort to ride for Pella. It was a hard ride of several days before the whitewashed walls of the city came into view.

Pella baked in the early August sunshine and shimmered in the heat-haze rising from the lake that formed its southern border. The lake had shrunk to half its size, with plains of dried mud stretching along every shore. A channel was dredged throughout the summer months to keep the harbor connected to the River Loudias and the sea, and a ship sat at the dockside, unloading figs and olives from the south.

Philip skirted the lake and entered the city through the grand south gate, to be met with wild adulation by the population. News of his successes had spread quickly, and the people poured into the streets to applaud their king. He was a popular ruler; the more so since his seizure of the Thracian gold and silver mines at Mount Pangaeus earlier in the year, and the new prosperity they were bringing to the city. Philip beamed his pleasure at the welcome, raising an arm in acknowledgement, nodding slightly as he caught sight of people he knew. Here and there, he exchanged a joke with the crowd, roars of laughter greeting every word. His progress slowed to a crawl, and a troop of the city guard marched ahead to clear a path through the throng.

Philip slowly worked his way through the town toward the palace, which dominated the most westerly of Pella's two hills. He knew Myrtale would be watching, and had deliberately chosen to turn his arrival into a grand promenade through the town, rather than enter through the northern gate that abutted the palace. The woman needed to be reminded who she was married to.

Myrtale was watching. She'd been in her dayroom when one of the maids had come rushing up, excitedly babbling the news of Philip's approach. With a flick of her wrist, Myrtale dismissed her attendants and walked over to the window. From here, she overlooked the monumental entrance to the palace.

Philip was coming through the copse of trees that had been planted to shield the palace from the noise and dirt of the city below. He had left the crowds behind and was now accompanied only by his bodyguards. A few of the palace gardeners had gathered at the side of the road, and several of the senior staff were hurrying out a gaggle of domestic slaves, growling at them to start cheering.

Myrtale scowled. She turned and looked at Aristander, who had followed her to the window. "So the dolt has returned, and now I suppose he'll want to claim my son."

Aristander muttered something noncommittal, drawing another scowl from Myrtale. Despite her best efforts, the priest still swore allegiance to the king.

"You must help me, Aristander. I don't want my son to turn into another drunken Macedonian oaf." Myrtale's face was twisted with disgust.

Aristander gave a helpless shrug. "What can we do, madam? Philip is the child's father, after all."

Myrtale glared at the priest. In Epirus, no one would dare to address the king by only his name. The lack of formality at this court infuriated her, and, yet again, it was Philip's fault; he actively encouraged it.

Aristander's cheeks burned and he quickly corrected his mistake. "The King is the ruler of this country, madam, and if he chooses to involve himself with the upbringing of his son, we cannot stop him."

Myrtale knew he was right. Her voice became softer in an attempt to be persuasive; she was desperate now. "He listens to you, Aristander. Use your influence to convince him that his son would be best served by staying with me. I can bring him up as a true prince; one he'll be proud of."

Aristander frowned. "I will do what I can, madam." He turned and walked to the door, his shoulders slumped. He paused. "This loathing that you feel for the King, madam, can only end in tragedy. Why not attempt reconciliation? He still has great respect for you."

"Respect?" snarled Myrtale. "And is your concern prompted by your wish to save the royal marriage, or your fear of being caught in the middle?" It was an unnecessary rebuke, but she couldn't help herself.

She glowered as she watched the priest leave. It still surprised her how quickly she had come to despise this land and its overbearing people, with their boorish pretensions at being Greek. She hated their crude customs, and the guttural, unintelligible tongue that twisted their own king's name into Bilip. How she longed to return to her own beautiful, untamed land.

But now she was the mother of the heir to the throne. One day her son would be king, and she was determined that he would not grow into another loutish northerner. She would keep Alexander away from his father as much as possible, and bring him up as an Epirote prince in her own image.

She hurried down the staircase from the royal quarters, chiding her maids as they hastily prepared her to greet the king. She could hear Philip's voice booming across the courtyard; he would soon be in the Great Hall. With a last glance in a hand mirror, she entered the hall herself, through a rear door reserved for royal wives.

"There you are, wife!" Philip turned as she appeared. The Great Hall was the most imposing room in the palace. It was vast, with frescoes lining the walls and a pebble mosaic covering the entire floor. Philip's marble throne stood on a raised dais at the far end, the fresco on the wall behind depicting centaurs hunting wild beasts. Visitors entered from the opposite end through two large oak doors, intricately carved with figures of battling warriors. The room was designed to impress. This was where the King of Macedonia received tribute, foreign ambassadors, and lesser kings.

Philip was stood in the center of the hall, surrounded by a horde of grinning scribes, soldiers, and pages. He had turned the palace at Pella into the administrative center of Macedonia, and it seemed to Myrtale that the entire male household had crowded through the doors. Determined not to be intimidated, she strode across the floor.

"Joy to you, husband, and I trust you are well?" She ignored the pages as they jostled each other to get out of her way. Philip nodded and stretched his arms toward her. They held the embrace for a few seconds, for the benefit of anyone looking for signs that the rumors of a rift were true.

They drew apart, Philip placing his hand on her shoulder. "Should you not be resting? What do the doctors say?"

"The doctors are well satisfied, husband." She found his false displays of affection irritating.

"And the baby, my son. How is he?" Philip's grip on her shoulder tightened. "Where is he?"

"He is fit and well, but will be asleep now and should not be woken. The wet nurse is with him and will acquaint you when he wakes for his feed. You will be able to see him then." She saw the look of disappointment in Philip's eyes and felt a moment of triumph. She had managed to stamp her authority in front of the whole household; she was in control of Alexander now.

Anger flashed across Philip's face. She nearly laughed at the knowledge that he'd realized what she'd done, but gave her husband a deliberately smug look instead. She knew Philip was too experienced a diplomat to compound the humiliation with a public show of rage, but he would need to reassert his supremacy, if only to teach her a lesson. Myrtale braced herself.

"Of course, wife. We must put the child first." Philip gave her a benign smile and stepped up onto the dais to address the whole room. She wondered what he was planning.

"We live in great times, my friends," he announced. "In recognition of this, I order three days of celebration throughout the land: one for the birth of my son, one for the victory of our armies in battle, and one for our fine victory in the games." The smattering of applause that greeted his words made Philip grunt.

Myrtale smiled. State-funded feasting was a way of life for palace employees and he'd need something more than that to put this audience on his side. This could prove expensive. Her smile stretched into a grin.

Philip was silent for a moment. "Very well. I also authorize the striking of a new silver coin to commemorate our victory in the games. On one side it shall bear an image of our victorious horse, on the other the head of my immortal forebear, the mighty Zeus." It was well known that the royal house of Macedonia was descended from Hercules, the son of Zeus, and therefore from Zeus himself. Myrtale snorted; it was also well known that Philip's great-grandfather had manufactured the ancestry of the royal house of Macedonia.

"And I decree that this medal should be distributed only to the jockey, and to those assembled here today, as witnesses to our success." This time the cheering drowned Philip's words. A coin minted in limited numbers would be worth far more than its face value, and there were collectors in the south who would pay highly for such a souvenir.

"And now a wager must be settled, mustn't it, wife?" He flashed her a grin. "Yes, my friends. We have one among us who did not believe that a Macedonian could prevail in the games, and was so sure of it that she agreed a wager even as our athletes marched out of the city. Don't you remember, wife?"

Myrtale did remember. The bet had been made following the approval of Macedonia's entry into the Olympic games, usually open only to Greek states. Securing a successful (if expensive) vote had been a coup in Philip's campaign for acceptance by the Hellenic world, and she had only proposed the bet to annoy him. But, if she had won, he would have allowed her to bring her own retinue of ladies-in-waiting from Epirus. As she had lost, she would have to stop keeping snakes in her room and restrict them only to her worship in the temple. It annoyed her that she would be giving up a habit Philip found particularly off-putting, and it annoyed her more that he was making the bet public. These foul-mouthed Macedonians would take offence that she'd been so sure they would fail at the games.

She smiled at the grinning Philip. "Yes, husband," she agreed, trying to seem unconcerned. "You were right and I was wrong. I should have had more faith in your athletes."

"Good! Good!" Philip rubbed his hands excitedly. He again spoke to the whole room. "And you proposed, did you not, that should there be a Macedonian victory at the games, you would honor our sportsmen with your own name."

A buzz ran around the audience. It had long been a matter of gossip that the queen had failed to accede to the tradition of giving up her maiden name at marriage.

Philip took a deep breath. "People of Macedonia," he announced. "The Queen wants it known that from this day forward she will answer only to the name Olympias, in honor of our achievements in the Olympic games."

The courtiers loudly voiced their approval, while Myrtale felt as if she'd been slapped in the face. Philip smirked at her, oozing triumph. A mere queen dare not call the king a liar in public; he'd outfoxed her and was reveling in it.

She glared at him. He'd not only alienated her from the Macedonian people for not believing in their ability, but, worst of all, had robbed her of her own name. The king had decreed it; from this day forward, she would be known as Olympias.

Olympias swept out of the hall without a word.

It was late in the afternoon before Philip was taken to see his son. He was ushered into the nursery, a room filled with women. They turned and stared at him expressionlessly, and it was Philip's turn to feel uncomfortable. He stood hesitantly by the door, vexed that he, the King of Macedonia, was uncertain what to do in these strange female surroundings.

"Where is the child?" He had hoped the tone of his voice would impose his authority on the women, but instead it just sounded unnecessarily loud and vulgar. He could feel his cheeks reddening. Through the mob, he saw a cot against one wall, with a nursemaid lifting a bundle out of it. He heard a baby's whimper and then the tiny bundle was placed in his arms. An old crone of a midwife tutted crossly and adjusted the position of his elbow.

He gazed into the face of his son. Alexander stared back for a moment, then yawned and closed his eyes. Philip chuckled with delight and a titter went around the women. The tension in the room vanished and a chair was brought forward. He sat with his son for nearly an hour, as the daylight faded outside the window and the maids lit torches around the walls. Finally, a nurse stepped forward and returned the baby to its cot. Alexander was still asleep as his father crept out of the room.

A few days later a tradesman brought news to the palace that Philip found faintly disturbing. The temple of Artemis at Ephesus had burned to the ground at the same time as Alexander's birth, and the city's priests were proclaiming that the destruction must herald the dawning of some great misfortune for Persia. Philip's soothsayers were ecstatic. This could only mean, they declared, that the child had been chosen by the gods, and would lead the Greeks in freeing their sister cities from the yoke of Persian tyranny.

Olympias looked smug for days, and began hinting that Zeus himself had fathered Alexander.

Philip retreated to his private quarters to assess the news. Yet again, he was troubled by the birth of his son. He had always thought that one day he would unite the Greeks and free the colonies that had been lost to Persia by the King's Peace, a humiliating treaty that had been forced on Greece some thirty years before. But if Alexander was destined to lead the Greeks, what did this mean for Philip?

Unwilling to think any harm toward his baby son, he dispatched a soothsayer to seek guidance from the oracle at Delphi. The reply was disconcerting; he was advised to pay homage to Zeus, and warned he must lose the eye that had spied on his wife as she lay with the god.

Chapter Three

The Treasury

Before Alexander reached his first birthday, he had a sister, Cleopatra. Her conception had been Philip's revenge on Olympias for spreading doubts about Alexander's paternity; there would be no such stories about her second child. Olympias vowed it would be the last time he would make her perform the duties of a mere wife, and she no longer even bothered to put on a pretence in front of the court. She and Philip lived separate lives.

The palace at Pella was also home to Philip's other wives, careful to avoid each other, especially Olympias, as much as possible. The children didn't care; the palace was their playground. Alexander and his sister grew up in the company of the half-witted Arridaeus and several more sisters belonging to the other wives. Then there were the children of Lanice, the noblewoman who had been entrusted with his care and who loved him like her own, and the numerous offspring of Artabazus, a Persian exile.

Alexander spent many hours with the ageing Persian and his family. The children would gather around to listen to his stories of life in the court of the Great King, as the Persian emperor was titled, and exchange grins as the old man exaggerated his exploits in battle and in the bedchamber. Barsine, his adolescent daughter, would pass around milk and sweetmeats, and make loud tutting noises whenever her father's stories became too bawdy for young ears. Ten years older than Alexander, she seemed so sophisticated and cultured to the young boy. One day, in a fit of childish passion, he told her he loved her. She laughed and ruffled his hair to make him cross.

And he was a likeable lad, seemingly unaffected by the open hostility that now existed between his parents, but with the petulance of a child that always got, and thus expected to get, his own way. Although short by Macedonian standards, he was not unduly small when compared to the meat-starved Athenians to the south. His skin was pale, albeit with a sun-baked red tinge to the face, and he had inherited his father's cheeky grin, and a smile that revealed a row of pearly white teeth. His countenance was engaging, with flaring nostrils, full lips and a high, slightly bulging forehead crowned by a mane of soft, tawny hair. But his eyes were his most striking feature. Dreamy and distant, when something caught his interest they could burn with an intensity uncomfortable to watch.

He was well-liked by the palace staff and, despite his mother's attempts to keep her children aloof, often to be seen chattering to the maids as they cleaned or scrounging treats from the cooks in the kitchen. Olympias loudly blamed it on Philip, who seemed to be equally at home in any situation, be it entertaining foreign dignitaries in an elaborate court function or singing crude songs with a squad of archers around a campfire.

Not that he was there that often. In the three years since he'd rushed home to see his baby son, Philip had spent most of his summers on campaign and his winters reforming the army. Freed by the wealth that came with possession of the mines at Mount Pangaeus, he no longer had to rely on unskilled and reluctant peasant conscripts to swell his ranks in time of war. He could afford to recruit and train a permanent, professional army, and was putting them to good use by steadily nibbling away at his neighbor's possessions.

Safe in Pella, Alexander was weaned on the exploits of his father. Reports of battles and conquests regularly reached the palace, the messenger still wearing the dust of the road as he swaggered to the center of the crowded Great Hall.

The gathering was quiet, expectant; the routine well rehearsed.

The messenger first surveyed the pages and civil servants who surrounded him, a smile on his lips. He swelled out his chest.

"Friends, shall I tell you how the King valiantly led the phalanx through a breach in the enemy's wall?"

A roar answered him. He grinned.

"Or shall I tell you that at this very moment, he is bringing home ten thousand head of barbarian cattle and as many slaves?"

Olympias stood before her husband's throne as though about to claim it for her own. She looked bored. She snorted contemptuously, and then muttered something about attending to something more important as she strode from the hall.

Alexander, standing with the king's children on one side of the throne, stayed. Excitedly, the toddler grabbed Arridaeus by the sleeve and propelled his elder brother forward. They joined the pages and attendants as they surged around the messenger.

"How many slain? How many captives? How many cartloads of plunder?"

The Royal Pages, all sons of Macedonian nobility, also sought news of fathers and brothers serving with the Companions. One was pulled from the crowd and led away to a quiet corner by a somber-looking secretary of the cavalry. Alexander watched curiously as the boy suddenly burst into tears, but was too excited to worry about such a thing for long. He rushed to find Barsine and tell her the latest story of his father's heroism.

Another messenger reached the palace, but this one did not swagger into the Great Hall. He insisted on seeing the senior ministers in private, and then the commander of the city guard was summoned. Rumors spread through the palace. The king had been wounded; he'd been captured; he was to be executed; he was dead.

Wailing women were hired from the city. Dressed in black, they stood in the courtyard and beat their breasts in despair. After a while in the blazing sun, they moved into the shade and demanded a jug of wine every hour. By evening, they were drunk and had to be expelled from the palace.

Olympias sent a slave to Lanice, ordering her to bring Alexander to her quarters. The nurse arrived with one hand tightly gripping

Alexander, the other ushering Cleopatra and Lanice's younger children. They stood watching with shock on their faces as she hammered to be let in at Olympias' door.

Now the children played in Olympias' dressing room, with Alexander on his mother's lap. He was trying to show her his latest toy, a small terracotta model of a warrior complete with moveable arms and legs.

Next door, in her dayroom, two male slaves stood behind a bolted door with a large wooden chest shoved against it. They carried short swords uncomfortably at their waists. Two ladies-in-waiting sat silently in a corner, looking frightened and bewildered. The windows were shuttered and bolted, the room dark and gloomy.

Alexander wriggled off his mother's lap and ran to the bedroom door. "Can I go and play with the snakes, Mama?" He was speaking to Lanice. Olympias was too preoccupied to notice and made a waving motion with her hand. The boy disappeared into the room, calling to Lanice's children to follow. They all drew back in horror at the mention of snakes, except for Proteas, Lanice's youngest son, who hurried after him.

"Madam, what news of the King?" asked Lanice as soon as Alexander was out of hearing. "Is he dead?" She took the queen's hand.

Olympias stared at the nurse wearily. She felt like she'd aged a thousand years in the last hour. "Not dead, leastways, not yet. But he's been wounded, badly. His doctor has operated on him but cannot say if he will live." Her voice faltered. "What am I going to do, Lanice? It's too soon; Philip can't die yet. Alexander is still too young to succeed." She glanced in the direction of the bedroom. "And whoever takes the throne will not let him live."

There was a noise at the door, the sound of raised voices. One of the slaves ran into the dressing room, his face white with fear. "There are soldiers at the door, mistress!"

Olympias stood. Somehow, she had the toy warrior in her hand; Alexander had already managed to break the end off its sword. "Take the children into the bedroom, Lanice," she said quietly.

"And lock the door." There was no sign in her voice of the tension she felt. She placed the toy on the dresser and walked through the tiny hallway that led to her dayroom. One of the ladies-in-waiting was sobbing; they both looked up at her imploringly.

"Leave here at once!" she shouted through the door. "This is the Queen's private apartment and you have no right to be here."

"Madam, we are here to offer you protection. You don't need to let us in, if you don't want to. We shall stay outside and guard the door." Olympias recognized the voice. She hadn't spoken to Artabazus before, but the heavy eastern accent was unmistakable. She wondered what to do. The Persian had only been at the court a short time, but she knew he was already a favorite of the king and that Alexander spent a lot of time in the company of his children. He could probably be trusted, and it was still too early for any rival to make a move. They would more likely wait until Philip was confirmed dead, just in case they killed the son and then the father recovered.

"Who is with you?"

"Memnon, madam. He was my captain in Phrygia. He is loyal to me, and to the King." Olympias knew nothing of Memnon, other than he was a Greek mercenary who had spent much of his career in Persian pay. But she needed allies and decided to take a chance.

She beckoned to the slaves. "Open it." The door was unlocked and the bolts drawn back, and the two men entered. They were both dressed for battle, Artabazus with a breastplate over his Persian robes while Memnon wore the full armor of a mercenary captain. Artabazus had a girl with him.

"Joy to you, madam." Artabazus spoke the Greek greeting, then bowed in the Persian fashion. "This is my daughter, Barsine. She will take any messages that we need to send." The girl smiled nervously.

Memnon looked around the room, rattling the door bolts to check for signs of weakness and then tapping the soft wood on the window shutters. "We cannot stay here," he said. "We've got to get the child out of the palace and to somewhere that can be defended." He walked through to inspect the dressing room.

"We don't yet know this city, madam," said Artabazus. "Is there a house where you would be welcome, perhaps one with a gate and a strong outer wall?"

Olympias shook her head. "I rarely leave the palace and do not know anyone in the town."

"What's that building on the lake, madam?" Memnon had returned and joined the conversation. "The one on the island. It looks like a prison."

"The treasury, you mean." Olympias smiled. "It's the King's treasury. I've only been there once, when I first arrived. The King wanted to show me his wealth." She gave a weak laugh.

Memnon looked at Artabazus and nodded. "That's the place. A treasury will have thick walls and only one entrance, and it can only be approached across that bridge."

"It does seem the best possibility," Artabazus said. "Do you know how many guards it has, madam?"

Olympias shrugged. "I only saw scribes and slaves. There were two or three soldiers on the bridge, I think."

"There'll be more now," said Memnon. "The commander of the guard will have posted more soldiers at the treasury as soon as he heard about the King, if he's any good anyway." He had gone to a window and was peeping through a gap in the shutter. "I say we go now, rather than risk waiting until the morning."

Artabazus agreed. "We must leave now, madam. Get your son and bring food enough for three days."

Olympias obeyed the Persian. Alexander was brought out of the bedroom, shouting with delight when he saw Barsine. The slaves disappeared to the kitchens to acquire food, while the ladies-in-waiting packed a few clothes. Memnon eyed the party that was assembling in the sitting room. "We can't take all these, madam. Your son only."

Artabazus nodded in agreement. "We can only take Alexander and yourself, madam, and the two slaves if they can be trusted with those swords." He turned and indicated Proteas. "We'll take his friend as well. He'll be company for the boy. All the others must stay though, and will be safer here anyway. They won't be troubled once the boy is gone."

Olympias saw the sense in his words. She and Lanice bid farewell to their respective children, Olympias giving Cleopatra a hug and chiding her to do as the nurse told her. She thanked the ladies-in-waiting and said she would send for them as soon as it was safe, but could see they were relieved to be among those left behind. With Alexander unlikely to live more than a few more hours, the farther they could distance themselves from him the better.

The palace was quiet. A few heads turned to watch the party leave, but none challenged them. That wouldn't become a risk until Philip's death was officially announced and allegiances were revealed.

Memnon led the way. Then came the two slaves, with Alexander and Proteas cocooned between them. Alexander kept turning to look at his mother and Barsine, a puzzled look on his face. They whispered words of comfort. Olympias was glad they'd also brought Proteas. It could buy valuable seconds if assassins didn't know which child to kill.

Artabazus brought up the rear, occasionally stopping to stare into the darkened street behind them.

But Pella was also quiet. A curfew had been declared and the guard was out in strength to enforce it. A building was burning on the dockside, but the looting that had caused it had been rigorously suppressed. Alexander stared fascinated as they passed a row of warehouses, each with a corpse swaying gently from the hoisting beam that jutted out from their upper floors.

The treasury was a squat, flat-roofed building, set on an island that lay a short distance out across the lake. As Memnon had surmised, it had been the city's prison until Philip had chosen it to house the wealth now flowing from Mount Pangaeus.

The commander of the city guard was taking no chances with the mob, and a full squad was assigned to guard the bridge that led out to the island. The soldiers watched the small group approach, those at the landward end picking up spears and replacing helmets on heads. The sergeant in charge of the squad raised his arm as they approached the barricade that had been erected in front of the bridge.

They stopped at the barrier. "Do you know me? I am Queen Olympias, the King's senior wife, and this is Prince Alexander, his son and heir. Let us pass." The sergeant turned to look at his comrades; they gave him blank stares.

"I have orders not to let anyone pass, mistress. Not unless they have the permission of the commander." He looked nervous and uncertain.

"Your commander is a servant of the Queen's husband, idiot! She doesn't need to seek his permission." Memnon was using his most authoritarian officer's voice.

"Perhaps, sergeant," said Artabazus, his tone more conciliatory. "You should send a messenger to inform the commander of our presence. He'll want to reinforce the guard once he knows that both the Queen and Prince Alexander are on the island and need protection."

The sergeant jumped at the chance to pass this problem on. "Yes, I'll do that," he said, and turned to call forward one of the others. They had a brief discussion and the man set off to find the commander.

Artabazus spoke again. "It may be some time before the soldier returns, sergeant, and we have children with us. We cannot stand here. Let us take shelter in the building, and if there is a problem," he surveyed the armed troops on the bridge, "we wouldn't be able to prevent you forcing us to leave."

The sergeant hesitated, and then nodded reluctantly. The barricade was parted and they crossed the bridge under the reproachful stare of the soldiers. These were militiamen, called upon to defend the city's buildings when required, and there was little doubt they did not want this added burden. They could handle rioting neighbors armed only with sticks, but protecting a prince could bring assassins and professional troops down upon them.

The gate to the treasury compound was locked. One of the soldiers called out and the duty scribe's head appeared at a grille in the wall. Memnon opened his mouth to speak but didn't have to. The clerk had worked in the palace enough times to recognize both Alexander and the queen.

They were inside the treasury within a few moments. The scribe bid a greeting to the queen, then hurried to a position of safety on the roof.

Memnon gave a little cry of delight. The building was ideal. It was one large, windowless room, divided up into separate, caged recesses. A desk and chair stood in the center, while in a back corner was a small living area for the duty scribe, containing a cot and a stool. A candle had been placed in a niche above the cot, and a plate with the remains of a meal sat on the stool. Nearby, a ladder gave access to a trapdoor and the roof. In each of the recesses were several large wooden chests, tightly bound with straps and bearing heavy locks. They contained the wealth of Macedonia. A convoy of mules arrived from the mines in the Pangaeus Mountains nearly every day, laden with gold and silver.

Artabazus offered the chair to Olympias, while a slave brought the stool over and placed it next to the desk for the Persian to sit on. The children explored the building in the first rush of excitement at being in a new place, but soon tired and Barsine settled them down in the cot. The blanket was smelly and stained. Memnon climbed up the ladder and onto the roof.

"What do we do now?" Olympias voiced her thoughts. Artabazus had been looking at the children, and adjusted his position on the uncomfortable stool.

"By morning the whole city will know we are here," he said, "but I think we're reasonably safe for the moment. This place is too public for anyone to do anything, until the King is dead anyway."

Olympias gave a half-smile at his frankness. Was it that obvious Philip meant little to her and she was only concerned for her son?

"What we really need to do, madam, is to get Alexander to safety, and that means exile. At least, until he's old enough to return and claim his throne."

She nodded agreement. "He would be safe in Epirus. King Arybbas is my uncle and would give us refuge, and supply an army when the time comes."

Artabazus shook his head. "Epirus is the other side of the Pindos Mountains, madam. We wouldn't be safe on the open road and there isn't time to plan such an expedition anyway; we need to find somewhere now. We can't go north. Your husband's brothers are in Thrace and it is they we must fear most. So it must be south, or . . . or we could go east, to the sea." His face brightened. "Yes, of course. We hire a ship and sail to safety. It's perfect. We're already at the docks and there must be three or four ships not a stone's throw from where we sit." He was becoming animated, his arms beginning to wave about. "We sail south, and carry on all the way to Epirus if need be. As for paying for our passage . . ." His gaze swept over the crates of gold.

Memnon appeared at the trapdoor and clambered back into the room. He was surprisingly agile for a big man in full armor. "The guards are gone," he said matter-of-factly. "There's only the sergeant left, and I think the only thing keeping that scribe up there is the drop from the roof." He sat on the desk and grinned at them as it creaked slightly under his weight. He reminded Olympias of her husband, and she wasn't sure if that was a good or bad thing.

"In the morning," continued Artabazus, "I will send Barsine to talk to the ship's captains. With enough gold, one of them will be willing to undertake such a journey."

Memnon agreed; he'd been listening to the conversation while on the roof. "But we also need to make contact with the army," he added. "They have the right to elect the next king and our biggest threat is that they choose someone straightaway, most likely someone already in the camp. Parmenion, for instance, or Antipatros. Either could make a claim for the throne themselves and then we'd have the army hunting us down. Madam, is there anyone in the army you can trust?"

"Not in the army. But Aristander is with my husband and he I can trust."

"The King's soothsayer," said Memnon thoughtfully. He looked at Artabazus. "I will ride to the camp at Methone, find the soothsayer and, through him, try to contact the King. If he is too ill or already dead, I will approach Parmenion." He turned back to Olympias. "If necessary, madam, I will offer the regency to Parmenion, to rule in Alexander's name."

Olympias nodded her agreement. Parmenion ruling as regent would remove his immediate need to kill Alexander, and the same could not be said if Parmenion was ruling as king.

The decision made, Memnon jumped to his feet as if ready to leave now. "Madam, can you write a letter of introduction to this Aristander for me?"

The scribe departed at first light, muttering something about it being the end of his shift. No replacement arrived. Alexander woke and demanded to go up on the roof. Olympias refused, and the tone of her voice ensured the child wouldn't put up his customary persistence.

It was early morning. The sun shone down on Pella but the solid walls of the treasury kept the occupants cool. The commander of the guard placed more men on the bridge, and a large crowd gathered as word spread that the king's son had taken refuge on the island. Many expected trouble and had come to watch the event. Peddlers moved among them, selling stuffed figs, sweetmeats and trinkets. A cutpurse was caught in the act, and beaten to a pulp by an enthusiastic mob who'd grown bored with the inactivity on the island.

There were too many onlookers for either Barsine or Memnon to attempt to leave. It was a serious blow to the group's plans and Memnon cursed out loud that he'd waited until daylight.

The hours passed, and then the guard commander arrived at the bridge. He addressed the crowd, Memnon straining to hear what he was saying.

"People of Pella, I bring joyous news. A messenger has arrived from our camp at Methone, and the King is alive and well. This very morning he rose from his bed and inspected the troops. Return to your homes and prepare for a feast to celebrate his recovery."

The crowd stood their ground, unconvinced. If anything, their numbers swelled at the news that something was happening at last. The commander crossed the bridge and stood at the gate. He hailed Olympias, and Memnon stuck his head to the grille to answer.

"Did you hear that?" the commander asked. "The King is alive. He is out of danger and plans to return to Pella to recuperate. He'll be here within a few days."

A hurried conference took place around the desk.

"How trustworthy is the commander?" asked Artabazus.

Olympias shook her head. "I don't know. I've never had cause to speak to the man. My husband appointed him to the post, for what that's worth."

"Any man can be bought," said Memnon.

"Exactly." Artabazus stroked his beard thoughtfully. "We'll be defenseless once we leave these walls, and I don't think we should do so on the word of a stranger. We need to hear the situation from someone who is absolutely dependable, who cannot possibly be bought."

"Lanice," said Olympias. "She's too fond of Alexander to be part of any plot against him."

"Yes, she would be ideal." Artabazus turned to his daughter, who was trying to keep the two boys amused. "Barsine, I have a job for you."

The girl stood, a trace of apprehension on her face.

"I want you to go up to the palace and find Lanice. You know her? She's Alexander's nurse; the woman we saw last night."

"Yes, I know her, Father. We take the children to play in the gardens."

"Good. Find her, and find out what is happening. Has there been a messenger this morning? If so, what was the message? There must be rumors in the palace, and Lanice will have heard them. Find out everything she knows."

"Yes, Father."

"And don't take any chances." He held his daughter's arm. "If you feel threatened or Lanice can't be found, come straight back. Her disappearance will be the evidence we need."

It was an anxious two hours before Barsine returned, with Lanice. Alexander slept in his own bed that night, well scrubbed and perfumed, but scratching the fleabites he had acquired from the scribe's cot.

Philip returned to Pella two days later. Crowds lined the streets to watch him being brought in, propped up on a litter on the back of a mule-drawn cart. They watched in silence, those who caught sight of his face not betraying their thoughts in front of the troops that marched either side of the cart.

The procession reached the palace and stopped in the courtyard. Olympias ordered that Lanice keep Alexander in her apartment until she had assessed the extent of Philip's wounds; she didn't want the boy scared.

Philip was lowered from the cart and placed on the ground in front of the queen. He was awake, one side of his face covered with a bandage. Blood seeped through the cloth, with more staining the sheet that covered his legs.

"You are well, wife?" Philip's voice was weak. A steward knelt down with a flask of wine to quench his thirst.

"I am well, husband. And you?"

Philip smiled, one corner of his mouth hidden by the bandage, wine dribbling from the other. "Yes, wife, I am well." He lay back and put a hand to his temples. "I want to thank you." He propped himself back up onto his elbow. "I want to thank you for looking after my son."

Olympias said nothing. She watched Philip being carried to his quarters, and then went back to her own. She had learned her lesson, and her two slaves had returned from the treasury with enough gold in their food sacks to fund a line of horsemen. On the day Philip finally fell in battle, she would have Alexander safely across the mountains before her husband's body was even cold.

Philip knew how real the threat had been. His half-brothers had spies in the army as he had spies in their camp, and the news of his wounding must have quickly reached their ears. They almost certainly had alerted their agents in Pella to look for an opportunity to slay the king's heir; it was, after all, what Philip would have done in their place. Much as he hated to feel a debt to his wife, taking refuge in the treasury had surely saved Alexander's life.

His recovery was swift and, after only a few days, the gash on his leg healed sufficiently for him to hobble around the palace on crutches. But the bandage remained on his face. It was some time before Philip of Acarnania announced that the wound had healed sufficiently to remove it permanently.

Philip saw his new face for the first time, and stared at the reflection grimly. The arrow had bounced off a stone parapet and slashed down, catching him as he scrambled up the rungs of a scaling ladder. The barb had scraped a furrow down the side of his face and, starting at the temple, the wound ran through his eye and down the length of his cheek.

He stepped closer to the mirror and tried to examine the scar in detail. Each time he turned his head to look with his one good eye, so the side with the scar was turned away from the mirror. He snapped at the stewards and they brought hand mirrors, holding them at angles so he could see his face reflected from one to another.

The scar glared back at him, bloated and ugly. The blow had shattered his cheekbone, leaving a cratered depression in the skin, while his empty eye socket had been stitched closed, causing a break in the scarlet weal that ran down his face. Philip sighed. He had always been proud of his good looks and the effect they had on both men and women. Those days were over, he supposed, and he'd be buying his pleasures from now on.

The scar fascinated his son. Alexander would follow Philip around, climbing onto his knee and wanting to touch it, or asking whether it hurt. On these occasions, Philip would sometimes regard the boy questioningly. The oracle had spoken truly; he had lost the eye that had spied on Alexander's mother and the mighty Zeus. So how much more was true? Was Philip destined to lose his future for the greater glory of his son?

Chapter Four

Quizzing the Persians

Greece descended into yet another civil war, this time stemming from something as trivial as the non-payment of fines. A meeting of the religious council at Delphi demanded that the city state of Phokis settle its outstanding charges. They refused and the dispute escalated, with the shrine at Delphi being seized by the Phokians, who then used its vast treasure to hire a huge mercenary army.

A sacred war was promptly declared against Phokis. Sparta, with her own fines to pay, backed the Phokians and, one after another, the Greek states became embroiled. Philip came in on behalf of the council. An experienced general and natural leader, he soon become a major figure in the war, and began to be spoken of as a possible leader of a united Greece.

And Alexander grew into a young lad. Lanice tried to teach him respect and courtesy to others but, more and more, he came to realize, and exploit, his exalted position. Many times, he caught the reproving eye of Artabazus, and even earned a tongue-lashing from Barsine. Olympias heard of the incident but took no action; it would teach Alexander to be shrewder in his dealings with others.

From his father and his father's generals, he began to learn the art of war. Long evenings were spent in the Great Hall, perched on the end of his father's couch and sipping watered-down wine as he listened to their drunken ramblings and tales of past victories.

"First," said Parmenion, slurring his words and wiping wine from his beard with the back of his hand. "We sent half the cavalry on a long sweeping maneuver to the right, forcing the enemy to stretch their line to cover the threat to their flank." He swung his arm to demonstrate the point, nearly sliding off his couch and allowing Antipatros to butt in.

"But we held back our troops in the center and left, waiting for the gap we knew would open up in their overstretched ranks." The child stared at the general with wide eyes and open mouth. "And when we saw it, we drove a wedge through that gap with a lightning charge by the Companions, and followed up with the unstoppable mass of the phalanx."

"And then, boy." Philip reached over to stroke his son's hair with wine-soaked fingers. "We slaughtered them in their thousands as they broke and fled from the field."

But the palace at Pella was not just a military command center. Philip's wealth attracted artists, diplomats, and scholars from all over the known world, and the king encouraged such an influx of culture. The palace became filled with Greek doctors and Persian philosophers; ambassadors from a dozen courts were in permanent residence; there were performances by Athenian actors, accompanied by musicians from Sicily and Asia Minor; Theban painters and sculptors sought commissions, and Corinthian architects and engineers expounded their ideas.

Alexander lived among them. He could converse equally well in both his native Macedonian and in Greek, the official language of the court, and had a smattering of Persian. He learned of distant countries and alien races, of fabulous statues, of palaces and temples. He heard tell of mysterious, ruined cities and ancient tombs that defied explanation, and of the sun-bleached bones that littered long-forgotten battlefields. The boy soaked up knowledge. He knew where the world ended in every direction, and could pinpoint on a map the mountains where Atlas held up the sky. Such was the cosmopolitan world of Alexander's childhood.

Runners arrived at the palace, with the news that a Persian fleet had been sighted approaching the estuary of the River Loudias. Three warships, crammed with warriors. The commander of the city guard dispatched messengers to alert King Philip, who was inspecting troops in Thessaly. Scouts reported that two of the ships had anchored at the mouth of the river; the third was sailing up the Loudias alone. The city relaxed a little. One ship would not be enough to mount a raid. Anxiety was replaced with excitement and speculation. What could be the mission of one Persian warship? What new development was in the offing?

The ship anchored in the middle of the lake, long and sleek, with a high stern and tall prow. A smooth, black, pointed ram glistened, just visible on the surface, and the pennant of the Great King fluttered from the topmost mast. Figures moved about on deck, the sun flashing on metal and gold.

The royal children gathered on the terrace to watch, Alexander hopping excitedly at the spectacle on the lake below. He leaned over to whisper in his sister's ear as she stood on tiptoe to see over the tops of the trees, scaring her with stories of rampaging Persians. Olympias, as the senior wife, ordered that a troop of the guard be placed at her disposal to defend the palace. She also summoned the keeper of the stables and instructed him to make ready the horsemen who would escape with Alexander, if the need arose.

A small boat could be seen being lowered into the lake from the deck of the Persian ship. Three sailors scrambled down ropes to crew it and a set of steps appeared, manhandled into place against the side of the ship. Two figures were helped down the steps and into the boat, their rich clothes and high hats signifying that they were nobles of the Persian court.

The boat made the short trip to the shore, where the commander of the city guard met them at the dockside with a guard of honor. More troops waited in the warehouses behind the dock, ready to fight.

The Persians introduced themselves as emissaries of the Great King, seeking an audience with Philip, King of Macedonia. Reluctant to be the one who informed them that the king, and therefore the army, was away, the commander delivered them directly to the royal residence.

The palace was in turmoil. Slaves hurried from room to room, placing bowls of flowers and fruit anywhere that the visitors might conceivably see. The senior ministers gathered together in one of the meeting rooms to discuss the situation. Olympias invited herself.

"In the absence of the King," said the secretary of the treasury, "Prince Alexander must meet them. He is the King's official heir, and anyone of lower rank would be deemed an insult."

"Impossible!" sneered Olympias. Although she jumped at any chance to promote her son, he was too young for such a task and she didn't want him making a fool of himself in public. "He is still a child, whereas I am both the King's consort and mother of his heir. I shall greet them."

The assembled men stared at her in dumbfounded silence. The procurer of provisions was the first to answer.

"Madam. To be received by a woman would be the greatest insult for the Persian nobles, and would be seen as an insult to the Great King himself. It cannot happen. Such an affront would be like a declaration of war."

"And being received by a baby isn't?" Olympias' temper rose. "He's only seven-years-old, for all the gods. What if he said or did something to insult them? Wouldn't that be as bad? It must be me."

Only the secretary of the treasury dared answer a queen who cursed.

"My colleague is correct, madam. A queen ruling in her own right would be acceptable, but your authority is as the King's consort. Having you receive them would be akin to slapping the Great King in the face. We cannot risk making an enemy of Persia while the sacred war still rages."

Olympias said nothing. The man was right, but she refused to admit it.

"It must be your son, madam," continued the secretary. "The Prince is seven, as you say, and so is officially a man under Macedonian law. It must be him. We shall be on hand to guide him, and any indiscretions can be put down to his age."

"Do not fret, Mother. I shall receive the visitors." Olympias spun around at the child's voice. Alexander stood there, tiny in the doorway and dressed in his play clothes.

The two Persians were ushered into the Great Hall. Their eyes took in the grandeur of the room at a glance, before being drawn to the child that stood before his father's throne. They'd been informed of Philip's absence and had, reluctantly, agreed to be received by his heir. But they had not been told how young Alexander was. They stopped and stared at each other, as if trying to decide if the Macedonians were mocking them. One opened his mouth to say something to the other, and then closed it again. The two men faced forward, removed their hats, and bowed to the boy.

Alexander had been speedily washed and perfumed, and now wore a crown of fresh flowers and the yellow colors of the Companion cavalry. One of his father's own costumes had been hurriedly cut to size and draped around him; it dragged on the floor.

"Joy to you, gentlemen, and welcome to Macedonia." The child's thin voice quavered slightly and he flashed a look at his mother; Olympias smiled her support. She stood just a few feet away, beside the king's ministers.

"Greetings, Prince Alexander." The elder of the Persians stepped forward. "And to your father, King Philip, ruler of Macedonia." He spoke Greek, with a rich, deep voice that resounded across the hall. For a moment, the child felt cowed by the authority in that adult voice. He looked at his mother again.

The second Persian spoke. "We come on the orders of the Great King, Artaxerxes the Third, Emperor of Persia. We seek an audience with King Philip to discuss important business." His beard came to a sharp point, and Alexander was startled to see it bob as he spoke. The room was silent, all eyes on the boy, but he was too flustered and overawed to answer. Olympias coughed.

It broke the spell. With one more glance in his mother's direction, he recovered himself. "My father is away attending to military duties, sir, and is not expected to return for many days. In his absence, I speak as his voice on affairs of state. What business is it that brings you to Macedonia?"

The Persians looked as though a blow had struck them. The one with the pointed beard dropped his jaw in surprise, the point curling on his chest. A murmur ran around the audience and Olympias stifled a grin of delight.

The elder Persian stared at the child expressionlessly. "My orders from the Great King were to speak to King Philip himself, sir." His voice had a harder edge to it, but all present noted that he addressed Alexander as sir.

The second Persian stroked his beard and half-turned toward his colleague. "If King Philip will not be returning for sometime . . ." There was a pause.

The elder Persian forced a smile. "We had not anticipated a long stay in your city, sir, nor a trek across country to find a king who is on campaign and could well be deep in hostile territory. In the circumstances, I am sure the Great King would not insist that we obey our instructions implicitly." He swallowed hard. "As you are King Philip's son and heir, and his authorized representative, I am certain we would have King Artaxerxes' approval to speak with you as with King Philip himself."

The room broke into a hubbub of noise and the ministers spun around to silence the crowd, furiously snarling at the noisiest of the onlookers.

Alexander grinned, swelled out his chest and puffed up his cheeks. He was enjoying himself now. He moved to the edge of the dais. "And what business is it you wish to discuss, gentlemen?"

The Persians still seemed unsure. They exchanged glances as though seeking each other's approval. The one with the pointed beard nodded for the other to continue.

"It concerns certain members of your household who are exiles from the Persian court, sir. They are the mercenary, Memnon of Rhodes, and Artabazus, former satrap of Phrygia."

The grin was wiped from Alexander's face. Artabazus was a wanted man in Persia, and had told him the story many times. How he'd been a satrap, a regional governor; how he had led a rebellion against the Great King; how he had been betrayed by his

Theban mercenaries; the flight to safety in Macedonia; the agonizing wait for his family to be smuggled out to join him.

"I know the men you speak of," said Alexander. "They are guests of my father, and are under his protection." He could sense how the mood among the onlookers had changed, that he was on dangerous ground now. Out of the corner of his eye, he saw the secretary of mercenaries stepping forward, ready to intervene if he said the wrong thing.

Alexander stared the Persian envoy in the face. "They have lived here some time," he said. "What is it that now brings them to the attention of the Great King?"

The Persian smiled. "You misunderstand our mission, sir. The Great King, in his wisdom, has granted them a pardon. We have been sent to command their return, that they may serve the Great King once again."

Again, a buzz went around the room. Alexander looked to the line of ministers for guidance as to his reply and saw they were all smiling with relief. He turned back to face the envoys.

"That is good news, sirs," he said, unsure if it was. "Perhaps we should summon the men in question, that they may hear the news themselves." He had directed the question at the chamberlain of the household, who nodded and left the room.

An awkward silence fell on the chamber; there was suddenly nothing that Alexander could discuss with the envoys until the men were present. The secretary of the treasury stepped forward with a suggestion.

"Sir," he addressed the boy. "It will take time for the men to be found, and then they may need to prepare themselves for the meeting. It will most likely be an hour before they are ready. I would venture that our guests," he nodded to the envoys, "would prefer to retire to more comfortable surroundings while they wait?"

The Persians welcomed the suggestion and, a few minutes later, were seated in one of the antechambers that lay behind the Great Hall. Here was where Philip would bring guests who were personal friends, or when the subject was too sensitive to be discussed in front of the court.

The two men were brought wine and sipped the liquid suspiciously; it compared favorably with the wines of Arabia, they lied. Alexander sat opposite them, on his father's couch. His feet didn't reach the ground, and he swung his legs nonchalantly. They made polite conversation, and the elder Persian had just begun to describe the Great King's wondrous gardens in Babylon when a gleam came into the boy's eye. He shot a glance at the Macedonian ministers hovering in the doorway.

"Tell me," he interrupted. "The Great King—is he popular with his people?"

The Persians stared at each other in surprise. "Yes," said the elder of the two. "The Great King is much loved by his people. They sing his praises from every corner of the empire."

Alexander nodded sagely. "And the army, they sing his praises also?" He gave the Persian the benefit of his penetrating stare and smiled sweetly. He was daring to interrogate his guests on the morale of the Persian army, and the look on their faces said it all. The secretary of the treasury gave a nervous cough and the secretary of mercenaries shuffled a step farther into the room.

"Yes, the army sings his praises also." The elder Persian spoke slowly, deliberately.

"I have heard that it's the largest army in the world. That must be a wonderful sight, to see so many men on the march. Have you seen that? Have you seen the army on parade?"

"I have, sir," the Persian answered cautiously.

"Where was that? In Babylon?"

"Yes, among other places." The younger man gave a warning cough.

Alexander refused to be deterred by the interruption. "And where would that be?" he asked. "Where else have you seen the army on parade?"

The Persian could not avoid such a direct question. He paused for a moment and then said, "Susa, sir." It was no secret that the

Persians maintained a large garrison at Susa, and it was too far to the east to be of any strategic importance to invading Greeks.

"Susa." Alexander stroked his chin thoughtfully, as though he was massaging a beard. The action was incongruous on a child. "Where is that? Isn't it on the road to Persepolis?" He looked over to the secretary of mercenaries for confirmation; the secretary nodded.

"And isn't that a royal road, gentlemen?" he continued. "Is it paved?" The Persians said nothing and Alexander knew his questioning was going too far. He forced a laugh to try and lighten the moment. "I've heard your Persian roads are well-maintained. Not like some of the tracks we have to travel on."

The Persians sat stony-faced.

A noise from the corridor broke the silence that had descended on the room. Artabazus and Memnon stood in the doorway.

Artabazus knew the elder envoy from his days at the Persian court and the two men greeted each other cordially. Memnon winked at Alexander, who had jumped to his feet. The two Persians also stood.

"Well," said Artabazus. "This is unexpected. I thought I would end my days here at Pella."

"You already know!" Alexander looked crestfallen. He'd wanted to tell them the news himself.

Artabazus laughed. "Yes, my child. We were apprised of the situation on the way here." He turned to the elder Persian. "And I am pleased to accept, sir. I look forward to going home and again serving the Great King."

"And I also accept, sir," said Memnon. "I welcome the chance to return to a military life. King Philip appointed me to the command of the training school here in Pella, but it's not the same." He laughed. "I can taste the dust of an army on the march already."

Alexander sat back down, and beckoned for the others to do the same. Memnon pulled chairs forward for himself and Artabazus.

"When does the Great King expect us to report for duty, sir?" asked Artabazus. "I have a family here, so cannot leave immediately."

"I can," quipped Memnon.

The elder Persian smiled. "As soon as you're ready. The Great King didn't specify a time limit for your return."

"Good. I expect it will take me a while to organize my brood, but then we will be on our way." Artabazus directed his gaze toward Alexander. "I hope to be able to say goodbye to your father before I leave. Is there any word on his return?"

Alexander shrugged, suddenly disinterested. A chilling thought had entered his young mind. "Barsine won't be going with you, will she?"

Artabazus smiled. "I'm afraid so, my boy. Now her mother's departed this life, I need her to take care of the little ones."

Alexander's face crumpled. There was an awkward silence as he sniffed back a tear.

"So what do you think of our young prince?" asked Memnon hurriedly.

The elder Persian smiled. "Oh, I think we have much to tell the Great King," he said.

Philip was euphoric when he learned of Alexander's handling of the Persian envoys, but it was fully three weeks before the business of war allowed him to return to the palace. Sweeping into the courtyard at the head of his escort, he immediately summoned the boy to the Great Hall. Lanice hurried him to the chamber, being intercepted by his mother before she reached it. Olympias was determined to be the one who presented him for his father's accolade.

She ushered him in to the hall. Philip was sprawled in his usual relaxed pose on the throne, quaffing wine from an enormous drinking cup with handles like wings. He rested it on one knee between gulps and joked with the courtiers who had flocked to the Great Hall as word of his arrival spread through the palace.

A broad grin split his disfigured face as he spotted his son. "Here he is!" he roared, standing up. He tossed the goblet toward a slave, splashing wine over those stood in the way. It settled in tiny pools between the pebbles of the mosaic floor.

All heads turned to look at Alexander. The child faltered, turning for reassurance to his mother. Olympias touched the back of his head and guided him toward the throne.

Philip took a stride forward. "Come here, my boy." He swept Alexander up and perched him on his shoulder. "This is my son," he announced. "Can you not tell? Already he has the mind of a king!" He grinned and placed his oak leaf crown on the boy's head, laughing as it slipped over the child's ears. "I trust you've made a full report to the secretary of logistics?" he bellowed. "He will need to know the state of these Persian roads when we're marching on Babylon!" A roar of laughter rang around the hall.

Alexander nodded eagerly, basking in his father's adulation while Philip gazed up into his son's shining face. The hall fell into a genial silence at this demonstration of a father's pride in his son.

Philip turned to look at Olympias. "Come forward, wife."

It was the first time he'd spoken to her for several months. She stepped up to the throne, her mind racing with all the possible surprises he might use this occasion to spring on her; discourse in front of witnesses could not be denied later.

"Yes, husband?" she said serenely.

"The boy reached his seventh year this summer, and is thus a man. I think it's time he was taken away from the company of women and turned over to a governor for formal training into adulthood." Philip turned to an aide, who produced a clay tablet. "I have made a list of several nobles, any one of whom would make an ideal governor for the boy. All of them are experienced in the arts of war and statesmanship, and some have sons of similar ages to the boy."

Olympias had been expecting this for some time. Philip was constantly trying to wrest control of Alexander from her, but his long absences on campaign had always allowed her to keep the advantage. But seven was the traditional age at which a Greek male became a man, and she'd known that Philip would not miss the opportunity. No doubt, his list of tutors would all be loyal Macedonians with estates far from Pella. But she was ready.

"Yes, my husband," she said. "I agree. I've been pondering this question also, and have already found the man."

Philip looked stunned, as did many others in the room. "You have?" He spoke slowly and put Alexander down. The child sensed the change in the tone of his father's voice and looked up at him, bewildered.

"Yes," continued Olympias. "The man I have in mind is someone who is already known to you. I speak of Leonidas, my uncle. I have already written to him, and he has gladly accepted."

"He has?" Philip stared hard at Olympias, and then turned to give Parmenion and Antipatros a leer.

He returned his gaze to Olympias and his face cracked into a broad smile. "You're right, wife. Leonidas certainly has the right credentials, and I think your uncle would be an excellent choice."

Olympias, puzzled, looked at Philip, then at Parmenion and Antipatros. Her husband merrily smirked at her, triumph written on his face, while the two generals stood expressionless, hiding their thoughts. The reason dawned on her in an instant of awful realization.

Talk of an alliance between Epirus and Sparta the previous spring had prompted Philip to lead a pre-emptive strike to keep Epirus out of the war. A Macedonian column had entered the country and occupied the Epirote palace at Dodona. King Arybbas had been placed under house arrest, and his nephew, Olympias' younger brother Alexandros, spirited out of the palace to reappear as a hostage in Pella a few days later. It was the reason for the last occasion Philip and Olympias had spoken: a blazing row upon Philip's return, conducted in the courtyard before he even had time to dismount from his horse.

But she should have known that Philip would take the opportunity to place a spy in the palace during his sojourn in Dodona, and her uncle had always been a weak man. With a sinking feeling, Olympias knew what she had done. She'd just given control of Alexander to Philip.

Artabazus was ready to leave. Two carts stood in the rear courtyard, waiting to transport the Persian's possessions to a large vessel moored at the dockside. A third cart would carry the family. Memnon had already left, eager to return to active service.

It was only in the last couple of days that Alexander had realized the full implications of the old man's imminent departure: Artabazus was taking his family so far away that he might never see them again. The child started following Barsine around, eager to spend every last moment he could with her. On the last morning, he found her busily supervising three slaves as they packed the bedding from her brother's bedrooms. He sat on a box being used to prop open a connecting door between the rooms, and watched her as she bustled about.

"Can I come and visit you in Persia, Barsine?"

"I expect so. If you want to." She picked up a pillow and stuffed it into an already full crate.

"But how will I know where you live? How will I find you?"

"I'll write and tell you," she said, a note of irritation in her voice. "Look, Alex, I'm busy. Why don't you run along and play? Your father told the boys they could each have a dagger as a going-away present, and they've gone down to the armory to choose them."

"I want to stay with you." He began to sob. "I don't want you to go, Barsine. I might never see you again."

She sighed resignedly at the sound of his tears and walked over to comfort him.

"No need to cry, Alexander. It'll be all right." She put an arm around his shoulders and raised a finger to his cheek. "Here, wipe away those tears."

Alexander sniffled, and lifted his eyes. "Will I ever see you again, Barsine?"

"Yes," she said, and kissed him on the cheek. "If the gods will it, I'm sure you will." She put her hand on his mouth, her fingers pushing each corner of his lips up into a smile. He gazed at her in adoration.

"The gods are going to will it, Barsine. When I grow up, I'm going to come and find you. And when I do, I'm going to marry you. That I promise."

Barsine would have laughed, but something in the child's eyes stopped her. She drew back slightly.

The moment had arrived. The two baggage carts were already winding their way down to the harbor and a small crowd had assembled in the courtyard to wave the family goodbye. Barsine's younger brothers were crowding onto the third cart, jostling each other for a place next to the driver, while Artabazus stood at the back, helping the smallest up. Philip stepped forward and embraced him, wishing him well; the king had delayed his return to the army so he could see the old man off.

The cart began to move and several of the palace children ran alongside, cheering and waving. Alexander tugged on Lanice's hand as he tried to follow them, but the nurse tightened her grip. It was not seemly behavior for a prince.

"It's not fair!" he cried in dismay. "You let Proteas go."

Artabazus was propped up at the back of the cart, his hand raised in salute as it turned into the gloom of the tunnel that led to the palace entrance. Next to him, Barsine gave a last wave goodbye. She was smiling, but there were tears in her eyes.

Alexander suddenly twisted, biting Lanice on the wrist and making her release her grip. The child dashed across the courtyard, his little legs racing after the cart that carried Barsine away. His toe stubbed against a raised flagstone and he fell flat on his face.

Shocked and in pain, he burst into tears and raised himself onto his hands and knees to look for Lanice. A stranger was standing over him, a small, shabby man with sunburned skin and a bald, shiny head. He reminded Alexander of the stallholders he'd seen in the market place. The man looked as though he'd come a long way. His clothes were covered in dust and he held onto two donkeys, one loaded down with a huge pack. He put out a hand and helped Alexander to his feet.

Lanice came hurrying over, looking anxious. She dusted the boy down and examined the grazes on his knees.

"This is a fine welcome for your great-uncle," boomed Philip, wearing his customary grin as he strode across the courtyard to join the group. "Alexander, meet your Uncle Leonidas. He's going to make a man of you."

Alexander looked up at the man, then at Lanice. A strange look had come into her eyes, one he hadn't seen before. He stared up at the man again, and then returned to Lanice. He reached out and put his hand into hers, and shuffled a step closer to the woman he called mother.

Chapter Five

Manhood

"Wake up! Wake up!" Alexander woke to find a candle shining in his face. He slammed his eyes shut and jerked up an arm to shield them, but Leonidas was ready. He grabbed the boy's arm and pulled him out of bed. "Get dressed," he snarled, "and be on the terrace in three minutes."

Dawn was still a faint flicker on the horizon as Alexander began his run. The guards at the palace entrance looked at each other and shook their heads in sympathy as the boy jogged past them. It had become a morning ritual. Alexander would run the length of the colonnaded terrace in front of the palace, then follow a circuitous path around the north wall of the city and back up on to the terrace for a final dash to where his governor stood waiting for him.

Then they would return to their quarters at a rear corner of the palace, where Leonidas had taken over part of a block next to the kitchens. Breakfast of a thin gruel would be followed by a bath in cold water, with the rest of the morning usually given over to martial training. There would be coaching in horsemanship, swordplay or archery when instructors were available, more exercise when they were not.

A light meal, then the afternoon was spent in the classroom. Tutors were hired from the town to teach Alexander the fundamentals of reading, writing and arithmetic, with history, geography and music being added as the syllabus expanded. Alexander finished the day by cleaning the three rooms that had been set aside for the boy's instruction: one as a bedroom that he shared with Leonidas, another as a gymnasium, and the third as a classroom.

On feast days, they would visit the palace temple to make sacrifice, always leaving before the feasting started. These were the only times that Alexander saw his mother, and rarely did he see Lanice or her family nowadays.

Time passed, and Alexander gradually settled into the routine of his new life. He noticed himself how much easier the exercises were becoming as he grew fitter, but still he was always hungry.

It was a hot afternoon. Leonidas had gone to make his weekly report to Alexander's parents and had left the boy with his reading teacher. The heat in the classroom was stifling, and proving to be too much for the old man. He told Alexander to read out passages from Euripides' play, the Bacchae, while he sat in the window and tried to get some air.

It took a while for the boy to notice, but then he realized he could hear snoring. He listened with glee for a few moments, staring at the parchment before him with unseeing eyes. Then he dared to look up. Yes, the old man was definitely asleep, his head resting on his wheezing chest, his breath gently hissing through an open mouth.

Slowly, very slowly, Alexander stood. He crept to the open doorway and glided down the stairs to the yard at the back of the kitchens. A team of slaves was preparing an ox for slaughter at the far end of the yard, but was too busy to notice him as he slipped by and hurried up the colonnade that led to the private apartments.

The boy grinned as he strolled past the bodyguard at the door of the room where Leonidas was meeting with his parents. This was the first time he'd been on his own since his uncle had arrived, and the sense of freedom was overwhelming. His father was home for once and would be bound to ask lots of questions, so he knew Leonidas would take more than the terse ten minutes he usually spent with his mother. He could allow himself a while yet before he had to be back in the classroom.

He found Lanice in her apartment. Her brother, Cleitus, was home from the army and telling her sons a tall tale about the war. Lanice and Cleopatra were weaving in the corner, the girl more interested in the yarn that Cleitus was spinning. She jumped off her chair as Alexander burst in, rushing over to fling her arms around her brother.

"Alex! I haven't seen you for so long!" She spun around to show him to Lanice. The nurse had risen to her feet, her expression both pleased and disturbed.

"Alexander, what are you doing here? Are you supposed to be here? You look so thin." She embraced the boy, and felt muscle under his skin.

Alexander beamed up at her. "What have you got to eat? You wouldn't believe how hungry I am."

He was soon tucking into the children's sweetmeats, while Proteas was sent to the cold cupboard, returning with a pair of chicken legs and some cheese. Alexander devoured them eagerly.

Lanice watched him eat, unable to hide her shock at how skinny he had become. His cheeks had sunk into his face and his collarbones were sticking out from under his skin, while his podgy little stomach had disappeared. But there was a new air of confidence about the boy and no doubting the muscle building up in his arms and shoulders.

Cleitus came over and joined them at the table. "So, Alexander, how are you getting on with your uncle?"

The boy made a face and shook his head. "I hate him. No matter how well I do something, he always says it wasn't good enough and I'll have to do better next time. He's never satisfied." He spoke through a mouthful of roast chicken.

"And he steals my things," he added, with barely a pause. "He's taken all my clothes and perfumes and makes me wear slave's clothes." He looked down at his rough woolen tunic with distaste. It was fastened at only one shoulder, the other kept free for labor. "This exomis is so uncomfortable that even a goatherd would refuse to wear it. He only lets me put on my good clothes when we come over to the temple."

Lanice tutted. "Really, Alexander, you shouldn't talk about your mother's uncle like that. What if someone heard you?"

"Oh, I don't care," said Alexander nonchalantly. "Besides, I am the King's son; who would dare report me?" He gave Cleopatra a sly grin, looking the image of his father.

He suddenly realized the time. "Uh-oh, better get back. See you when I can!" And he was gone.

He raced back through the palace, taking a shortcut through the foundations of the new bathhouse his father had commissioned, but knowing he had taken too long. He breathed an oath to Hermes; he would need divine help to get to the classroom before his uncle. He prayed that his father had asked lots of questions.

He was too late. He turned into the yard, his heart sinking as he saw Leonidas and the teacher at the foot of the stairs. The old man was muttering something about a misunderstanding while Leonidas paced up and down, hands on hips. A dozen slaves were scurrying in and out of buildings, looking for him.

"Alexander! Where have you been? What is the meaning of this?" Leonidas was furious. "Your father feared you'd been abducted and has turned out the guard to look for you. What game do you think you're playing?"

The old teacher looked at Alexander and shook his head in resignation. Picking up his bundle of manuscripts, he shuffled off, cringing as Leonidas continued his tirade against the boy.

His father summoned Alexander the next morning. A scowling Leonidas ordered him to dress in his best clothes, then marched him to the king's morning room where his parents were waiting for him. They sat side by side, the closest the boy had ever seen them. He was directed to stand while Leonidas took up a position by the door, his arms folded.

Philip gave the boy a long, hard stare. "Well," he growled softly. "What have you to say for yourself?" He was wearing his oak leaf crown; he meant business.

Alexander shrugged; there was little he could say. "I was only gone for a while and never left the palace. I was with Lanice the whole time." It came out as a whine.

"Do you realize how concerned we were?" Olympias frowned at him. "We didn't know where you were or what had happened to you."

Philip hadn't taken his eyes off Alexander, making the boy squirm under the scrutiny. "Nothing like this must happen again. Is that understood?" Alexander nodded dumbly. "Your uncle is acting on our behalf, and is to be obeyed as you would obey your mother or I. Such behavior will not be tolerated again. Now leave us and wait outside. We wish to speak to your uncle."

Alexander avoided looking at Leonidas as he squeezed past him into the corridor. The door was shut behind him. He pressed his ear to it, hoping Leonidas was also about to receive a reprimand; that would be worth hearing. But the thick wood blocked all sound from within. Disappointed, he turned and pressed his back against the wall, allowing himself to slide down until he squatted on the floor with his arms resting on his knees. He focused his eyes on the cracks in the plaster on the opposite wall and began to hum softly. The duty bodyguard glanced down at the boy, and then he, too, resumed his contemplation of the opposite wall.

"Take a seat, Leonidas." Philip waited while the man pulled up one of the spare chairs that lined the room. Leonidas sat erect, his back bolt upright and his knees pressed firmly together. He looked at both Philip and Olympias expressionlessly. Philip sensed his wife was about to start the dialogue, and got in first.

"The pressures of kingship," he began, "have necessitated that I've not spent as much time with Alexander as I might have wished, and this may have prevented me giving the boy as much guidance as might have been desirable. I think, however, that I know my son well enough, and that I know how to bring out the best in him." He could imagine the sarcastic comments forming in Olympias' mind.

"In my experience," he continued, "it would produce better results if you try to encourage the boy, rather than bully him.

Reason with him and let him see why you want him to undertake this task or achieve that goal. When he can understand how he will benefit from performing, what to him, may seem an unnecessary chore, he will be more amenable to the drudgery of carrying out that chore. Do you not agree, wife?"

"Why, yes, husband," replied Olympias meekly, taken by surprise by his articulate reasoning.

Philip grinned inwardly; it was not often he could leave his wife lost for words. He warmed to his task. "And it wouldn't hurt to reward him now and again. Give him a treat or at least a decent meal; the boy looks half-starved!"

Olympias attempted to join in the conversation. "You're pushing him too hard..."

Philip drowned her out. "You must remember, Leonidas, that the boy has been brought up in a royal palace and, as my heir, is used to always having his own way and never being chastised. Yes, I will admit that he's possibly become an unruly child." He paused, as though giving the thought consideration.

"But now you've arrived, and suddenly everything has changed. He's no longer being treated with regard; he's been taken away from his friends and those who would show him deference; he's forced to perform rigorous physical exercise. Hardest of all, he's being ordered to undertake tasks that would normally be assigned to the lowliest slave. He doesn't realize this is training to prepare him for the hardships of life on campaign, and it's little wonder he rebels at the first chance that presents itself to him. I would have done the same in his position."

Leonidas said nothing, and Philip wondered if anything he'd said had penetrated the man's skull. Olympias took advantage of the momentary silence.

"We have decided," she announced in her most superior voice, "that we will appoint someone to assist you." Finally, there was a reaction from Leonidas. He opened his mouth to say something, and then seemed to think better of it.

But Philip wasn't going to let Olympias take the initiative. "It will ensure," he chipped in, "that Alexander always has supervision.

Even when you have other duties and are not able to be present." Olympias scowled at the interruption.

"Exactly," she said frostily.

"And it will also give the boy contact with someone who is, technically at least, subordinate to him." Philip was unstoppable today. "The problem is that you're my wife's kinsman, so able to treat Alexander as an equal. But an assistant will, even when supervising him, have to accord the boy the respect that goes with his rank." He smiled encouragingly. "After all, I don't want my son to forget who his father is." He shot a glance at Olympias; she ignored the look.

There was silence. Philip had covered all the points he and Olympias had agreed upon before the meeting; he had nothing further to say. Olympias had given up trying to compete.

"Very well," said Leonidas, taking the hint and standing up. Their eyes bored into his back as he left the room.

Philip pulled himself to his feet. "I think that went rather well," he decided. Olympias looked up at the man she hated.

"Yes, husband, and you did very well indeed. For a moment I almost remembered why I married you." She smiled, and offered her hand to Philip.

Rather surprised, he took it and helped her rise from her seat.

"For all your faults, husband, you do have Alexander's best interests at heart." She gave him a very light kiss on the cheek.

They walked toward the door together.

"Can I choose Leonidas' assistant, husband?" Olympias was putting on her coyest voice; Philip grinned at her audacity.

"I suppose so. But try to do better than when you chose Leonidas."

Lysimachus reported for duty three days later. The man had served as a mercenary in Philip's army for several years before retiring to Pella, and had gained access to the palace on the strength of his military service. No one was quite sure what his principal trade was, but he seemed to make an adequate living on the edges of court life. That he was Olympias' man; Philip had no doubt.

Alexander was in the paddock practicing the javelin with a new Spartan instructor, when he spotted Leonidas coming down the path from the stables. There was another, bigger man with him, hurrying to keep pace with his uncle's peculiar, quick-stepped gait.

"Alexander, come here." The boy wondered what it was this time; he hadn't been allowed a moment's rest since they'd returned from the meeting with his parents. He turned and trotted over to the side of the path, giving the man standing beside Leonidas an inquisitive glance.

"Alexander, this is Lysimachus, my new assistant." Alexander gave the man a longer look. This was the first he'd heard about any assistant, and, from the look on Leonidas' face, the boy guessed it was not his uncle's idea.

The man was tall, towering over Leonidas, and well built, fat even. He was already perspiring in the morning sun, beads of sweat running down the sides of his face. He had wiped an arm across his brow at some point and the hairs on his forearm were plastered to his skin.

"Joy to you, sir." Lysimachus grinned at the boy. He had two teeth missing.

Leonidas gripped Alexander by the shoulder and stared him in the face. "Lysimachus is to be my deputy and you will obey his instructions as you would mine. I will not tolerate any further nonsense. Is that clear?" Alexander nodded glumly. Now there would be two of them hectoring him all day.

Leonidas gave a rare smile. "It seems the boy has finally learned his place," he commented to Lysimachus. He touched the man on the elbow. "Come, and I will show you your duties."

He started back up the path to the palace. Lysimachus half-turned to follow him, then hesitated a moment. He pulled a sweetmeat from the pouch around his waist and tossed it to the boy.

"From your mother," he mouthed.

More treats followed. Each dawn Lysimachus would make the trek up the hill from his lodgings in the town, usually arriving while Alexander was still at his morning exercise.

Every day the assistant stopped at the agora to buy a treat of some sort from one of the market traders. One day it would be fruit or a sweetmeat, the next a slice of cheese pie or a stuffed vine leaf. Then came the wait for the right moment. Alexander and Lysimachus would maneuver like sparring partners, exchanging glances and whispered words as they judged when to pass the food without Leonidas spotting the transaction. Alexander became adept at consuming the treat in seconds. He'd tear off mouthfuls and gulp them down virtually unchewed, licking crumbs, grease or juice from his fingers.

Sometimes it would be impossible; Leonidas was always there. On these occasions, Lysimachus hid the treat in Alexander's trunk in the bedroom that the boy shared with Leonidas. Alexander found these to be the best kind of treats. Waiting until sure his uncle was asleep, he nibbled on the food, savoring it, making it last. Listening all the while for signs of movement from the snoring Leonidas.

Months passed and Alexander grew fitter and stronger. Each month he was visited by Philip of Acarnania to be measured: chest, waist, biceps, thighs, weight, and height. Each month his physique developed, but each month he just did not seem to grow. It began to cause comments in the palace and prompted Philip to order a full examination of his son.

"What do you think?" he asked. Philip stood in his dayroom, while Olympias sat on a couch in the corner, a scowl on her face. Philip of Acarnania pulled his ear away from Alexander's chest.

The doctor shrugged. "I can find nothing untoward. His physique is developing normally. He is, in fact, extremely fit for his age."

"But he's so small. Look at him." Olympias indicated the naked boy in the center of the room. "His sister is the same height as him already."

"As I said, madam, he appears physically fit." The doctor packed his tools away and turned to face the queen. "In my opinion, he is merely a late developer and there's no cause for concern. You watch. One day he'll suddenly shoot up." He smiled and nodded toward Philip. "And be taller than his father."

Olympias snorted at that, while Philip grinned.

"What do you think, Alexander? Will you be taller than me one day?"

The boy managed a half-smile. "Just give me time, Father." He'd had enough of being poked and prodded, and talked about as if he wasn't there.

Philip's gaze returned to the doctor. "It is worrying, though. I could understand if he was some pasty-faced Athenian youth, but not someone who spends as much time exercising as he does." He walked over to grasp his son's bicep. "Look at that, Philip. Pure muscle."

The doctor nodded agreement. "As I said."

"It's that Leonidas," growled Olympias. "He's starving the boy and it's stunting his growth. Feed him properly and then we'll see him grow." She smiled as Alexander gave a slight cheer.

"Is that possible?" asked Philip.

"Perhaps." The doctor leaned against a wall, arms folded. He shrugged again.

Alexander stared up at Philip, tempted to beg for more food. If only his father knew how he longed to just sit and eat.

"Very well," said Philip decisively. "I don't want to upset Leonidas' training schedule, so won't order him to increase Alexander's rations. Instead, we'll give the boy a new duty. He can serve food with the Royal Pages at all state banquets in future, and I'll have him wait on me personally to ensure he gets something extra." He ruffled Alexander's hair as the boy's face broke into a grin. "We have a reception for the new Etruscan ambassador tomorrow night; we'll start him with that."

"Leonidas will just deny him the little food he does get to make up for it," said Olympias. "You know what that man's like."

"We'll tell Leonidas that it's to improve the boy's etiquette and his understanding of court protocol. He won't be there to eat, but to observe."

Olympias looked unconvinced. "If you say so, husband." She turned to her son. "Are you going to get dressed, then?"

Banquets were almost a routine when Philip was in the palace, and the extra food they brought made Alexander feel positively bloated. It also gave him the chance to mix with the Royal Pages, boys his own age, and to keep abreast of affairs in the outside world. His father's return from each campaign was an event he looked forward to eagerly.

His duties were to serve the king's couch, which usually consisted of Philip and his latest fancy, usually an officer of the Companions. Wine would be followed by food, followed by entertainment and more wine. There were always plenty of opportunities for the boy to feed his face between the serving pantry and the Great Hall.

He swallowed a last morsel of chicken breast as he placed the plate on the low table in front of his father's couch. Philip glanced at the bite-sized notch in the roasted fowl and smiled at his son.

"Tried to escape, did it?" he asked, teasingly.

"Yes, Father," answered the boy. He stepped back and picked up an empty fruit platter, wondering if he could get it back to the pantry before the last of the sweetmeats disappeared. The Royal Pages were like wolves.

"He addresses you as Father?" The new representative of the Amphictyonic Council raised an eyebrow enquiringly.

Philip laughed. "Of course. This is my son. Come here, Alexander, and introduce yourself."

"So this is Alexander?" The envoy sat up on his couch and looked the boy up and down. "Your name has been mentioned by the pilgrims at Delphi. They say you're a rival for any Spartan boy your age."

"That's right." Philip beamed with pride. "And he can sing. Find me a Spartan who can do that."

"You sing, too?"

Alexander nodded. "Music is part of my instruction, sir."

"Come, show our guest." Philip pulled himself to his feet and eagerly led his son to the center of the hall. The room hushed, and the boy flushed as all eyes focused on him.

He began to sing, a ballad to Theseus. Each note was sweet, each word crystal clear. The audience was enraptured, and silence fell on the hall as he ended the last note.

The cheering burst like a thunderclap. "More! More!" The word became a chant.

Philip raised his arms in mock outrage. "Such a cherub's voice can only be achieved once in an evening. Let the poor boy rest."

Alexander, grinning from ear to ear, bowed and retired from the hall. The applause still ringed in his ears as he sauntered down the corridor.

He was certainly enjoying life more now. He had regular contact with others of his own age, and Lysimachus was providing the extra little comforts that made the day bearable. Lysimachus was becoming invaluable.

Leonidas seemed to think so, too. He may not have wanted an assistant but the man had proved to be both competent and reliable, to the point that Leonidas began to relax his grip slightly. He took to leaving Lysimachus with Alexander one or two nights a week while he went into the town, becoming a frequent visitor to the brothels that lined the back streets behind the shrine to Aphrodite.

He would return long after the boy had gone to bed, blundering clumsily into furniture as he tried to find his own cot in the darkness. Alexander would be woken to the stink of cheap wine and even cheaper perfume.

But it was a small price to pay to have Leonidas away from the palace for a whole evening. Three hours without his uncle's constant carping, with the added bonus that Lysimachus would always take the opportunity to give him a proper meal in the kitchens. Olympias only paid him for a daily supplement to Alexander's diet, but the man had his own reasons for wanting to treat the boy so regularly.

Yet again, Leonidas had bathed and perfumed himself, and was making the long trek down the hill to the town. The guard at the side entrance gave a knowing smile as the man passed, his bird-like step even faster than usual. Lysimachus paused long enough to be sure there was no possibility he might return for some reason, then took the boy over to the kitchens.

They sat at the huge table that took up the center of the kitchen hall, Lysimachus watching as Alexander tucked into a platter of sardines, followed by a dessert of figs and nuts.

"Is that good, my young sir?"

Alexander looked up and nodded happily, juice dribbling down his chin. Lysimachus smiled fondly at the boy, then his eyes lit up as he spotted a Thracian slave carrying a bundle of wood for the ovens. The youth was tall, like all his race, and still wore his hair tied in a tribal topknot. He placed the firewood in the storage space by the hearth and smiled at Lysimachus.

"Here he is, my young Atlas." Lysimachus beckoned him over. The youth came and sat on the table by the older man. He was facing Lysimachus, with his feet on the bench and his knees parted. The assistant placed a hand on his knee and stroked it softly.

Alexander watched them curiously. Effeminacy was despised and intimate relations between men of a similar age frowned upon, but in a society where women rarely left the home and admiration of the male physique was actively encouraged, it was common for an older man to turn to a younger. Intellectuals in places like Athens promoted the notion of platonic pedagogy, but it was rarely such. Alexander swore that when his time came, it would not be Leonidas.

"Why Atlas?" he enquired.

Lysimachus grinned and gripped the slave's thigh. "Look at those muscles. As strong as Atlas himself."

Alexander slurped another mouthful of figs while he considered the statement. "What about me, Lysimachus? Who do I remind you of?"

Lysimachus laughed aloud. "You could only be Achilles, who else? And I am Phoenix, your humble tutor." He bowed slightly and Alexander giggled, delighting in the comparison. Lysimachus knew well enough that the hero of Troy was the boy's idol.

Alexander's face glowed with pleasure. "What about my father? Who is he?"

"He is Peleus, of course. As Peleus was the father of Achilles, so is not the King your father?"

"And my mother?" Alexander liked this new game.

"Why, the Lady Olympias can only be compared to the noble Helen of Troy."

Alexander nodded agreement, then grinned.

"What about Leonidas?" He chuckled wickedly, but Lysimachus refused to be drawn into slandering his superior.

He stood, shaking his head. "No. No more. And I think, sir, that you should hurry and finish that meal. It's getting late, and time I put you to bed," he said, looking at the Thracian.

It was turning into a cold winter. Alexander shivered in the schoolroom, trying to stop his teeth chattering as he studied the Anabasis by Xenophon. The story of how that great general had led his army to safety from deep within Persian territory was standard reading for Macedonian officers, and one of Alexander's favorite tales. But it was just too cold for him to concentrate properly today, and the thin woolen garment that Leonidas had issued to him was insufficient for weather as severe as this. His history teacher sat wrapped in a thick cloak, snug and warm. Thankfully, the short winter days meant that torches would soon have to be lit; they would provide some measure of warmth, at least.

There was a slight tap on the door and Lysimachus entered. He looked at the tutor for permission to interrupt, and then beckoned to the boy. "Your governor wishes to see you, sir." Alexander wondered what he'd done to warrant such a formal request. Except for when Leonidas was within hearing, Lysimachus always called him Achilles now.

He stood, searching the assistant's face for some clue. Lysimachus avoided looking at the boy as they walked the few paces to the bedroom in silence.

"Come in, boy." It was his uncle's voice, and Alexander knew from the tone that he was in for another beating. He looked up at Lysimachus once more but the man was keeping his eyes lowered. With a resigned droop of his shoulders, Alexander entered the room. His sparse furniture was in disarray, his cot dragged out from the wall and the blanket pulled onto the floor. Both his trunks were open, with the lids flung back and his clothing and possessions strewn beside them. Leonidas stood by the trunks, a goat cheese pastry in his outstretched hand. "What is this?"

Alexander said nothing. Lysimachus must have hidden the pastry in his trunk that morning, but he was not going to inform on him. As Achilles would not have betrayed his faithful Phoenix, so Alexander would not betray Lysimachus. He would rather suffer the punishment himself; it was a matter of honor.

"Answer me, boy."

Alexander looked up at his uncle. "I bought it, sir."

"Bought it!" snorted Leonidas. "With what?" The boy had no money.

Alexander shrugged. "My mother gave me some obols last time I saw her. I used them."

Leonidas looked as if he was considering the possibility for a moment, and then sneered. "So, where exactly did you buy this, then?" He looked down at the pastry in his open palm, then back at the boy. "Tell me that, if you can. You cannot leave the palace, or has the agora moved into the courtyard? Perhaps they've set up stalls in the Great Hall. I must start shopping there myself!" He sniggered at his own joke.

Alexander thought it best to stay quiet. He stared at the floor, letting his uncle's invective wash over him.

"Do you know what I think? I think you're a thief. I think you sneak over to the kitchens and steal, like a common criminal. Is that not the truth, boy?" He was almost screeching.

Alexander looked up in surprise. Even a fool would have suspected Lysimachus was involved, and he'd expected that at any moment his uncle would turn on the man, still standing downcast by the door. But if Leonidas believed he was stealing from the kitchens, then why not settle for that?

He nodded, and heard Lysimachus expelling a long breath. "You're right, sir. I've been taking food from the kitchens nearly every night." He suddenly had a flash of inspiration. "But I was only doing what you taught me, sir. Didn't you tell me my training was no harder than Spartan boys receive, and aren't they encouraged to steal food from their neighbors? I was only doing the same."

Leonidas stared at him incredulously. It was true. Spartan instructors actively encouraged their wards to use their initiative and steal extra food; it was one of the reasons for not giving them sufficient to eat. There was silence in the room.

"Very well," Leonidas said finally. "I shall overlook it this time, but it must stop, you hear me? It's not fitting for the King's son to be caught stealing from his own kitchens." He crushed the pastry in his fist and let it fall to the floor. "Now clean this mess up," he said, stomping out of the room.

The boy was euphoric; he had tricked his uncle and gotten away without punishment.

"What a fool!" he said, picking up the crushed pastry and stuffing it into his mouth. "It's not fitting for the King's son to be caught stealing," he mimicked. "More likely, he doesn't want the gossip that would follow if people thought he kept me so hungry I had to steal food."

Lysimachus put his hand on the boy's shoulder to calm him down.

"Thank you, my Achilles," he said. "But you realize it must stop? I can bring you no more treats. It's too risky."

Alexander nodded, and then grinned. "That's alright. I'll just carry on stealing from the kitchens."

Chapter Six

The Peace of Philocrates

The sacred war was drawing to a close. The city-state of Phokis, the vast treasure it had looted from Delphi spent, neared collapse. Athens and Sparta, grown wealthy by supplying the expensive mercenaries Phokis had squandered her fortune on, became keen to abandon their floundering ally and withdraw from the war before it was too late.

Philip sensed the mood was right and instructed his agents to let it be known he was willing to open negotiations. The Athenians responded, arrogantly at first, dictating their own terms. Philip gleefully put a swift stop to that by launching a fresh offensive. Alarmed at the Macedonian advance, Athens buckled, its governing Assembly dispatching a series of diplomatic teams to Pella.

The afternoon sun streamed through the window of the anteroom where Philip was preparing to meet yet another party of Athenian envoys. He was tired, having only just arrived from Thermopylae, but flushed with success. He'd managed to bribe the Phokian commander into surrendering the pass, and now the road to the south lay open to his army.

He rubbed his hands in anticipation. "How many are there?" he asked.

"Ten, and this time they've brought Demosthenes," answered Antipatros. He and Parmenion stood at the door. "According to the housekeeper in their lodgings, he's boasting that his oration will leave you speechless." The old general turned to Parmenion. "What's he supposed to have said?"

"That he will sew up your mouth with a reed."

Philip arched his eyebrows. "So Demosthenes has finally decided to put in an appearance, has he?" He scratched his beard thoughtfully. "And who is leading them?"

Parmenion smiled. "Philocrates, of course." All three of them laughed; Philocrates was Philip's man—bought and paid for.

Philip took another swig from the gargantuan wine cup in his hand. "Well," he said. "Give me a while longer and then the fun can begin. I'll let you know when I'm ready." He closed his eyes and swung his feet up onto the couch.

The Athenians waited in another room, tucked behind the monumental entrance to the palace. They had been in Pella for two days, waiting for King Philip to arrive, then the news had come that morning; he'd returned and was ready to see them. Now they waited on wooden benches as a cold spring wind blew in through a door-less archway. They had been there for three hours, and were in little doubt it was deliberate.

Demosthenes was fuming. "How dare he!" he muttered. "How dare this upthart keep us waiting?" His frustration at the delay was aggravating his lisp. "We, the reprethentatives of the greatest city on earth, are kept waiting by thith Mathedonian sponge. I'd lay a wager that's why we're delayed; they're trying to thober him up."

The others said nothing in reply. For years, Demosthenes had kept up this personal crusade against King Philip, making slanderous speeches, publishing wild accusations, warning the Assembly against him at every opportunity.

He paced the room irritably, knowing what the others were thinking. They couldn't understand his private vendetta against a man who, to many of them, seemed a reasonable, just, and fair ruler. And Philocrates was not to be trusted. More than once, he'd voiced the opinion that a strong leader of a united Greece might be no bad thing, given the disparate collection of warring cities that currently ravaged the country.

But Demosthenes was a true patriot, a man who loved his city. He feared Philip, and the threat to Athenian democracy and freedom that was everything Philip represented. In his dreams, he saw Macedonian warriors marching through a burning Athens. He saw them looting its treasure, and slaughtering and enslaving its people. He saw an army of savages with King Philip at their head. That was why he hated Philip.

"Remember that I am the youngeth, so I have the right to shpeak lasht." The lisp was becoming intolerable and he caught sight of two of Philocrates' aides smirking at each other. He pulled a couple of tiny pebbles from the bag at his waist and placed them in his mouth. It was a trick he'd adopted to force him to articulate his words.

"I will show this barbarian the power of the word over the sword," he continued. "He may think he has us begging for peace, but it will be the Macedonian who's on his knees by the time I finish with him. I'll have him begging us to share our Athenian enlightenment with him. This non-Greek!" He almost spat a pebble out.

None of the others doubted him. Despite his speech impediment, and their own intense dislike for the man, he was acknowledged as the greatest orator of his time. If anybody could turn this humiliation into a victory, it would be Demosthenes.

The Great Hall had been prepared for the meeting. In the center stood a row of chairs for the Athenians, with an open space behind for their aides. Directly opposite, and in front of the raised dais that housed the throne, was another set of chairs. These were for the Macedonian generals and ministers. The king would be on his throne, looking down on all of them.

The chamber was already full, the entire court lining the walls. Nobody wanted to miss this ultimate moment of Macedonian glory, the humbling of the mighty Athens.

The great doors were opened and the Athenians filed in, ushers showing each one to their seats. Demosthenes was placed near the end of the row and angrily marched to the center seat, sitting down with an audible thud. The Macedonians were already in their places, staring implacably ahead.

An usher made the announcement and the Macedonians rose for their king. Philocrates also stood and the Athenians followed his lead. Only Demosthenes was left sitting, determined not to be cowed into an act of deference to the man he hated. Then his resolve broke and he, too, got to his feet. He consoled himself by nonchalantly folding his arms.

Philip entered through the door at the back of the dais. He wore a crown of gold oak leaves and cavalry armor over a light tunic, and was surrounded by his bodyguard, each carrying a spear. His wives and children followed behind—all of his wives and all of his children. Demosthenes snorted contemptuously; such degenerate behavior would not be tolerated in Athens.

Philip sat and gestured for his appointed heir to join him, Alexander eagerly taking his place beside his father's throne. The king nodded to Antipatros to resume his seat, a signal for the rest to sit.

"May I say joy to you, gentlemen, and welcome to Macedonia." Philip's voice boomed across the hall. "I must apologize, as I understand you've been kept waiting for sometime." He looked at Parmenion, as though seeking confirmation of the fact. "It was unavoidable, I'm afraid. My army was engaged in disarming the Phokian garrison at Thermopylae, and such things always need close supervision to avoid a bloodbath. You know what soldiers are like if left alone."

He paused to stare at the Athenians, while they glanced at each other in shocked disbelief. The meaning behind his flippant remark was clear. The Macedonian army was through the pass at Thermopylae; they were in marching distance of Athens.

Philip broke their contemplation. "Now I will try to keep this brief, gentlemen, as I can see that some of you are still suffering from your revelries of last night." A titter of laughter ran through the audience as Athenian eyes were lowered to the floor and cheeks burned red. King Philip knew about last night; everybody, it seemed, knew about last night.

They had been invited to dinner at the home of a Macedonian noble in the city. All but Demosthenes had gone, and his excuse that he did not wish to be corrupted by these barbarians had been proved justified. Wine had flowed, a slave girl brought in, and events had gotten out of hand. Even worse, the slave had been an Olynthian, a freeborn Greek, captured at the fall of that city two years previously.

Only Demosthenes stared ahead, struggling to contain a smirk at the discomfiture of his colleagues. He had, after all, warned them. He focused his eyes on Philip and wondered if the man had engineered the party.

Philip stared back, his face as expressionless as Demosthenes' own. "I would like to hear what Athens thinks," he said. "Who wishes to speak first?"

One after the other, the envoys stood and took their turn to speak. But there was little they could say, not now that Philip's army held the pass at Thermopylae. They were defeated, and they knew it. A few pleaded their case, defending Athens' claim to the city of Amphipolis and warning against allowing Thebes to profit too much from the war. Others salved their consciences by making half-hearted pleas to spare Phokis from the fate that had befallen the Olynthians. Most were more preoccupied with the reception that would await them when news of their humiliation reached Athens. Already, accusations were being prepared against each other. Finally, it was Demosthenes' turn to speak.

He slipped a pebble under his tongue and stood. He had spent days preparing his speech and was not going to be cheated of his moment. He, alone, would put this barbarian in his place.

"And you are?" asked Philip, as if he didn't know.

"I am Demosthenes. Perhaps you have heard of me?" The Athenian looked about the hall smugly; his fame would have reached even a backwater such as this.

Philip gave him a long stare. "And what do you have to say, Demosthenes?"

The Athenian swelled out his chest. "In these troubled times," he began, lifting his voice as though addressing the Assembly at

Athens. "It falls upon the true Greeks among us to . . ." Philip was picking his nose. The man was actually sat there with his finger up his nose. Demosthenes stood with his mouth open.

Philip acted as if nothing was amiss. He plucked the digit from his nostril and stared at the Athenian enquiringly. Demosthenes composed himself and began again.

"In these troubled times . . ." Now Philip was sucking the finger, twirling it around his mouth, gleaning nourishment from it. Demosthenes looked down at the blank faces of his companions. It was as though only he could see what the man was doing. "In theeve troubled times . . ." The finger was inserted back into Philip's nose. Demosthenes willed himself to concentrate; he was determined he would be heard.

"In these troubled times, it falls upon the true Greeks . . ." Philip had slumped back into his seat and let his thighs slide forward, as though getting comfortable. The Athenian stood at eye height to the king's knees. Philip slowly parted his legs, and Greek males did not own underwear.

It was no good; Demosthenes had totally lost the thread of what he was saying. A smatter of giggling rose from the Macedonians lining the walls.

Philip leaned forward in his chair. "Is anything wrong?" he asked in a concerned voice. "Are you feeling unwell, perhaps? Would you like a drink of water?" The audience was whispering excitedly.

Demosthenes was lost in his own thoughts. He knew his compatriots would be enjoying his confusion as much as the Macedonians. His penchant for outspoken speeches and vitriolic personal attacks had made enemies of all of them over the years, and they would be relishing this humiliation. He needed to sit for a moment and recover his composure, but Philip wasn't going to give him the opportunity.

"Well, come on, Demosthenes." A sarcastic tone had crept into his voice. "Are you going to speak or not?"

The man peered up at Philip, his mind in a daze. He shook his head wearily and sat down.

Philip sneered in triumph. "In that case, I suggest we all withdraw so I may consider my reply." He stood, beckoning to Parmenion and Antipatros to follow.

After a short recess, the Athenians were recalled to the hall. Philip took his seat and surveyed the envoys, while Alexander ran to take his place by his father's side.

"Gentlemen. I have listened to what you have to say and have considered it very carefully. Now these are my terms." The authority in the king's voice echoed around the Great Hall.

"I propose," he said, "the following: Athens will withdraw its troops behind its borders immediately, and recall all mercenaries serving with the Phokians; Macedonia will retain control of Amphipolis and all land captured thus far; Phokis is mine to deal with as I think fit. Finally, Athens will propose that Macedonia receives the votes Phokis currently holds on the council at Delphi.

"Oh, I nearly forgot." His exaggerated expression of astonishment belied the weakness of his memory. "And I will sponsor the next Pythian games. Athens will propose that also." This last item was the most valuable prize for the Macedonian king, to preside over a truly Greek event.

"In return, you may keep the island of Euboia, and I will ensure that Thebes does not take the opportunity to encroach on your borders." He smiled magnanimously and ruffled Alexander's hair; the boy beamed up at his father proudly. "Now, what do you say to that, gentlemen?"

The Athenians looked at each other in silence, knowing they were in no position to argue. Phokis was finished while Thebes grew stronger, and now Athens itself was threatened; the Macedonians were in control of the pass at Thermopylae.

Philocrates stood. "It is a gracious offer, sir, and I'm sure my colleagues find it as acceptable as I do." There were a few murmurings among the envoys but none spoke out, so Philocrates smiled at the king and sat back down. He had earned his pay this day.

A state banquet was laid on for that evening to celebrate the swearing of the oaths that sealed the armistice, and, as usual at these events, Alexander was called upon to perform for the guests. Being a special occasion, it was decided that he should sing and Proteas accompany him on the lyre. Afterwards, the two boys would debate the works of the playwright Euripides, a particular favorite of Alexander's. He was fast approaching his ninth birthday, and forward beyond his years.

The party was already well underway by the time the Athenians arrived. Two Companion cavalrymen threatened each other with daggers, while someone had vomited against a wall, a slave wiping the splatter off a fresco. Philip had his arm around one of the younger Companions and was singing a love song in his ear, substituting his own lewd words for the original chorus.

The Athenians took up the corner reserved for them. They sat upright on their couches, feeling too uncomfortable to lounge, and, quiet and subdued, they sipped their wine and watched the antics of these vulgar northerners. Grimacing, Philocrates beckoned to a slave and instructed him to dilute their wine krater with water. The Macedonians were infamous for drinking their wine unmixed, but it was too strong for southern palates and had been the Athenians' downfall at the party the night before.

Antipatros, in turn, watched the Athenians. Like them, he didn't have the stomach for drinking that characterized his compatriots. To compensate, he had taken it upon himself to become the voice of reason at these events, ensuring that the excesses of the others didn't go too far and they all got home safely. He suffered for it, often being the butt of Philip's drunken jibes, but it was always appreciated the morning after.

He called over a slave and sent him to fetch Alexander and Proteas from where they waited in Lanice's apartment. Then he set about the task of penetrating Philip's drunken brain and reminding him that his son was due to perform.

Eventually he guided the king to his throne and quieted the gathering. The two boys were brought in, Alexander bold and confident, Proteas rather overawed and nervous. They walked to the center of the hall, where two stools waited for them. Antipatros noticed that Alexander was picking up Leonidas' fast-paced step. The other boy had to hurry to keep up.

Philip beamed at his smiling son. "Come on, my boy," he slurred. "Show the Athenians what you can do."

Alexander sang as sweetly as a bird, his high, lilting voice floating through the air as though wafted on the breeze. Proteas plucked gallantly at the strings of his lyre, doing remarkably well considering his lack of practice.

The song came to an end softly, Alexander lingering on the final note. There was silence in the hall for a moment, and then the usual raucous applause. Companions sprang to their feet demanding that the boy sing again, while Parmenion strode over to the two boys and hoisted Alexander onto his shoulders in jubilation. The room hushed as Philip made to speak, and Demosthenes struck.

"He sings like a girl!" sneered the Athenian. "Or a eunuch! Is that it, boy? Come on, lift your chiton and let's see what you have down there." He turned to his companions. "I wager we'd find nothing." Then, suddenly leering at the boy, "Except for a sore ass!" He grinned and made an obscene motion with his finger.

Parmenion lowered Alexander slowly to the floor, the boy trembling in disbelief, his cheeks bright red and his lip quivering. All eyes turned to the throne, but Philip was too shocked and too drunk to speak immediately. He sat in stunned silence.

Demosthenes' eyes swept the hall, a triumphant sneer on his face. Philip finally stumbled to his feet, but his fuddled brain was incapable of a suitable retort.

"My son is a man!" he roared, "as much as any man in this room!" He swung his arm about wildly, nearly falling over. He'd been drinking steadily since the meeting had finished that afternoon.

He lurched his way to the center of the hall. Pushing Proteas aside, he gripped Alexander's shoulder, the boy wincing as his father's fingers dug into his flesh.

"My son is a man. And one day he'll be a king, King of Macedonia!"

Parmenion joined the fray. "And still he can sing better than any of your southern spawn. Find me an Athenian boy who can sing like that!"

But Demosthenes had the upper hand. "I could find many, and many more who could do better," he said dryly. "As for being a king, what sort of king will this songbird make?" He sucked on the pebble in his mouth and eyed Alexander with contempt. "What will he do, warble his enemies to death?"

Antipatros feared violence; the mood among the Macedonians was turning ugly and several had already risen to their feet, daggers drawn. "You're a guest in this house, Demosthenes," he shouted, "but you have abused our hospitality. I suggest you and your friends leave. While you still can!"

The Athenians needed no encouragement. Fearful for their lives, they bundled Demosthenes out of the doors and fled across the courtyard, with an enraged king screaming obscenities at them from the center of the hall.

"As for the rest of you!" Philip snarled, turning on the Macedonians. "I didn't notice any of you rushing to defend my son's honor. Get out! Get out of my sight!" The scar on his face throbbed a bright red.

They spilled out into the corridors and dispersed to every part of the palace, only Parmenion and Antipatros daring to stay. Philip finally relaxed his grip on his son's shoulder.

"And as for you." He looked down at the boy, the anger drained from his face. "The Athenian was right. A king should not have the time to excel at anything so unimportant as singing; only to enjoy the music that others make."

It was an unnecessary thing to say, and Philip would have regretted it the next morning if he'd been sober enough to remember, but it had been said. He turned away and stalked out of the hall, the two generals following behind. Antipatros looked back, to see the boy stood alone in the center of the empty hall, his shoulders slumped and cheeks flushed with shame. A tear was forming in his eye.

"Tell my father I shall never sing or play music again," he whispered.

"Come in, boy."

Alexander entered his father's study. Philip sat at his desk, going through some training figures. The king was naked, waiting while Philip of Acarnania prepared a poultice for a venereal infection he'd picked up from somewhere. Parmenion sprawled on a couch, eating an apple.

Philip picked a scroll up from his desk and wagged it at the boy. "I received a letter this morning, from Isocrates. Do you know who he is?"

Alexander shook his head.

Philip smiled. "So there is a limit to the extent of your knowledge. He's an Athenian philosopher, my boy, and as well known in learned circles as our friend, Demosthenes. But he apparently thinks more highly of me." He indicated the scroll.

"This is an open letter, read out to the Athenian Assembly last week, with copies distributed throughout Greece. In it, he calls upon me to lead a Greek crusade against Persia and retrieve the colonies of Asia Minor. He says that the Persians are weak and cowardly and it would be an easy campaign, with rich plunder to be had for the taking. He also points out that it would not only unite Greece at last, but would provide living space for all the mercenaries who would no longer be needed for Greece's internal wars. Two problems solved at once." He glanced at Parmenion and the two exchanged smiles.

"What do you think I should do, Alexander?" he asked.

The answer was obvious. "Lead the crusade, Father. You would both win back the colonies and be acknowledged as King of all Greece." The boy sensed it was not the right answer after all. "That is what you want, isn't it?"

Philip shook his head imperceptibly. "Not their King, but merely the commander of their army. And how long do you think my influence would last once the campaign was over?"

He wagged the scroll again. "This Isocrates is either a fool or incredibly naive. Does he really think I'm going to volunteer to be the unpaid leader of their surplus mercenaries, for the greater glory of their city-states? Oh yes, I might receive a few words of praise in the Athenian Assembly, though not even that if Demosthenes has anything to do with it." He leaned forward and almost seemed to lower his voice conspiratorially.

"I will win back the colonies, Alexander, but this is not yet the time. Listen to me, my boy, because it may well fall upon you to carry it out. Never turn your back on the Athenians or Thebes or Sparta. You cannot move against Persia until you have first secured Greece. Is that understood?"

Alexander nodded, unsure if he'd just received a lesson in tactics or an admonishment for his stupidity.

Philip sat back in his chair and held up the scroll again. "Meanwhile, someone as eminent as Isocrates, no less, has told the whole of Greece that I'm the right person to be their leader. He's planted the idea in their heads for me, and I wonder how many battles I will not have to fight now, thanks to Isocrates?" He broke into his ugly grin. "And everything I do from now on? Why! I'm doing it in the interests of Greek unity and the sacred crusade."

Chapter Seven

Ox-Head

"We are of the opinion," said Philip, "that our son has outgrown the homespun teachers you're hiring from town. We've decided to engage a full-time tutor for him, and will be dispatching messengers throughout the civilized world to advertise the position and invite applications. Of course, we will only consider the most scholarly of academics." He turned to look at Olympias, who nodded her agreement.

"You must understand, Leonidas, that it's not mere arrogance that prompts this decision." Philip eyed the governor, sat in his usual, stiff-backed pose. "Alexander will be King one day and, if he's going to hold onto this kingdom, he needs the best education money can buy. And that money will not be wasted. Alexander is bright, very bright."

"I'm inclined to agree, sir. I've seen the boy in the classroom myself, winning an argument with a blustering teacher on a point of Greek grammar. I shall inform the boy upon his return from his duties. Will there be anything else, sir?" The king shook his head, and Leonidas stood and left the room.

"Well, that was easier than I'd expected." Philip poured himself more wine from the pitcher by his feet.

"He'd obviously heard rumors. You've not exactly kept it secret."

"I suppose not, wife. Still, I'd have thought he'd see a tutor as a rival."

"Oh, he does." Olympias stood and smiled down at her husband. "Well, health to you, husband," she said, uttering the traditional farewell. "And don't think I mean it."

Philip gave her his lop-sided grin in reply. He sat for a while after she left, finishing off the wine. It seemed a shame to waste it.

The news would please the boy, he mused. He almost wished they'd summoned Alexander to the room as well; that would have put Leonidas in his place.

He'd been weakening the governor's authority for sometime, giving Alexander his own suite of rooms in the palace with Lysimachus as his personal steward. He was, after all, no longer a child, and nothing less befitted a Macedonian prince.

Philip had ensured his continued control over the boy by placing him in the page's quarters, well away from the royal apartments. He had good reason to be so cautious. His spies kept him informed of the queen's constant attempts to poison his son's mind against him, and the boy was fast becoming old enough to be a threat to his father. Philip couldn't afford to lose him now.

Alexander was now in his twelfth year, and his attitude to his parents had subtly changed. Philip's continued military and diplomatic successes had made Macedonia the predominant power in Greece, but it no longer brought the boy the pride it had in childhood. More and more, he was looking to the future, and each new triumph for Philip was one less opportunity for his own reign. It seemed almost as though his father was doing it deliberately.

"Of course, he is," said Olympias. "He's jealous of you. He knows you're destined to outdo him, so keeps parading these so-called victories of his in an attempt to prove he's as good as you are."

Alexander sat in his mother's dayroom, eating a pastry and drinking watered wine. It had become a habit, Olympias taking it upon herself to regularly summon him to her quarters and work on his young brain.

She kept up the torrent of sweetmeats and propaganda. "You realize you've inherited nothing of use from him. You excel at everything, why? Not because of him. It's all due to the illustrious pedigree I've passed down to you.

"Think about it. Your skill with the sword, spear and bow is only natural to a descendant of Achilles, while your aptitude for running and riding is instinctive to one who can trace his ancestry to the widow of Hector, Troy's mightiest warrior. Your noble looks, astuteness and intelligence, of course, came from the princely rulers of that very same city.

"You were born to greatness, Alexander, and will be greater than that man Philip can ever hope to be. Always remember he is merely your mortal guardian, and need I remind you who your true father is?"

Alexander laughed and shook his head. "I get the point, Mother." He enjoyed these sessions. Granted, the aim was to turn him against his father, but her stories fascinated him and made sense to a youth on the verge of adulthood. He was destined for great things, and even his paternity pointed to that.

He watched his mother as she scolded a slave who'd spilled a drop of wine, and smiled at her antics. He'd never had the opportunity to spend much time with her before, and she'd always seemed rather distant to him as a small child growing up with Lanice. He knew she cared for him, but now he was finally getting the chance to know her properly. Beneath her haughty exterior, and despite the wild accusations that regularly rose from every quarter of the palace, she had the same concerns and aspirations he'd encountered among the wives of his father's courtiers. And her human weaknesses made her somehow seem more reachable. She was just a mother who wanted the best for her son.

Alexander still reported to Leonidas for daily instruction, but now his evenings were his own and he regularly mixed with the pages, gathering around him a quite substantial group of friends. Although they carried out certain menial duties, the Royal Pages were only nominally servants, many having their own slaves and substantial wealth. They were the sons of the Macedonian gentry, gathered at the palace as hostages for the continued loyalty of their fathers and brothers. Most would graduate into the ranks of the

Companion cavalry, and all dreamed of one day becoming one of the king's personal bodyguard, of wearing the purple cloak restricted to the seven most trusted of Philip's companions. They regarded themselves as courtiers rather than hostages, and all were eager to befriend the future king, even if he was some two or three years younger than many of them and still a child in their eyes.

Favorite among the duties of the pages was to act as bearers and beaters when the king and his entourage hunted the deer that abounded in the parks of Macedonia. Sometimes they would be lucky enough to be included on an expedition into the highlands, searching out the bears and lions that still roamed the forests. These occasions brought the opportunity to spend a few days away from the palace, and Alexander was not slow to persuade his father that he should be included.

Shepherds had reported a lioness in the area over the previous weeks and the local guides confirmed it was still present, tracking it to a sprawling cypress wood that clung to a steep hillside. It should make for a good day's hunting.

The Royal Pages strung themselves along the edge of the wood, Alexander at their center. Behind him stood Alexandros, his mother's brother. He was the eldest and leader of the troop, and also had special instructions from both Philip and Olympias to watch out for his nephew.

The hunting party, massed on the slope above them, was in jovial mood, toasting each other with large volumes of unmixed wine and confident of a successful hunt. A few eyed the pages greedily, though careful to keep their comments between themselves. After all, the king's son was among them.

Alexandros raised his arm and looked to the king, who gave the nod for the hunt to begin. In unison, the pages began to yell, and stepped forward into the trees. All were naked except for a white cloak, sunhat and spear, conventional hunting attire for Macedonian youths.

Immediately the treetops came alive as a host of squawking, flapping birds fled the cacophony below. Small animals scurried through the undergrowth for the safety of their burrows, mice and voles, a rabbit, a fox. The lioness broke cover, bursting out of the forest, snarling and sending the pages scattering. The dogs were released and, with a roar, the hunting party swept down the slope in hot pursuit, again scattering the pages. Many of the hunters shrilled the Macedonian battle cry, "Alalalalai!" as they passed. This was what they lived for; this was better than war itself.

The woods fell quiet, with the pages farthest down the slope chasing after the pack, the rest knowing they had no hope of catching up. They began to gather in small groups, disappointed that their day's hunt had ended so quickly.

Phrygius was the first to see it, and stopped dead in his tracks. To his right, Leonnatus saw it a moment later and gave a cry of warning. The boar stood motionless, its piggy eyes unswervingly watching the two youths. It was an old animal, the biggest either of them had seen. Phrygius backed away slowly, gingerly swinging his spear in a wide arc before him. The boar watched, unimpressed.

More pages were drawn to the area by Leonnatus' cry, appearing through the trees to either side of the beast. It became agitated as it saw its escape routes blocked.

Phrygius eyed the animal warily. "Have you killed your boar yet, Leonnatus? That one would make a worthy prize."

According to ancient Macedonian custom, a boy was not considered worthy to recline at table with men until he had speared a wild boar. Like the tradition of wearing a cord in place of a belt until he had killed a man, the custom was falling out of fashion in the wake of Philip's Hellenization program. Few of the pages currently at court had performed either ritual.

Leonnatus shook his head. He was a big bear of a youth, already an accomplished wrestler. "You know I haven't, Phrygius, and I would dearly love to claim this one. Look at the scars on those flanks; I wonder how many he's killed?" Leonnatus was smiling, but his eyes betrayed his misgivings.

"The boar is mine," shouted Alexander as he ran in front of Leonnatus. He stood at no more than chest height to the youth.

Alexandros was a few paces behind. "Alexander! Get back. This is too dangerous for you; stay away." He should have known better.

Alexander grinned and closed on the boar, his spear raised.

"Alexander, no!" Leonnatus tried to grab the boy but his hand clutched empty air. Startled by the sudden movements, the boar backed into the bushes, becoming entangled in the undergrowth and slipping as a hoof slid on a patch of moss. It squealed in rage and fright.

Alexander gulped as he realized, too late, the danger he was in. He tried to turn and run, but barged into a tree, scraping his knee on the bark. A bellow came from the undergrowth as the animal tried to free itself, the tops of the bushes shaking frantically from side to side.

"It's going to charge!" Phrygius hurled his spear and saw it clatter uselessly among the shrubbery.

The boar burst from the bushes and charged at Alexander. Trapped with his back against the tree trunk, the boy had no time to do anything but point his spear in the direction of the animal.

The boar, eyes wild and unseeing, never saw the spear. The point made contact with the animal's tusk, shoving the shaft back against the tree trunk. With its base wedged against the trunk, the point slipped sideways and entered the boar through its snout. Sliding through the animal's innards, it erupted from its underbelly in a torrent of blood and entrails.

The weight of the beast smashed into Alexander, crushing him against the tree. Both animal and boy slid to the floor. There was a stunned silence for a moment, then the pages rushed forward, every one of them shouting.

They pulled Alexander to his feet. He was trembling with shock and his breath came in gasps, the wind knocked out of him by the collision. His ribs ached and his back and buttocks were scraped and bleeding from contact with the tree trunk, but he was otherwise unharmed. The boar's tusks had somehow missed both chest and stomach.

The babble continued, the boys clustering around Alexander, examining him for signs of injury, not believing he had escaped so lightly. Attention turned to the boar, lying lifeless at their feet. Their voices raised an octave as the panic of the previous few moments turned to exultation at the thrill of the kill, and one or two discreetly used their capes to hide the sudden surge in their loins.

"Look at the size of this beast!" Perdiccas grabbed the butt of the spear and raised it, trying to lift the animal. It slid farther down the shaft, into the ooze of its own intestines.

"Well, you've killed your boar, Alexander, and that's more than I have." Leonnatus slapped him on the back. The boy winced, but continued to grin.

"There will be feasting tonight—we eat roast boar!" shouted Proteas, as he watched two of the pages heave the spear up onto their shoulders. The boys wobbled under the weight of the animal, skewered between them as though already on the spit.

"Wait! This is not good." Alexandros drew a few surprised stares.

"What do you mean, Alexandros?" Phrygius gestured toward the carcass. "Alexander has killed his boar; how can that not be good?" The pages fell silent, puzzled at Alexandros' attitude.

"Listen to me." Alexandros was worried, the concern in his voice evident. "No one can know that Alexander killed the boar on his own. We must say we did it together."

The pages looked at each other. "Why is that, Alexandros?" Craterus asked the question for all of them, his tone revealing his rising irritation.

Alexandros shrugged resignedly. "Have you killed a boar yet, Craterus? Or you? Or you?" He pointed to one boy after another. "Nobody has killed a boar for years. Phrygius is the only one here who has, and that was before he came to court.

"And why?" He turned and stared straight at Phrygius. "Because the King disapproves. He thinks it's another example of your country's backwardness, something else for the Athenians to despise. So what do you think he's going to say when he discovers we've let his son perform a rite that's now only practiced by the children of the hill tribes?"

There was a murmur of agreement; they hadn't thought of it like that.

"No!" Alexander screamed the word at them. His cheeks had flushed red and he was quivering with fury. He'd just risked his life for this prize and was not going to be cheated of it. "What are you saying, Alexandros? I did it, on my own. I killed the boar." He stabbed a finger at his uncle. "You! You're just jealous!"

Alexandros shook his head. He reached out a hand and took a step toward the boy. Alexander took a step back.

"Alexander, listen. You know as well as I what your father thinks. You're his son and he expects you to set an example to the people. Do you think this is an example he would approve of? And what would your mother say?"

The boy tried to think of a reply, but didn't have his father's way with words. Instead, he snarled like a dog, his lips drawn back and teeth bared. His eyes, usually so deep and dreamy, blazed like the fires of the underworld.

"No! No! No! No! No!" He spat the words at Alexandros. "I won't have it! The boar is mine. I killed it, and I have earned the right to recline with the men. You cannot take that away from me." For a moment, he looked like he was about to stamp his foot.

But Alexandros had convinced the others. "Come on, Alexander," said Proteas. "You know Alexandros is right. If the King finds out we let you face the boar alone, he will never forgive us."

"Yeah," came a nameless voice from the back of the group. "It'll be all right for you. The King will give you your place at table with the men, but it's us who'll suffer for it. We're the ones who will be scrubbing your plates with the slaves afterwards."

There was a silence, the color draining from Alexander's face as though he had been suddenly deflated. For his glory, his companions would suffer. Such glory would be worthless and his shame would be that of Achilles at Troy, when he allowed Patroclus to go out and die in his name.

"You're right; I should have realized." Alexander's voice was barely a murmur. He surveyed the group, his comrades. "We hunted the boar together, and that is how it should be."

There was an audible sigh of relief, the boys unsure what had just happened but glad it had.

"We tell the King the animal attacked us and we hunted it only to protect ourselves," said Alexandros. "Alexander was injured in the confusion, but not by the boar and was never in any danger." A chorus of nods and smiles greeted his words.

They reached the campsite to find the hunting party had returned empty-handed, the lioness having escaped them by climbing a nearly vertical cliff face. "Like a goat," they joked. Attention focused on the boar, still skewered on Alexander's spear. Darkness was falling as it was set up on a spit over the fire, adults and boys gathering around to enjoy the smell of the meat as it roasted.

Philip was in a jovial, drunken mood. He placed his hand on Alexander's shoulder. "Perhaps we should have been the beaters and you the hunters. Maybe some of your luck might have rubbed off on us."

"What are you going to call your hunting party, Alexander?" called Amyntas from across the flames. "You will need a name." Five years older than his cousin, Amyntas had recently graduated to the Companion cavalry. He seemed to hold no grudge toward the boy who would succeed to the throne that had once been his, and some of the pages did not even know the story of his brief reign.

Amyntas had been the infant son of Macedonia's previous king, Philip's elder brother, and had succeeded to the throne upon his father's death in battle. Philip had been appointed regent, but his evident abilities and the need for an adult ruler had soon led to the backing of the army in an offer of the throne. Philip had baulked at murdering an infant, the obvious next step to securing his kingdom, and had allowed Amyntas to live. But a king could never take chances. The youth may not show any outward sign of ambition, but all his slaves and all his lovers were in the king's pay.

Philip shot a look at his nephew, and then laughed. "A good point, Amyntas. All Macedonian gentlemen of quality belong to a hunting club. It's got to be Hercules," he said to his son. "All the best clubs are dedicated to Hercules, but Hercules-the-what?"

Alexander shrugged. "We hadn't thought of forming a club. Are we allowed to?"

Philip chuckled. "Well, I don't know the rules on such things but you will one day be King, my boy, and it's time you learned that if a king doesn't like the rules, he changes them."

"The name is obvious," shouted Parmenion. Drink was getting the better of him and he was slurring his words. "It should be Hercules-the-Pig-Sticker!"

And so, in the best traditions of Macedonian hunting clubs, the members of the Pig-Stickers sat down to eat meat with the men that night. Alexander sipped his wine unmixed for the first time, and hoped it was an acquired taste. He felt closer to his father than he had for a long time. He watched the man.

Philip was approaching middle age, but not yet slowing down despite the years of unchecked debauchery. Almost ceaseless campaigning kept his body sleek and muscular, but old wounds gave him pain and his good looks had long since vanished. His flesh was covered in scars and his gashed face hideous with its single eye.

And still his men loved him. Not just these noblemen, who surrounded him at court and called him Philip to his face, but also the rank-and-file of his army, who followed him into the field and willingly died to further his glory. Alexander wondered if he would be able to command that much love and respect when his turn came. There was much he could still learn from this man, whether he was his true father or not.

That Alexander had slain the boar became common knowledge within days of their return to the palace. All the pages had relatives at court, and brother told brother and son told father. Philip was soon informed.

He pondered what action to take. To admonish the boy, in public or private, would destroy the affinity they had felt since the hunt. Philip was planning to be home for the winter, and the thought he might finally be able to spend some time with the lad was pleasing to him; it would be a shame to spoil that. The story did not seem to have spread beyond the palace, and that witch Olympias seemed to be unaware of it. Besides, his son had killed his boar, and that was something to make any father proud. He would keep silent.

The winter passed pleasantly, father and son making up for the years they had lost. On Philip's orders, Alexander would be released from his studies so they could go riding together across the plains that surrounded Pella, with only the bodyguard in attendance. Sometimes they spent the night at the villa of one of the many courtiers who'd been granted land close to the palace, yet another of Philip's strategies to Hellenize his nobles.

On one such outing, the pair shared a couch in front of a roaring fire. The owner had discreetly retired his household early, leaving only a single slave to attend to the guests. The duty bodyguard struggled to stay awake at the door, while the others were already asleep in a pile of sheepskins on the floor. Philip was making the most of this intimate moment with his son.

They were playing Tavli. Alexander threw a tantrum the first time they played this forerunner of backgammon, sweeping the pieces from the board when he realized too late that nothing could stop his father from bearing off all his men. But Philip calmed him, and began to explain his moves to the boy. Just a few games later Alexander beat his father.

"I've won! I have, haven't I?"

"You certainly have, my boy. I might be able to pull a few pieces back, but whatever I do, you'll be ahead at the end."

The boy jumped to his feet, his arms waving in the air. "I've won! I've won!" he called to the sleepy guard.

Philip smiled at his son's jubilation. He'd let him win, but knew he would soon need to use the loaded dice in his own favor instead of the boy's. He learned too fast.

"Now, how about finishing that pastry, and then we'd better turn in. Tomorrow, I think we'll go back to that opened tomb we found. If we've got thieves in the area, I want them caught."

"Can I go inside this time?"

Philip laughed. "Maybe, but only if we can find a fortune-teller first and buy you a spell for protection."

Philip dismissed the slave and settled down next to his son. He pulled the blanket up to the boy's neck and Alexander was soon asleep, cradled by his father's arm.

Winter gave way to spring. The clearing weather prompted the highland shepherds into driving their flocks back to the mountains from winter pastures on the plains. Philip, yet again, vainly tried to pacify the lowland farmers, enraged at this annual trampling of their crops. Much as he liked to think he ruled one country, he knew he still had a long way to go.

But the unexpectedly mild spring allowed him to turn his mind to other matters. Events in Epirus were causing concern, and he had the feeling it could be time to return to that country.

King Arybbas was becoming increasingly unpopular with his people, and several Epirote nobles of royal blood were emerging as rivals. It was probable he would soon be deposed by one or another of them, with the likelihood of the country being torn apart by the civil war that would certainly follow. Philip needed Epirus to safeguard his flank in any operation against the south, and could not afford to see her weakened or ruled by a new king with sympathies that lay with Philip's enemies. He called a meeting of his war council.

Within a week, the plain beyond Pella was thronging with traders of all kinds. An army preparing for war needed supplies, and carpenters, armorers, leatherworkers, all set up their workshops. Others, drawn to wherever there might be a buying public, soon followed them. Stalls selling sweetmeats and pastries sprang up; peddlers of overpriced trinkets moved among the crowds; quacks performed miraculous cures on their stooges. Then there were others, male and female, who sat in booths with open doors, encouraging the interested to step into the tiny space inside.

The trading camp took on a festive air as the people of the town flocked through the gates for a welcome day out after the rigors of winter, and the gentlemen of the Pig-Stickers quickly found their way to the carnival.

Alexander munched on an apple, sniggering with the others as they spotted Leonidas surreptitiously entering one of the boxes, a woman shutting the doors behind him.

"No need to hurry back to the palace now, Alexander." Proteas leered in the direction of the booth and made an obscene gesture.

"I'm not so sure," replied Alexander with a grin. "Knowing my uncle, he'll be back outside in two minutes." The group laughed.

Their attention was drawn to a crowd gathering at one end of the site. The yellow cloaks of a troop of Companion cavalrymen could clearly be seen above the heads of the crowd, followed by the purple of the bodyguard. King Philip was visiting the camp.

The royal party rode up the main thoroughfare through the encampment, slowed both by the mud and by the cheering citizenry that flocked to greet their leader. Philip was still as popular as ever and happily acknowledged his people, a broad smile on his crooked face.

Alexander watched his father pass but, as had become usual on these occasions, was unable to feel pride in this demonstration of his father's popularity. Instead, his thoughts again turned to his own reign. Would King Alexander be able to command as much respect?

Philip was heading for the farthest end of the camp, to where the horse dealers had set up their paddocks. The small group of youths naturally gravitated in that direction. It was always useful to be in the king's eye, especially when they could be seen to be on good terms with his son.

By the time they arrived, the rest of the court had joined Philip. Parmenion chatted to a visiting mercenary general, Demaratus of Corinth, about the merits of the Boeotian helmet versus the Corinthian, while Aristander pretended to stifle a yawn as a soothsayer from the south recounted a visit to the oracle at Siwa in Egypt. Philip of Acarnania delighted some junior members of the

Companion cavalry with descriptions of the more outrageous wounds he had treated in his time.

The king was with the secretary of the cavalry. A number of horses were being led around a paddock, the minister occasionally stepping forward to inspect one more closely. Few failed. One after the other they were approved, with slaves marking their flanks and scribes recording the transaction. The horses were of poor quality and obviously destined for the Prodromoi, Philip's light cavalry.

All the while, the king was involved in other negotiations. Traders lined up with examples of their work—a pole-turner who claimed he could supply fifty pike shafts a day, a blacksmith selling leg grieves, another with stabbing swords. Soldiers were responsible for buying their own kit throughout the rest of Greece, but Macedonian recruits received a free issue of basic equipment. It was yet another part of Philip's strategy to give his army an advantage. Those who could not afford to outfit themselves weakened his enemy's forces, while he could always count on fielding substantial numbers of well-equipped troops.

Alexander drifted over to his father. His companions followed eagerly, jostling each other aside as they strove to be seen as part of the prince's inner circle of friends.

"Joy to you, my boy." The wine on Philip's breath was unmistakable. "Tell me what you think of this?" He was inspecting a large round shield, of a type unfamiliar to Alexander.

He took the shield from his father. It was made of a sturdy wood, with a thin outer covering of bronze that cried out to be painted in regimental colors. It was much larger and heavier than the small bronze shields fastened to the elbow by the men of the phalanx.

Alexander shook his head. "I'd guess this was for use by a unit of hypaspists, though it's large even for them." Intrigued, he looked up at his father.

Philip chuckled lightheartedly. "No, it doesn't belong to the Shield-Bearers." Named for the shields they carried, the Hypaspists were Philip's elite guards regiment. Armed with short spears, they could be used on uneven ground where the phalanx was too unwieldy to operate.

Craterus called out from the group, eager to prove his knowledge. "It's a hoplon, sir, a hoplite shield from one of the cities in the south." Philip scowled at the youth's interruption; the moment between father and son had been broken.

He took the shield from Alexander and handed it back to the crestfallen merchant. "Yes, the lad's correct. Go and sell this to the Athenians. It has no place in my army." There was no sign of contempt in his voice.

"But I'm glad you were able to see it, my boy." Philip turned and placed a hand on Alexander's shoulder. "One day you will all face such shields on the battlefield." He was addressing the group now. "And for as long as you do, you know you will win. Our own army also used the hoplon when I became King, but I changed that. I took away the hoplon and gave the phalanx the puny arm bracelet they carry now. Why?" He stared directly at Craterus.

The youth blushed. "I don't know, sir," he lied.

Philip gave him a smile of satisfaction. "You'll go far," he said. There was a snigger from some of the others and someone digged the youth in the ribs. Philip turned his attention back to the group.

"Then I'll tell you why. It's because I also gave them the sarissa. That pike is fully half as long again as those carried by our enemies, and in a shove between phalanxes, we can cut them down before they even get close enough to reach our front rank. It gives us the edge in every battle, and will continue to do so until the fools realize and copy us." His ugly face split into a grin. "But the sarissa needs two arms to hold it, so we threw away the hoplon!"

The boys broke into a chorus of dutiful laughter, but already knew the effectiveness of the sarissa. They'd heard their fathers tell how the massed ranks of the phalanx had burrowed deep into the Thracian line; how the mounts of the famed Thessalian cavalry had shied away from a wall of sarissae; how a Phokian phalanx had collapsed and been trampled into the dust by a Macedonian regiment that had not even broken step.

A slave approached the king's entourage, a bodyguard barring his way. Aristander took the man's message and nodded.

"The horse is ready, sir."

"Ah! Come, Alexander. This should be worth seeing." Philip withdrew his hand from his son's shoulder slowly, letting his fingers slide down the boy's arm as if about to hold his hand. "According to the dealer, this horse is worth thirteen talents." He grunted and added, "I have bought cities for less."

The whole group strolled toward the farthest paddock in the line, Philip with his entourage, Alexander with his band of companions. Behind them trailed a substantial throng; the king's public appearances usually drew a crowd.

A small hut had been set up at the entrance to the paddock, with canvas stalls located to either side of it, each large enough to stable several horses. A small pennant flew from the hut, the ox-head emblem of Philonicus of Thessaly, horse-breeder of repute.

Philonicus stood at the entrance to the paddock, his smile and widespread arms of greeting masking the troubled look in his eyes.

"My King, joy to you. I trust you and yours are well."

Philip nodded. "And joy to you, Philonicus. It is good to see you again. It's been far too long since you pleased us with your presence." The king's greeting was genuine; he'd been buying horses from the breeder for many years. "So, what have you brought me this time?"

Philonicus gestured toward the stables. "It's the most magnificent horse I've had the pleasure to handle, sir. A trifle temperamental granted, but a truly rewarding mount in expert hands." He looked sharply at Philip, to make the point.

The gesture was not lost on the king; he was easy to flatter. "Well then," he said, glancing down at Alexander. "Let's see the beast, shall we?"

A groom led the horse out, while another walked to one side. Philip's eyes narrowed and he whispered in Alexander's ear. "See that, boy? The second groom feels the need to carry a training stick and is careful to stay forward of the hind legs." Alexander nodded.

But the horse certainly was magnificent. Pure black, except for a white patch on its forehead, it towered over its handlers. Its belly was sleek and groomed, the legs strong and muscled. It eyed the rowdy throng gathering beyond the rope that marked the edge of the paddock.

"Well, it's certainly a thoroughbred. There's no mistaking that," Philip said, impressed. "You never fail to deliver, do you, Philonicus?" The trader managed a smile.

"Imagine if you will, sir, reviewing your troops from a mount as superb as this, or leading your cavalry in the charge, or watching a city burn." Philonicus was a professional. "And when the ladies see you astride such a beast . . . ?"

The horse was as good as sold. Philip turned to the head of his stables eagerly. "Let's see what he can do."

The trainer stepped forward, the horse watching his approach carefully. It turned its whole body to face him as he came alongside, its rump barging into the second of Philonicus' grooms. The man jumped quickly, uttering something unintelligible. It sounded like Egyptian to Alexander.

At the sound of the raised voice, the horse flicked its head up and pulled on its reins. The groom holding them was the next to curse the horse, this time in Dardanian.

The animal understood the words less than Alexander, but knew what harsh voices meant. It backed away from the threat of more pain, the ugly Greek bit cutting into its mouth as it strained on the reins. The Dardanian groom in front was pulled helplessly forward, the Egyptian behind slapping the stick under the horse's hocks in a vain attempt to control it.

A roar of delight erupted from the crowd; this was unexpected entertainment. Bets were taken on who would win, the horse or the two hapless slaves. Philip's trainer turned and looked at the king, and shook his head imperceptibly.

The affair degenerated into farce as Philonicus hurried over to try to retrieve the situation, and skidded on a pile of dung. It took several more minutes of uproarious laughter before the horse was brought under control again.

Unlike his hooting companions, Alexander watched these events unfold in silence. Despite his years, he was an accomplished horseman—the king's son could be little else. He wondered what horrors could have been inflicted on an animal to make it so troubled. It was a terrible misuse of such a fine horse.

He glanced up at his father. Philip was also silent, his expression grim.

The trainer tried again. He stood a few paces in front of the animal, uttering soothing noises. He took a step forward, then another. It seemed to be working. The horse eyed him suspiciously but made no attempt to back away.

The trainer advanced one more step, taking the reins from the groom. He lifted his arm slowly and passed the reins back over the horse's ears. "There, boy. Easy does it."

The horse saw the raised arm and felt the brush of leather. It heard the male voice and caught the man's breath in its nostrils. It again shied away, this time rearing up on its hind legs menacingly. The trainer let the reins drop, the horse snorting and taking the opportunity to canter a few paces away.

The trainer walked back to Philip, shaking his head as he went. "This animal is not suitable for riding, sir. Given time, perhaps, we could train it for a chariot team, but even then I have my doubts." He gave a disparaging shrug. "It's so nervous it's afraid of its own shadow."

Philip nodded agreement, then turned to give Philonicus a long, withering stare. The trader shrank visibly. "I am not pleased, Philonicus. I thought we were friends, but you have tried to dupe me with a rogue animal like I was some fat Athenian ripe for the taking." His tone, already harsh, was becoming angry. "Can you explain yourself? What's the meaning of bringing me such a beast?"

"I'm sorry, sir. Please forgive me," said the trader, his eyes downcast. He sighed and raised them. "The horse has already been returned as unmanageable by two buyers, sir, and the fools have ruined the animal. The lash marks on its rump are still visible if one knows where to look."

"And?" Philip's voice was low, menacing.

"I had to sell for more than my usual profit margin to recoup my losses, sir, and only a king has that sort of money. But I wouldn't have charged you as much as thirteen talents," he added, hurriedly.

"Asking that much gave me the leeway to accept the price you would bargain me down to." He smiled dolefully. "Unfortunately, the horse failed to behave today."

"Unfortunately? Do you realize I could have you arrested on a charge of trying to endanger the King's person?" Philip flung his arm in the direction of the horse, now quietly watching them. "You would have me ride that into battle? So, are you in the pay of my enemies? They'd have been awarding you gold crowns as it carried me onto their spears. That horse is a killer, Philonicus, and I'd wager no one could ride it."

That was all it needed.

A spark came into Alexander's eyes. He would tame the untamable beast. "What a waste!" he said, then louder. "What a waste of such a splendid animal."

Philip spun around. "What do you want, boy?" he snapped. "I can do without one of your performances."

Alexander was taken aback; his father never spoke to him like that in public. But this was too good an opportunity to miss.

"You're being too hasty, Father. There's nothing wrong with the horse that can't be corrected with a bit of skill and patience." He turned to face the crowd and announced, "I will ride the horse."

There wasn't a word from the king's entourage. They looked to Philip for a lead, but not so the citizens of Pella. The prospect of seeing this arrogant young prince fall on his ass was more entertainment than they'd seen for a long time. They roared their delight.

"So, you're going to ride the horse, are you?" There was a sneer in Philip's voice. "A horse that the head of my stables, a man who was a champion jockey before you were even born, says cannot be ridden. And you're going to ride it?"

Alexander nodded. His father's reaction told him he was overstepping the mark, and he was less buoyant now, more conciliatory. "The horse is afraid of adults, Father, but I am not an adult. I'm too short, and my voice is not yet broken. The horse won't see me as a threat, won't even feel my weight on his back."

Philip stood and stared at his son in silence, then his face cracked into its unsightly lopsided grin and he shook his head in wonderment.

"You never cease to surprise me, do you? Very well. Let's see if you are that perceptive; let's see if you're right. But be careful, that horse is wild. I don't want to have to face your mother and explain a broken head." He motioned to the trainer to help.

"No adults." Alexander waved the trainer away and walked toward the horse, now quietly chewing on a cud. He began to hum, very quietly, melodically. He heard Demaratus of Corinth call out.

"Ride that horse, Prince Alexander, and I shall buy it for you."

Alexander moved nearer, his arms lowered. The horse watched him closely, more curious than suspicious as this tiny figure could not possibly be a danger. For endless minutes, Alexander stood next to the horse, humming gently. The spectators grew bored with the inactivity and started chattering among themselves, while Philip folded his arms.

"I wonder how long this is going to take?" he commented to the trainer.

Alexander gently raised a hand and placed it against the horse's neck. He let it slide up to the bridle, curling his fingers around the strap. He took a pace to his left, then one more. Squeezing the bridle slightly, he took a third step, and the horse followed. A ripple of applause ran through the crowd. Philip exchanged glances with the trainer.

Horse and boy strolled across the paddock, and Alexander began whispering into the horse's ear. "What's your name, boy? What name did they shout as they thrashed your back?" He stroked the horse's neck. "I promise, you will never hear that name again." He looked up at the patch on the horse's forehead. It resembled the ox-head brand of Philonicus' stable, stenciled onto the rump of all his stock. "Shall I call you Ox-head? No, that's a Greek name. I shall call you Bucephalus, our word for ox-head. You're going to be the mount of a Macedonian prince, and you deserve to have a Macedonian name."

He slipped off his cloak and let it fall to the ground; he didn't want to risk anything flapping over the horse's eyes and startling it. He ran his free hand along its back. "Will you let me mount you, Bucephalus? Or will you dump me in a cowpat, in front of all these people? No, you wouldn't do that to me." He gripped the horse's mane and lightly slid onto its back. The horse barely moved.

The crowd began to cheer, but then abruptly fell silent at the sight of such a tiny figure astride such a beast. Philip gestured to the trainer, anxiety written on his face.

Alexander saw the trainer and a groom moving toward him, and pressed his knees against the horse's flanks. "Come, Bucephalus. We don't want their interference."

Bucephalus took one look at the approaching adults and responded to the pressure of the boy's knees. He trotted, slowly at first, across the paddock. Alexander held on, gaining confidence and with a smile on his lips.

The horse increased his speed, the trot becoming a canter, then a gallop. A groan of dismay rose from the crowd as the gallop became a mad dash toward the far side of the paddock. Philip was shouting now, calling on the Companions to fetch their horses and follow. He ordered Philip of Acarnania to ready his bag of potions, and swore revenge on Philonicus if anything happened to his son.

Bucephalus galloped on, feeling the wind whip his ears and barely conscious of the tiny weight across his back. He reached the farthest edge of the paddock, a tiny stream marking its boundary, and slowed to cross.

As with the others, the dash had taken Alexander by surprise, but he was quick to react; if he was to control the horse, this was the moment.

He reached down and gave the horse an encouraging pat on the neck. "That was good, boy, but now you must take me back." He dragged the reins, trying to make the move as nonchalant as possible. It worked. The horse swung his head, accepting the change in direction.

Alexander knew the horse was his as they trotted back the way they had come. He could hear the cheering, could see the crowd surging into the paddock. It began to dawn on him just what he'd managed to achieve. He'd tamed a horse that his father had been afraid to even mount.

He cantered up to where Philip stood waiting. The king was alone, the noblemen of the Companion cavalry struggling to contain the mob. Everywhere Alexander looked, there were grinning faces. He slid from the horse, totally at ease.

"Well, Father?" He was careful to stand away, keeping Bucephalus at a distance from any adults.

"Well?" Philip turned to face the crowd. "Well?" he bellowed, a roar going up in reply. He turned back to his son, and Alexander saw that look sweep across his father's face again, the one he'd noticed before. Philip spoke again, quieter this time, so only Alexander could hear him.

"If this goes on, I think you'll need to find yourself a kingdom of your own, my boy. This one's proving too small for the likes of you."

The comment took Alexander by surprise. He stared up at his father, unsure if he'd just received an accolade or a warning. Philip let the words sink in for a second or two, and then laughed.

"Demaratus said he would buy you the horse if you rode it, Alexander, and he's a man who keeps his word. So it seems the horse is yours, and well-deserved too." He gestured toward the crowd. "Now, go and enjoy your triumph."

"Joy to you, wife. You know why I have asked you here?"

Olympias shook her head as she sat on the couch that had been offered her. She gazed around Philip's dayroom, feigning disinterest. "Something to do with my son, I assume."

"That's correct. I have decided on the successful applicant for the position of tutor, and wouldn't dream of making the announcement public without informing you first."

Olympias gave him an imperious glance. "That's good of you, husband. And I take it you've chosen Isocrates?"

He smiled. "No, the man is in his nineties. I want someone educating my son who can finish a lesson without taking a nap halfway through." Besides, Philip hadn't forgotten the philosopher's naivety in his call for him to lead the crusade against Persia.

Olympias raised her eyebrows. "Then, who?"

Philip took a moment to answer, enjoying the look on his wife's face. It was rare he could surprise her these days.

"I have received applications," he continued, "from every corner of the Greek world, many accompanied by bribes and effusive flattery." He was rewarded with another surprised stare. "But I have decided on a rising star of the academic world, a philosopher named Aristotle. He is not only hailed as the foremost student of Plato, but I already know him. Aristotle's father held a position at court as one of my own father's physicians, and we met on occasion as children."

"And you expect me to approve him? You're slipping, husband. You're not supposed to admit he's your man."

Philip's smile broadened. "You wouldn't say that if you knew the fee he's asking. As I said, we were children. I haven't seen him in years."

"So, convince me. What are his fees?"

"That is between me and Aristotle, but I will say this: he is a native of Stagira. I see you've heard of that city, and that would be because I flattened it a few years ago. In addition to his fee, I must rebuild Stagira. Do you have any idea how much that will cost me, wife?"

Olympias could venture a guess. "Well," she said. "If I can't have my own man educating my son, I can at least have one who is neutral. I approve. Aristotle, it is."

A messenger bearing the offer of appointment was dispatched to Aristotle's academy on the island of Lesbos. It was the same messenger Philip always used when communicating with the philosopher. They'd been using this same messenger since Aristotle had joined the court of a certain Persian despot called Hermeias several years earlier. Hermeias ruled a territory on the coast of Anatolia—that would make an ideal jumping off point for any campaign against Persia.

With the army fully equipped and eager to march off the sloth of winter quarters, Philip led them onto the road to Epirus, and the bond between father and son was broken for the last time. Alexander also lost Alexandros, not just his uncle but also his confidante and mentor. The youth was to accompany Philip on his return to Epirus.

It was a short and relatively bloodless campaign. King Arybbas rapidly fled into exile in Athens and Alexandros was installed as the new king, and Macedonia's puppet.

It was a shrewd move, and one that Philip had been grooming Alexandros for since the day he'd snatched him as a boy from the palace in Dodona. King Arybbas had always been too unreliable, but now Philip had a king on his border who was both acceptable to the people of Epirus and completely trustworthy. It also kept the peace with Olympias; her brother was now the ruler of her homeland.

Chapter Eight

The Gardens of Midas

Alexander nearly laughed aloud when he walked into his mother's dayroom and saw his new tutor for the first time. Aristotle stood in the center of the room, dripping wet from the rain that still drummed on the roof.

He wore traveling clothes, a woolen tunic covered by a gargantuan cloak. Even damp from the rain, Alexander could tell the clothes were both well made and expensive. Aristotle had removed his hat to reveal a pate of wispy hair and, with his thickly crimped beard, he looked to Alexander like he'd put his head on upside-down. He was tall and thin, very tall and very thin. Spindly legs emerged from beneath his tunic, skinny and hairy, and splattered with the mud of the road. It was another Leonidas.

Olympias gave her son a frosty look, a warning to wipe the smirk from his lips. "Alexander, I sent for you to welcome your new tutor. Do so."

Alexander looked up at Aristotle; he didn't even reach the man's chest. "Joy to you, sir, and welcome to Pella. I have heard much about you. Is it true that you studied in Athens under the great Plato? I look forward to taking instruction from a true scholar." Behind him, Leonidas bristled.

Aristotle's eyebrows rose imperceptibly. "And joy to you, Prince Alexander. I have heard much about you, too." The man had a slight lisp, and the smirk returned to Alexander's lips.

Tuition started the next morning, and ended abruptly. Aristotle quickly declared that the schoolroom was totally inadequate, the location next to the kitchens demeaning, and that the boy needed the stimulation of others of his own age.

Alexander found the whole affair comical. Aristotle had appeared in class wearing an outfit of the finest linen, a material usually reserved for women's clothes. He wore large expensive rings on nearly every finger and a gold chain around his neck. With the lisp and upside-down head, the man just couldn't be taken seriously.

Olympias placated the tutor, telling him a room would be made available for lessons in the pages' quarters, and those boys who could be spared from other duties would join Alexander in class. But the palace buzzed with gossip about the soft southern dandy while Leonidas joked with Lysimachus and rubbed his hands.

"I doubt this pimp will last long," he quipped. "He'll soon go back to the whore-house he came from."

Lessons began afresh the next day. Craterus and Leonnatus joined Alexander in the schoolroom for the morning lecture, while Proteas sat in for an hour in the afternoon. Two others were in class the next morning.

It was far from ideal. Rarely did the same boy attend consecutive lessons, while Aristotle's Macedonian was rusty and few of the pages were fluent in Greek. Those who could understand what he was saying were unable to keep up with the subject matter.

Alexander often found that he and the tutor were carrying on a discussion alone, while the others fidgeted or stared out of the window in bored silence. He found his companions' lack of knowledge irksome, until he realized why; they could hardly be expected to keep pace with the son of a god.

Then Philip's dealings threatened to backfire on him and he was forced to return to the palace and attend to business. He had been backing a nationalist government in Egypt for years and had also begun funding rebels in Cyprus, but the current Great King was proving to be more belligerent than his predecessors and set on recovering his lost territories. Even now, a Persian army was gathering in the region known as the Troad, the Aegean coast of Anatolia. Rumor had it they would invade Cyprus and then march on Egypt, or even Greece.

"Matters are coming to a head," said Philip, pacing his study. "Athens is proposing an alliance and joint action to aid the insurgents, and this I do not want." He leaned against his desk and stared at Parmenion. He and Antipatros were the only two of Philip's advisors to be summoned to this most secret of meetings.

"I'm not yet ready to face Persia," continued Philip, "and cannot hope to be until I have the whole of Greece pacified. Key to that is Athens, and their willingness to offer refuge to King Arybbas has not been lost on me." He smiled. "They say Demosthenes led the cheering as the Assembly unanimously passed the motion. It is an open act of defiance, gentlemen, and I know better than to put any faith in the promises of such an ally."

"What are you going to do?" asked Parmenion.

Philip poured himself more wine before answering. "The only thing I can do. I shall negotiate an understanding with the Great King that gives him a free hand to deal with Egypt and Cyprus as he pleases. A Persian agent is in town for that purpose and I'll be meeting with him this afternoon. That's where you come in, Antipatros. The Athenian emissary is also expecting to meet me this afternoon, to discuss our new alliance. Make sure he is indisposed for a day or so, by which time I'll have returned to the army."

The general smiled. "I know a brothel that will make him think he's become a god, given enough cash. Leave it to me."

"Word of this will get out, Philip," cautioned Parmenion. "It will cause resentment in Athens and be seen as weakness, both by our enemies and allies."

"Yes, I know. And have no doubt that being forced to submit to the Great King is a blow to my pride, but I'm willing to suffer humiliation now if it will give me victory later." He shrugged. "And when the alternative is to march against a Persian army with the Athenians guarding my back, I know which I prefer."

"Very well," said Parmenion. "And what do you want me to do? I take it you called me here for a reason."

"I want you with me when I meet the Persian. See if you can glean anything out of him about the Great King's intentions in the Troad. I think we can assume our friend Hermeias' days are numbered. He's become too powerful to be left alone for much longer."

Parmenion nodded. "It's lucky Aristotle's no longer under his patronage. Bringing him to Pella was timely good fortune."

"Don't I know it," agreed Philip. "I was always careful to only let Hermeias be aware of my tacit support, but my communications with Aristotle were free and frank. Thankfully, whatever now happens to Hermeias, Aristotle is safely out of reach of the Great King's torturers."

Philip drained his wine cup and placed it on the desk, a signal that the meeting was over. "Well, shall we get started, gentlemen?"

And then the deed was done, and the rebels in Egypt and Cyprus had been abandoned to their fate. Philip prepared to return to the army, but summoned Aristotle that evening. The tutor had been kept well out of sight while there'd been a Persian agent in the palace, but had been asking for a meeting from the moment he learned that Philip was at home. The king was aware he had grievances.

The two men met in Philip's dayroom, and clasped each other as old friends.

"Joy to you, Aristotle, and it is good to see you at last. It's been so long, but you've not changed at all." It was true; Aristotle looked as bizarre as the king remembered from his youth. Philip ushered him to a couch and called for wine.

"And you look well, sir." The tutor was trying not to look at the king's slashed, disfigured face. Philip chuckled; he knew.

"Well, maybe I'm not so pretty as I once was, but that is the price one pays. Still, let's not speak of that. Please take a seat, my friend, and call me Philip. My friends call me Philip." As did a number of his slaves.

He was keen to know how his son was progressing, and Aristotle cautiously took a sip of wine, mixed with water for his benefit. "I can speak freely?"

"Of course." Philip took a swig of unmixed wine and braced himself for whatever was to come.

"The boy is very intelligent, but may not benefit from my tutelage as much as he could." Philip looked at him enquiringly, his crooked face making the stare seem malevolent. Aristotle continued hurriedly.

"I take it you've heard that I arranged for some of his friends to join the lessons?"

Philip nodded.

"I'd hoped they would provide sufficient stimulation for the boy, but they have other duties and consider it a chore. It is not satisfactory." Aristotle put his cup down and sat upright on the couch, giving an earnest connotation to his words.

"I would like to bring a few scholars to Pella, boys who are his academic equal. He likes to be the best at whatever he does, and they will make him work if he wants to be the top student in my class."

Philip roared with laughter. "That's an excellent idea! He needs a challenge to perform at his best, you don't have to tell me that. Yes, I give you full authority to arrange it."

"There is one other issue. The schoolroom is inadequate, and far too noisy. The palace itself is too noisy." Aristotle paused, and took a deep breath. "What I would like is to take the boy away from the city altogether, to somewhere with fewer distractions."

Philip mused this latest request. It was a different matter altogether. Alexander was protected within the confines of the palace, but would not be so elsewhere, and the son of a king lived with the threat of assassins and kidnappers.

For all that, Philip was taken with the proposal. Here was a chance to finally get the boy away from the clutches of his mother. "Do you have somewhere in mind?" he asked.

Aristotle shook his head, caught by surprise at Philip's easy acceptance of the idea. "I was seventeen when I left Macedonia and only really knew Pella." He smiled and picked up his cup. "Perhaps you could suggest somewhere?" he queried hopefully.

Philip could. A strategy was already forming in his mind that would achieve a number of goals at one go. "There is a place that might be suitable, a hunting lodge near the Sanctuary of the Nymphs in Mieza. Do you know it?"

"The town, yes, but not the sanctuary." Mieza was a picturesque and prosperous town about a half-day's ride to the west of Pella. The area was so rich in vineyards and orchards that it had acquired the name Gardens of Midas after the king of legend. The tutor's smile broadened.

"The lodge is only a short distance from the town," continued Philip, "but quite secluded. I rarely use it now and, with some modification, it could be turned into a splendid little academy. What do you think?"

Aristotle was beaming. "It sounds perfect. When do you think we'll be able to move in?" He was sitting on the edge of the couch, his knees twitching excitedly.

Philip smiled; Aristotle's eagerness was infectious. "Oh, I think it could be ready for you before the waxing of the next moon. I'll tell my treasurer to release the funds and send a work party up there immediately. There is one point I have to make clear, though."

The smile was wiped from Aristotle's face. He nodded warily and took a sip of wine. "And that is?"

"I have to consider the safety of my son. As he will no longer have the security of living within the palace, I will arrange to have a small garrison sent to Mieza to guard the academy. There is a cavalry officer, Cleitus. His sister was Alexander's nurse and they would both die to protect him. I'll put him in command."

Aristotle smiled his relief. "Yes," he agreed. "It would be wise to have troops close by. Such a thing would not have occurred to me."

"But that will not be sufficient on its own," continued Philip. "I will also replace some of your scholars with my pages. They have all received weapons training and will be immediately available should any incident arise."

Aristotle's shoulders drooped. "Well, if you think it's necessary." He took another sip of wine, then nodded. "You're right, of course. How many were you thinking of, though? I shall want to preserve the academic integrity of my class."

Philip laughed. "Aristotle, I think you underestimate my boys. They're all the sons of noblemen and have received an adequate education. Don't worry, my friend. I'll choose only the most intelligent, those who won't shame themselves unduly against your scholars."

The matter was settled, and the two men relaxed and reminisced about their childhoods for a while. Then Aristotle made his excuses and left. He said he had many arrangements to make, but he couldn't keep up with Philip's drinking.

Philip drank on alone for a while, a satisfied smile on his face. He'd finally found a way of getting the boy away from Olympias that she wouldn't be able to argue with. Not only that, he had suddenly created a new elite among the pages. They'd all want to be one of the select few, and their fathers would be paying handsome bribes to ensure they were.

There was one other bonus to the arrangement. The boys would be closeted in their own little world, with an academic exposing them to the best that Greek culture had to offer. Maybe Philip's generation still clung to the old ways, but Alexander's peers would become as sophisticated as the highborn of Athens.

Pleased with himself, he called for his latest fancy, a newly appointed officer of the Companion cavalry. The young man arrived promptly and they retired to Philip's bedroom, with a krater of wine and orders not to be disturbed until morning.

The relocation caused the expected uproar. Every page wanted to be a part of the cadre, and some regretted their reluctance to toady up to the obnoxious little prince in the past. Alexander insisted he be allowed to choose his own classmates and Olympias was quick to agree; it guaranteed Philip would not be able to select his own people. Philip, on campaign again, consented to his son's demand, but sent word to Leonidas to ensure Alexander did not have the chance to spend too much time with his mother. He didn't want her overly influencing the boy's selection.

Alexander basked in his new power, relishing the flattery and inducements heaped upon him. It made little difference to his final choice. He already knew who he was taking and those he would be leaving behind. The gentlemen of the Pig-Stickers were his band of brothers, his clan, and it was his duty to choose from their number first. Aristotle's only stipulation was that they must be of reasonable intelligence and competent in Greek; the Macedonian language was to be banned from the classroom.

Proteas was first to be chosen. Friends since they had shared a cot in Lanice's bedroom, he was guaranteed a place. Craterus, Perdiccas and Phrygius were natural choices. He had been forced to ponder before including Leonnatus, as the youth's size might make him too much of a challenge on the sports field. Iolaus and Marsyas, two more members of the Pig-Stickers, made up the rest of his band.

On Philip's orders, three more youths joined the group. Ptolemy, Philotas and Cassander were about to graduate to the army, but were assigned to Mieza as Alexander's personal bodyguard instead. Although they were older than the rest of his companions, Alexander knew all three well and didn't resent it. Cassander was the son of Antipatros and brother to Iolaus, while Philotas was the youngest of Parmenion's sons. Philotas had a further mission; he was to be Philip's eyes and ears at Mieza.

The day of the move came, and several large wagons assembled in the courtyard. Alexander and his chosen companions supervised the loading of their possessions, their excited chatter contrasting with the silence of the other pages and the envious looks as they passed by on their way to their daily duties.

By mid-morning the wagons were ready to leave. The convoy trundled out of the courtyard, laden with the goods and slaves needed for the establishment of the new academy. Two chairs had been placed on the back of the largest wagon. Lysimachus occupied one; he was to continue his role as Alexander's steward. He leaned over the side, waving to the crowd that had assembled to watch them leave. Aristotle sat stiffly on the other chair, fingers anxiously gripping the rail as the wagon clattered and jolted over the flagstones. He looked like he wasn't going to have a pleasant journey.

The boys didn't leave with the wagons. There was one more errand to perform first, and then they would follow on horseback later that afternoon. They assembled in the rear courtyard, dressed in adult robes and wearing garlands of flowers in their hair. They each held an olive branch and were in jovial mood.

They turned at the sound of festive music. A procession came through the archway from the living quarters and headed across the courtyard. Cleopatra led the way, in the position of honor reserved for virgins. She carried a jug in one hand, while the other balanced a tray on her head containing several small baskets of offerings. It was the first time Alexander had seen his sister for several months. She was nearly a woman now and kept to her quarters; it wasn't seemly for a woman to have a social life.

Arridaeus came next, Alexander smiling as he spotted the shuffling figure. It was good to know his mother must have given her permission for him to be present. Although she didn't approve, she knew Alexander was fond of his idiot half-brother.

Arridaeus had been given the task of leading the goat. The animal meekly followed the bumbling youth as he tugged on its lead, its horns gilded and its body adorned with ribbons. It was chewing on its tongue, oblivious to its fate.

The procession was strung out behind. Alexander could see his mother, followed by Lanice, who carried a smoldering incense burner on a tall stand. Cleitus followed, escorting Lanice's youngest children. Proteas was one of Alexander's chosen and the girls were there to say goodbye to their brother. Behind them came the musicians, playing pipes and lyres.

A dozen friends and relatives of Alexander's companions made up the rest of the procession. They included a few of the pages, putting aside their envy to bid farewell to their friends. Leonidas brought up the rear.

Alexander was surprised to see the man. He'd been adamant that Leonidas was not to go to Mieza and Olympias had taken particular pleasure in informing her uncle that his services were no longer required. They'd expected he would return to Epirus, but there was no indication of it thus far.

The boys joined the procession, Alexander walking alongside his sister. He turned around to face Arridaeus and did a half-skip to the music, making the boy grin and stutter something. They continued on to the far corner of the courtyard and turned into the small garden that stood in front of the palace temple.

Aristander waited for them on the temple steps, while a table and benches had been set up in the garden and a cauldron bubbled in one corner, tended by a group of slaves. Three of the males came over to join the seer, now acting in his capacity as a priest.

Cleopatra mounted the steps and handed the jug to Aristander. A slave helped her lift the tray off her head, giving her back the middle basket before carrying it over to the table and laying out the contents of the others. They contained honey cakes and sweetmeats for the feast. Another slave took the incense burner from Lanice and placed it beside the altar that stood outside the temple door.

The procession gathered around the steps and Arridaeus handed the goat over to the third slave, the youth waving goodbye to the animal as it was led up the steps to stand beside the altar. A small fire burned on the slab, making the goat nervous.

Aristander moved among the group, ritually washing their hands with water from the jug that Cleopatra had carried. He remounted the steps and stood before the goat, jerking his wrist to splash the remaining liquid over the animal's head. It immediately shook itself dry, to a chorus of approval from the congregation; the nodding of its head was a sign that the animal consented to being sacrificed.

They fell silent, raising their hands and exposing their palms as Aristander led the prayer.

"I call on Dionysus, also known as Bacchus. Hearken, o lord of vegetation, who teaches mortals to cultivate the grape and ferment the wine. Hear us, son of Zeus, bestower of contentment on those who do you honor, and imparter of madness on those who spurn you. Indulge us, god of good cheer and the bacchante. Hear me, also, any other god who may be present." The temple included a shrine to Athena, the royal family's second deity, and it didn't do to risk offending anyone.

"Accept these offerings, o Dionysus, as a measure of the piety of those present. Today, some of them will be leaving us, and we implore you to watch over these poor travelers and grant them a safe journey. Guide them on their way and bless them with a successful venture."

Alexander looked through the open temple doors. Despite the shadows, he could just make out the statue of Dionysus in its niche, staring back at him.

Cleopatra held the remaining basket up for Aristander, who scooped out a handful of barley grains and scattered them on the altar fire as an offering. He returned his hand to the basket, slipping it beneath the grains to remove the sacrificial knife that had been ceremonially hidden beneath them. He was careful to keep his back to the animal, which was becoming increasingly nervous and had excreted on the temple porch. Two of the slaves had taken up a position on either side of the goat, steadying it by the horns. The third stood behind, holding a large boulder in both hands.

Aristander circled around behind the animal and deftly cut a lock of hair from its forehead, throwing it onto the altar fire and uttering a magic spell. The hair shriveled in the flames. He gestured to the slaves that he was ready.

The boulder rose and fell, striking the goat squarely on the skull. Stunned, the animal buckled under the blow as the first two slaves hoisted it up by the horns, exposing its neck. Aristander jabbed once, piercing the throat. Blood spouted from the wound and the slaves heaved the animal forward, directing the flow toward the altar. The women in the congregation immediately let out an ear-splitting cacophony of shrieking, wildly ululating their tongues between their teeth. Olympias was the loudest; she was a priestess of Dionysus.

Blood fizzed on the fire and splattered down the altar, collecting in the bowl that had been placed in front of it for that purpose. Aristander picked up the bowl and poured it onto the flames as a further offering, making the fire hiss and spit.

The slaves worked swiftly, turning the animal over and splitting its belly. Kneeling in blood, they expertly drew out the innards, while Alexander and his companions surged forward, each brandishing a five-pronged fork.

The slaves stuffed pieces of offal onto the forks, Alexander receiving the heart as guest of honor. The boys crowded around the altar to roast their trophies over the fire, the smell of barbecued meat drifting across the garden.

The slaves continued to butcher the goat. The thighbones were removed and wrapped in fat, Aristander reverently placing them on the fire as the god's share of the offering. The party would consume the rest of the animal.

Already people were beginning to wander over to the table, picking at the sweetmeats and pouring themselves wine as the slaves hefted chunks of meat over to the cauldron. The musicians struck up a tune and Alexander joined his mother and sister to await the feast. They sat in silence for a while, enjoying the music.

Arridaeus shuffled over, careful to keep Alexander and his sister between him and Olympias. She scared him.

"I wish I was coming with you, Alexander. It sounds like it's going to be fun." He flung a glance at Olympias as she made a sound of contempt.

Alexander smiled and touched his half-brother's shoulder affectionately. "Well, you can always come and visit us," he lied. "It's not that far away."

Arridaeus grinned, already looking forward to it. He took a swig of wine, spilling some down his front. "Oh good, more food." He hurried over to the table, where a slave was carving a steaming cut of meat.

"I don't know why you tolerate that fool," Olympias said, loud enough for everyone at the table to hear. Arridaeus wisely kept his back turned.

"Hush, Mother, he'll hear you." Cleopatra put a hand on her mother's lap in admonishment. "He's not so bad really, quite sweet sometimes."

"Sweet?" snorted Olympias, but didn't pursue it. "So, what are your plans for your next triumph, Alexander?" She was still boring her maids with the saga of her son's taming of a horse that Philip had been afraid to mount. "I somehow think the opportunities will be limited in a backwater like Mieza."

Alexander leaned forward to see past his sister and answer Olympias. His mother was starting to show her age in the sunlight; he hadn't noticed the bags under her eyes before. "I agree, Mother, but I'll be concentrating on my studies and doubt there'll be time left for anything else anyway."

"And you make sure you do. These Macedonians may not be much competition," she said, looking pointedly at Alexander's companions, "but this Aristotle is bringing in his own scholars as well. Don't let some peasant's spawn outshine you in the classroom. Remember who your father is, and by that I mean your real father."

Alexander and Cleopatra exchanged smiles. Their mother didn't miss a trick.

"Yes, Mother."

The celebration continued, stoked by a steady supply of cooked meat and unmixed wine. Olympias began to sway to the music, ordering that a drummer be summoned so she could perform a sacred dance.

Cleitus came and sat beside Alexander. "It would be better if you don't let your companions stay too long, or yourself for that matter. We don't want to be on the road after dark."

Alexander nodded. "We'll be ready." He liked the way Cleitus had come to him as the leader of the group. "I just have something to do and then I'll be leaving, and the others won't stay long once I've gone." It was natural arrogance that made him say it, but it was true.

The boy stood and crossed the garden, weaving a path through the gathering. His companions were becoming steadily drunker, unused to the volumes of unmixed wine they were imbibing that afternoon. Alexander smiled as he saw Craterus puking over a convenient hedge. Were it not for the presence of women, it could be a scene from the Great Hall.

He mounted the steps to the temple. A slave was clearing the charred ashes from the altar as another mopped blood from the porch. He found Aristander just inside the door, left open so that Dionysus could also enjoy the festivities. It was much cooler inside, a breeze wafting through from an open door at the rear.

Aristander looked enquiringly at the boy; the ceremony was over and sightseers weren't encouraged within the temple. "Is there something you require, Alexander? I am at your service." There was goat's blood spattered on his white robes.

"Yes, there is." The boy hadn't yet decided whether he liked the priest or not. Aristander was a trusted friend of both his father and his mother, and anyone who could achieve such a unique position was to be both respected and suspected. "I would like to make a private offering to Dionysus."

Aristander's eyebrows shot up. "What do you have in mind?" The boy was empty-handed.

"You have incense?"

Aristander gestured to a slave to fetch the incense basket. "It is expensive, Alexander. You understand that?" Frankincense could only be imported from the east and the Great King controlled all those trade routes, and set taxes as he pleased.

"I can pay." It was true; he now received an allowance and would claim the cost as expenses.

"Very well, but limit yourself to no more than a scoop or two." The priest ushered him to the altar in front of Dionysus' statue, where another slave was already lighting a fire.

The first slave returned with the incense basket and took up a position next to the priest. He had quickly wrapped a robe over his tunic and placed a wreath on his head in preparation for the unexpected ceremony. It made Alexander realize he'd left his own garland out in the garden. He took the wreath from the slave's head and placed it on his own, then raised his hands as Aristander invoked the god and introduced him as the supplicant.

"This is Prince Alexander, heir to the throne of Macedonia. He has always been devout in his worship and has sacrificed to you on every feast day. Grant him this day, his petition."

The priest sprinkled a few grains of incense onto the fire, making it flare up. "What request would you like me to make, Alexander?" he asked.

"I would rather say my own prayer."

"You want to make an oath?" The surprise in Aristander's voice made the boy look up from the flames. "That would require another blood sacrifice."

"Not an oath; a prayer. But I want to make it myself."

"Well, it's irregular, but I suppose I can permit it." Aristander took a step back from the altar.

Alexander faced the statue that towered over him. Dionysus, bearded and impassive in purple robes, gazed out through the open doors.

"My name is Alexander and I am your brother, as I, too, am a son of Zeus. King Philip is merely my mortal guardian, a father in name only." Out of the corner of his eye, he saw Aristander's jaw drop.

The priest hurriedly waved the slave away and stooped to speak in the boy's ear, his voice hushed, urgent. "Are you sure about this, Alexander? This is blasphemy."

Alexander ignored the interruption. "As the heir to a king I am expected to be the best, but as a son of Zeus I must be more than that. I must excel at everything and fail at nothing, and anything less would be a reflection on our divine father himself. It is a heavy burden and I entreat you, as both my god and my kinsman, to lend me your support and guidance.

"Tonight I take my companions to Mieza. They already look to me as their leader, but that is not enough. One day I will be the King and they my generals and ministers. They must both love and respect me, and the best opportunity to achieve that is at

Mieza. With your patronage, I can gain their respect by being unsurpassed in the classroom and the stadium, but that will not win their love. I can only do that by being a true friend. Guide me in my associations with them. Let me be exceptional without arrogance, impart advice without conceit, and be honorable unto death. Only then can I hope to gain the same loyalty that my mortal father already assumes from his subordinates."

He was finished. The heresy he had just committed weighed down on him and he suddenly felt afraid. He scooped incense onto the fire to placate the god, one handful, two, a third. If Dionysus took exception to anything he'd said the consequences would be unimaginable, but he had needed to say these things. He knew much of his popularity was due to who he was, while the devotion that Philip was able to command from his subjects continued to puzzle and infuriate him. He could never hope to be a better king than his father without that same fidelity.

Aristander said nothing as Alexander continued to shovel incense onto the flames. The cost of the spice was prohibitive, but he was as afraid of divine retribution as the boy was. The fire roared and pungent smoke stung their eyes. They heard footsteps on the marble floor and turned, expecting to see Dionysus himself bearing down on them. It was Leonidas. He looked at Alexander with contempt.

"Have I taught you nothing?" A sneer curled his lips. "I told your father this would happen if he let you have money of your own." He gestured at the half-empty incense basket. "And who is going to pay for this? Not you, that's for sure. It will be your father, and I shall make certain he knows who's wasting his money. You're a wastrel, boy, and always have been."

Alexander's blood boiled. Even at this late stage, the man couldn't resist having another stab at him. For years, he'd been forced to suffer his gibes and degradations in silence, but no more. He exploded, the tension of the previous few minutes fueling his rage.

"How dare you speak to me like that? You have ceased to be my governor and ceased to have one jot of authority over me. Why are you still here, even? Don't you realize that everyone hates you?" His eyes narrowed to slits and his voice became like ice. "You should mind your words, Leonidas, for one day I will be King." He lapsed into silence; his blatant threat had surprised even himself.

Leonidas struggled to speak, visibly shaken by the unexpected outburst. "Well," he said finally, his voice tremulous. "And when you are the King, you will be able to burn all the incense you want." He turned and walked unsteadily to the door.

"And I will, Leonidas," spat Alexander as he watched him go. "And I will."

He would never see Leonidas again, but would make his former governor a fabulously wealthy man many years later, with a convoy of frankincense from a newly conquered Egypt. Alexander never forgot a grudge.

Aristotle's scholars were preparing for bed when the group arrived at Mieza that evening. One, named Callisthenes, was introduced as Aristotle's own nephew, while the other two were brothers, Erigyius and Laomedon. All three were veterans of Aristotle's former academy on the island of Lesbos, as was Theophrastus, an assistant tutor who had accompanied them. The Macedonian contingent looked them over and felt confident. The scholars were bright and Laomedon was fluent in Persian, but the brothers looked to be somewhat older than the Macedonians and they all had the nervous air of outsiders.

They had brought Aristotle's wife with them from Lesbos. It caused some surprise among the boys. From his foppish clothes and mannerisms, they had assumed that Aristotle preferred to be the female. It ended the running joke that had been performed whenever he turned his back on the class.

A fourth scholar appeared two days after their arrival. Nearchus, a Cretan youth with skin burned brown by the sun, rode into the courtyard and confidently announced that he had arrived. He was the son of an admiral, tall and strong, and Alexander eyed him suspiciously.

The boys had a dormitory above the schoolroom in one wing of the lodge, Aristotle taking an apartment in the other wing. The slave's quarters and the kitchens were at the back, with a small garden beyond. A central courtyard gave the boys an assembly area, and a walled gate, security. Cleitus and his detachment occupied a house in the town, a short distance away.

They soon settled into a routine in Mieza. The summer schedule was to spend the cooler morning hours on the sports field under the direction of two paidotribes from Athens. These sports instructors wore their traditional purple robes and carried a stick that had been split at one end. They put the boys through their paces, waving the split ends of their sticks in the face of anyone they thought wasn't trying hard enough. The afternoon was spent in study under Aristotle or Theophrastus, or one of the assistant tutors who were routinely hired from Mieza for the more mundane subjects. After bathing for dinner, they would first assemble for prayers at the nearby Sanctuary of the Nymphs where, at Alexander's request, a shrine to Athena had been installed alongside that of Dionysus, the resident god.

The sanctuary was formed around three caves in a cliff face, with a broad plateau in front. Inside the largest cave were the shrines to the gods and the multiple statues of the nymphs, with lesser shrines and storage lockers in the adjoining caves. The boys were forbidden to approach except for their daily prayers.

The plateau stretched some width, before plunging down to a soft-flowing stream. Centrally positioned on the plateau was a portico, designed to give relief to weary pilgrims. It consisted of two colonnaded platforms connected by a shorter platform at one end, while a tiled roof gave shelter from the elements and stone benches stretched along each of its three sides.

It was a perfect spot, and the boys soon talked Aristotle into conducting lessons in the shade of the portico, when the heat of the sun made the schoolroom stifling.

On one such afternoon, they raced each other to secure the coolest, most shaded bench. Since their move to Mieza, it was no longer imperative to be seen next to the prince. Aristotle walked behind them, talking to Laomedon in Persian.

He called them to order and began the lesson. For a while, he spoke about his research during his time in Anatolia, telling them of the differences he had noted between the types of flora found on the coast and those found in the mountainous regions. He paced up and down, walking between the benches, turning to look directly at one boy or another as he spoke.

He was waiting for someone to ask a question, as he was sure they would. Iolaus obliged him. "But why are they different, sir?"

"That's obvious." Philotas had a slight note of contempt in his voice. "They have to deal with different climates, snow in the mountains and salt air and storms on the coast." He leaned forward in his seat to sneer at the younger boy. Iolaus was sitting next to his brother and Philotas changed his mind when he saw the look on Cassander's face.

"Yes, that's true." Aristotle strode up to Philotas and stood over the youth, determined not to allow any situation to develop. "But do plants have hearts? If, as we believe, the heart is the source of all thought, how does a mountain plant know that it will need to survive the cold for long periods?"

Philotas stayed silent. He had no answer to that.

"What you have to understand, boys, is that nothing exists where it should not, and a bird cannot exist underwater any more than a fish can fly. In nature, everything is ideally suited to its environment; there can be no other way."

"But a man could survive in the desert, sir; if he had enough water." Proteas looked puzzled. "So could his horse, for that matter. According to you, every man who ventures into the desert should die."

Aristotle smiled and shook his head. "No, I'm not saying that at all." They were showing more interest than he'd expected, and far more than any of them had shown in the classroom at Pella. The move to Mieza was certainly proving to be a boon.

He moved over to Proteas' bench. "Think about what you've said. A man, no, a man—and his horse." He looked around the group with eyebrows raised, drawing the hoped-for titter of laughter. "A man and his horse can survive in the desert, but, and you said it yourself, only if they have enough water. The man needs to bring the means of their survival with him, otherwise he would last no longer than his horse would." There were a few nodding heads.

"And that's what makes man unique." Aristotle almost said it with pride. "A man can survive in the desert because he has the forethought to bring water with him, but his horse cannot survive without the extra water the man has brought for it. A horse does not have the capacity for intelligent thought, and that is why it is a beast of burden."

"But many animals show intelligence, sir, especially horses." Alexander sounded indignant. "My own Bucephalus, for instance." He was still the only one who could do anything with the animal.

"Do they?" Aristotle seized on the statement. "When you call your horse or your favorite hound, does it come running because it loves you or merely because it recognizes the sound of your voice?"

"More likely because it thinks you have food." The class broke into laughter at Ptolemy's remark and a smiling Aristotle agreed.

"Exactly, my young friends. Plants are more advanced than the base materials because they have that defining element we call life, and enough consciousness to draw nutrition and grow. Animals can feel emotions like desire and fear or," he nodded at Ptolemy, "answer your call because they know you're a source of food. But man stands above all the plants and animals that he shares this world with. Man has that higher faculty, the ability to control his emotions and actions, and only the gods themselves are on a higher plane."

Aristotle's arms swept outwards. "Imagine if you will, a line. At this end," he raised his left hand, "is existence. And at the other," he swung his right hand upward, "is consciousness. And all matter lies somewhere on this line.

"Let me take it further. At one end is existence without consciousness, at the other is consciousness without existence." He was losing some of them already, puzzled looks creeping into their eyes. "Existence without consciousness. What do I mean by that?" He strode up to Laomedon; the boy could be counted on to save the lesson.

"Something that lives without knowing it's alive, sir?" the boy ventured.

"That's almost right. Not something that lives, but exists. Life is a higher plane altogether." Aristotle picked up a pebble. "Consider this stone. It doesn't know it exists. The caves behind you don't know they exist, nor the benches you're sitting on." He looked around the class. "They exist without consciousness. Does everybody understand what I mean by that now?" There were nodding heads and some relieved smiles. "So what do I mean by consciousness without existence?"

"Something that can live without a body, sir; the gods." Philotas was the first in the scramble to answer.

"Maybe, but don't the gods have bodies?" Aristotle gave them time to think by strolling over to examine the lion-headed rainspouts on the portico's roof. He suddenly turned. "Philotas?"

"Well, yes, they do. Our own bodies are modeled on them."

"Not yours." Cassander took his revenge for the slight against his brother.

Aristotle continued swiftly, before any bickering could break out. "Philotas was right both times. It's true that the gods have bodies, but they are equally comfortable without them. They take mortal form for our benefit, not theirs. How many of you could gaze upon a god in his true form and not go mad?

"The gods are the supreme example of consciousness without existence, or, to be more accurate, without being. So we have the two extremes." He raised his hands again. "Base materials such as stone and earth that merely exist, and then the gods, who don't even have the need for anything as primitive as a corporeal shell. Agreed?" His face was becoming more animated, his lisp more pronounced.

"And the rest of us lie in between. Soil is of the lowest value. Above soil are the plants and above plants are animals." His hands were thumping up and down. "Above animals is man, and only the gods are above man. Any questions?" He flung his arms down and surveyed his audience as though expecting applause.

The boys had no questions, merely murmuring their assent. "I'm surprised we didn't think of that ourselves," remarked Phrygius. "It explains many of life's little mysteries."

Aristotle was both pleased and disappointed by their acceptance. He'd been formulating the theory throughout his research of the wildlife in Anatolia and would have welcomed a modicum of contention, but it was not the real purpose of this lesson.

"Now it follows that, as each group has its place in the line, so each member of a group has its place within that group. Would everyone agree that a flower is superior to mere grass?" Again, the nodding heads. "And that an animal that hunts is superior to an animal that is hunted?" He paced back and forth. "A hawk is above a dove and a lion is above a deer. Now what about man?"

There was a moment of silence before Nearchus voiced the obvious answer. "A man is above a woman, sir."

"Yes, and?" Aristotle hurried over to him, arms flapping, encouraging him to continue. "What else?"

"The free man is above the slave?" This from Iolaus.

Aristotle swung around to face the boy. "Good, and?"

Iolaus struggled, and then his face brightened. "And a warrior is above a . . . a farmer."

"And?" Iolaus was spent, so Aristotle looked the group over for another victim. "Craterus—and?"

"A civilized man is above a barbarian, sir." The boy grinned as he saw the tutor's reaction to his answer.

"Exactly! Well done, Craterus." Aristotle began pacing again. "A civilized society is infinitely superior to a barbarian one, and who are the most civilized people on earth, my boys?"

"The Macedonians." Everyone sniggered at Leonnatus' remark, except the new arrivals from Lesbos.

Aristotle was not to be deterred by Leonnatus' flippancy; the point he was trying to make was too important for that. He waited for the noise to subside.

"Not just the Macedonians, and your father would agree with me on this, Alexander." He spun around and stared at the boy.

"You will one day be King and it's important you understand this. The Greeks, my boys, are superior to the barbarians."

He walked over to gaze down at the stream that babbled past the sanctuary, giving time for his words to sink in, then turned and returned to his charges.

"King Philip prides himself on being Greek, and he is right to be proud. To not be Greek is to be nothing, worthless, and I'm not just talking about the savages to our north. I've lived among the barbarians, my boys, and my time in the Troad was long enough to observe the mockery that passes for civilization among the Persians.

"Oh yes, they may have fine buildings and wear fine clothes, and there may be scholars and artists among them, but they are not Greek. They do not have that quality," he searched for the word, "that essence, which is uniquely Greek. Go to any city along the coast of Anatolia, and you will know whether the population is predominantly Greek or Persian, instantly. Be proud of your heritage, my boys, and defend it. It is fitting for the Greeks to enslave barbarians, but never for a barbarian, any barbarian, to enslave a Greek."

Perdiccas looked puzzled. "But lots of Greeks are slaves, sir. My father has some from Olynthus, and a couple of Phokians."

"Yes, but they are Greeks enslaved by other Greeks, not barbarians."

"And your own city of Stagira was enslaved, sir. The whole population, by King Philip." Ptolemy's statement drew a murmur from Iolaus and all eyes focused on Aristotle.

The tutor felt his cheeks reddening beneath his beard, but he'd known someone would be bound to mention Stagira and had an answer ready.

He raised his fists again. "When a fisherman pulls his catch aboard, the fish that slips the net becomes superior to those who remain to be eaten." He made a sweeping motion with his right arm. "That fish moves above them in the order of things. If a lion injures a paw, it moves down the order and becomes inferior to the prey that can now outrun it." Now a downward motion with his left arm. "But that change in position may only be temporary. The fish may well be caught the next day and the lion will return to its rightful place if it can go without food long enough for its paw to heal." The hands joined together.

"And so it is with the people of Stagira. Through war they are now slaves and, whether deserved or not, of lower status than free men. But it will not always be so." He was pacing again. "When my work here is done, King Philip has promised to rebuild my city and release my fellow citizens from bondage. They will be free men again; free Greeks retaking their rightful place in society."

There was silence. The plan to rebuild Stagira was well known; every new city was a useful outpost against Macedonia's enemies. But releasing the slaves was news to the boys. One or two had fathers who owned slaves taken at Stagira.

Aristotle heard the silence and immediately regretted his partisan outburst. Freeing that many slaves would be a costly and difficult undertaking, and Philip had agreed to it only reluctantly. Even then, he'd refused to make it part of the formal contract. It was a private bonus, conditional on him being satisfied his son had received the best of educations. It was not wise to have made it public knowledge this early. Aristotle speedily ended the lesson.

"Have you understood me, Alexander? Greece has the highest level of civilization in the world, and it will one day fall on you to protect that precious jewel against the barbarians. It is something your father has so far failed to understand. Do not wage war on other Greeks; your enemies are to the east."

Alexander understood. He had his doubts about considering the likes of Athens as an ally, but he knew where his true enemies lay. Even if his father was too spineless to face up to Persia, he was not. He would be the one to avenge the humiliation of the King's Peace. He would be the one to free the Greek colonies.

Chapter Nine

Rivals

The long summer evenings were the boy's favorite times. They would go riding almost every evening, chasing each other across the plain in imitation of the great equestrian events at Olympia, sometimes hunting foxes and deer, sometimes taking their bows to stalk birds and rabbits.

The camaraderie that Alexander craved was slowly beginning to develop among this small band of similarly aged boys, sharing experiences daily and isolated as they were from the outside world. He was still too young to sense it fully, but finally his companions were including him because he was one of them, not because it was expedient for their future careers to curry favor with the king's heir.

The boys heard the news as they returned from hunting—King Philip would be visiting the academy the next day. A bevy of slaves had been sent ahead from the palace and were busy erecting a small encampment of tents in the field next to the stables.

The boys were thrilled. Mieza was rather rural and quiet after life at the palace, and any diversion was welcome. They chattered excitedly as they were served their evening meal that night, speculating on who would be with the king and hoping to see family members among his entourage.

Alexander ate quietly. The news had taken him by surprise and he was not happy about it. Mieza was his own little empire and he ruled it free of the shadow of his father; he resented the intrusion.

Craterus nudged his elbow. He had become closest to Alexander in the twelve months since their move from Pella, and now shared his couch at meals. They were the same age and Alexander felt more affinity with him than with the older boys. Their friendship had prompted some gossip and a few lewd remarks among the others, and only he dared ask the question many of them were thinking.

"You're quiet, Alexander. Aren't you pleased at the prospect of seeing your father again?"

"Will that man not leave me alone?" Alexander's statement silenced the room. "It seems like there isn't a month goes by that we don't hear of some new victory or other. At this rate there'll be nothing left for me but to try not to lose the kingdom my father created for me." He chewed slowly on a piece of pork before adding, "And now he comes to rub my nose in it."

Craterus stared at him. "I'm sure he doesn't mean to do that, Alexander." There was little else he could say, so didn't try. The room was quiet as the boys finished the rest of their meal, their joviality broken.

Alexander's remarks had startled them. Envy of a king by his heir was to be expected and had always been apparent in Alexander, but this was the first time he'd spoken publicly of it. Even more revealing had been the invective behind his words. The boy was now in his fourteenth year and would soon be old enough to challenge his father; he obviously couldn't wait. The time was approaching when they would have to decide which side they were going to choose.

The boys assembled in the tiny courtyard of the academy the next morning, Alexander at the end nearest to the entrance arch. Ptolemy, Philotas and Cassander had formed a bodyguard around him, wearing sheathed swords instead of the knives they usually carried. Aristotle waited in the shade of the porch with Theophrastus and the paidotribes, while his wife made a rare appearance at the window of their upstairs apartment.

They heard the faint sound of cheering in the distance, and a slave posted on the roof shouted the news that the king was in sight. Alexander grimaced.

Cleitus and his twenty-man garrison stood in line outside the wall, raising their spears in salute as Philip swept into the courtyard. The bodyguard and then a troop of Companion cavalry followed, filling up the courtyard and milling about trying to find room to dismount.

Alexander stepped down from the porch and moved forward to greet the king as the boys raised a cheer. Philip remained on his horse for a moment, towering over the assembly; he knew how to dominate a situation. Then, with athleticism surprising in such a big man, he leapt from the horse in a single movement and stood in front of his son. He grinned at the boy.

"So, this is where you've been hiding!" He shouted the words so that everyone could hear and was rewarded with laughter from the boys.

"Joy to you, Father, and I trust you had a safe journey?" Alexander smiled and took a step forward, ushering him in the direction of Aristotle.

An introduction to the students and staff was followed by a tour of the academy, Philip expressing lively satisfaction with the remodeling work carried out on his lodge. He then surprised everyone by asking to sit it in on a typical lesson.

The boys filed into the schoolroom and took their seats. Philip entered and sat at the back, looking incongruous perched on a stool. A number of Companions congregated outside, some peering through the door curiously while others looked bored as they chatted in small groups. An occasional laugh penetrated the room and Aristotle bid Theophrastus go outside and ask them to move out of hearing of the students. The assistant re-entered the classroom and stood by the door.

Aristotle cleared his throat. He looked nervous. The lesson was unexpected and the presence of the king intimidating.

"I had not planned for any lessons today, boys, but as we are here I would like to introduce you to the categories. It will give you the chance to see how you can use logic to your benefit." He looked over at the king's son; there was no doubt who he would be concentrating on today.

"Alexander, suppose I was to give you a riddle to solve. Tell us how you would go about discovering the answer."

Alexander shrugged petulantly, his father's presence making him feel on show. "How can I say, sir, until I know what the riddle is?"

Philip chortled with laughter. "That serves you right, Aristotle. You should know the boy better than that by now. Good answer, my boy!" Alexander continued to face his front.

Aristotle tried again. "Very well, let us give you something more solid. Suppose you're leading an army through the desert, no, through enemy territory. You are short of food and an impassable mountain range is barring your way. What would you do? How would you get your men safely to the other side of the mountains?"

"That one is easy, Aristotle." Philip was in a buoyant mood, the academy being all he'd hoped for. "Bribe a goatherd to show you the path he uses for his goats. And let me tell you, boys. There is always a goatherd—and he can always be bribed." The class greeted his quip with laughter while Aristotle gave him a dry look. It would never have occurred to Philip he was disrupting the lesson.

"Yes, but we don't all have the benefit of your military experience, sir. What would you do to save your army, Alexander?"

This was more to the boy's liking and his mind turned to the great general, Xenophon. The story of how he had led his troops out of Persian territory was still one of his favorites.

"I would send out scouts to look for a way around, sir, others to search for a way across. And I would do as the King suggests, and round up the locals to bribe or beat a path out of them."

"Bravo, my boy!" Philip was exultant. His pride in his son meant he was the only one in the room who didn't notice that Alexander had called him by his title.

"Yes, I'm sure you would lead your army out of danger with that approach." Aristotle began to slowly pace the room, eyeing each of the boys individually. "Now let us consider what you have done, how you arrived at that course of action. You will need your tablets, boys."

They all reached down and picked up their wax tablets and writing sticks, with Philip making a show of searching for his, to more amusement from the class. Aristotle exchanged a smile with Theophrastus. With the king in this mood, the future of the academy was assured.

Alexander did not smile. His mother was right; the man was a buffoon.

When all had settled down again, Aristotle continued. "There are ten logical steps to reasoning. I am not saying you will need to use all of them for every problem you encounter or, as Alexander just demonstrated, that you will even be aware you're using them at all, but you should know what they are and in which order they should be used. Write these down:

"The first category is substance, the next quantity, then quality, then relation. Everyone has got those down? Good. They are followed by place, time, and situation." Leonnatus was struggling to keep up so Aristotle paused a moment. "Finally come condition, action, and passion."

Aristotle walked among the boys as they finished scratching the list onto the soft wax of their tablets. He checked spelling here and there, sighing when he saw a Macedonian word. Not all the boys were as fluent in Greek as he'd hoped they'd be.

"So what do I mean by these words? Substance is the object of our investigation, perhaps a man or an elephant. Examples of quantity would be its size or volume, for instance two cubits high or five medimni of elephant dung." That drew the intended laugh. "Such attributes as an object's color fall under the category of quality, and double, half, equal to are examples of an object's relation, or how it relates to other substances and the world around it.

"We will deal with these four first. Let us consider substance. It is the cause of our problem, in this case the mountain that Alexander must cross. Quantity is how many of the substance there are. Well, there are several peaks, a complete mountain range. As for quality? These are not mere hills but high enough to be capped with snow. Do you see how this is building? By taking each piece separately, we can build a complete picture of the problem. Consider how you could take this approach for any question.

"Suppose I wanted to build a chair. I would first need to decide its substance. Well, it's a seat. Quantity? Just the one chair, so I can afford to use expensive, imported wood. See how that has taken us into quality? Now what about its relation?"

There was no immediate answer but he had set the boys thinking. He continued to the back of the class and exchanged a smile with Philip. The king looked pleased.

He rose from his stool. "I've seen enough to know my son's education is in good hands, Aristotle. Now I wish to visit the sanctuary and make an offering to the nymphs, so I will be on my way and leave you in peace. You will join me tonight for some refreshment?"

"Of course, sir. It would be an honor." Aristotle flapped his hands for the boys to stand as their guest departed.

"Philip, call me Philip." Before he left, the king extended the invitation to the class, and only Alexander didn't burst into a gleeful grin. He had a frown on his face, and this time his father noticed.

The party took place in Philip's pavilion. The boys were already sprawled across couches when Aristotle and Theophrastus arrived, eating meat and drinking unmixed wine like adults. They welcomed their tutor and his assistant, doubling up to make a couch available for them.

But the pair didn't stay long. Several female musicians had been hired from Mieza to provide comfort for those who wished it, and two were already naked while another demonstrated what else she could do with her flute. The two academicians were out of place among the carousing Macedonians, and left as soon as it was polite to.

Philip shared his couch with his latest conquest, a young mercenary officer from Thebes. He pressed his thigh against the man's crotch as he joked with Parmenion, but kept an eye on

Alexander. The boy was drinking with Phrygius and Craterus, and every now and then would glance across the room at his father, turning away as soon as their eyes met. Parmenion had already passed on Philotas' account of Alexander's comments at dinner the night before, and Philip had received the report with a look like thunder.

An officer from one of the phalangite regiments stumbled to his feet and staggered outside to be sick, then Amyntas sauntered past with his hand buried beneath the chiton of one of the musicians. He winked at his cousin's party as he passed, the boys replying with a cheer. Others were leaving, either through drink or lust. Philip was not drunk, not tonight. He called a slave to him.

"Tell my son I wish to see him in my private quarters." He got to his feet, placing a restraining hand on his companion's shoulder when the man made to follow him. "Join me when my son leaves."

Philip passed through the passageway that led to his personal quarters and wearily sat in his easy chair. It reminded him of Aristotle's lesson and he smiled as he stroked the wood. These philosophers spoke such drivel sometimes.

"You wished to see me, sir?" Alexander pushed aside the canvas flap and entered. Philip looked up, the smile vanishing from his lips.

"Since when have you called me sir?" said Philip, indicating for the boy to sit. Alexander remained standing, a defiant look in his eyes. "Sit down!" The revelers in the anteroom heard Philip's roar. Alexander sat down meekly.

"What is it, Alexander?" Philip had regained his composure immediately. "What's the reason for this behavior? Haven't I provided the best that I can for you? Aristotle is the foremost scholar in Greece, and as for that." He gestured in the direction of the academy. "Do you have any idea how much that place is costing me? All I want is to give you the best start possible, and this is the thanks I get. Why?"

"The academy was your idea, not mine. I was quite happy at the palace."

Philip gave him a long, hard stare. All Philotas' reports stressed how much Alexander was enjoying the academy. "Very well. If you hate it here so much I'll send you back."

"I didn't say I hated it." Alexander's tone was immediately more conciliatory. "I appreciate the efforts you've made and I have nothing against you, Father. It's just that I sometimes wonder if you really want me as your heir."

Philip was stunned. "Whatever makes you think that?"

"The things you do." Alexander shifted uneasily in his seat. "I am to be your successor, the next ruler of Macedonia. You should want me to be a good king and build on your achievements, yet it seems like you're deliberately trying to make it harder for me. How can I expand my kingdom if there's nowhere left that you haven't already conquered?"

Philip continued to stare at his son with his one eye, and then laughed. "Is that really what this is all about?" He thought back to the prophecy the oracle had made at Alexander's birth and added, "Don't worry boy; there'll be plenty left for you. Why are you complaining anyway? Would you rather inherit a strong kingdom or a weak one? The stronger I leave Macedonia, the easier it will be for you."

"For me? Then why do you continue to have sons? I am your heir, so why do you need more? You've had two sons in the last year alone, and these children are a threat to my inheritance. Amyntas, too. You took the throne from him, yet you allow him to stay by your side."

"Amyntas is only a threat to you. He's your problem, not mine." His son's whining was starting to irritate Philip. "If you feel so threatened by competitors, then perhaps you should try that much harder so you become king through merit rather than just because of whom you are." He saw that look come back into his son's eyes, and relaxed his tone a little.

"Besides, these others are mere babies and their mothers are not even royal wives. They are no threat and, let's be realistic, in all likelihood you will have succeeded me long before they reach an age where they could be a threat." Philip leaned forward in his seat, his hands clasped and his elbows resting on his knees.

"You're my appointed heir, Alexander, and I earnestly hope it's you who inherits my throne, but I cannot be sure you will. You've seen Arridaeus. He's my firstborn and was once my heir, but look at him now. Something could happen to you and what would I do then?

"What you must understand is that I have a duty to Macedonia. I cannot afford to be a king without an heir, as that would be inviting civil war. It may not be in your interests, but I have to have more than one son, just in case."

Alexander reluctantly nodded agreement. "Your words make sense, I suppose, Father."

Philip sat back in his chair, relieved. "Let me give you some advice. Kill Amyntas the moment you learn of my death, and then kill your brothers. All of them—starting with Arridaeus."

The boys were having their morning practice on the sports field, so did not learn about the new arrivals until they returned to the academy and found slaves pushing furniture around the dormitory in an attempt to squeeze in two more beds.

Theophrastus entered with the new boys and introduced them as Harpalus and Hephaestion. They were pages from the palace and already known to most of the group; there were calls of greeting from some of the boys. Alexander knew them by sight but neither had been part of his circle at Pella. He had spoken to Hephaestion once or twice, but never to Harpalus. The boy had one leg shorter than the other and walked with a hoppity gait. It had excluded him from a lot of the more strenuous activities at the palace and Alexander had not considered him worth bothering with.

Barely a week had passed since the king's visit and it was obvious to everyone why the two boys had been sent from Pella—it was a lesson in humility for Alexander. Philip paid for the academy and he would decide who went there, not his son.

There was a tension among the boys for the next few days. Alexander treated the newcomers with an aloofness they did not deserve, pointedly turning his back on Harpalus when the boy spoke in class for the first time.

The cripple seemed to accept his lot. His disability had been a barrier at the palace and there was no reason to think it should be any different at the academy. Hephaestion came from a different mould. He was a tall, good-looking boy and had never had a problem making friends. His own self-confidence had caused him to reject the toadying up to Alexander that had characterized life at the palace, and he wasn't going to let the insufferable little prig upset his life now. Like it or not, he would need to come to an understanding with the boy.

He found Alexander in the stable block, attending to Bucephalus. Although a lad had been brought in from Pella for the task, the prince still liked to groom the horse whenever he could.

"I saw you ride him. That first time, at the fair."

Alexander span around at the sound of the unexpected voice, his face changing to a scowl when he saw who it was. "What do you want?" he mumbled.

Hephaestion didn't answer immediately, strolling up to lean against the edge of the stall. "You must have been the only one there who didn't think you'd be thrown. How did you know he'd let you ride him?"

Alexander shrugged, being deliberately churlish. "I didn't. For all I knew he was going to throw me."

Hephaestion looked incredulous, and then gave a single laugh. But it was a pleasant laugh, not scornful. "You jest, surely. Then why did you do it? You could have been killed."

Justly proud of his achievement, a smile curled Alexander's lips. "I took a risk, yes, but it was a calculated risk. I could see he'd been mistreated, but by adults." He patted Bucephalus' neck as he spoke, making the horse give a little snort. "I wasn't an adult, so why should he be afraid of me?"

Hephaestion shook his head in wonder. "Well, all I can say is that you're braver than I am." He gazed up at the horse. "He is a beautiful animal, and he still only lets you ride him?"

Alexander nodded proudly. "The stable boy tried to mount him a while ago, but Bucephalus wouldn't keep still long enough. In the end he had to walk him down to me at the lower paddock." He chuckled at the memory.

A slave appeared at the stable door to summon them for cleansing prior to evening prayers at the sanctuary. The two boys walked to the bathhouse together, Alexander reaching the door first and holding it open for Hephaestion to follow. The boy smiled his thanks as he walked through, and continued to smile as the slave prepared their baths. He had achieved his task.

The students breathed a sigh of relief as the thawing of relations. No one would have claimed that Alexander and Hephaestion had become friends, but the exaggerated politeness and civility with which they now treated each other was apparent to all.

Only Harpalus failed to benefit from the new mood. Alexander may have stopped being openly hostile but saw no reason to be pleasant to the cripple. Hephaestion felt some responsibility for his traveling companion so suggested he come on a hunting expedition. Harpalus declined at first, but was encouraged when Proteas and Perdiccas lent their support. The following evening, Harpalus received some surprised looks and a few words of welcome as he and Perdiccas rode up to join the others at the start of the hunt. Alexander murmured something to Craterus but made no public comment. Harpalus had been accepted into the group.

A new air of unruliness entered the classroom in the weeks following Philip's visit. The youths had been slightly in awe of the privilege they knew they received by being part of the academy, but Alexander's defiance of his father and the ructions over the new arrivals had proved to be the catalyst for the normalizing of their behavior. They were simply a bunch of boisterous and inquisitive schoolboys, eager to challenge authority and see how far they could go. Aristotle and Theophrastus struggled with the change.

"It's getting out of hand and something must be done." Theophrastus stood in Aristotle's study, anger etched on his face. "It used to be the odd sniggered remark or a yawn or two on a warm afternoon, but now they're quite prepared to talk amongst themselves while I'm lecturing. I spotted two of them in town yesterday, when they were supposed to be taking instruction from the history tutor."

"It's still only the Macedonians, I take it?" Aristotle sat at his desk, documents scattered in front of him. "I've not yet had any trouble with the boys we brought from Lesbos."

"No, they're still loyal to you. They've not had the privileged upbringing these Macedonian assholes have had. It's Alexander's fault. He's the cause. I say punish him as an example to the others. It's the only way."

Aristotle pondered a moment. "No, turning him against me will just make matters worse. You're letting your dislike of the boy cloud your judgment, Theophrastus, but you're right about one thing: I have to do something or risk losing the academy."

The boys filed into the classroom that afternoon and took their places. Leonnatus, Proteas and Phrygius were missing. The trio had sneaked off to go hunting birds after the morning exercises and were unlikely to be back before evening. The others chatted idly while they waited for Theophrastus to arrive. It promised to be a dull afternoon.

Aristotle appeared at the door. The boys looked at him in surprise; he always left the mathematics lessons to Theophrastus. Not only that, he was dressed in riding clothes, complete with boots on his feet. An interested buzz went around the classroom.

He gave the boys ten minutes to prepare their horses and assemble in the lower paddock. They were ready in plenty of time; their curiosity was aroused and nobody wanted to miss this, whatever it was. Aristotle smiled as they rode up in a rabble, chattering excitedly and with grins on their faces. He had succeeded in catching their attention.

"My boys, it's a nice day so I thought we would spend the afternoon outside. I'm hoping to show you examples of some of the things I've observed in my studies of animals, so you might say we're going hunting. Does anyone object? You were supposed to be studying mathematics this afternoon, and I can take you back to the classroom if you prefer?" He joined in the laughter that answered his words.

Ptolemy led the way as they rode toward the slopes of the Bermius Mountains, their usual hunting grounds. The region around Mieza was renowned for its wine, and it was a pleasant ride along a path lined with vineyards. Not for nothing was the area known as the Gardens of Midas.

Aristotle was content to follow the boys; they were the hunters and knew where the prey was. They had never seen him on horseback before and he was aware of the sniggering glances that kept coming his way. He didn't care if it kept their interest, but wished his bare legs didn't look so white and gangly.

He started the lecture as they rode. "The one thing I've discovered in my studies is the immense diversity in nature. Some creatures have two legs and others four, while some have none and slither across the ground. Some animals are carnivores, others not. Some have fur and others have skin like leather. Some have horns and others tusks, and some can fly while others swim in the sea.

"With all these differences, there is only one conclusion that can be reached, which is that nature provides every creature with the best tools it needs for its survival. Every animal is ideally suited to its environment, and that environment will mould its appearance and habits. For instance, have any of you hunted boar?" The question was rhetorical (he'd heard the story of the Pig-Stickers enough times) but it served its purpose in making the boys laugh and give each other knowing glances.

"The swine of Mount Athos are much fiercer and bolder than their lowland counterparts, and even a sow will best a lowland boar. This is because the harsh climate of the mountains produces a much hardier animal than the milder temperatures found on the plains. So, you can see how otherwise identical creatures can have differing temperaments.

"Now, why do you think animals exist? What is their purpose?" He threw the question open to the class.

A number of the boys answered similarly. "To provide food for man, sir."

"Yes, but they will not see it that way." His statement drew an unintentional laugh. "Well, it's true. What do you think inspires a bear to wake up in the morning?"

"Hunger, sir. An animal needs to eat every day or it will starve." Riding alongside Aristotle, Erigyius was the best placed to answer. "They will wake up if for no other reason than to find food."

"Yes, but there is another incentive equally important to every animal, and that is to reproduce and continue the species. Animals have no higher level of existence than that, and the habits of animals are always either connected with the procuring of food or with the breeding and rearing of young."

They were climbing the slopes of the Bermius Mountains now, and Ptolemy led them off the track and into the woods. Aristotle fell silent, preferring to concentrate on the task of staying mounted as they picked their way through the branches. He wanted the boys to enjoy themselves, but not by seeing him unhorsed.

Ptolemy acted as scout, dismounting from time to time to search for tracks. Still, it took a while before they spotted some deer among the undergrowth. They reined in their horses and turned to Aristotle in triumph.

"Ah, you've found some wildlife, and about time, too. I was beginning to think I was back hunting with the Persians." The jibe drew laughter and the deer looked up in alarm, forcing Aristotle to wait a few moments for the animals to settle again.

"Now the most striking feature of the deer is its antlers," he began. "Look at that stag. We can tell he's less than six-years-old because his antlers have not yet reached their full growth, and that doesn't happen until that age. But he's more than two because deer don't have antlers before then, merely a slight protuberance.

See there? Surely, that buck is the offspring of the stag we see here. I would say that this is an animal of some four or five years. He is in his prime and these hinds are his harem."

"What a prize! And I don't even have a spear." Craterus voiced the thoughts of several, but Aristotle gave him a reproachful look.

"They aren't for hunting, boys, not today. Look at them standing there, allowing us to share this moment with them. It would be a desecration to kill any for sport." He became aware of the stares the boys were giving him and hurried on with the lesson.

"It may look like bone, but the antler is actually a horn, and a unique horn at that. The horns of other animals are hollow except at the tip, but the deer's antlers are hard and solid all the way through. And that is not all. The deer is the only animal that sheds its horns, which it does annually, growing a new set by the next breeding season. All other species have one set of horns which they retain permanently, and if they are damaged or cut off, they will not re-grow."

"But with so many differences, sir, how can you be sure that antlers are horns? If they have nothing in common with the horns of other animals, then maybe they are something else altogether." It was the first time Alexander had spoken and Aristotle was quick to seize on it.

"That's a very good question and one I have pondered myself." Alexander's cheeks glowed at the implied praise. "But it's something you'll have to trust me with, I'm afraid. Antlers are horns; I made an extensive study and could not find otherwise." Aristotle chuckled deliberately. "With such an enquiring mind, perhaps you'll be the one to prove me wrong one day?" Alexander blushed a second time.

The lesson continued as they followed the deer through the trees. "You will notice that the color of an animal's horns matches the color of its fur. The same is true of nails, claws, and hooves, but teeth and bones are always white. This I have found to be universal.

"No animal has both tusks and horns, and no saw-toothed animal, such as the lion, has either.

"The more teeth a species has, the longer will be its natural lifespan. I believe that the male of the species has more teeth than the female and have found this to be the case in man, pigs, sheep, and goats. It is an area of research I am still pursuing, and I have many more species to study before confirming this as a rule.

"As animals grow older their teeth get blacker, but the horse's teeth grow whiter with age. It's the only animal I have observed this in."

All the while Alexander kept close by, listening attentively and asking pertinent questions. Aristotle wallowed in his pupil's newly revealed interest; Bucephalus was the only animal he had seen the boy pay any attention to before. The others were happy to leave the two of them to it. Animals were for hunting as far as they were concerned.

They came onto a track and followed it down to a tiny village. Aristotle halted them, and they bought bread and goat's cheese and two skins of kykeon, a gruel-like beverage made from barley, herbs, and water. The villagers were eager to sell all they could at the inflated prices the townies were willing to pay.

Just behind the village, they found a shady spot by a stream and sat down to eat their meal. The food tasted good but the kykeon was a peasant's drink that made their breath stink. Nearchus drank heartily; it reminded him of his boyhood on Crete.

Aristotle continued the lesson as they ate. "Being an island, Lesbos gave me the opportunity to study marine life in great detail. We tend to think of all fish as belonging to just one genus, but there are some puzzling differences that question that idea. For instance, you all know what a dolphin is?" They nodded; a fresco in the public bathhouse at Pella showed Poseidon in the guise of a dolphin. "And a whale?" Another nod.

"Fish lay eggs, but dolphins and whales gives birth to live, fully-formed young. Not only that, the baby is nourished in the womb by a placenta in the same way as the young of animals. No other fish does that but every animal does. Dolphins and whales have lungs and breathe air, and have blowholes to expel the water they ingest while feeding. No other fish breathes air or has a blowhole.

"How then, can dolphins and whales be of the same order as other fish? I believe that they should actually be classed with the beasts of the field. They are animals that live in the sea."

"But how?" Alexander was sat just behind Aristotle. "What are animals doing in the sea? It doesn't make sense."

Aristotle craned his neck around and gave the boy a sideways look. "Come and sit next to me, Alexander." Hephaestion made room for him.

"Now I have spoken before about how everything has its place in relation to everything else, and it follows therefore, that there must be points where different classes meet. That's what I think is taking place with dolphins and whales. They must be in the position where fish meet animals. Sharks also give birth to live young, but without the placenta. Does anyone see what that implies?" He looked only at Alexander, the boy's intense face revealing his total absorption in the tutor's words. This was his question and the others kept their silence.

"The shark is on the other side of the divide," he answered, "the last of the fish. The shark is the highest form of fish and the dolphin the lowest form of animal. It makes sense; they even look similar." Alexander gave a grin of satisfaction at his reasoning.

"Maybe, and where does that conclusion lead you? If that's the case, what can you say about the point where two classes meet?"

The boy's expression turned to puzzlement. He thought about it for a moment, but then shook his head.

"Think, my boy." This much interest in a subject needed to be encouraged and Aristotle was determined to coax an answer out of him. "Use the categories the way I have taught you. The dolphin and the shark are your substance, but what is their relation? How are they different and how are they similar?"

"They look alike and give birth the same way," pondered Alexander. "They both look like fish but give birth like animals, one more so than the other." His eyes had that distant look that always overtook them when he was deep in thought. "Is it that they therefore belong to both classes? No, that they have characteristics of both classes, so . . . they are a merging of the two classes! Yes, they're the point where one class becomes another. The shark is more fish than animal, the dolphin more animal than fish. That's it, isn't it?" He beamed in triumph and was rewarded with the tutor's smile.

"Maybe you're right, but the truth is I don't know." Aristotle laughed at Alexander's disappointed look. "I agree, my boy. I think the classes don't just sit side by side, but that there's a merging of some sort as you suggest, and sharks and dolphins are the proof of that merging." Aristotle stretched out his legs. The ground was becoming uncomfortable.

"But think of the questions that arise. If dolphins are animals, why do they live in the sea? Is there a fish that lives on land and has legs? Did the dolphin once live on land? Did it once have legs? If nature can mould a hardier boar for life in the mountains, is it also capable of turning legs into fins for life in the sea? And where does the whale fit in?" He shrugged. "It's a mystery."

"So if I was to go swimming every day, sir, would my legs turn into fins?" Ptolemy was being facetious and Aristotle knew it.

"Possibly," he answered with a smile.

"But how can a leg turn into a fin?" Alexander was puzzled, and more than a little peeved. Aristotle had asked a question without knowing the answer.

Aristotle turned his attention back to the boy. "And that's the biggest mystery of all. The best example I could come up with is that of the gelding and the eunuch. They were born male, but mutilating just one small part is enough to cause a major change in their appearance. They become more female in both form and action." He ignored a snigger from Iolaus. "So, if the alteration of one organ can make an animal virtually change sex, perhaps a change to another organ can make a limb turn into a fin."

He looked around the group. "You must remember, boys, that this is still only a hypothesis and it will be some time, if ever, before I'm satisfied I can answer all the questions it raises."

The boys absorbed his words in silence. Aristotle was revealing ideas still only half-formed in his brain, and making them privy to concepts that the rest of the world could not even imagine. Never had the gulf between their lives now and the prosaic existence they had led in the palace been so great; they were truly an intellectual elite.

It was after dark when the group returned to the academy. Aristotle wished good health to the boys and retired to his quarters, satisfied with his day's work. Craterus cadged them a supper of an apple each from the duty kitchen slave and they mounted the staircase that led to their dormitory. Phrygius, Proteas and Leonnatus were woken by the noise and forced to listen enviously to animated accounts of what they had missed; they would not skip a lesson again. Then the candles were snuffed and the room was silent, save for Laomedon's snoring. The boys slept well that night.

Chapter Ten

Arete

The next few months passed quickly, the group kept busy by Aristotle and his staff. Although still unruly at times, they tended to save it for their leisure hours now, paying attention when in the classroom. The boys appreciated their privileged position more than ever before and had no wish to waste it. Aristotle's excursion had paid off better than he could have hoped.

With the onset of winter, they were forced to cut back on their hunting expeditions, turning instead to the town of Mieza for their evening entertainment. Complaints about their rowdy behavior filtered back to Aristotle, who forbade Alexander to go into the town after dark. The boy, of course, refused to be left out.

They had discovered a brothel on the far side of town and it soon became their favorite haunt. The building stood at the end of an alleyway that led off a street of workshops, and you wouldn't feel too safe walking the area alone after the traders had closed their shops and retired to their homes in the rear.

But Alexander felt no fear as he followed his companions through the empty streets, only excitement and nervousness. It was his first visit, though most of the others had already been, the dormitory rocking with coarse laughter at the wildly exaggerated stories of their prowess and the vulgarity of the three-obol women.

They entered through a door that led into a narrow hallway, making smutty comments as they stumbled into each other in the darkness. A door opened and the hallway was flooded in light.

"Joy to you, little brothers," said an ageing madam as she beckoned them into a lighted room. They filed in, grins on their faces, and Alexander looked around him. The room was large, with couches against three sides. A diagonal pattern covered the stone floor and frescoes of cavorting bodies decorated every wall.

The madam ushered them to the couches, Alexander finding himself next to Leonnatus. There was movement through a door in one corner and three girls came in carrying trays, a cheer greeting their arrival. They were dressed in flimsy chitons, their bodies clearly visible as they handed out wine. Alexander raised his broad, flat wine cup to his lips and took a sip. The wine was cheap and he tasted sediment in his mouth.

Cassander raised his own cup and called out, "Are we Athenians? Bring in some big cups." He was referring to the southerner's habit of progressing from shallow cups to deep cups during the course of a drinking party. It drew a laugh from the others and the madam forced a smile. The cups were her attempt at imitating the symposiums of upper-class society and the jibe wasn't appreciated.

"Never mind the big cups; bring in some big women!" Leonnatus gestured his meaning by putting his hands on his chest, raising another cheer from the boys.

The madam hurried to oblige him. This was the largest number of youths to have visited so far and they could easily get out of hand. The sooner they'd been packed off to separate rooms, the better. She stood at the door and beckoned to the girls assembling in the corridor.

They processed into the room and formed a semi-circle, surveying the boys with alluring smiles. Alexander grinned. The girls were younger and prettier than the hags he'd seen in the back streets of Pella, and all wore versions of the see-through slip. Nothing was being left to the imagination.

"Which one do you want, Alexander?" The room hushed at the question. It was his first time and a low, bear-like growl of encouragement emanated from the throats of his companions. He felt his cheeks burning red.

"Do we have a virgin?" The madam clucked and homed in on the boy, while the girls giggled at the prospect. Leonnatus raised his arm to point an index finger down on Alexander's head, to more laughter from the boys.

The madam beckoned to one of the girls. "Thalia will take care of you; she's good with first-timers. Why—she's almost a virgin herself." There were chortles from Philotas and Laomedon, who'd both had her on their last visit.

Thalia stepped forward. She was a young and quite attractive Scythian, with tribal tattoos on her arms and a pleasant smile. The madam had named her after one of the muses of legend, as her true name would have been too awkward for civilized tongues.

Alexander felt a stirring beneath his tunic as she extended her hand and pulled him up from the couch.

"Ask for a kubda, Alexander," called Phrygius, his voice unnecessarily loud. The air was thick with testosterone.

The others took up the cry, "Kubda! Kubda!" The pair exited the room to the chant.

Alexander followed the girl up the corridor. She knew how to walk, a slow saunter that swayed her backside to full effect. He felt himself mesmerized by the sight as she led him into one of the many side rooms. It was tiny and sparsely furnished—a barely-made truckle bed, a stool with a few clothes slung across it, a loom in the corner that held a half-spun woolen garment.

But Alexander had no eyes for the room. He was transfixed by the girl's body and excited by the throbbing in his loins. "Three obols," she said in a thick foreign accent. "Three obols for kubda."

He hurriedly pulled the coins from his pouch and, at her direction, handed them to a child who had appeared at the open door. The boy ran off down the corridor to deposit the money in the owner's strongbox.

Thalia closed the door and pulled up her chiton, indicating that he should do the same. He stood naked before her a moment later, but she wasn't looking. She'd already turned and bent over the stool, gripping it with both hands and splaying her bottom for him in the classic kubda position.

It was all over in a brief frenzy of shoving and panting. The girl splashed some water over herself from a bowl and donned her dress. "Come again, little brother," she said as she sat down at the loom, her back to him. As his lust subsided and his breathing returned to normal, so Alexander felt flat and dissatisfied. He had that same sense of shame he felt on those occasions when he gratified himself in private. He dressed and returned to the lounge.

Hephaestion was already there, reclining with a drink in his hand. He grinned as Alexander entered. "So how did it go, little brother?"

Alexander leered as he sat down. "It was great; I rode her like a dog." He wasn't going to reveal his true thoughts to Hephaestion. He gave the youth a puzzled look. "Haven't you been in yet?"

Hephaestion took a sip of wine before answering. "No, it's not for me. I have little interest in women."

Philotas returned, then Erigyius and Laomedon. The two brothers had had an Egyptian girl together and regaled them with the story of her insatiability. Leonnatus walked in, decided he was ready to go again, and went in search of the madam. The room filled with the boys, their raucous chatter prompting the woman to shoo them into the street with warnings to consider the neighbors and keep the noise down.

It was an amiable ride back to the academy, but Alexander was lost in thought. Even though he had wanted the Scythian girl and enjoyed it, there'd been something cold and empty about the encounter and it left him with a sense of disappointment. He was confused.

A group went back the next night, but Alexander made his excuses. He would have to go again or his absence would raise questions, but he wasn't ready to repeat the experience just yet. The knowledge he would be expected to be a regular visitor from now on didn't thrill him.

He waited for the others to leave and then sought out Lysimachus. His pedagogue was in the stables, trying to repair a split bridle. The leather was old and worn, and Alexander made a mental note to buy him a new one the next time he went to the market in Mieza. They exchanged pleasantries for a few moments and then Alexander broached the subject.

"We all went into Mieza last night."

"So I heard." Lysimachus didn't look up from his stitching.

"We went to a house in the Street of Potters. It was a brothel."

Lysimachus put the bridle down and looked into the boy's face. "What is it, Achilles? Tell your Phoenix." He was sitting on a bale of hay and gestured for Alexander to do the same.

They didn't see each other as much these days and it had been sometime since Lysimachus had addressed him by his pet name. It relieved the awkwardness he felt. "There was a girl, a woman. It wasn't what I'd expected."

"It never is, my boy. What was the problem?"

"I can't say. I enjoyed it, but . . ." He tried to find the words to describe his feelings. "It didn't seem right. She was nothing to me and I was nothing to her. It was like we were no more than animals."

Lysimachus laughed. "You didn't think it would be love, did you. You won't get that from a whore." A flare of anger came into Alexander's eyes and he added, "No, I'm not mocking you. I would never mock you, my Achilles.

"I think the problem is you expected too much. It's only natural, as it was your first time and you anticipated great things. But she was only a whore, Achilles, and as you say, you were nothing to her. Don't worry, my boy. In time, and with the right woman, you'll find that it's a wonderful thing."

There was more on Alexander's mind. "I wonder if it should even be a woman. Hephaestion prefers men and perhaps I'm the same."

Lysimachus considered the thought. "Perhaps," he said, "but then you said you enjoyed this whore. Many men in Greece take pleasure in other men's bodies, your own father for instance, but that doesn't mean they have no interest in women. Go ask any man in the army; it's a standing joke that King Philip takes a new wife with every campaign."

That was a sore point with Alexander. "Yes, but that's because he has to produce heirs. His wives only see him when he's at the palace. Whenever he goes away he takes a man with him."

"What do you expect? He's with the army!" Lysimachus chuckled. "Take my word for it, my boy. Your father enjoys women every bit as much as men, and I'm sure you'll be the same."

"But what if I only like men? What if I'm like those painted she-males who gather in that street behind the Sanctuary of Aphrodite in Pella?"

"Not you. You'll be more like the warriors of the Sacred Band of Thebes. They fight side-by-side with their lovers, and no foe is more feared on the battlefield."

A brightening smile spread across Alexander's face. "Or like Achilles and Patroclus." Any thought he might be imitating his hero was guaranteed to please the boy.

"There you go," said Lysimachus.

Aristotle was late for class. The boys whiled away the minutes enjoying an outrageous story of the previous night's antics from Leonnatus, but it was unlike the tutor to be so late and eventually they became curious enough to send Iolaus to look for him. He returned with Theophrastus a few minutes later, and the news that Aristotle had received a letter while they'd been on the sports field. According to Theophrastus, he had read the document, retired to his apartment, and had not been seen since.

Callisthenes, being his nephew, and Alexander led the delegation that mounted the steps to the tutor's apartment. A maid answered the door but refused them entry, saying her master had withdrawn to his study with instructions he should not be disturbed. Aristotle heard the noise and emerged as they tried to question the slave further. He was grim and said little, telling them to return to the classroom and he would be along presently. Only Callisthenes was allowed to remain.

The two of them entered the hushed classroom twenty minutes later, Callisthenes avoiding their enquiring eyes as he made his way to his stool. Aristotle replaced Theophrastus at the front of the class and stared down at a wax tablet he held in his hands. It was fully two minutes before he spoke.

"My boys, this day I have received tragic news. Hermeias, my old friend and colleague, has been cruelly put to death by the

Persians." There was a murmur among the boys. Although they had long known the satrap's days were numbered, it was still a shock. Alexander wondered how his father would react to the death of his ally.

"How did it happen?" he asked for all of them.

Aristotle sighed. "He was lured to a meeting with a Greek mercenary named Mentor. You may know of him? His brother, Memnon, was once a guest of your father in your childhood." The boy gave him a puzzled look. He'd been too young to remember the night in the treasury and only recalled Barsine and her father from those days.

"A pity, as it would be wise to recognize the faces of such scum. It would appear that Hermeias and Mentor met as officials of the Great King, then, while Hermeias was enjoying his hospitality, Mentor suddenly turned on his guest and arrested him." The boys gasped; such a betrayal was against all they believed in.

Aristotle smiled in grim satisfaction. "Yes, you might expect such a thing of a Persian but not a Greek, even a Greek in Persian pay. Hermeias was taken to Susa and turned over for torture but, despite their worst excesses, he refused to reveal what he knew and was finally impaled on a stake at the Great King's orders. His last words were that his friends should know he died a true gentleman and scholar." Aristotle fell silent.

"I'm sorry, Aristotle." Alexander didn't know what more to say. The others murmured their condolences.

"How is your wife?" asked Craterus. She was also Hermeias' niece.

"She is as well as can be expected in her grief. Thank you, Craterus." He looked down at the tablet in his hand, and sighed heavily. "My boys, I have composed a hymn in memory of Hermeias and would like to recite it to you."

There were a few surprised looks but no one dissented.

"I have called it Arete, as it is a hymn in praise of virtue, and all those who aspire to it." He paused again, his Adam's apple bobbing with emotion. He gulped and then began.

"Arete, you whom the mortal race wins by much toil; you are the fairest prey in life.

"For the beauty of your form, it is an enviable fate both to die and to endure toils violent and unceasing.

"On such a prize do you set the mind: equal to the immortals, better than gold, than noble ancestors, or languid sleep.

"For your sake, Hercules, the son of Zeus, endured much in deeds hunting after your power.

"Through longing for you, Achilles and Ajax committed themselves to the house of Hades.

"Because of the gracious beauty of your form, Hermeias, the nursling of Anatolia, forsook the sun's rays.

"Therefore, the muses shall exalt him, famous in song for his deeds, and immortal."

Cassander was first to break the silence that followed. "That was beautiful. It stirs the senses." There were murmurs of agreement.

"More than that." Alexander's voice was thick with emotion and there was a faint glistening on his cheek. "You have captured the essence of that which every man should strive for." He looked around the room. "I pledge to make every effort to live like my noble ancestors, Hercules and Achilles. I, too, will place honor and virtue above all else and will willingly suffer and die for my cause."

"That is a noble aspiration, Alexander, and one that you would all do well to follow." Aristotle was fighting back the tears. Theophrastus took a step forward and placed a comforting hand on his shoulder.

The boys said nothing, but even those who hadn't entirely succumbed to Aristotle's poetry knew they had just crossed a threshold. They were now more than mere colleagues or members of an exclusive club. They had become a band of brothers, and there would be no place for anyone unwilling to live by their ideals—by Alexander's ideals.

It was decided they would forego the brothel that evening in respect for Hermeias, instead trekking to the sanctuary and sacrificing to Hades and Athena for the soul of the departed. The next night it was business as usual.

Alexander declined with confidence, citing the morals of Achilles as his reason. It drew a few remarks as the others made their way into town, but they weren't surprised he had now managed to elevate himself above the pleasures of the flesh.

Alexander read for a while but the writing on the scroll was faded and the candlelight made his eyes ache, so he decided to go to the bathhouse instead. He was surprised to find Hephaestion and Perdiccas there; he'd assumed everyone had gone into town. It was obvious he'd walked in on something and made to leave.

"No need to go, Alexander. We're nearly through anyway." Hephaestion sounded tipsy. He was slouched in one of the hipbaths that lined the walls of the circular building, drinking wine while Perdiccas sat in the alcove behind and massaged his neck. Perdiccas had a knee on either side of Hephaestion's shoulders and his feet rested against his stomach. Hephaestion's forearm rubbed the other boy's thigh each time he took a sip of wine.

Alexander hesitated, and then filled a vacant bath from the pool that occupied the center of the room. He undressed and placed his clothes in the niche situated above each alcove, conscious of the other two watching him. Although the boys saw each other naked every day, this time it felt different.

Hephaestion poured wine into a cup and passed it across to him as he settled into the bath. "Would you like a massage, Alexander? Perdiccas is very good."

Alexander said nothing, merely shaking his head. He unwrapped the cloth he stored his strygils in and chose one shaped for the upper arm. The bronze implement opened up the pores but he put it down after a while and let himself relax. The heat of the braziers combined with the warmth of the water and the steam that filled the tiny building.

He heard the door being closed and opened his eyes. Perdiccas had gone, and Hephaestion was lying in the center pool, his head and arms at Alexander's feet. The youth was pouring a bottle of pungent perfume into his bath.

Hephaestion put down the empty bottle and began to gently knead each toe in turn. Alexander's first impulse was to pull his legs up, but he found himself unable to move. Hephaestion slid his fingers along the boy's feet, encouraged by the lack of a rebuttal.

Alexander's mind was in turmoil. He stared down at Hephaestion, who stared back with a slight smile on his lips. Alexander opened his mouth to speak, but the sensation of the fingers against his soles was pleasant. He said nothing. Hephaestion continued, leaning forward to move his hands up to Alexander's knees. Then they slipped below the water and stroked the length of his calves.

That had the desired effect. Alexander stayed silent but his body spoke for him. Hephaestion's smile turned to a grin and he slid himself over the end of the bath.

It wasn't long before the others became aware of the new relationship. There were a few jealous jibes from Craterus, who saw his own special bond with Alexander disappearing, but the others accepted it with little comment. Most were rather relieved at the development, as the thought of having to live with a sanctimonious Alexander hadn't been a welcome one.

The lengthening evenings heralded a resumption of their hunting forays. On a whim, Alexander bought two Dardanian wolfhounds from the market in Mieza. They were huge beasts with evil tempers and fleas to match, and a passionate loyalty to the boy.

The foul weather had lasted all day and there was no question of venturing out into the hills that evening. A few of the boys rode into town, while the rest enjoyed a game of knucklebone dice in the dormitory. It was their favorite indoor pastime, played with colored beads flung into the air and snatched as they fell. It derived its name from the goat's knucklebones that were used in antiquity, and still favored by the poor.

The skies cleared a little as darkness fell, so Alexander broke off from the game to take the opportunity to walk his dogs. Their exercise was usually in the form of sinking their teeth into a fleeing hare, and retrieving a stick was a novelty that soon wore off. They watched their master fling it for the umpteenth time, and promptly sat down in the mud.

Alexander laughed and turned to walk up the path back to the academy, whistling for them to follow. They raced past him and detoured to investigate a likely rustling in some bushes, so he pulled his cloak up to cover his head against the increasing drizzle and left them to catch up. As he reached the garden, he noticed a light in the potting shed that Aristotle had converted into a workshop.

He approached the tiny wooden building, where the tutor kept his specimens and sometimes brought animals for dissection. The shutters had been closed over the only window but lamplight flickered through gaps in the boards. The door was barred from the inside.

He rapped his fist against the door. "Aristotle, are you in there? It is I, Alexander." There was no reply but he heard movement from inside and the lamp was extinguished. He grasped the handle of his dagger.

"Who is with you?" It was Aristotle's voice.

Alexander relaxed his grip on the dagger. "Nobody, I'm alone." He heard the bar being removed and the door opened a fraction.

"No dogs! Keep them out!" Alexander did as he was told, sliding in through the gap in the door as the hounds yelped with indignation at being left outside.

Aristotle relit the lamp. He stood by his workbench, on which lay a bloody cloth. His saw and sharpened dissection knives were laid out next to the cloth, one stained with blood and matter.

"What you see here, I must swear you to keep silent. Is that understood?"

"Of course, Aristotle. You have my word." He couldn't take his eyes off the cloth, and had already guessed what must lie beneath for it to be so secret.

Aristotle removed the sheet and Alexander stepped forward to examine the fetus. The baby was tiny and grotesque, barely formed. Aristotle had slit the belly open to expose the tiny bones of the rib cage, and the heart and other innards were lined up alongside the oversized head.

"How did you get it?" The dissection of any human corpse was illegal and carried severe penalties.

"I have an arrangement with a midwife in Mieza. Whenever she attends a miscarriage, she brings it to me. This is the third, and the youngest so far. Look at its fingers, Alexander. What do you see?"

He looked, and then looked again. "All the gods! They're webbed, like a frog." He looked up at the tutor. "What does it mean?"

Aristotle shook his head. "I cannot say, other than it's yet another example of the connection between man and the animal world. There are so many similarities, but also so many differences. It seems like the more I find out, the more questions I have. I fear I'll never have all the answers."

He picked up a scalpel and continued with the dissection, while Alexander jotted the occasional note on a wax tablet as Aristotle dictated. It was fully an hour before the boy opened the door and let the dogs in to dispose of the carcass. When they'd eaten their fill, he gathered up the remains and hurled them into the cesspit that served the academy. He returned to find Aristotle wiping down the workbench. They walked through the garden in silence, comrades with a shared secret.

Lysimachus had returned from yet another trip to report Alexander's progress to Olympias. Over time, he had also effectively become the academy's postman, ferrying letters between the boys and their relatives. His return was always welcomed.

He handed his horse to a slave and guzzled from a flask of wine. It was a half-day's ride from Pella and he was covered in mud from the road. He longed to sink into a bath but knew he would not be left alone once the boys heard he'd returned.

He found them in the middle of a geography lesson at the sanctuary, and grinned as they spotted him and ran over. He sent the relief tutor from Mieza home early and ambled over to a bench, the boys muttering impatiently at his sluggish distribution of their letters from the satchel around his neck. He did it deliberately, laughing at their insults.

The portico in front of the caves was soon a babble of murmuring voices as the boys read their letters aloud, as was the custom when reading.

Lysimachus reached into his satchel and handed a scroll to Alexander.

"This will amuse you, my boy. It certainly gave your mother a laugh." Alexander looked it over curiously. It was written on parchment and too formal to be from his father.

He unwrapped it and began to read. After a few words, he laughed and glanced at Lysimachus. "It's a letter from Isocrates. Have you read it?"

Lysimachus shook his head. "Your mother made me aware of its contents, though. It's an attack on Aristotle, I understand. Isocrates tells you to beware of traveling philosophers, or something like that." They both laughed.

The Athenian had been deeply aggrieved at his failure to secure the post of Alexander's tutor, and the fact he was in his nineties was a flimsy excuse as far as he was concerned. Now the letter was a dig at the successful candidate.

Alexander read aloud. "I implore you to ignore quibbling academics and hair-splitting sophists, and concentrate on practical argument instead. What rot!" he declared, looking up.

Their laughter was attracting a crowd and the boys gathered to listen as Alexander read out the choicest excerpts for their entertainment. They laughed with him, but a few exchanged glances at some of the advice the aged philosopher was giving, especially when he made the point that a king should rule by command, not persuasion.

They had reason to agree with Isocrates. One of Aristotle's favorite lessons was in eristics, particularly the ability to argue a case from both points of view. He was hoping to instill a sense of fair-mindedness in the future king.

Alexander shined at the art, and he and Callisthenes would make a game of debating a proposition, then suddenly switching stances at Aristotle's direction. But they were the only ones who found it amusing. The rest took the Macedonian attitude that a man who could show two faces at one time could not be trusted with either. Aristotle would have none of it, but should have heeded their counsel. Eristics would one day lead to the death of his own nephew, Callisthenes, at the hands of a scheming King Alexander.

"Have you had any word from the army?" Iolaus hoped for news of his father.

Lysimachus chuckled. "Oh yes, I certainly have. As you already know, King Philip has spent most of the last year securing the border with Thrace. Well, you'll be pleased to hear he's taken another wife, a Thracian princess this time." A light-hearted jeer came from the boys. "He's also established three new outposts along the frontier, only he's not settling them with colonists but with the dregs of Macedonia. Apparently, one of the settlements has already been nicknamed Thugsville by the Thracians. Maybe next time they'll think twice before challenging Macedonia's borders." The boys hooted with laughter at his words.

"But there is a serious side, as his actions in Thrace are causing more problems with Athens. Yet again, Demosthenes has spoken against King Philip in the Assembly, claiming it's all part of a Macedonian plot to seize the Athenian colonies along the Thracian coast. I don't know if that's what the King intends, of course, but the possibility is enough to have Athens worried. They need those harbors for their fleet. Without them, they risk losing control of the supply routes for their grain, and that they cannot allow." The mood among the boys became more subdued. Although the shipyards along the Chalkidiki coast were continually producing new vessels, the Macedonian navy was still far from strong enough to face the mighty Athenian fleet. It was a campaign that Philip could not yet win.

Lysimachus sensed their disquiet and hurried to reassure them. "The Athenians have sent a captain to organize the defense of their colonies, but nothing more as yet. Boys, I have other news; the King has a new favorite."

Gossip at last, and a chorus of voices asked the same question. "Who?"

Lysimachus grinned. "The King's eye has been taken by a new arrival to the Companion cavalry. Does anyone remember Pausanias of Orestes?" The startled looks told him they did. The youth had been a Royal Page until graduating to the army the previous fall, and they'd all worked alongside him at the palace.

"It would seem the King's bed is a ladder to success, as there's already talk of him taking the next vacancy that arises in the bodyguard. And if the King does go to war with Athens, that vacancy may not be long in coming. My boys, Pausanias may well be wearing a purple cloak before the end of the year."

Lysimachus grinned again and stood with a flourish, as though making a grand exit. It amused him to stir these young nobles up occasionally and he had certainly done that, leaving a muttering of envy and anger behind him as he strolled back to the academy. It was every page's dream to wear the purple cloak of the bodyguard, and Pausanias would win it for baring his bottom.

Alexander felt like giggling with elation, but was careful to say and do nothing as he absorbed the resentment around him. It would soon dawn on the boys that they'd been out of circulation for too long, and their best chance for advancement now lay with him. If there were any waverers among his colleagues, King Philip had just ensured they would stay in his son's camp.

Chapter Eleven

End of the Idyll

The war with Athens didn't happen, but it was an uneasy peace. Philip continued to increase the Macedonian presence in Thrace, while the Athenian captain proved to be little more than a pirate. Philip demanded he be recalled to Athens and the Assembly debated the matter. Midway through the deliberations, Demosthenes stood up and made the speech of his life; the captain stayed.

First Ptolemy, and then Philotas and Cassander left to join the army as summer came to an end, Aristotle deciding they had grown too old to be pupils. Perdiccas and Phrygius joined them the following spring, while Proteas and Craterus were promoted to the role of Alexander's bodyguard. Philip recruited Harpalus as his new mole; the youth had a head for figures and tastes to match.

None of the graduates were replaced, and it wasn't difficult for the remainder to guess that their days at Mieza were numbered. Aristotle could not be drawn, but news that a colony had been established in the ruins of his hometown told them all they needed to know.

Despite their underlying excitement, the routine at the academy continued as normal.

The boys assembled in front of the academy for their morning jog, running on the spot and rubbing their hands in the pre-dawn chill. They were cold and eager to get started, but no one dared move until the paidotribe gave the order. The sports instructor stood by the gateway, engaged in conversation with one of Cleitus' guardsmen, deliberately keeping them waiting. Spinning around, he waved his split stick at the boys.

"Take off!"

They raced up the path, turning and following the ditch that bounded the first of the orchards. The instructor and the guard watched as Alexander moved past Nearchus to take the lead. As they disappeared out of sight, the guardsman made a comment about the sight of so many naked buttocks at one go. The paidotribe laughed, and began to make his way down to the lower paddock.

Alexander was already there when he arrived, as always. Nearchus and Proteas were competing for second place with the rest strung out up the slope. Leonnatus brought up the rear; he wasn't built for speed.

Alexander played with his hounds, which had been taken for a walk by Harpalus, his usual pastime when the others were exercising. The boys gathered around him as they finished, bending their heads between their knees and filling their lungs with air. Alexander was barely out of breath, a product of his years with Leonidas.

"I don't know how you do it," Nearchus gasped. "Every morning I try to beat you, and every morning you leave me standing. Tell me, are you in league with Hermes?" Alexander laughed at the taller boy.

"He should enter the Olympics," added Proteas. "I've said that before."

"And so have I, sir." They fell silent at the paidotribe's voice. "Why don't you? You're certainly good enough."

Alexander looked at the man. "Quite simply, the Olympics are open to all and it would not be seemly for a prince to compete with illiterate peasants. Even worse, can you imagine if I lost to some goatherd? If I could compete only against kings and princes, then perhaps I might consider it."

The paidotribe grimaced; he came from a long line of goatherds. "Get those mutts off my field," he snapped at Harpalus. "I don't want to be stepping in their turds."

The boys practiced the discus and javelin for a while, the sheer strength of Leonnatus coming to the fore in these events. Then the paidotribe split them into two groups, some for a wrestling bout and the others for boxing. The wrestlers gathered around the vats of olive oil and sand that stood in the lower corner of the field, smearing the greasy liquid over their bodies as they paired off for the first round. Alexander and Hephaestion would fight each other, their giggles prompting a sharp rebuke from the paidotribe when they lingered too long sprinkling sand over each other's bodies. They grabbed a pick from the pile and hurried over to join the others in preparing the wrestling pitch.

Leonnatus was in fine form, the prospect of a bout spurring him on. He swung his pick heartily, plunging it into the hard earth and gouging out large chunks of turf. He didn't notice the split in the handle as he swung it above his head once more, and the end flew off. It soared through the air, the point skewering Iolaus through the thigh. The boy fell to the ground with a scream.

There was pandemonium for a moment, before the nervous-looking paidotribe restored order. He pushed through the gaggle of boys gathered around Iolaus and examined the wound, the boy screaming again as he tried to remove the pick. He left it where it was, calling for Alexander to run and warn Aristotle, and for the others to help carry Iolaus back to the academy.

Alexander ran like never before. He found Aristotle tending to his beehives in the garden and blurted out the story, heedless of the insects that swarmed around his oiled skin. Aristotle removed his wide-brimmed straw hat, adapted for beekeeping by the addition of some transparently thin linen netting. His face was ashen.

"Go to my apartment and ask the maid for my physician's chest, and then bring it to me in the kitchens." Alexander did as he was told, smearing greasy sand on the chair in Aristotle's study as he helped the maid retrieve the box from the clutter under his desk. He ignored the flushed looks of Aristotle's wife. She hadn't been this close to a naked youth since the last feast day she had attended on Lesbos.

Aristotle already had the huge table in the kitchen prepared when they brought Iolaus in. The pickaxe blade still stuck out of his thigh, blood spurting from the wound and trailing across the stone floor. Leonnatus carried him in his arms, mumbling apologies with every step. He placed Iolaus on the sheet that Aristotle had laid out ready for him.

"Everybody outside; I need space to work." Aristotle was already tightening a tourniquet around the leg, trying to stem the loss of blood. "Why wasn't this done earlier?" He gave the paidotribe an appalled look. "Are you trying to kill the boy?" The paidotribe said nothing as he sheepishly backed out of the room.

He was the only one to leave. The boys stood back from the table, but had no intention of abandoning a comrade in such a state. Iolaus' face was pale and drained of blood, his eyes barely open. His breath came in short gulps.

"Can I do anything, Aristotle?" Alexander could feel himself becoming irritated at his inability to help. He needed to do something.

Aristotle gave him a sharp look. "Yes, you might be useful." He glanced around the room, noticing the boys hadn't left. "Callisthenes, go down to the stream and find me some sphagnum moss."

Aristotle placed a few drops of liquid on a cloth and held it under Iolaus' nose; the boy quickly fell into a drowsy incoherence. Craterus was detailed to hold the leg steady and Leonnatus was placed at Iolaus' shoulders with the same task. Aristotle was ready to extricate the pick. He gave Alexander a surgical instrument, with hurried instructions on how to use it to prize the wound open.

Iolaus murmured and trembled as the pick was removed, but failed to come around. A wine-soaked sponge was inserted into the gash, and then Callisthenes returned with the moss and Aristotle prepared it in a small pestle. Within a few minutes, the wound had been cleaned and Alexander was using another instrument to clamp it, marveling as the tutor sewed the skin together as though it was a garment.

Another twenty minutes, and Aristotle had applied a foul-smelling poultice, made with herbs from his box and from the garden. A few minutes more, and he'd mixed a potion and trickled it into Iolaus' mouth. A stretcher was brought from the storeroom and Iolaus was carried to the dormitory. He was weak, but he would live. It remained to be seen if his injury would curtail a military career.

Aristotle began replacing the lids on his herb bottles and washing the bloodied instruments. The boys had accompanied the stretcher and only Alexander remained.

"I want you to teach me."

Aristotle turned and looked at the boy. "Teach you what?"

"All you know about medicine. You just saved Iolaus' life. He'd have died without you and next time you may not be there."

Aristotle smiled. "It takes years to learn everything, my boy. I only know this much because my father was a doctor and taught me. That was his chest. I think he had hopes I'd follow him into the profession." His eyes grew misty at thoughts of childhood. "Besides, it's not part of the syllabus." He returned to washing his instruments.

"Then teach me in the evenings. I'm willing to learn in my own time."

Aristotle sighed, and smiled again. "Very well. First lesson; take those rags," he indicated the bloody pile on the table, "and put them in the furnace. Then come back and I'll show you around the herb garden. But first, go and put some clothes on."

Relations with Athens continued to deteriorate through the winter, with a Macedonian merchant ship being seized and its crew sold into slavery. The Athenians repeatedly ignored Philip's demands that the cargo be returned, and then they kidnapped a Macedonian diplomat and held him to ransom.

Alexander received orders to travel to Pella while the boys were gathering at the sanctuary for the afternoon lesson, and the portico became a buzz of excited chatter as they discussed the development.

"Do you think the King will give you a command, Alexander?"

"Why aren't we coming with you?"

"Don't leave us here to rot while you win all the glory."

Alexander smiled. "You have it wrong. I'm not recalled permanently, only for a few days. The King is sponsoring a new gymnasium in my name and wants me to be present at the dedication ceremony, nothing more than that. I'll be back within a couple of days." The eager look in his eyes betrayed his own excitement at the news.

The boys came to order as Aristotle came down the path from the academy. He, too, had heard the news and was in somber mood. He knew this day had been coming, but had hoped for longer; Alexander's education was far from finished.

"My boys, today I will talk to you about the nature of kingship. What is a king? Is he an absolute ruler or the servant of his people?" The boys flung sideward looks at each other. Aristotle had studiously avoided the issue of monarchy as an institution, despite the odd mischievous attempt to draw him on the subject from time to time. That he chose to speak now was proof he believed the academy was soon to close.

Aristotle certainly did, and knew this was probably his last chance to shape the future king. "Firstly, let us examine what we mean by the term ruler. It could be said that the master of a household is effectively the ruler of that house. He is responsible for all who dwell there, and makes decisions that affect their lives. Now why is that? What gives him the right to choose his daughter's husband, or to sell this slave and buy that one?

"I will tell you. He has the right because they are incapable of organizing their lives for themselves. There is no question that a child needs adult supervision, and the slave is the same. As with children, most have an imperfect sense of reasoning and need a master to lead them for their own good. And what of women? They have a deliberative faculty, true, but the male is, by nature, more capable of leadership than the female. Women can, and do, run their own lives, but it's a governance without authority and will suffer from the lack of male guidance." Aristotle was walking up and down each wing of the portico, first looking at this boy, then that one, but they all knew who he was talking to.

"So what of a king? I likened the master of a household to a king, and you can see there are similarities; a king is simply the master of a household of thousands. I earlier asked whether a king is an absolute ruler or a servant of his people. The answer is that both are true and that a king, leastways a good king, will perform both functions ably. Surely this is a contradiction, Leonnatus?"

Leonnatus sat up sharply, caught out by the unexpected question. "Yes, I suppose so," he mumbled.

Aristotle shook his head violently. The youth had answered as he'd hoped.

"You will notice that I said a good king, and that is the crux of kingship. A good king understands that he rules for the benefit of his people, while a bad king rules only for himself. A good king rules justly, while a bad king rules by inspiring fear." He was stood alongside Alexander but with his body turned so he faced the opposite bench. The boy stared straight ahead, his face expressionless. Only the flush of his cheeks intimated that Aristotle's words were getting through.

"Now with so much power and responsibility, what sort of person should be a king?" He began pacing again. "Only those with the highest possible virtues—honor, courage, honesty, integrity are to name but a few. Above all, he must always value the welfare of his people above his own."

Aristotle had returned to the open space in front of the class.

"Does such a man exist? You need only read Homer to know he existed once. If he existed then, he surely can exist again. And such a man can only become a king. There is no other choice for him."

Aristotle fell silent, the comparison to Achilles ensuring that his lesson would leave its mark. He may not approve of the concept of monarchy but if Alexander must be a king, then let him be a good one.

One by one, the boys turned in their seats and looked at Alexander. He sat among them, his face scarlet.

They gathered at the stables to see Alexander off. He felt embarrassed by the farewell and kept insisting he would be returning in a few days, but Lysimachus had loaded a donkey with his possessions, just in case he wasn't.

Aristotle and Theophrastus came up the path from the academy, the boys moving aside to let them pass. Alexander felt his heart thumping.

"This is it, my boy," said Aristotle with a smile. "You leave now to become a man."

Alexander grinned but his eyes betrayed his feelings. "Maybe so, and maybe I'll be back in class in a few days. The King has said nothing about my not returning."

"Whether you return or not, today is your first step on the road ahead." Aristotle took a scroll from Theophrastus and handed it to Alexander. "Take this with you to remember me by. I've been preparing it for some time, and think you'll like it."

The boy unwrapped the scroll and began to read. It was an abridged version of Homer's Iliad, a traveling companion. He looked up at his tutor, his eyes beginning to mist.

"Thank you, Aristotle, and have no doubt I shall keep this with me wherever I go. I'll read it every night, and think of you."

"You were my best pupil. Now just remember everything I have taught you." Aristotle extended his hand in farewell. "Health to you, Alexander."

"And you have been like a father to me, Aristotle. More so, as my father may have given me life but you have taught me how to live." They shook hands.

"Health to you, Father."

Alexander and Lysimachus mounted their horses and led the donkey through the crowd. The boys followed them down the road for a short distance, continuing the barrage of comments and catcalls. Then they were alone, save for a posse of Cleitus' guardsmen. Alexander looked at Lysimachus and smiled.

It was strange to sleep alone that night. It was as if he could almost hear the silence and he craved the snoring and animal noises of his companions. He managed to doze fitfully for no more than an hour, and then lay awake until dawn, watching the lightening of the sky through the cracks in the shutters.

He decided to rise and go for a run on the terrace, with each step expecting to see Leonidas' sour face appear around the corner. After bathing, he sought out his father. Philip had already lurched and stumbled his way to bed by the time he'd arrived the evening before, prompting Olympias' greeting for her son to be barbed with more than the usually venomous tirade against his father.

Philip was dictating a letter in his dayroom, seemingly unaffected by the alcohol still swirling through his veins. He jumped up to greet his son as a steward showed him in.

"Joy to you, my boy. You had a pleasant journey I trust?"

"Yes, Father, and now I await your orders."

"Orders?" Philip turned to look at Parmenion and Antipatros, both lounging on couches against the wall. Parmenion looked the worse for wear, and had a bowl within easy reach. "I have no orders, Alexander, other than you accompany me to the opening of the gymnasium this afternoon."

"So I am to return to the academy?"

"Of course. You're still only in your sixteenth year, and I intend that you will receive at least as much education as those brats in Athens. They don't finish their schooling until the age of eighteen, and neither will you."

A smile split Philip's ugly face. "Then again, you're of an age now that you should be shouldering your share of royal duties, so I may not be able to allow you to attend full-time. The function this afternoon will be the first of many, my boy, and you're about to find out that being a king is not all glamour and glory, but also endless hours of making speeches and entertaining boring dignitaries."

He chuckled at his own joke. "But don't worry, opening a gymnasium ranks among the better functions. I've arranged to have a trial of boxers for our Olympic team after the opening ceremony, and it should be quite good. Who knows? Perhaps I'll have a go." He chuckled again, and Parmenion put a hand to his mouth and grabbed for the bowl.

The speeches were as boring as his father had predicted. A large crowd had gathered, listening attentively whenever Philip's eyes were upon them, stifling yawns and picking noses as soon as he looked away.

The boxing tournament was what they'd come for, and it proved worthy of their expectations. The winner was awarded a crown of laurel leaves by Philip, and strode to the center of the gymnasium to receive the adulation of his backers. He struck a heroic pose, despite the blood on his face. Alexander noticed how the man had his head tilted slightly to one side, mouth open and eyes raised as though looking to the heavens. It was an effective pose, giving the man a godlike air. He noted it for future use.

Afterwards, father and son walked back to the palace, which turned into an event in itself. They entered the agora through its grand gateway and crossed the open space together, which prosperity had turned into one of the largest marketplaces in Greece. Merchants shut up their shops and streamed through the arches that lined every side of the square, while civil servants poured out of their offices on the north side. They thronged around Philip and his son, held back only by the bodyguard. Philip greeted them good-naturedly, joking with a citizen here and there and accepting a present of fish from a trader. A stall was overturned in the crush.

Alexander kept his thoughts to himself as he watched his father's actions, trying to understand the magnetism that drew the crowd to him. Philip noticed the gaze and bent to whisper in his son's ear. "They may cheer me today, Alexander, but if the mines in Pangaeus ran out, would they still cheer me tomorrow?" The boy absorbed his father's words of wisdom.

He ate in the Great Hall that night, drinking unmixed wine and roaring encouragement with the others as a contortionist from the islands performed a somersaulting sword dance, and then used her feet to fire an arrow from a bow.

He could not match the veterans of the Companion cavalry and it was still quite early when he made his excuses and staggered to his feet. He was too drunk to notice the bawdy comments and knowing leers as he left the hall. He stood in the tunnel that led to the main entrance for a few minutes, letting the draught revive him, before stumbling up the staircase and through the maze of corridors to the royal apartments. He fell into bed, asleep in moments.

He awoke, aware of a knocking at his door. He reached for the dagger under his pillow, the movement bringing a hangover pain to his eyes.

He managed to raise himself onto the edge of the bed. It was still dark outside. Stumbling through to his dayroom, he called, "Who is it?"

"Alexander, open up. It is I, your mother. Don't keep me waiting."

He pulled back the bolts and unlocked the door, to find his mother stood in the corridor with a woman. Olympias swept into the room, sniffing disgustedly at the smell of alcohol. "I see you intend to follow after your father," she said, before turning to the other woman to add, "I don't know why I even bother with him." The woman smiled but said nothing.

"What do you want, Mother?" Alexander's head was splitting.

"This," Olympias announced, "is Callixeina. She is experienced and will teach you the ways of the world. Perhaps then you'll forget that boy, what's-his-name. She is my present to you." She turned with a magnanimous flourish and left the room, stopping at the door to add, "Don't worry. She's been examined by Philip of Acarnania and is clean."

Alexander was left alone with the woman. She looked to be nearly thirty, attractive and full-bodied. She slipped her chiton off with a practiced movement of one hand and stood naked for his inspection, a trace of a smile on her face.

"Does my father know about this?" Alexander could barely move his head without a blinding flash behind his eyeballs. He needed to throw up.

Callixeina smiled. "I believe the King is paying for me, sir." She nodded toward the bedroom. "Why don't you lie down and leave things to me." His head was swimming and he was in no position to argue, so did as he was told. She climbed on top and rode him, uncaring whether his moans were of pleasure or pain.

He slept for a while afterwards, shaking off the effects of the hangover. When he awoke, he bathed and sought his father. The king was in a meeting in the planning room and the guard at the door barred his way. Nobody was allowed into those meetings without an invitation, not even the king's own son.

Alexander waited impatiently in the anteroom, and then stormed off to find his mother. She was in her dayroom, compiling a list of items for a merchant she was sending to Athens on a shopping expedition.

She could see the boy was fuming. "What is it, Alexander? Don't you like the girl? I can get you another if you want."

"What do you think you're doing? What gives you the right to decide who I sleep with?" He had never raised his voice to his mother before, and she was shocked.

"Alexander, what's got into you? Is this what they taught you in the academy?" She was blustering, a trace of disquiet in her eyes.

Alexander became more conciliatory. He, too, had been rather taken aback at his outburst. "You must understand, Mother, that I am a man now, and a man must be allowed to make his own decisions. You no longer have the right to make them for me."

Olympias relaxed, and smiled. "It's not that, my son. I just don't want you spending all your time with boys. After all, I want to have grandchildren one day. Besides, it was your father's idea to hire the girl, so go and have it out with him. You know what he's like. I have to go along with what he says."

Alexander knew his mother well enough to doubt her innocence, but little would be achieved here and he had assuaged his anger. He simply said, "I choose my own friends, Mother," and left.

Olympias returned to her shopping list, a smile on her face.

He arrived back at the planning room to find the meeting was just breaking up. The door was open and Philip's officers were filing out, their numbers telling Alexander that the meeting must have been more than a simple strategy session. He slipped past them into the room, acknowledging the odd greeting here and there. Philip stood beside the large table that took up one wall of the room, with a relief model of Greece laid out upon it. He was talking to Antipatros and a general named Attalus.

"Alexander, my boy. And how was the wench?" He exchanged a grin with Antipatros.

"I have already told my mother, and now I must tell you. I am a man now; I choose my own friends and I choose my own bedmates. I must ask you not to interfere."

Philip gave him a stupid look of surprise, then turned to his companions and guffawed. "The boy has balls after all! All this I've been hearing about him spending his time with one boy, I was beginning to think I'd bred the King of the Fairies." He turned back to his son. "We've had this conversation before, have we not? A king must produce heirs, and that goes for the heirs too. You have a duty to sire children, and your personal preferences do not come into it."

Alexander opened his mouth to reply but didn't have the knack of finding the right words for the occasion. His father always managed to express himself better, be it jokes, speeches, or profound statements.

"Besides," continued Philip, "it was your mother's idea. She chose the whore," he gave his son an exaggerated look, "and then sent me the bill! Take it up with her if it's not to your liking."

It was pointless to continue the argument, so Alexander turned to leave. Philip stopped him.

"I was going to send for you anyway. Come over here and look at the map a moment." Alexander eagerly did as he was bid; any involvement in military affairs was welcome.

"You've heard of our problems with Athens?"

He nodded.

"Well, matters are coming to a head. Demosthenes," Philip sneered the name, "has talked the Assembly into negotiations with Persia. And I must be more of a threat than I thought, because the Great King is seriously considering making an open declaration of hostility against me. I could find myself fighting on two fronts if he sends an army into Thrace."

Alexander stared at the map. Colored wooden blocks were scattered across the landscape, signifying the opposing forces. A large number congregated on either side of the straits of the Hellespont. "What are you going to do?"

"The best chance of stopping a Persian army is when they are still crossing the Hellespont, and key to that is holding Byzantium and Perinthos." Philip gestured at the map; the two cities dominated the straits. "But now Demosthenes has persuaded both cities to join a new alliance of Greek states headed by Athens. They are supposedly allied to me, so I intend calling on them to honor their agreements and supply me with ships to fight piracy in the Aegean." He smiled grimly as he added, "And we shall see who they are more afraid of, Athens or me."

Alexander shook his head in wonder. The more he heard, the graver the situation became. He was beginning to realize just how sheltered they'd been in Mieza. "And if they refuse?"

Philip leaned against the table wearily. "Then I will take Byzantium. I have to have the city on my side, and a show of force may well discourage the Persians. That's where you come in. Byzantium is well defended and could take a lengthy siege, which I shall have to command personally. But I can't afford to leave Macedonia without a ruler for too long, not the way things are. If I have to go, I propose making you my regent with full powers to rule in my name. I'll leave Antipatros to serve as your advisor. What do you say?"

Alexander was speechless. "Yes, Father," he managed to murmur. "It would be an honor, and I will not fail you." He glanced around at Antipatros, who was smiling encouragement.

"Good, then that is settled." Philip straightened up; his old bounce returning. "You're to stay at the palace for now, until we know which way the Byzantines are going to jump. I want you to spend time with myself and each of my ministers, to receive instruction on your duties as regent." He smiled at his son. "Happy?"

Alexander nodded dumbly.

Chapter Twelve

The Valley of the Strymon

Caught in the middle, Byzantium and Perinthos chose to ignore Philip's demand for ships. Athens voted special honors for the cities and a gold crown for Demosthenes, while Philip mobilized the Macedonian fleet and gave Byzantium a warning to comply. The Byzantines strengthened their walls.

Once they knew that Alexander wasn't coming back, the students at Mieza abandoned the academy and joined him in the palace. Only Callisthenes remained, before he also rode to join the prince on the urging of his uncle. The academy remained open for a time in case the students returned, but now Aristotle devoted his days to research. The paidotribes returned to the south, while Theophrastus traveled to Thebes and took a job as a tutor until he was able to find something better. He had already begun writing the first in a series of pamphlets criticizing Alexander.

Olympias continued to send Callixeina to her son's room each night. She slept in his bed, while Alexander slept in Hephaestion's. It wasn't long before Philip found out and sent the whore packing back to Thessaly.

With the onset of spring, the merchant sent to Athens by Olympias was arrested as a spy and tortured into confessing. Though Philip found his wife's fury amusing, he knew the affront was aimed at him. Byzantium was being reinforced with Athenian ships and buying mercenaries with Persian gold. It was time for war.

The king rode out of Pella at the head of his Companion cavalry. Those left behind assembled on the colonnaded terrace in front of the palace, watching from their vantage point and listening to the cheering that rose from the city. The force filed through the eastern gate and wheeled about to ride in the direction of the coast, and ships to Thrace.

Alexander watched them disappear into the distance, the sun glinting on spears and armor. "Health to you, Hephaestion," he murmured.

Iolaus overheard the remark but said nothing. Virtually all the former students had been drafted into the Companions, Hephaestion at the insistence of Olympias. Iolaus and Harpalus, whose disabilities precluded them from military service, Proteas, Marsyas and Callisthenes remained as Alexander's personal staff. Cleitus also stayed behind with five thousand men, to defend the city in case of trouble.

Antipatros strode over to the new regent of Macedonia. "Well, Alexander, are you ready to assume your duties?" He smiled and swung out his arm, as though inviting the boy to take his place on the throne that waited for him in the Great Hall.

Alexander pulled himself off the fluted column he'd been leaning against. "Oh, yes," he said with a grin. "I'm ready."

The weeks passed quickly, Alexander kept busy by his duties as regent. His mornings were spent in his father's study, signing bills and authorizing payments out of treasury funds. Antipatros usually sat with him during these sessions, monitoring the transactions and putting forward reasons for or against making a particular purchase.

One afternoon a week, he met with the king's ministers to discuss upcoming problems. The meetings were rather dull but Alexander listened to the words of these experienced civil servants attentively, eager to learn the business of being a king. Olympias also had lots of advice for the youth, but he resisted her attempts to manipulate his government. He may love his mother, but he knew better than to trust her.

He and his remaining comrades spent most afternoons in the small palace gymnasium, working up a sweat and then scraping it off in the bathhouse afterwards. Their evenings were spent in the Great Hall, though with the army in Thrace, the sheer lack of numbers meant the carousing was subdued.

At all times the conversation would inevitably turn to the news from Byzantium. It was not good. Philip had besieged Perinthos as the easier of the two cities, but his army was now stalled in front of its walls. Even worse, the seizure of nearly two hundred Athenian grain ships at anchor in the Hellespont had seemed a good prize at the time, but the outrage and fear it provoked in Athens had brought an open declaration of war with Macedonia.

There were other problems, closer to home.

Alexander sat with Antipatros in his father's study, studying the scroll in his hand. Finally, he asked the general, "So how strong are the Maedi? Could they threaten us or is this just a raid?" A single Thracian tribe didn't seem much of a menace to him.

"They're not particularly strong, but it's the mere fact they're raiding our borders that's the problem." Antipatros stroked his beard, a worried frown on his forehead. "They've been quiet for years but will have also heard the news from Perinthos. They know the bulk of the army is far away and in trouble, so they're testing us. Does Macedonia have anything left? That's what they're asking themselves. And when they find we have nothing, not just they, but all the Thracian tribes will descend upon us."

"We have Cleitus, and there are fifteen thousand men guarding the southern passes."

"We don't touch the troops on the passes!" Antipatros put paid to such insane thoughts. "And Cleitus is needed to defend the city if the Athenians managed to get this far." The general shook his head. "We can't waste his troops on garrison duty in Thrace."

"Use them for a swift campaign, then. Send Cleitus on a quick strike to immobilize the Maedi, with orders to be back before Athens has time to discover he's gone." Alexander stood up to emphasize his point. "It would also keep the other tribes quiet. They won't dare rise up if we make an example of the Maedi."

"If it could be no more than a raid, then yes, that could work. But it would be a gamble. What if he was unable to withdraw or even defeated completely?"

"That's a chance we must take. To do nothing is to give our enemies time, and the longer we give them, the stronger and more confident they will be when we eventually have to face them."

Antipatros looked at the youth, a smile flickering on his lips. "I can see you've studied your Xenophon. Very well, we dispatch Cleitus with orders to strike against the Maedi, do what damage he can, and be back here before the waning of two moons."

"I'll go with him." Alexander's words were flat, toneless; they didn't betray the emotion he felt. He desperately wanted to see action for himself, to take his first head and truly become a man according to the ancient Macedonian custom.

Antipatros stared at the prince. "No, your father would not allow it, and neither can I."

Alexander racked his brain for excuses. "We must prove to our enemies that we're serious, and Cleitus is only a captain. Putting a captain in command will seem like we're weak." He was still standing, his heart pounding. "Come on, Antipatros; it'll be safe enough. Cleitus will do all the fighting while I'll be in the rear, no more than a figurehead."

Antipatros shook his head, unconvinced. "No, it's too dangerous. If the Maedi managed to lay an ambush, you'd be in as much danger as any soldier. No, I can't allow it. Your father may have made you regent but he made me responsible for you." Antipatros also stood up, and the two faced each other.

"I'm sorry, Alexander, but that's the end of it. Now, if you will excuse me, I must go and find Cleitus." He turned and left the room, ending the argument.

His mother had been easier to convince than Alexander expected. Some fast-talking about the merits of winning a victory while his father floundered in front of Perinthos had caught her imagination, while assurances there would be five thousand men between her son and the enemy tempered her maternal anxieties. Antipatros wavered under the combined pressure, and so it was that Alexander found himself riding alongside Cleitus as they entered the valley of the River Strymon and received the first reports that the Maedi had been sighted.

As regent, Alexander was the senior officer, but he was only nominally in command. Cleitus gave the orders and had explicit instructions from both Olympias and Antipatros to protect Alexander. He tactfully placed the youth in command of the rearguard and sent him down the column, causing sneers on the faces of the troops as he rode past them. Alexander could imagine the remarks on their sniggering lips and his blood boiled at the disgrace, but he did as he was told for now.

He reined in and joined the others of his party at the front of the supply train. Proteas was now his official bodyguard, while Iolaus and Marsyas had been appointed to act as his stewards. Harpalus and Callisthenes were along for the ride. Lysimachus also rode with the youths, under orders from Olympias to ensure her boy escaped any disaster.

There were scuffles between the scouts of both sides, the distant shouting and sounds of clashing steel sending a buzz of excitement through the marching Macedonians. Alexander felt his heart accelerate and gave his companions a look of false bravado. They looked as nervous as he felt.

Cleitus ordered a halt and deployed a vanguard while he waited for clearer reports of what he was up against. The scouts returned, one with a bloodied arm, another waving a Maedian head like a flag, to guttural cheers from the troops.

The news was encouraging. The enemy scouts had been driven off before they could spot and number the Macedonian column, and a main force of no more than a few thousand Maedian tribesmen was encamped beyond a bend in the valley. They were preparing to move but looked disorganized.

Cleitus conversed briefly with his officers. They knew the Maedians of old, and an attack was imminent. Skirmishers were sent across the river, archers to harass the enemy from the safety of the far bank, and javelin men to protect against any flanking move by the enemy. Cleitus split the column, sending most to take cover in the trees while a few hundred phalangites advanced up the valley, gripping their sarissae below the point and trailing the spiked metal butts in the dirt. A smattering of scouts rode in front, and the pack mules plodded behind. Fifty horsemen, all the cavalry that Cleitus had, guarded the supply train. They looked like a tired advance column at the end of a long day's march. The trap was set.

Alexander dismounted and moved through the trees behind the main force, Lysimachus flanking him and advising caution when he impatiently tried to push through a file of pike men. The youth was becoming desperate, having already watched as his colleagues were drafted into Cleitus' horsemen. Even crippled Harpalus was going to fight, while he was forced to hide in the bushes.

There was shouting from the river; the Maedians had been sighted.

Alexander put his hand on Bucephalus' neck and whispered reassuringly in the horse's ear as the sound of fighting echoed across the valley. The enemy was charging the reduced phalanx, unaware of the larger Macedonian force readying themselves in the trees to their left. Alexander craned his neck but could see nothing, his view blocked by trees and troops.

A trumpet sounded in the valley, the signal from Cleitus. A roar rose from the mass of men in the trees and they surged forward, expertly forming line after line of a new phalanx at the run. They advanced on the Maedians unbidden, their pikes gripped at shoulder height. The tribesmen on the left turned to meet the threat but were squeezed back against the river as they tried to escape the inevitability of the sarissae, each of which was six strides in length.

It was a slaughter. Those not skewered on the point of a sarissa were drowned in the river, while the few who made it to the far side had their throats slit by Macedonian skirmishers. Hundreds of panicked Maedians streamed back up the valley.

But Alexander's eyes were elsewhere. The Maedian horsemen had bypassed the column and were even now engaging the small force of Macedonian cavalry. Savages surrounded Cleitus, while Alexander could see that both Iolaus and Callisthenes were unhorsed and struggling to escape the stabbing spears of Maedian horsemen.

He mounted Bucephalus in an instant, galloping down the slope toward the melee before Lysimachus could react. He leveled his lance, blood pounding at his temples and his eyes smarting wildly as sweat ran into them from beneath his shiny new helmet. He was unaware his mouth was emitting the Macedonian war cry, "Alalalalai!" as he homed in on a Maedian horseman who had cornered Iolaus behind a string of pack mules. Only the frantic bucking of the terrified animals prevented the tribesman from delivering the deathblow.

The Maedian heard the cry and turned, too late. Alexander drove his lance into the man's belly, but the force catapulted him backward off Bucephalus as his dangling legs failed to find a grip; in an era before stirrups, he had just learned a valuable cavalry lesson. He smashed into the ground but was up in a moment, drawing his sword and searching for Bucephalus.

Men from the phalanx streamed back to aid the cavalrymen as Lysimachus pulled up alongside. "What do you think you're doing?" he shouted and, for a moment, Alexander thought he was going to reach down and hit him. Then Lysimachus recovered himself and anger was replaced with relief. He dismounted and looked the youth over. He had lost his helmet and his shoulder was numb from the fall, but he was otherwise unharmed.

Lysimachus knelt by the wounded Maedian. The man was spread-eagled on the ground, the lance standing upright from his belly. Blood pumped from the wound, making a puddle around the man. He raised his head to mumble something, and then died.

Lysimachus rose and drew his sword. He looked at Alexander a moment as though seeking permission to perform the deed, and then sliced the man's head off at the neck. He picked it up by its matted hair and offered it to the youth. "Well, you have killed your man, my Achilles."

"What did he say?" asked Alexander, gingerly taking the object from him and holding it out so that it didn't drip blood on his legs.

Lysimachus shook his head. "I don't know their language."

Troopers spotted the youth with his trophy and ran over. "The Prince has made his first kill! He's a man; find him a belt!" More soldiers gathered around and took up the cry. It didn't matter that the practice of a boy wearing a cord until he'd killed a man had been discontinued under Philip, or that a breastplate concealed Alexander's waist; the men wanted to celebrate the rite.

Cleitus rode through the crowd. He'd been wounded in the arm but paid no heed to it as he dismounted and told Alexander to sheathe his sword. The youth did so, placing it in the sheath that hung from a sash across his shoulder. Cleitus stepped forward and removed the sash, lifting it in the air for the men to see. They cheered, and continued to cheer as Cleitus placed it back over his head. Alexander had become a man.

They made camp and cremated their fallen comrades, a priest offering prayers to aid them on their journey to Hades. After dark, Alexander removed the Maedian's head from its stake outside his tent and walked to where the body of his enemy still lay. He wasn't sure what compelled him to do it; just that he knew he should. He hefted the corpse over his shoulder and carried it to the flickering ashes of the Macedonian funeral pyre, where he stoked the embers and stood in silence until both body and head had been consumed. The sentries informed Lysimachus and he stood by, close at hand but out of sight.

Most of the survivors of the battle fled north to defend their own villages, and the Maedian fortress fell without a fight the next day. Despite containing a chieftain's residence, it proved to be little more than a number of huts within a wooden stockade, little different to the hundreds of such structures that could be found atop mountain slopes throughout the highlands of Macedonia.

Alexander stood with Cleitus, watching as a few old men were put to the sword and those fit for work were herded into slavery. There was little in the way of booty and phalangites cheerfully lit torches to burn the place to the ground.

"Wait!" Alexander hurried forward to stop them. An idea had just occurred to him and he turned to Cleitus. "Burning one village will not stop the Maedians coming back. The King always leaves an outpost to control the locals, and we should do the same." He waved an arm about him. "Make this our outpost. We can leave, say, a hundred volunteers, and send colonists when we get back to Pella. We'll leave them some of the female captives as well; that should be a good enough inducement."

Cleitus laughed. "I think the Maedi have learned their lesson, but it does make sense, I suppose. Very well. If you can find a hundred volunteers, we'll do it."

"And we call it Alexandropolis?" He wanted to see the reaction on Cleitus' face, and was not disappointed. Philip was notorious for naming new colonies after himself, and for Alexander to do the same could only be construed as a challenge.

"I somehow think your father may have something to say about that."

The whole city of Pella turned out to greet the return of the conquering hero. The victory made a welcome change from the depressing news coming from the Hellespont, and the added gossip that Alexander had named a colony after himself lent a festive air to the reception. He led his troops into the city, his head tilted in the same heroic pose as the boxer he had seen just a few months before.

Olympias greeted her son at the monumental entrance to the palace. She was exultant, ordering Philip's other wives and children to line up with the palace staff along the length of the colonnaded terrace. Alexander, aware that he still didn't know how his father would react to his effrontery, smiled and let her enjoy the moment.

Whatever Philip actually thought, in public he made a show of lauding his son's initiative. There was little else he could do with his army bogged down outside Perinthos and the prince installed in the palace.

Alexander found the lack of a rebuke encouraging, and took steps to take further advantage of his father's absence. He knew the king would waste no time in re-imposing his authority when he did finally return, so set about creating a power base of his own, one that would be too strong for Philip to break.

"Well, sir?" He put down his wine cup and gazed into the face of one of Pella's leading citizens. "Do I have your support?"

"It is a most generous offer, sir, and one I shall seriously consider." In return for a pledge of loyalty, the merchant had just been offered a contract to supply Macedonia's army with grain for the next five years. It would make him a rich man. "I feel, though, that I cannot accept without consulting my partners. I must talk to them first." The man stood up and stumbled hurriedly toward the door. "I wish you good health, sir."

Alexander stared at the man's back as he left the room. It was the fifth such rebuttal he had received that day. It seemed that bribes and promises of future rewards weren't enough to buy the citizens of Pella.

It was a clumsy attempt at a coup, and one that could not fail to come to the attention of his father.

For the first time in his career, Philip was struggling. Perinthos was a natural hilltop fortress and its walls remained solid, despite the increasingly ingenious siege machines the Macedonian engineers continued to produce. Now there was disease in the camp. He turned his attention to the stronger Byzantium, if only to revive his troop's interest.

In his tent outside the walls, Philip listened to the reports from Pella with a mixture of anger and hilarity. "Is this the boy I spent half my treasury on educating? Did the fool think I wouldn't hear about it?" He drained his drinking cup and wiped the dregs from his beard. "Doesn't he know I have Pella sewn up? I know everything about everyone in that city."

"He's young, Philip, and still has a lot to learn," placated Parmenion. Attalus was also present. The general came from a powerful family and was steadily rising to prominence in the army. He said nothing, but neither he nor Parmenion would lose sleep that the youth had finally managed to fall out of favor with his father.

"Young?" Philip replied, slurring the word. "Not so young he can't plot against me at the first opportunity. I bet his mother is behind it. That witch can't wait to see me dead and her son on the throne." He giggled drunkenly. "It would serve them both right if I was to name Amyntas as my heir instead. He has just as much right as Alexander."

Philip of Acarnania looked up from dressing the king's latest wound, and glanced at Attalus and Parmenion. Everyone knew that Amyntas would be a fool not to challenge Alexander for the throne when the time came, whether he was the named heir or not. The two generals avoided the doctor's eyes, their faces expressionless.

"You can't do anything while we're stuck here, Philip." Parmenion steered the conversation in another direction. "Wait until we return to Pella and reprimand him then. It shouldn't be much longer now the Persians have lost interest. Byzantium must surely fall soon and then we can go home."

"You're right as always, Parmenion, but I think it might be wiser to bring him here in the meantime and leave Antipatros as regent. The boy will find it harder to plot against me when I'm in the next tent."

The summons caught Alexander by surprise, though he should have expected it. That Philip would hear of his dealings was certain, that he would bring the youth to where he could keep an eye on him an obvious next step.

Philip had kept up a string of correspondence since leaving for the Hellespont, mostly affable and mostly containing advice, so Alexander was not alarmed by the call. He was slightly annoyed that his tenure as regent had ended so quickly, but excited at the prospect of finally joining the army, and of seeing Hephaestion again.

His orders were to bring reinforcements, though there were precious few of them to spare. A single battalion of barely-trained conscripts followed the prince out of Pella, and few lined the streets to see them off. The switch to Byzantium had proved to be as unrewarding as the siege of Perinthos, and that things were not going well for Macedonia was evident to all. It was a miracle that Athens had not invaded already.

With the Athenian fleet dominating the Aegean, it took a month to reach the army by the overland route, and by then the war was over. The barking of the city's strays foiled a promising night raid on Byzantium, and Philip finally decided to call it a day. But the lifting of the siege brought an unexpected reward, as the first contact with Byzantine envoys indicated they might be willing to renew the alliance with Macedonia. A lack of commitment on the part of the Athenians had a lot to do with their decision.

Reluctant to return to Macedonia with nothing tangible to show from the campaign, Philip detoured north and carried out a lightning raid on the Scythians. The foray was a success and he turned south laden with booty and slaves. Alexander found the army encamped on the open plain of the southern steppe.

Philip interrupted a meeting to rush from his tent when scouts brought news of Alexander's column. Father and son embraced in the center of the camp, with grins on every face and any thought of a reprimand forgotten.

The king was keen to show off the spoils of war, and guided his son to the far side of the camp. Here there were no grinning faces, only thousands of sullen barbarian women and crying children.

"You saw the horses when you came in?" asked Philip.

Alexander nodded; the huge herd of animals corralled outside the camp had been impossible to miss.

His father grinned. "There are twenty thousand of them, all mares, and as many slaves here." He chuckled and added, "All mares again. Not a bad haul, don't you think?"

"Not bad," agreed Alexander. "But why only females?"

Philip laughed and put an arm on his son's shoulder. "A single stallion can impregnate a thousand mares, so why bring home a thousand stallions when I only need one? With a stock of twenty thousand mares, I can keep the cavalry supplied with as many new mounts as they could possibly want."

Alexander smiled at the reasoning. "And the women?"

"From what I hear, you already know the answer to that. What did you do to persuade your men to colonize, what did you call it, Alexanderpolis?"

Alexander started slightly at the mention of the name but could tell his father wasn't mocking him, even with the mispronunciation of the name.

"Alexandropolis, and I gave them the women. That's what you're going to do with these?"

"Exactly. I can usually find enough men willing to go and colonize the borderlands, but not women, so I shall use these instead. It'll be a better life than they'd have as slaves, and they even get to keep their children. They will soon regard it as home."

"That's clever," said Alexander. "It makes sense."

"Of course it does, my boy. You may hold a territory for years but you will only ever be an occupying army. So, you try shipping in colonists, but they merely create a Macedonian enclave in the middle of hostile locals. If you want to truly pacify your conquests, populate them with a mix of your own men and enemy women. When their husbands are soldiers in your army, those women will soon become your most loyal subjects."

Alexander nodded sagely. "That's a tactic worth remembering," he said. And he would, marrying thousands of his men to local women in the campaigns to come.

A feast was called for that evening, to be held in the open air so the other ranks could participate. Alexander wandered the camp with his father, quaffing jugs of wine and exchanging pleasantries with the soldiers gathered around each campfire. When they needed refills, they stood in line behind the rank and file, Philip roaring with laughter at an old joke cracked by an even older phalangite. Alexander managed a convincing smile, and knew this was an invaluable lesson. This was why Philip could order his men to go forward to certain death.

A commotion in the lines of tents attracted their attention. A row had broken out, apparently involving some Macedonian phalangites and a group of Theban mercenaries. One of the Scythian captives was at the center of it; she cowered half-naked between them. Philip strode over purposefully. "Lads! Lads! What's the problem? There are plenty of these sluts to go around."

A sword flashed in the torchlight. Philip froze, and then dropped to the ground, narrowly avoiding a flailing blade as the two groups scuffled around him. His shadowing bodyguards were caught out by the unexpected fracas and only Alexander was close. Drawing his sword, he rushed into the melee and felled a Theban, then a Macedonian. It was enough to buy time for the bodyguard to arrive and form a wall of swords around the king.

Alexander looked down. "You can get up now, Father. The danger is over." Philip got to his feet, and said nothing.

As the evening progressed, the former students of Mieza sought Alexander out. Philotas had received a promotion; Phrygius sported a bandaged arm; Laomedon jealously guarded a sack of gold coins. They gathered around the fire outside Alexander's tent, drinking Scythian wine and catching up on news. They all knew of his victory over the Maedi.

Alexander stood next to Hephaestion, their arms rubbing slightly. He could feel the hairs on his forearm bristling at the touch and there was a buzzing in his head from his closeness to the youth he had missed so much. He was barely listening to the conversation and failed to answer, to hear even, when Nearchus asked him a question. There was silence for a moment, and then Ptolemy yawned and said something about it being a long day. The others followed his cue, draining their drinking cups and bidding each other good health. Hephaestion crouched down to feed some leftover meat to a stray dog that Alexander had adopted on the march. They both looked up at their master.

Philip was preparing for bed when Philotas stopped off at his pavilion to inform him that Alexander was with Hephaestion. Philip thanked him, then walked through the opening that led to his sleeping quarters. Pausanias sat up in bed, waiting for him. Philip cracked a grin as he climbed in next to the bodyguard. "Well, that bit of news will piss off his mother."

The ambush was Philip's fault. They were passing through the land of the Triballi, a barbaric people known for their hairiness and regarded with contempt by everyone. Despite demands from their king that the Macedonians pay a fee for crossing their land, Philip felt little need for his usual safeguards and allowed the army to become strung out, with wide gaps opening up between the units. The long supply train trailed farther and farther behind, with only lightly armed prodromoi cavalrymen as an escort. Philip and Alexander spent the day hunting. In the late afternoon, they spotted groups of Triballi warriors moving across the plain, prompting jokes about hairy asses from the Companions. Philip laughed with them but ordered the party to return to the column as a precaution. He didn't like the numbers he was seeing.

The supply train was already under attack by the time they joined the main force. There was smoke on the horizon from a burning wagon, and terrified prodromoi galloped past as Philip reined in his horse.

"Attalus! Bring up the hypaspists, and be quick about it." He turned to the Companions and yelled, "We haven't come this far to lose our booty to barbarians, boys." And he was gone, leading the Companions in a headlong gallop. Alexander kept pace with the bodyguard, his own small group of companions mingling with Philip's.

They came over a rise to find the Triballi dispersing with the horses. The captive women were also fleeing, having first turned on their jailers and littering the plain with dead prodromoi. Ahead and to the right of Alexander, a contingent of Macedonian infantry faced a Triballi rearguard.

Filled with rage at the loss of his spoils, Philip charged into the midst of the action. The Companions followed, running down fugitive women who got in their way. A band of mounted Triballi turned to counter-charge the Macedonians and the opposing cavalry met head-on, snarling up the majority of the Companions in a fierce melee. Alexander's sword cut thin air as he swiped at one warrior, and then sliced through the arm of another. He strove to keep up with Philip, who, incensed at the loss of his plunder, swept through the enemy like a man possessed. Alexander and the bodyguard were the first to emerge from the fracas behind him.

Philip rode between the Triballi rearguard and his own infantry, sword raised and shouting to his men. The Macedonians gave a roar and advanced to rally around the king, but the Triballi reached him first, surrounding him and pulling at the reins of his horse. He toppled over and disappeared from view.

A groan of dismay went up from the Macedonian infantry, convinced the king must already be dead. They began to falter and turn, abandoning his body to the enemy.

Dead or not, the seven men of the bodyguard would die before deserting their king. They ploughed into the Triballi, smashing swords down on exposed heads and ignoring spear thrusts to their legs in their determination to reach the body. A horse shied up as a blade penetrated its flank, the rider sliding off its back and into the mass of warriors. Alexander, just behind, heard his death cry.

The bodyguards reached Philip, hacking and chopping at the Triballi gathered around him. Alexander leaped from Bucephalus and stepped into the path of a Triballian warrior, grabbing the point of his spear and pulling the man to him. He was a big, hairy brute, and Alexander saw the surprise in his eyes at the strength of the little Macedonian. He ran him through with his sword.

Pausanias had also dismounted and stood over Philip in an attempt to shield him from the blows of the Triballians. Two more bodyguards joined him and another rode up from the other side, the encirclement being enough to clear the enemy from Philip's body. Companion cavalrymen were also arriving and the Triballians backed off. The danger was over.

They finally had the chance to look down and see if Philip was still alive. He was conscious, but only just. He had fallen under his horse and the carcass had saved his life by blocking spear thrusts into his vital organs. But there were cuts to his face and hands, and a spear had skewered his leg to the horse's rump. A shattered thighbone was visible through the blood that pumped from the wound.

Alexander went to work immediately, trying to remember all that Aristotle had taught him. Removing the spear, he applied a tourniquet to the leg and splashed the contents of a water skin over the gash in an attempt to clean it. Other than tightly binding the wound with a bandage, there was nothing more he could do without physician's tools, so he set himself to inspecting the minor injuries. He was aware of Philip opening his single eye and staring up at him.

The Companions gathered around, looking concerned and asking stupid questions. At Alexander's instruction, they loaded the king onto the back of a wagon and set out to locate Philip of Acarnania.

They found the doctor with the main column. He ordered that Philip should not be moved so they stood their ground for three days, continually harassed by the emboldened Triballi on their new horses. At first, the doctor doubted whether the leg could be saved, but they sacrificed a bull and Aristander led the army in prayers. The gods were pleased, and Philip of Acarnania emerged from the king's tent to announce that he was conscious and lucid, and keen to get back on his feet.

The people of Pella dutifully lined the streets to watch the return of their king, but the silence was almost audible. Philip could still not walk and had to be strapped to his horse. He was wearing full armor for the procession and sweated in the heat, with his beard damp and mouth hanging open. They watched the man sway and wondered how much longer he could last.

Chapter Thirteen

Sacred War

Philip spent the rest of the summer at the palace, waiting to return to full health, and waiting to see if the Athenians would come. Neither happened; he was left with a permanent limp and Athens failed to realize just how vulnerable Macedonia had been that summer. He called a council of war.

His officers filed into the planning room and took their places along the walls while Philip stood at the door, greeting them. He chatted to a junior officer for a moment with Pausanias looking on, jealously alert to any threat to his position as the king's consort.

Alexander arrived and confidently strode across the empty center of the room to stand beside the map table. It was his rightful place as prince and heir.

Philip entered and the door was closed behind him, sealing it from the outside world. He stood for a moment, as though counting heads, and then lurched across to the map table. He may have felt as confident as his son, but the limp spoiled the image.

"Gentlemen, joy to you and welcome. Some of you may be wondering why I've called you together today." He leaned against the table for support. "Well, it's because I know what they're saying in the agora, at the symposium, and in the brothels. They say I'm finished." He gazed around the room, his one good eye settling on one face after another as if looking for the guilty. "Let me tell you, gentlemen, they are wrong. My leg may be taking a while longer to heal this time, but I can still ride a horse and I can still thrust with a sword. And I can still fulfill all the functions of a king—ask any of my wives!" The quip brought the intended guffaw from the officers and Philip allowed a moment for their laughter to subside.

"There has also been talk that Macedonia is finished and any day now we will be invaded and enslaved. What rot! It's true we've been through a trying time lately, but that's over now.

"And I will tell you why. Yet again, Athens has dithered. Yet again, the Assembly has talked and proposed resolutions, and yet again, they've sat on their hands and done nothing. It is exactly what I expected of them. They've missed their chance, gentlemen, and now it's too late because the army is back in Macedonia and rested. Let them come—and we will slaughter them."

He stood over the map table and waved a hand airily in the direction of the east. "As for Persia? Pah!" The exclamation brought a slight chuckle from the gathering and Philip turned back to his audience, pleased at their reaction. "We now know where the Great King stands, don't we, Parmenion?"

"Not beside Athens, that's for sure."

"That's right. Persia backed away from Byzantium as soon as the Athenians declared war on us. The Great King may have no objection to supporting an ally of Athens, but it's bad for his reputation to be seen as allied to the city itself." He waited for another ripple of laughter to subside.

"He's proved he won't ally himself with Athens and will stay out if they are involved, so we now know we don't have to worry about a Persian horde crossing the Hellespont behind our backs."

"And just in case," Parmenion called out. "Byzantium is back in the fold." More laughter.

"So what do we do now? How can we turn this to our advantage?"

"Sit on our hands like the Athenian Assembly!" Parmenion shouted to order. There were cheers this time; the double act was generating an almost festive air in the room.

Philip grimaced in mock horror. "That's something we won't do."

"Then seize this opportunity and strike while our enemies are divided."

"But we're not barbarians, Parmenion. Surely we don't make war without just cause?"

Aristander took his cue and stepped out from the crowd. "Sir, this morning a messenger arrived from the council at Delphi. The people of Amphissa have been cultivating the sacred fields and refuse to stop or even pay recompense. The council, remembering how you upheld the law in the war against the thieves of Phokis, again requests your aid. Sir, will you help?"

"But can't Athens support Delphi?"

"They didn't even send a representative to sit on the council, sir." There was a titter from the crowd; the charade was pure entertainment.

"Then I accept. I, for one, will not stand by and see the shrine despoiled a second time. Gentlemen, we march south to protect Delphi and exact proper respect from Amphissa. And if Athens refuses to join us in our sacred charge, then we shall deal with them once and for all.

"And then," Philip once more leaned against the map table for support. "We can rest. We can retire to our estates and spend our days tending to our gardens. You don't agree, Parmenion?"

"I cannot rest knowing that Persian gold and Persian mercenaries cost Macedonian lives in the siege of Perinthos. We should demand an explanation, and recompense for our losses."

"You're right, we should. Perhaps I should dispatch an emissary to Persepolis to demand just that." Philip grinned wickedly. "But I can't see the Great King paying up, not if he wants to keep his throne. And a refusal will be what, Parmenion?"

"I'd say, a legitimate cause for war." The general looked around the room. "And with that, we'll be free to prepare for the campaign we have all longed for. We'll be spending this winter preparing to cross the Hellespont, and will land in the Troad next spring!"

The applause was rapturous, everyone surging forward to mob Philip as he hobbled into the center of the room to acknowledge their cheers. He turned to say something to Alexander, but closed his mouth at the sight of the scowl on his son's face.

Alexander sought his companions immediately after the meeting, finding them in the palace swimming pool. They had been eagerly awaiting news of the meeting and jumped out to crowd around him as he crossed the rear courtyard. Their mood changed when they saw the look on his face.

"What is it, Alexander?" asked Perdiccas. "What did the King say?"

He told them.

"And?" asked Hephaestion, looking puzzled. "Isn't that good?" He turned to the others. "We go to war—together!" They could hardly conceal their glee, Proteas stifling a laugh.

"Don't you see?" Alexander turned on Proteas, reluctant to raise his voice to Hephaestion. "My father is going to liberate the Anatolian colonies next year. That mission was mine. It was about the only thing I had left, but now, yet again, he's going to steal my victory. He is the one who will avenge the King's Peace and be glorified throughout Greece, not I."

Hephaestion frowned. They all frowned. "No," said Hephaestion. "Now I think you're being ridiculous. The King's glory is as much our glory, you included, and you should be pleased we're going to have the honor of participating in such a crusade. That's what I think."

Alexander's cheeks flushed as though he'd been slapped in the face. His mouth opened but he said nothing. Marsyas finally broke the silence, with a mumbled suggestion they should go hunting for birds in the reeds by the lake. They all jumped at the idea, glad for any excuse to change the subject.

They had their first row that night, Alexander forbidding Hephaestion to ever speak to him like that in public again.

The army marched slowly south and occupied the pass at Thermopylae. They were in no hurry. Even now, Philip still hoped he could bring Athens around by diplomatic means and took pains to do nothing that might provoke them. But the mere presence of Macedonian troops south of the pass sent fear through the city, and Demosthenes' vitriol in the Assembly ensured that the pacifists were shouted down. More worrying for Philip, the Assembly voted in favor of sending an embassy, led by Demosthenes himself, to Thebes.

The Thebans were still nominally allied to Macedonia and he had counted on their compliance to give him access to the south, but they had already made a half-hearted attempt to block him at Thermopylae and now there was a danger they would side with Athens. It was an alliance that Philip feared.

His own diplomats reached the city first, and made their case while Demosthenes fretted and fumed in the waiting room outside the Bouleterion, the Theban's assembly hall. The Macedonians put forward a convincing argument that guaranteed Thebes a share of the spoils merely by allowing Philip to pass through their territory. They felt confident they'd won the Thebans over, but they had reckoned without Demosthenes.

He stood before the voters of Thebes and sold out Athens' own allies. In return for their support against Philip, Athens would help the Thebans overcome the other city-states of Boeotia, despite the long-standing treaties of friendship the Athenians held with most of them.

The Bouleterion debated. An alliance with Athens offered the chance for Theban expansion, while they would be the junior partners in any alliance with Philip. The marble slab, on which the treaty with Macedonia was inscribed, was brought into the Bouleterion and ceremonially smashed.

Athenian mercenaries were immediately dispatched to help their new allies strengthen the defenses in the mountain passes, while more headed west to cut Philip off from the Gulf of Corinth and a possible link-up with his southern allies.

The Macedonian advance halted and Philip called his senior officers to his pavilion.

"I have decided," he announced, "to wait out the winter. I learned the futility of trying to batter down city walls at Byzantium and Perinthos, and have no wish to spend this winter encamped outside Athens. Questions?"

"It gives the Athenians six more months to prepare for us," said Attalus. "Their walls will be as strong next spring as they are now, if not stronger, so I don't see what can be achieved by waiting. I say we should attack now." There was a murmur of agreement.

Alexander turned to face the general. "Yes, but I don't think the King intends assaulting the walls of Athens. Am I right, Father?"

"That's absolutely right, my boy. Do you know why?"

"The city will fall by default if we can tempt their army out into the open and destroy them, but the citizen-soldiers of Athens will not emerge during the winter months. That's why you want to wait."

"There you have it, gentlemen." Philip smiled at his son. "We leave a holding force and return the army to their home barracks. They spend the winter with their families, and come back refreshed next spring."

"But are you sure the Athenians will come out next spring?" asked Attalus, a peeved look on his face. "Their strength is their walls, not their army."

"They'll come out," answered Philip. "A siege means the whole population will suffer and, even if they win, their city could be left in ruins. They'll prefer to fight on neutral ground."

"It also guarantees that Thebes will fight," added Alexander. "That won't be the case if they skulk behind their walls and leave the Thebans to face us alone."

"Very good, my boy. I hadn't thought of that."

"What about Persia?" Parmenion asked. "This means there'll be no expedition to recover the colonies next year."

"We can't have everything, I'm afraid. Yes, Parmenion, I am also putting back the expedition by a year."

Philip glanced around, looking for signs of dissent. Alone among his officers, Alexander was smiling at the news of the postponement.

The army returned to the comfort of winter quarters. Like most of Macedonia's nobility, Alexander and his friends idled away the winter months hunting and drinking. The format of his future court was already beginning to take place. There were those, like Perdiccas and Ptolemy, who would be his future generals, and others, like Iolaus and Callisthenes, who would be his stewards and administrators.

Philip was aware of the clique forming in his midst, but did nothing to break it up. He was on reasonably good terms with his son again and hoped to keep it that way. Besides, Philotas and Harpalus were keeping him abreast of their activities.

Spring arrived, and Philip made his move. The campaign had barely begun before he arranged for a dispatch to fall into Theban hands, advising the king of a rebellion in Thrace. Philip was seen to be hurrying the bulk of his army north, leaving Parmenion with a mere holding force. The Thebans relaxed and the Athenians congratulated themselves, awarding Demsothenes another gold crown.

As planned, Parmenion marched by night; catching the Thebans by surprise and slaughtering the garrison at Amphissa while half of them were still otherwise engaged in the city's brothels. By the time the news reached Athens, the Macedonian army had seized the Gravia Pass and was spilling out onto the Boeotian plain. The allies had no choice but to abandon the mountain passes and fall back to a new defensive position on the plain at Chaeronea.

Philip was in no hurry to follow. He had, after all, just won a sacred war, and now had the whole summer in which to subjugate Athens and Thebes at his leisure. He oversaw the tearing down of the walls of Amphissa as he had pledged he would, and then traveled to Delphi to receive the grateful thanks of, and a crown of golden oak leaves from, the council.

And then the army marched for Chaeronea.

Philip's enemies had chosen their position well, strung out across a valley with their flanks protected by steep slopes on either side. The Macedonians would have to climb a rise to reach their positions, and a pass through the mountains to their rear afforded an escape route if the worst happened. As the only unit with any real combat experience, the three hundred lovers of the Theban Sacred Band took the position of honor on the right wing, the sword side, while the ten thousand hoplites of the Athenian contingent were massed on the left, the less prestigious shield side. The Theban infantry and their Boeotian levies held the center.

They were reasonably confident. Demosthenes stood in the midst of the Athenian phalanx, proudly wearing his hoplite armor for the first time. He sipped from his flask and joked with the men around him. It was late summer and they were already starting to sweat in the dawn sunshine.

The Macedonian officers emerged from Philip's tent and dispersed to their units. They, too, were confident. Athens had not fielded a citizen army for twenty years, and the novices who faced them this morning were unlikely to stand long against the veterans of the Macedonian phalanx. Sworn to die before they would retreat, only the Sacred Band posed any threat, but Philip's battle plan would take care of them. They were too few in number to make any difference anyway.

Alexander and his father were the last to leave the tent. They stood at the entrance, staring across at the burnished ranks of the Athenians.

"You know what you have to do?"

"Yes, Father. Wait until the gap opens up, then break through, strike them in the rear and isolate the Sacred Band. But are you sure the plan will work?"

Philip smiled. "It worked ten years ago against the Illyrians, and I see no reason why the Athenians should be any different."

Father and son clasped each other, and then Philip limped down to take up a position behind the Regiment of Hypaspists, his Royal Guards, on the Macedonian right wing. His gammy leg precluded him taking his usual place at the front of his troops. Meanwhile, Alexander mounted Bucephalus and rode over to the head of the Companion cavalry. He knew the import of this day. He was barely eighteen, yet his father had made him a general and given him command of the Companions. As if that was not enough, the success of the coming battle would depend on his judging the right moment to charge. A smile flickered on his lips.

A discordant trumpet blare signaled the start of the battle. The massive blocks of the phalanx in the center of the Macedonian line stepped forward, leveling their pikes purposefully as the steady tramp, tramp of twenty-four thousand pairs of feet echoed across to Alexander. Light showers of Boeotian arrows fell among them but their step did not falter.

Philip's hypaspists also advanced, and the front ranks were climbing the rise toward the Athenians within a few minutes. As Philip had counted on them doing, the inexperienced citizen-soldiers surged forward to meet the foe, throwing their own ranks into disarray. As planned, the hypaspists fell back in front of this onslaught.

They withdrew down the slope, the Athenians pressing them every step of the way, but still failing to fully exploit the Macedonian retreat; they needed encouragement. Philip, at the rear of the hypaspists, raised an arm as though trying to steady his troops. It was the signal for a dozen volunteers in the rear ranks to drop their spears and flee. He lowered the arm, and a dozen more followed.

The Athenians, from their vantage point higher up the rise, saw the fleeing guardsmen over the heads of the others. They gave a cheer and the first hotheads flung themselves at the spears of the hypaspists. Philip raised his arm again, and another score of guardsmen joined the deserters.

The Athenians charged en masse at the sight, their commander riding through their ranks and shouting encouragement to the few who still hesitated. A slow-motion chase ensued, the Macedonians shuffling backward, the jeering Athenians prodding them along with their pikes.

Philip had formed up his line at an angle so that his hypaspists on the right wing had already engaged the enemy while the men of the phalanx were still advancing in the center. It was deliberate. The phalangites continued their advance as the hypaspists fell back alongside them and, unnoticed by the Athenians in their eagerness to follow the enemy, the phalanx was coming between them and their Boeotian allies.

The Boeotians in the center found themselves standing well behind the Athenians. The left hand units were forced to move across to fill the empty space opening up in front of the Macedonian phalanx, forcing units to their right to also move. And so it continued, with the hypaspists drawing the Athenians ever farther down the valley, and the hapless Boeotians spreading out in an ever widening line. The veterans of the Sacred Band could see the danger, and shouted and waved their warnings, but only Alexander was watching. He raised his lance and pressed his knees into Bucephalus' flanks.

The Companions surged through the widest of the gaps opening up between the Boeotian units. Alexander swung his lance to his left, and a contingent of Companions peeled off to engage the Sacred Band head-on. He pointed to his right, and the main body wheeled around and smashed into the rear of the Boeotians. It was the cue for Philip to halt the withdrawal of the hypaspists and urge his men forward.

Alexander continued his diagonal dash across the battlefield, before turning his remaining men and charging into the rear ranks of the Sacred Band. He felt Bucephalus shudder from a sword slash but the horse didn't falter. Leaping off his back, Alexander slapped him across the rump to send him out of the melee to safety.

Already the Athenians were in confusion. Seeing the enemy in their rear, any pretext at a coordinated defense quickly evaporated and their only thought was to escape the remorseless advance of the Macedonian guardsmen. They streamed toward the pass that was the route back to Athens.

The men of the Sacred Band did not run, and neither did they offer themselves for ransom or give themselves up to a life of slavery. They stood in ranks and died where they stood, each pair fighting to the last to defend his own, and his partner's, honor. Alexander could not bear to see such heroes die. He stopped and turned; Hephaestion was by his side, as he knew he would be.

"Can't you see, Hephaestion? It could be us standing there. We're slaughtering Achilles and Patroclus a hundred times over."

Hephaestion nodded. He had a gashed shoulder and held a hand to the wound. "The Athenians have broken and the field is ours. Why don't they surrender?"

Alexander knew why, but there was little point in trying to explain. If Hephaestion didn't know, he still had more to learn than Alexander had thought. He looked across at the mass of Athenians pouring into the pass, and was stunned to see the Macedonian infantry advancing at a walk, making little attempt at pursuit. "Look, they're letting them escape. What is the King doing?" He turned to find Bucephalus; the horse had not strayed far. He stood patiently waiting for his master, disregarding the blood that seeped from the wound in his neck.

Alexander found his father following behind the hypaspists and chatting to Attalus as if he was on an afternoon stroll. "They're getting away!" he yelled, pointing in the direction of the pass.

Philip looked at him impassively, as though disapproving of a wayward son interrupting his conversation for a triviality. "That's right, and that's my intention. Calm down and come down here, and I'll explain why. Do you know your horse is wounded?" Attalus smirked and held Bucephalus' bridle as Alexander gave his father a petulant look and dismounted. A small number of hypaspists gathered around to watch.

Philip spoke to the group. "I could give chase, and not one of those men would reach Athens. But what would it gain me? Tonight, there would be ten thousand widows and twice as many orphans in Athens who would want me dead, and how big a garrison would I need to keep the city in check then?" He grinned at a grizzled guardsman, who had slapped his palm to his brow and made a face in mock consternation at the thought.

"But all I intended doing today," he continued, "was to pacify Athens and Thebes, not destroy them. Well, Thebes perhaps." There was a chuckle from the men at that. Philip gazed around him. "In a few months we march for Persia," a cheer, "and I cannot afford to tie up large numbers of men garrisoning Greece. I want

Athens on my side or at least neutral." He gave another grin. "And most of all, I want their ships."

Alexander bristled as the men cheered Philip's words. His father had managed to make him seem a fool in public and, yet again, he didn't have the turn of phrase to deliver an appropriate retort. He stayed quiet but the look on his face said everything.

"Of course," said Philip, reading the look. "My plans would have been meaningless if we'd lost today. And who do we have to thank for our victory, lads? Whose charge swung it for us?" He took his son's wrist and raised it.

"Alexander!" The cry was raised, and quickly taken up across the field. Men turned at the noise, keen to relieve their tension after the battle. "Alexander! Alexander!"

Philip urged his son to mount Bucephalus so the men could see him. "He is the King," he shouted above the cheers. "I am merely his general." Alexander rode slowly through the ranks, smiling at the men who shouted his name and his father's chiding forgotten.

Philip rewarded the heroes of the battle, Alexander included, while his men raised a victory trophy of captured weapons and armor in the center of the battlefield. Then the Macedonians sacrificed for the souls of their dead and feasted in the acropolis of Chaeronea, overlooking the valley.

It turned into an uproarious celebration of their victory, with Philip wrestling a gigantic hypaspist for a wager in the center of the marketplace. The man let his king win, and then took the gold that Philip had promised him in the clinch. The drinking continued unabated into the night, with Alexander and his gang legless as they staggered from the feast and peered over the battlements, to laugh as Philip led a frenetic conga line of Companions down to the valley below.

In his drunken state, the king had decided that such a victory deserved nothing less than a torchlight performance of the revelry of Comus, an ancient Dionysiac procession. He sang and lurched his way through the Athenian dead, closely followed by the line of dancing Macedonian nobles, and it wasn't long before he reached the captives, two thousand of them, corralled against a steep wall of the valley.

Philip's taunts were rapid and vindictive, encouraged by the laughter of the Companions. The Athenians endured this added misery with heads bowed, except one. The figure rose from their midst and made his way toward Philip. The bodyguard hurriedly moved in front of the king, who stood grinning stupidly at this unexpected act of defiance.

The man gave a long stare at the wretchedness about him, and then looked Philip full in the face. "Fate has given you greatness, King Philip, yet it seems you choose to squander it. I wonder, would Homer have cast you as King Agamemnon—or as the petty Thersites?"

To be likened to the worst character in Homer's Iliad was a slap across the face for Philip. He was immediately sober, pulling his tunic down to cover his backside and straightening his oak leaf wreath from where it had slipped over one ear.

"You are right, sir," he said, without a trace of a slur to his words. "It is contemptible to mock brave men. To whom do I have the honor of speaking, may I ask?"

"My name is Demades. I am a member of the Assembly and you may have heard of me."

Philip had. He possessed full dossiers on any Athenian of note and Demades was an orator second only to Demosthenes, and with an added quick-wittedness that the other man lacked. He could also be readily bribed.

"I know of you, Demades, and have received nothing but favorable reports. It is rare to find a man of honor and integrity in these times and it's a pleasure to meet you at last, notwithstanding the circumstances."

Demades said nothing. He was too unpretentious to be fooled by flattery, and the rapidity with which the Macedonian had shaken off his intoxication had taken the man by surprise. Philip smiled, aware of the reasons for his silence.

"Come, Demades. It would be my pleasure if you dine with me tonight. We have much to discuss."

As the days passed, Philip thanked the good fortune that had led him to Demades, for the reports from Athens were disturbing, to say the least. He had expected the city to immediately sue for peace on any terms, but their fear of Philip (aided by a speech from Demosthenes) proved to have the opposite effect. They were strengthening their defenses for a siege, and offering freedom to any slave willing to take up arms and fight for the city. Demades was dispatched to Athens with Philip's terms.

Philip summoned Alexander to his pavilion. He was reclining on a couch in his private quarters and gnawed at a roasted chicken leg, tearing at the meat and speaking with his mouth full. "Come in, my boy. Are you hungry?" He gestured toward an overloaded plate that had been placed beside him. "Help yourself." Antipatros was also in the tent, working his way through a second plate.

Alexander declined, and stood awkwardly in the center of the room. "Sit down, Alexander. There's no need for formality here." Philip swung his legs off the couch and made room for him, and father and son sat side by side. "Demades returned this morning, and the Assembly has accepted my terms with gratitude. And so they should, as I'm asking for nothing but their friendship."

"Return of their dead, release of the captives without ransom, no garrison, and we will not even cross their borders," grunted Antipatros. "They must be praising Athena for their good fortune."

"I'm sending Antipatros to Athens as escort for their dead," continued Philip. "I want you to go too, as my representative. There are people I want Antipatros to see while he's there, and you are to present the public face while he's doing that."

Alexander considered the surprise request. "Wouldn't it be better if you go? You are the King, after all." He felt rather put out that he would only be supporting Antipatros. "Besides, we're the victors, so why should we go to them?"

Philip smiled. "If only it was that easy. You've heard they were preparing for a siege, I take it?" Alexander nodded. "Well, Byzantium has proved the folly of besieging strongly-walled cities, and I have no wish to tangle with the fortress that is Athens. What's more, their fleet would still be at sea, supplying the city and threatening to land troops in our rear. A siege could last indefinitely, and that I cannot afford. I must have peace with Athens."

"All the more reason to go yourself, then. You're the King, while I'm just a prince. You would make more of an impression than me."

Philip laughed. "Look at me, boy. What sort of an impression do you think this battle-scarred face would make on the Athenians? I want an alliance with them, not to give their children nightmares."

"It would also send the wrong signals," added Antipatros. "The Athenians perceive your father as the oppressor, and it's better if they don't have to suffer the sight of him marching into their city."

The convoy left the next day. Alexander and Antipatros, with a number of Companion cavalry and fifty hypaspists as a bodyguard, escorted the wagons containing the ashes of the Athenian dead. The freed captives followed, two thousand strong.

Antipatros glanced back down the column and grinned. "I can't believe they demanded their clothes and equipment back; the cheek of it." There were a few laughs of agreement from the leading ranks of the Companions.

"And I can't believe that the King agreed," answered Alexander. "He had Aristander going from tent to tent, trying to persuade the men to hand them over. Those were legitimate spoils of war."

"He needs to keep Athens sweet, I suppose." Hephaestion, like all of Alexander's circle, had volunteered to be part of the escort. "Are you looking forward to seeing Athens, Alexander?" he asked.

"It will be an experience and I would dearly like to worship at the statue of Athena, but that'll be out of the question." Only Athenians were permitted to enter the Acropolis, wherein stood the giant statue of the goddess.

Antipatros lowered his voice a tone. "I shouldn't worry, if I was you. Give it a few moons and, no doubt, it will have been replaced with a shrine to your father."

Alexander shot a glance at the general. Philip had begun to talk in terms of deification of late and, certainly, it did no harm to encourage the concept of his divinity among his enemies, but the very idea of a mortal offering himself up as equal to the gods offended the sensibilities of someone as pious as Antipatros. Alexander had heard rumors of an exchange of words on the subject, but the remark was the first proof of any rift between the general and the king. He savored the thought that he might have a new ally.

They stopped short of the city and camped for the night, not wishing to arrive in darkness. The freed Athenians kept going, eager to get home, and it worried Antipatros that the Macedonian contingent would be arriving at the gates of the city alone. Demades reassured him. As long as they had the wagons containing the ashes of the fallen, they were certain of a welcome the next morning.

They broke camp at first light and approached Athens from the northwest, passing the festival town of Eleusis and falling silent as they reached the first of the tombs that lined the Sacred Way. The summer haze lifted and Alexander caught sight of the Acropolis, perched on a huge outcrop of rock in the center of the city. Its buildings gleamed a dazzling white in the sun.

Now he appreciated why his father had been so keen to avoid a siege. The walls of Athens stretched away to his right, all the way to the massive naval installations at the port of Piraeus. There were even walls in front of the walls, outer bastions to protect the gates. A siege would have been futile.

Thousands of heads lined the battlements before them, craning their necks for a first glimpse of these barbarians from the north. The famous Dipylon gate stood open. "If this is a trap, we're finished," hissed Phrygius.

He was right. There would be no escape once they passed between the two outer towers and entered the open courtyard within the gate. High walls would surround them, with little room to turn.

"Nobody is to draw their sword unless I do," Antipatros called down the column. There wasn't a sound from the crowds on the battlements or from those who lined the street as they passed through the gate and followed Demades up the Panathenaic Way. It was as if the whole city had been struck dumb.

The procession trooped into the agora, the huge market square. This was as close to the Acropolis as the Macedonians would be allowed. Here they were to hand over the ashes of the fallen, for them to be taken up to the citadel and honored before Athena in the sanctuary of the Parthenon building.

The people of Athens were streaming into the agora for the handover ceremony, still quiet and sullen, still a beaten people. At a sign from Antipatros, the Macedonians dismounted. The wagons were brought forward and Alexander held the harness of the lead ox.

"People of Athens," he shouted. "I give you your dead. They died honorably, and you should be rightly proud of them."

He winced as he heard Antipatros hiss a curse. It wasn't the speech they'd rehearsed. To ask the victor for the return of your fallen was seen as a symbolic admission of defeat, and his announcement that he was giving them back their dead must sound like pure arrogance to the Athenians. But it was too late now.

A figure stepped out from the shadows of the Painted Stoa, a building whose walls were lined with trophies of Athens' victories. It was Demosthenes.

The orator slowly walked toward the young man. "Joy to you, Princh Alexander. On behalf of the people of Athens, I thank you for allowing uth to have our dead back." There wasn't a trace of sarcasm in his voice and, despite the impediment, Alexander didn't realize who the man was.

"It is my honor to return such heroes, sir."

Demosthenes climbed onto the back of the wagon and slipped a pebble under his tongue. Picking up one of the smaller urns, he held it aloft for all to see and began the lament.

"Time, whose overseeing eye records all human actions, bear word to mankind what fate we suffered.

"How, striving to safeguard the holy soil of Hellas, upon Boeotia's famous plain we died."

It was an epitaph so moving the Athenian Assembly would vote to inscribe it on the monument to their fallen. There was silence in the market square as Demosthenes completed the oration and replaced the urn.

"How long do you think before we're back to burn this place?" murmured Ptolemy. Cassander nodded in reply. There had been no acknowledgement of defeat, no hint of regret at their actions. The very choice of Demosthenes to deliver the speech was an indication of the feeling within the city.

The wagons were led away to begin the climb up to the Acropolis, and Demades worked hard to inject a more festive air to the proceedings. He welcomed the Macedonians as Athens' new friends, pointedly reminding the crowd that King Philip had agreed not to cross the border or station ships in the harbor of Piraeus.

The people knew how lightly they had escaped in defeat and how easily that could still change, so a band was summoned and the mood lightened a little with the music. Official speeches of welcome followed, along with an announcement that the Assembly would confer honorary citizenship on King Philip and his son, and their statues would be commissioned and set up in the agora.

An impromptu sports tournament was arranged at the racetrack that ran diagonally across the agora. Someone or other mentioned Alexander's athletic prowess and, egged on by his comrades, he reluctantly found himself representing Macedonia in a challenge race. His misgivings were assuaged slightly when he learned that his opponent was an Athenian of some repute, an Olympian athlete.

"At least there'll be no disgrace in losing," commented Hephaestion as he took Alexander's clothing from him.

Alexander eyed his opponent. The man was tall and lean, with long legs that would outpace his own. "Win or lose, it's a challenge I think I shall enjoy."

The race was to be two stadium lengths, a comparatively short distance. At the signal, Alexander dashed forward and took an early lead, but his opponent was good, too good. At the turn, the Athenian was several strides ahead and increasing his lead. The man glanced back, then again as he drew closer to the finish, turning his whole body this time in a movement that forced his pace to slacken. Alexander drew level, and then stopped dead. The Athenian stopped too, then shrugged and crossed the line.

"I should have known better," fumed Alexander as he walked off the track and grabbed his clothes from Hephaestion. "They'd ordered him to let me win. There can be no honor in such a victory."

"You did once say that you'd only race against kings," reminded Phrygius. "And you were right."

"Of course I was right. And let that be a lesson to me: I should listen to myself in future." The casual arrogance of the remark brought laughter from the group, the anger Alexander had felt dissipating as he laughed with them.

The Macedonians were parceled out to a number of private residences throughout the city that night. Alexander and his companions were invited to a symposium at the Academy, and the youths jumped at the chance to see the place where Aristotle had been educated.

Xenocrates, the head of the Academy, was their host, with the acclaimed actor Thessalus among the guest list. Isocrates was also there. The aged philosopher was almost a hundred, and the oldest man they had ever seen. He could barely walk and his hearing and eyesight were poor, but his mind was still agile.

Slaves ritually washed their feet and then the guests sang the traditional hymn to Dionysus, the god of wine. Thessalus was appointed lord of the feast. He oversaw the mixing of water and wine in the krater, declaring that each guest would be required to drink three cups before the food was served or pay a forfeit. Isocrates was exempted, as his bladder was well beyond such feats.

But the party was subdued by Macedonian standards, with only one flute player and no entertainment. The boys smirked as they sipped their watered-down wine and listened politely as Thessalus engaged Alexander in a discussion about the significance of tragedy in the theater.

Isocrates mildly rebuked him for hogging the star guest, and then pointedly asked after Aristotle, who was still in Macedonia.

Alexander remembered the disparaging letter the old man had sent him in Mieza, and was careful to answer diplomatically.

"I believe Aristotle is planning a return to Athens, sir," he said. "But I haven't spoken to him for some time so cannot be more precise."

Isocrates chuckled at the thought of the return of the traveling sophist and left it at that. He turned the conversation to the news from Persia.

"You have heard that Artaxerxes is dead?" he asked. They all grinned in acknowledgement. The news there was a new Great King had swept through the palace at Pella. Their faces were a blur to the old man, so Xenocrates intimated that he believed they had.

"Good news travels fast," said Isocrates with a smile. "Murdered by his own vizier, it is said, and now the vizier's puppet sits on the throne. It would seem to me there has never been a better time to recover the colonies from the Persian yoke. I spoke with your colleague, Antipatros, this afternoon, and he indicated that King Philip could well be considering such an expedition."

Alexander's face changed. "Well, my father seems to have more important things on his mind these days." There'd been talk that Philip had taken a new lover from the ranks of the Companions. "But I expect he'll get around to it eventually." The enthusiasm of the others made up for any reluctance on Alexander's part.

"I heard that we'll return to Macedonia as soon as possible and start preparations," Proteas called from his couch. "Well, when affairs have been settled in the south." He blushed.

"I'd think an expedition of some sort for next spring is likely," added Nearchus, taking up the lead.

"But didn't we say the same last year, and the year before that?" Alexander's remark was politely ignored.

"With Thebes defeated and Athens as an ally, we're finally in a position to turn words into actions. This time I'm sure it will happen," said Ptolemy, a grin cracking his face.

"If only I can live long enough to see such a thing," sighed Isocrates.

"Xenocrates, I've heard that you lecture on government and I would like you to do something for me." Alexander had had enough and changed the subject as easily as if he had commanded it. The others fell silent, aware of his pique.

"I would like you to draw up a set of rules for royal government; a guide that a king could refer to when in doubt." There wasn't a sound in the room as his words sank in. For Alexander to talk of his own reign was virtually speaking treason.

Xenocrates cleared his throat and sat upright on his couch. "Well, yes, if you wish. Erm, what sort of rules did you have in mind?" He had no urge to become implicated in a plot against King Philip.

"Nothing specific; make it a general guide to things that a king should bear in mind when making decisions. When he should impose his authority, for instance, and when he should delegate."

"Excellent," cried Isocrates. "I can see King Philip has chosen his successor well. At this rate, all that remains is for him to become a god; I must write and tell him so." The old man was totally oblivious to the discomfiture felt by all but Alexander.

The remainder of the evening passed pleasantly enough. Thessalus told the story, to uproarious laughter from the boys, that Demosthenes was seen to catch his clothing on a bramble during the flight from Chaeronea, and had screamed, "Take me for ranthom!"

Isocrates fell into a doze, farting occasionally to giggles from the boys. Thessalus gently shook him awake to spare the old man more embarrassment. Xenocrates, meanwhile, was proving to be rather taken with Hephaestion, his conversation with the youth being conducted in ever more hushed tones.

The attraction was not lost on the others, with numerous sly grins and surreptitious glances at the two chatting in the corner. Alexander enjoyed an enormous sense of superiority at the sight of his smirking companions and the ridiculous conclusions they were jumping to. He felt no fear or jealousy, only an absolute trust in Hephaestion.

"We Athenians have always been pleasantly surprised," pronounced Isocrates, "to discover that Athena is a patron goddess of the Macedonian royal family. How did that come about?"

"I cannot say," answered Alexander. "All I know is that she ranks equally in our esteem with Dionysus, and the shrine in the palace at Pella came from my grandfather's palace at Aegae. It is our oldest shrine."

"Older than me, even." Isocrates smiled. "Did you know we have a shrine to Athena here in the Academy? It is an exact copy of the statue in the Acropolis."

"Is that so?" A gleam came into Alexander's eyes. "Can I see it? If I cannot visit the real thing, I can at least see a copy."

He was led to the shrine, a three-foot replica in an alcove to the rear of the Academy. He returned a few minutes later.

"That was beautiful," he murmured. "I can't imagine how wonderful the real statue must be. You're so lucky to be able worship at that, the most esteemed shrine to Athena. Oh, well."

"You're an Athenian citizen now, by order of the Assembly," remarked Isocrates casually. "Maybe not born and bred, but a citizen all the same, and you revere Athena more than many who've lived in this city all their lives."

"Is this wise?" asked Thessalus.

Isocrates chuckled. "What could they do to me, that wouldn't be a favor at my age?"

"As if you could make it up those steps." Thessalus smiled dubiously. "As well you know."

And so, as the city slept two hours later, the actor led Alexander through a side gate in the cliff face of the Acropolis and up a flight of steps to the citadel itself. The place was deserted at this hour, and the pair quickly crossed the open courtyards and slipped through a rear entrance of the Parthenon building. Thessalus positioned Alexander for best effect, and lit a torch.

A placid pool was directly in front of them, an immense shadow behind. As his eyes adjusted to the light, Alexander was able to see more. Thessalus moved around the pool and raised his torch.

"Can you see? In the daytime the doors are open and the sunlight reflects off the pool to illuminate the statue."

Alexander could see. He stood before the statue of Athena, towering high above him. Her head and shoulders were barely visible in the gloom, but the gold and ivory that covered her wooden body shone out. In one giant hand, she held a winged victory, the figure taller than Alexander himself. The other hand rested on a golden shield, with a coiled serpent wrapped around the inner edge.

Her face was a pale ivory, beautiful and magnificent, staring into the darkness as she kept watch over her city. She wore a golden war helmet, no more than a faint glint in the torchlight.

Alexander raised his hands in supplication, and prayed.

The Macedonians left Athens later that morning, making a triumphal return to camp the next day. It didn't last. Within an hour of his arrival, Alexander had been summoned to a meeting with his father. Philip was alone in his pavilion, and drunk.

"So first you tell the Athenians that you—you are giving them back their dead. Then you ask for rules of royal government from the head of their foremost place of learning. Whose royal government, I wonder? And then, of all things, you break into their most sacred place like some kind of thief. What did you think you were doing? I would now be besieging Athens if you'd been discovered, or more likely paying a ransom for the return of your corpse."

Alexander said nothing. He was in the wrong and the best thing was to just let his father get it out of his system. Philip was too drunk to sustain his anger for long.

"You're too impetuous, my boy. You never think things through or have regard for the consequences. Well, do you? I've spent twenty years building up this kingdom, and how long will it take you to lose it? And you can wipe that look from your face!"

Alexander turned to leave.

"Yes, that's right. Walk away like you usually do." Philip stumbled to his feet. "Let me tell you this, boy. If you leave this tent before I dismiss you, you can say goodbye to your inheritance. I have other sons, and can make plenty more." The jibe made Alexander spin around and glare at his father, who grinned at the impact of his words.

"I will have this kingdom and you won't stop me." Alexander spoke slowly, deliberately, almost hissing the words. "Think on this, Father. When you're nothing but charred bones in your urn, I will be the one sitting on your throne." He didn't look back as he left the tent, a stream of filth following him into the daylight as Philip roared out every swear word he had ever heard.

There would be no reconciliation this time and, although he did not publicly announce it, word spread that Philip was contemplating naming a new heir. The ever-ambitious Attalus was the first to come forward, offering his niece as a vessel for the king to produce truly Macedonian heirs.

But there was still work to be done before Philip could think of such things. Sparta, alone among the city-states, had declined his overtures for an alliance. He had written to the city to ask whether he should come as a friend or as a foe, and the Spartans had replied with their characteristic laconic humor, "Neither."

Philip could not leave a belligerent Sparta behind him but had no wish to become bogged down in a new war, not with winter approaching. He settled for a swift campaign to neutralize the city instead, and the army crossed the Isthmus of Corinth with a mission to lay waste to Sparta's lands and redraw her borders.

With barely a skirmish, the campaign left Sparta isolated and enfeebled, facing famine and with her border regions parceled out between her nearest neighbors—and oldest enemies. The moment had come to pull the Greeks together into a new alliance with Philip at their head, and so the newly formed League of Corinth met in that city as the first snows of winter fell on the hills.

They gathered in the magistrate's meeting hall, the doors slamming shut against the noise from the agora and a cold wind that funneled through the columns of the south stoa. The representatives huddled in their city groups. They knew what to expect; they'd been primed beforehand to avoid any embarrassing outbursts.

Philip took his seat at the head of the room, and opened the proceedings with a proposal for consideration by the league.

"I seek a common peace, gentlemen. An alliance in which each member state will rally to the aid of another in the event of attack, and support offensive action undertaken by the league." He was using his most magnanimous voice, and was rewarded with nods of assent.

"Policy will be debated by a steering committee of five members," he continued. "They will be elected on a regular basis, with safeguards to ensure that no one city dominates the committee. Each and every member state will be guaranteed certain rights and the autonomy to pass its own internal laws, where they do not interfere with the common good." Again, the nodding heads.

"And I will be the leader of the league's joint forces, its hegemon. As will my heirs. Do I have your agreement, gentlemen?"

The audience rose to their feet on cue, shouting their assent and calling for a monumental tablet to be prepared. They had little doubt the league was nothing more than Philip's tool for the subjugation of Greece, but it kept the Macedonian army outside their gates and they were more than willing to accept.

Philip left for Pella in triumph, leaving the league to debate the finer details. He did not return to Macedonia immediately. Instead, he made a detour to Olympia and commissioned the construction of a tholos, a circular monument, in honor of his victory at Chaeronea. This building, within the very walls of the Sanctuary of Zeus Olympus, he named the Philippeum. And why shouldn't he consider himself divine?

It turned into a long winter, with the palace at Pella becoming home to two camps, the followers of the king and those of the prince. Philip had the upper hand by far, both in power and in numbers, but he was worried. Whether he liked it or not, he still regarded Alexander as his heir, but an openly hostile faction within the palace was too dangerous to tolerate.

He let his gaze wander across the Great Hall to the cluster of couches commandeered by Alexander and his cronies. The boy was thirsting for power and a showdown would be inevitable unless he could keep a tight rein on his son's dealings, and that was becoming ever harder to do. As though aware of the eye upon him, Alexander broke off from talking to Hephaestion and raised his head. His stare met his father's.

In her apartment, Olympias began to hum. Slowly at first, she moved across the room, lifting the snake she held in her hands, dashing its brains against the wall as she turned. Her humming became louder and more insistent as she danced, her twirling more frantic. Dionysus watched from his niche, his wooden eyes focused on the priestess as she prayed for the death of her husband at the hands of her son.

Chapter Fourteen

The Land of the Agrianes

Alexander hammered on his mother's door, being let in by a startled looking lady-in-waiting. He stormed through the apartment and found Olympias in her dayroom. Cleopatra was with her.

"Have you heard? Now the old fool is accusing you of adultery and says I'm a bastard!" He stood, quivering with rage.

"Calm down, Alexander, and take a seat." Olympias waited for him to sit, then stood herself, walking over to idly straighten a mirror on the dresser. "It's more serious than you think," she said, turning to face him. "He's getting married again."

"To that drippy Cleopatra," blurted his sister. "You know, Attalus' niece. It's disgusting. She's only my age and even has my name. It's like he's trying to bed me." She shuddered.

"I wouldn't put anything past your father." Olympias' face twisted into a sneer. "Whatever his reasons, this Cleopatra is Macedonian born and bred. If she has a son, he will be pure Macedonian. Do you follow me?"

Alexander did. Many among the Companions would prefer a truly Macedonian successor, but all Philip's wives had been foreigners up to now. This marriage put his inheritance in jeopardy.

He grimaced. "I never thought he would actually do it, but he's really trying to dispossess me this time. But why is he accusing you of adultery, Mother? What has he to gain by that?"

"Can't you see? His attack is against you, and the more unpopular he can make me, the more unpopular he will make you by default. It's an old trick." Olympias sat down again.

"There's one thing he seems to have overlooked," mused Alexander. "By disinheriting me in favor of a son that isn't even born yet, he leaves himself without an immediate successor. And if he dies before the child matures, who will be the natural choice to rule as regent? Attalus would, as a blood relative of the boy."

"And then there's Parmenion," he continued, the anger returning to his eyes as the plot unfolded in his brain. "He's second only to Philip and could easily persuade the army to back him if anything happened to the King. So, who married Parmenion's daughter in the wedding month?" He made as if trying to remember. "Of course, it was Attalus. What a power base those two are building." He sneered. "Doesn't that old sot realize what's going on? He doesn't deserve to keep his kingdom."

"Your life will be forfeit if either Attalus or Parmenion take the throne," said Olympias flatly. "You can be sure of that. So we'll have to make sure you're the next King of Macedonia, won't we." She smiled, and Alexander knew what she meant.

In another part of the palace, Philip also smiled. "What troubles you, Parmenion?" He took a gulp of wine and waited for the general to reply.

Parmenion crunched on an apple and chewed slowly, pulling himself up onto the arm of his couch with an elbow. "Why are you disowning Alexander, and why now? He won't tolerate it and will only become a threat to your safety. You've already alienated Antipatros with that Philippeum of yours; can you afford to lose Alexander as well? Greece is ours and the invasion is only weeks away, so why cause trouble now?"

Philip laughed. "Do you think I seriously want to disown Alexander? No, much as he deserves it, I've put too much effort into the boy to turn my back on him now. Besides, who would I replace him with? Every son by my other wives has died in infancy, that witch Olympias has seen to that. She's only spared Arridaeus because he's retarded."

"But you have other sons. They may be illegitimate but that hasn't mattered in the past."

"Yes, and they're also pure-bred Macedonians, eh, Parmenion?" Philip grinned, aware of the general's leanings. Parmenion shrugged and took another bite of his apple, deeming it wiser to say nothing.

"I want Alexander to be my heir, Parmenion. He will be a strong king; I've seen to that."

"So what's this about, then? You've questioned his legitimacy."

Philip took a slug of wine and chose his words before speaking again.

"I have not questioned his legitimacy. I allow the rumor to remain unchallenged perhaps, but that accusation didn't come from my lips. The problem is that I can no longer trust Alexander. He wants my throne, and I know Olympias is plotting my death. Have you seen these?" He took a small disc from his purse and tossed it over to Parmenion.

The general looked it over. It was a cameo, showing the unmistakable portrait of Alexander, side by side with a woman—Olympias.

"She has a workshop in the city turning those out by the dozen," continued Philip. "She's getting the people used to the idea of Alexander and Olympias, Olympias and Alexander. Then she intends to kill me and rule for herself, as the power behind Alexander's throne."

"You have proof of this?" Parmenion tossed the cameo back. Philip made no attempt to catch it, letting it clatter to the floor.

He shrugged. "Who knows what thoughts that woman has in her head. As to whether Alexander is involved, I cannot say either. I have no evidence, but he's always huddled in some corner or other with those friends of his, and I wouldn't put it past him. I have got to remove Olympias and neutralize Alexander and his faction before they have the chance to act."

"Philotas hasn't reported anything."

"I know, and your son isn't the only ear I have among them. I mean the boy no harm, but I must break up that group of his and keep him at arms length, at least until the invasion starts." He chuckled. "I may want him to inherit my kingdom, but I would prefer that it be later rather than sooner."

"So why are you marrying Cleopatra?" Parmenion slung the apple core onto the table.

"Insurance," replied Philip. "You saw Alexander at Chaeronea. He leads from the front, like me. Both of us could easily be killed in Persia, and what of my kingdom then? I'd like to leave him here as regent, but he would never stand for that. I'd be accused of robbing him of his chance for glory, no doubt." Philip drained his drinking cup and smacked his lips. "So my insurance is to leave behind a substitute heir, just in case."

"What's to stop Olympias killing the substitute?"

"Olympias will be dead well before then." Philip grinned at the thought. "It's long overdue; I've only left her alive this long for the sake of the boy."

"And what of Attalus?"

Philip gave Parmenion a long look. "What of him?"

"He's becoming ever more powerful. When I allowed him to marry into my family, I didn't know you would be marrying into his. He already has a bloodline of his own to the throne, and now he will be an in-law to both you and I. He is ambitious, Philip, and my advice is not to trust him."

"I know that, my friend, and don't worry. I'm going to send him to Persia with the vanguard. He'll have no influence that far from court. And I will also have my most loyal man there to keep an eye on him."

"And that is?" As if the general needed to ask.

"Would I send anyone else, Parmenion? I want you to lead the invasion, with Attalus as your lieutenant."

The wedding feast proved to be sumptuous, as befitted a king of Macedonia. The guests gathered in the main courtyard at dusk, their heads crowned with wreaths of laurel and myrtle, the buildings garlanded with the same. Alexander stood with them. To refuse to attend would have cast more doubt on his position as Philip's heir.

They heard the cheering long before the king's chariot came rattling through the inner gate. The procession from Cleopatra's home had been a triumphal affair and it seemed like the whole city had turned out to pay their respects to the king as he passed.

Philip stood next to his new bride as Attalus guided the chariot across the courtyard and stopped before the open doors of the Great Hall. A torchlit procession followed through the gate, the bride's family and friends, and a good few gatecrashers. Helping Cleopatra down, Philip led his bride through the throng gathered in front of the huge oak doors.

The guests followed, eager to claim their place on one of the many couches that had been squeezed into the hall for the occasion. Philip waited with his bride on the raised platform at the far end, acknowledging the shouts of goodwill being flung at him from all sides.

Alexander marched down the center of the hall and stepped up onto the platform. Father and son stared at each other. Without a word of greeting, Alexander flung himself onto the couch to the left of his father's, the place of honor reserved for the chief guest. Philip said nothing.

The feast got underway without more ado. A choir sung the hymn to Dionysus while sesame seed cakes were distributed to the guests as an emblem of fertility. Cleopatra, lying on the couch next to her new husband, fumbled with her veil as she tried to eat hers.

Weddings were among the few occasions when women ate with the men, and the proceedings were restrained as a result. Not so Philip. He'd been drinking for hours and launched into an impromptu song about how his cock would be crowing long before dawn. His bride was thankful for the veil that hid her face.

He suddenly stumbled to his feet. "My friends," he slurred. "In honor of the occasion, I have decided to grant my new wife the married name of Eurydice. It is an ancient royal name and that of my own, dear, mother."

There was a burst of applause from the guests while Alexander glowered at his father, his cheeks burning red. The magnitude of the honor the king had just bestowed on his new wife wasn't lost on his son.

Philip grinned stupidly and opened his mouth to say more, but the task was beyond his alcohol-fuddled brain. He slumped back onto the couch.

Toasts followed, with Parmenion and Antipatros leading the gathering in wishing the couple a long and fruitful marriage. One of Philip's other wives (all except Olympias had dutifully accepted the invitation) welcomed the new bride into the household, and then Attalus stood up to make the toast on behalf of the bride's family.

"My friends," he began. "We are witnessing a historic occasion. Finally, the King has taken a Macedonian bride, and maybe now the gods will bless us with a legitimate successor to the kingdom."

Alexander was on his feet before Attalus had even finished the sentence. "So what am I? You dare call me a bastard, you moron!" He flung his drinking cup at the general, the contents splashing over the guests caught in the middle. Attalus grinned.

"Sit down and shut up, Alexander!" Philip was too drunk to tolerate another of his son's tantrums.

Alexander spun around. "He insults your son and you tell me to shut up? Maybe I should hope I am a bastard, 'cause who'd want a fucking father like you!"

Philip lurched to his feet, his face red with rage. "No one talks to me like that!" He grabbed at the sword he'd used for cutting the ceremonial bride loaf and pushed past the table that separated him from his son. The wine and his gammy leg ensured the lunge failed, his calf bashing against the edge of the table and sending him sprawling beneath Alexander's vacated couch.

Alexander stood over him. "Look at that," he announced to the stunned gathering. "Here is the man who will lead us from one continent to another—and he can't even cross the room." His voice was thick with contempt.

Antipatros stood up. "I think it would be better if you leave, Alexander. Return to your quarters and wait for the King's summons. He will expect an apology in the morning."

"An apology," growled Philip from the floor. "I'll have your head for this. You and that witch mother of yours."

Within the hour, Olympias sat on the back of a wagon outside the palace stables, a cold spring wind making her shiver despite her cloak. She looked about her anxiously. Alexander's explanation had been rushed and garbled, but there'd been no doubt he thought their lives were in danger.

He stood talking to one of his companions in the darkness, while more saddled their horses inside. He came over to the wagon.

"Are you ready, Mother? We're going to meet Lysimachus in the agora and he will drive the wagon. Ptolemy is going on ahead to warn him." He tied Bucephalus to the back of the wagon and jumped up into the driver's seat.

"What about Cleopatra? We can't leave her behind." Olympias hung on grimly as the wagon lurched forward.

"She's safe enough. The King won't harm her."

"You still haven't told me what happened, Alexander. I'm frightened."

He glanced back. "Don't worry, Mother. I'll explain it all when we're clear of the city."

Daylight found them on the track that led southwest to the Pindos Mountains and the border with Epirus. Lysimachus now drove the wagon, with Alexander riding alongside. Ptolemy and Leonnatus scouted ahead while the rest of her son's friends followed, those few who hadn't been with their families in the Great Hall. Harpalus, Callisthenes and Nearchus rode behind the wagon, while Erigyius and his brother Laomedon lagged behind as rearguard, watchful for any sign of pursuit.

Once safely inside Epirus, Leonnatus was sent on ahead to the palace at Dodona, returning the next day with an escort of Epirote cavalrymen. There was also a letter for Olympias from her brother. Alexandros was pleased to welcome them, but his words left little doubt he was unhappy with the situation and would prefer that their stay be a short one.

It wasn't unexpected. Alexandros couldn't turn away his sister and nephew, but he owed his throne to Philip and knew as well as they what the consequences of incurring the king's displeasure could be.

Alexandros revealed what posture he had decided to take when he met the party at the entrance to the acropolis of Dodona. As his sister, Olympias was invited into the palace and given a suite of rooms suitable for a long stay, but Alexander and his companions were to be quartered in a hunting lodge outside the walls. Pandering to their love of hunting was given as the reason and the accommodation was comfortable enough, but the message was clear: the prince was too dangerous a guest to be allowed inside the city.

Although he couldn't blame his uncle, it posed a problem for Alexander. The lodge was too open to be safe against Philip's assassins so there was little alternative but to move on, but to where? Harpalus offered the obvious solution.

"We have the oldest sanctuary in Greece as a neighbor. If I was you, I'd ask Zeus himself what to do."

Early the next morning, the group descended the slope below the palace and stood in silence as Alexander entered the confines of the ancient Sanctuary of Zeus. The oracle here was as old as time itself.

A priest took Alexander's fee and handed him a sliver of lead onto which he scratched his question. He was led into the inner sanctum, kept deliberately dark and filled with the smell of incense and unwashed feet. An old crone sat in a gargantuan chair in the center of the room; she was his intermediary with the gods. Dazed by a brew of ergot-infected barley, she took the message and staggered through a doorway into the garden beyond.

Alexander strained his eyes against the sudden glare of sunlight and made to step forward for a better view, but the priest restrained him. He could hear the woman babbling the question to the grove of sacred oaks, and then cackling in her drugged state as she listened to the answer that whispered back to her from the rustling of the leaves in the wind.

She turned and slumped against the door, lashing out at a second priest who rushed forward to support her.

"Almighty Zeus has spoken to me," she announced, burped, and stumbled back into the chair. "He bids his son to seek refuge among the enemies of his enemies."

Alexander waited for more, but there was none. The woman's head slumped forward and he could see she was falling into a stupor. The priest touched him on the shoulder and led him back out to his friends.

"Well?" asked Nearchus, as Alexander mounted Bucephalus and began to work his way back up the slope.

Alexander stopped for a moment and smiled. "I should apparently seek refuge among the enemies of my enemies. As my enemy is the King of Macedonia and everyone is his enemy, make of that what you will." He shrugged, and continued up the path.

His thoughts turned to Hephaestion, who'd been sitting with his family somewhere in the midst of the Great Hall. He'd left him a note but didn't doubt that Philip's spies had found it first.

The conversation did not resume until they were back on the track that led to the lodge. "You were well received in Athens. Couldn't you go there?" suggested Laomedon.

Harpalus glanced back. "They'd slam the gates in his face."

"Harpalus is right," agreed Alexander. "Athens would not welcome a fugitive from King Philip's court. It will be the same wherever we go. My father controls the whole of Greece."

"Then we should go north, to Thrace or Illyria," said Nearchus. "Macedonia has little control over the tribes beyond her borders."

Alexander laughed at the thought. "Yes, Nearchus, and they hate me as much as they do my father. My head would be on a pole within the hour."

"Not necessarily." Ptolemy spoke up for the first time since their arrival; misgivings about leaving Pella and the prominent position he'd earned in the Companion cavalry had kept him subdued until now. "King Langarus of the Agriane tribe would give you shelter." Alexander gave him an enquiring look.

"You never knew him," continued Ptolemy. "He was a Royal Page when I first arrived at the palace and we shared a dormitory for several years. He was there as a hostage for his people's loyalty, but the King released him to take over the tribe when his father died. We got on well together."

"How well?"

"He was my mentor." He didn't need to elaborate further.

"But would he take us in, even with you among us?"

Ptolemy shrugged. "I don't see why not. We can only try."

They continued to discuss the idea during the course of the day. No matter how lukewarm the welcome may be, in Illyria they would at least be beyond Philip's reach. Alexander kept going back to the words of the soothsayer; the Illyrians were Macedonia's most ancient enemy, and he would be seeking shelter among them.

As if it was an omen, Phrygius arrived that night with news from Pella. Hephaestion and the others were confined to their quarters and the palace was rife with rumors that the King was arranging Alexander's murder. There was more. Philip's new wife was with child and had been for sometime. A boy would be the Macedonian rival that Alexander feared. The news decided him; they would leave for Agriania as soon as could be arranged.

The land of the Agrianes lay deep within Illyria, with too many hostile tribes in between to have any hope of reaching it without incident. The group traveled by sea instead, sailing around the Peloponnesian peninsular and into the Aegean. They stole ashore in Thrace under cover of night, followed by a hard ride up the valley of the River Strymon, scene of Alexander's first military victory.

Disguised as Greek seamen from Byzantium, then as Thracian farmers returning from market, they somehow reached Agriania undiscovered. Ptolemy knew a few words of the language and offered himself up to a passing wagon driver. The others waited in a shepherd's hut for two days, and then awoke to the sound of warriors outside the door.

Ptolemy stepped from between them and introduced his old friend, King Langarus.

The capital of Agriania was little more than a large hilltop village, but it had sturdy wooden walls surrounded by a deep ditch—and thousands of Illyrian warriors between it and Philip's army.

The ways of the Illyrians were strange to the new arrivals. They ate sitting upright in chairs, women were invited to their drinking parties, and the more they drank, the more they tightened their belts. The Macedonians hid their smirks and settled into their new life, grateful for their welcome.

Spring turned into summer and then fall, and Alexander fretted in exile. His only news came via traders and cattlemen, fragments of rumors overheard in a hundred marketplaces. He took heart from the one fact on which they all seemed to agree: the new queen's child was a girl.

And then a wine merchant arrived. He was a citizen of Pella who had done business at the palace and knew many of their friends. The exiles welcomed their compatriot warmly, eager for news from home—and did he have a tale to tell.

They gathered around the fire in the hut they all shared, plying the man with drink. He needed little encouragement to speak.

"After you, shall I say, removed yourself from Pella, sir, it was assumed that King Philip would deal with you quickly." The merchant paused to await a reaction from the prince, and received a nonchalant shrug.

"We, too, assumed that."

"But it didn't happen. The King was busy with preparing for the invasion of Anatolia and seemed content to leave you alone, and that was a mistake. Illyrian tribes on Macedonia's border saw his inaction as weakness and began new raids. The King had no choice but to postpone the invasion and march against them."

There was silence for a moment. The invasion had been postponed; they hadn't yet lost their chance for glory.

"It is definitely postponed?" Alexander asked for them.

The man smiled. "They were campaigning the whole summer, sir, but when they came back, they brought a story with them." The merchant grinned, revealing rotten teeth. "You know the King's favorite, Pausanias?"

Now he really had their attention. They, too, grinned, and drew closer to the fire, as though conspiratorially.

"Go on."

"The King's eye has been turning to younger flesh of late and, during the campaign, Pausanias' jealousy finally led to a confrontation. The King spent the whole evening with a new officer of the hypaspists, and then Pausanias challenged them both, calling the officer a tart and a hermaphrodite. King Philip was outraged and the youth apparently reduced to tears."

"His name?" asked Harpalus.

"Also Pausanias."

"A nephew to Attalus?"

"That's the one."

There was a general chorus of jeers. The effeminate page had been destined for the civil service until Attalus intervened, his switch to the military being purely due to his uncle's influence. Leonnatus raised a limp wrist and placed the other lightly on his waist. They laughed at the caricature.

The merchant raised an eyebrow. "Apparently not, sir. In skirmishing the next day, he ran out from the ranks of the hypaspists and dashed toward the enemy line. Inevitably, he was cut to pieces, and everyone knew the reason for his actions; he had been proving his manhood."

They fell silent at the loss of a brave comrade.

"But the story does not end there, sirs. Now Attalus is vowing revenge on Pausanias for the death of his nephew."

Alexander heard of his coming long before Demaratus reached the village. The Corinthian was politely received by King Langarus, and escorted to the hut where Alexander waited.

"I bid you joy, Demaratus. It has been a long time." Alexander directed him to sit on one of the stools. "We Illyrians sit upright," he added with a grin.

Demaratus smiled and plonked himself down on the stool. "And joy to you, Prince Alexander. It certainly has been a long time. The last occasion I saw you must be the day you conquered Bucephalus. The horse still lives?"

"He lives, and I am eternally grateful to you for buying him for me. He is stabled in Dodona until I can retrieve him." Alexander looked pointedly through the door at the village outside. "It wasn't practical to bring him with me."

Demaratus gave a half-chuckle of agreement. "Yes, I can understand that, which brings me to the purpose of my visit. I take it you know I'm here on behalf of your father."

"His spies and rumormongers are everywhere," said Alexander with a smile. "Even here."

"Your father chose me to speak for him because I am known to you. Also, I have only recently returned to Pella from many years in Sicily. He believes that is sufficient proof I am not his man and not trying to deceive you." He looked at the prince enquiringly.

Alexander nodded. "I remember you as an honorable man, Demaratus. I trust your words."

The Corinthian leaned forward on his stool, making it crack alarmingly.

"Your father is very concerned at the situation, truly so. He asked me to convey to you his apologies for the unfortunate misunderstandings that led to this, and to assure you he still regards you as his heir. Should you agree to return to Macedonia with me, you have his pledge that your safety will be guaranteed and you will be restored to your rightful place as heir to the throne of Macedonia."

Alexander's heart jumped at the prospect of a return to Pella. The impotence of half a year in exile was proving too much for someone of his ambition—and the Illyrian penchant for human sacrifice sickened him.

"Why is he doing this?" His face did not betray his feelings.

Demaratus laughed. "I cannot say what is truly in your father's heart, but he told me his main concern is the effect this rift is having on the unity of Greece. When he learned you had taken refuge with King Langarus, he was content to leave the situation alone. As I understand it, he thought things had worked out rather well, with you safely confined to Illyria and your mother under the watchful eye of her brother in Dodona.

"But it didn't last. The recent uprising by the border tribes has proved that your sojourn in exile has hidden dangers, and both agents in the southern cities and visitors to the palace are confirming his fears. Your feud with your father is being seen as a source of hope to Macedonia's enemies, and the crusade against Persia cannot go ahead until it's resolved. You're still his intended heir, so it is plain unnecessary and needs to be stopped."

"You say I am still his intended heir, but would that be the case if his new Macedonian wife," Alexander slurred the words contemptuously, "had given birth to a boy?"

"Even if it had been a boy, and even if he has a boy in the future. A child king would be vulnerable and Philip cannot reasonably expect to live until one matures, leastways, not unless he retires from campaigning completely. I see little chance of that, so he needs to have an adult heir and you are that heir."

Alexander was grateful for the Corinthian's bluntness. "If I return, what of my companions?"

"They have the same assurances as you, and will be reinstated to their previous ranks without fear of reprisal."

"And my mother also?"

Demaratus smiled and shook his head. "Your father guarantees her safety for as long as she stays in Epirus, but he was adamant she wasn't to return to the palace."

Alexander grimaced. "I suppose I can't blame him. Very well, I accept the King's invitation to return."

The group said their goodbyes to King Langarus and began the journey to Macedonia in party mood. They had crossed the border within days and Hephaestion and Craterus met them north of Pella, the others at the city gates. Philip sent a request that Alexander accompany him to the gymnasium the next afternoon, that the city might see the proof of their reconciliation and spread the word.

The appearance had the desired effect, with a crowd gathering in the street as news spread that father and son were inside together. The atmosphere in the gymnasium was cordial but conversation sparse, the two factions finding it easier to gravitate to opposite ends of the floor. Alexander and his companions sprinted against each other in the colonnades, while Philip sparred with a Thracian boxer.

The onlookers surged into the building, eager to see if the news was true. Philip allowed them to encroach, to his regret. Three disgruntled phalangites pushed their way to the front of the crowd.

"Hey, Philip. So when are you going to pay us what we're owed, then?"

He ignored them, making a show of fending off a punch from the Thracian instead. The soldiers were not to be put off.

"Come on, Phil," the ringleader persisted. "Don't pretend you can't hear us, or are you deaf as well now? If you want us to fight in Persia, you pay us first."

They were starting to draw chuckles from the crowd and couldn't be ignored any longer. Philip paused and considered his answer; he couldn't tell them that two decades of constant warfare had finally drained his coffers.

He shrugged as if helpless. "You know how it is, lads. Launching an invasion is a costly business, but you'll be paid once we get there—with Persian gold. There'll be more than you can carry once we invade Anatolia. Look at me; I'm already in training so I can carry more." He grinned, confident that his charm would work its usual effect.

"And what do you expect us to live on in the meantime? I bet you never go without, up in that palace of yours."

Philip glared at the man. He prided himself on having no pretensions and being equally at ease with aristocrats and peasants alike, but it sometimes had its drawbacks.

But he was never flustered for long. He suddenly slapped the Thracian boxer on the back and raced him through the archway that led to the plunge pool. The two could be heard boisterously splashing about inside, while the entrance to the room was quickly blocked by a discussion-group of Companion cavalrymen. Unable to follow, the three phalangites stood muttering sullenly to each other for a while, and then first one, then the others, turned and faded back into the crowd.

Alexander watched them leave with a bemused smile on his face. "That man never ceases to surprise me," he said, turning to his comrades. "I think, gentlemen, that we have just had a lesson in how to destroy your enemy's ability to fight."

Chapter Fifteen

The Pixadorus Affair

The following months developed into an uneasy truce, with Alexander and his father together only at public functions or when the business of government dictated it. Not that Alexander had much of a role in the government of the kingdom. He was once again the commander of the Companion cavalry, but nothing else came his way.

He was content to bide his time and consolidate his position through the long winter months. His clique of friends re-emerged, much to Philip's annoyance, and Bucephalus was returned to him, with a message from his mother. She was well, but watched at all times. She cautioned him against replying; his position at court was too precarious and Philip could interpret any contact with her as a plot.

Alexander would have obeyed his mother, had it not been for the arrival in Pella of a troupe of actors led by Thessalus, the party guest who had led him up to the Acropolis to pray at the statue of Athena. He brought the sad news that Isocrates had passed away within a few weeks of the visit, the old man's dream unfulfilled; the colonies still awaited liberation.

Thessalus was keen to renew his acquaintance with the Macedonian prince, and an actor was perfectly suited for crisscrossing the countryside without suspicion. Before long, Alexander and his mother had a safe, if irregular, means of communication.

And there was more than mere gossip to tell her. The new queen was with child again, and the omens were pointing to a boy this time.

Philip's envoy traveled to Persepolis and demanded recompense from Persia for their support of Byzantium and Perinthos. The Great King politely declined, as Philip knew he would. Flushed with expectation, he returned to the south and reconvened the League of Corinth. The proceedings were well stage-managed. Expressing outrage at the refusal, Philip proposed a crusade to punish the Persians by retrieving the Greek colonies of Anatolia. The league backed him unanimously; the way had finally been cleared.

He returned to Pella and gave the order for the invasion force to be readied, announcing that Parmenion and Attalus were to depart before the summer with a vanguard of ten thousand men.

"Ready?" asked Alexander.

"I suppose so." Hephaestion smiled. "Are you sure the invitation was for you?"

"Prince Alexander and guest. I would assume there's only one Prince Alexander."

They entered the courtyard of Parmenion's townhouse gingerly. A steward met and escorted them inside, while a stable boy disappeared down a side alley with their horses.

Philip was lord of the feast, of course. He was already drunk. He wore a crown of wilted flowers atop his head and his disheveled robe exposed more of his body than Alexander wished to see. The king intercepted his son in the hallway and thrust a huge goblet into his hands, challenging him to drink or pay a forfeit. A small crowd spilled out from the symposium to watch, their cheers egging Alexander on.

He hefted the goblet and guzzled, letting liquid gush down his front and splash across the floor. The wine was sour and he could smell urine, but he dutifully drained the goblet and inverted it on his head.

"Bravo, my boy. There's not many have managed to empty it." Philip spun around, putting out an arm to steady himself against a wall. "What did I tell you, Parmenion? Could he be anyone else's son?"

Parmenion smiled. "Not with a gullet like that. And now, Alexander, we shall need your contribution to help refill it. Hephaestion hasn't had a turn yet."

The symposium was just one of dozens being held all over Pella, farewell parties for those officers fortunate enough to be part of the vanguard. Alexander had already attended a party for Proteas and had another scheduled for the brothers Erigyius and Laomedon; the three were the only members of his circle to be chosen for the expedition. Receiving an invitation to Parmenion's festivities had taken him by surprise. It had been apparent for some time that the general had joined the ranks of those who would prefer a purebred Macedonian successor.

The food was sumptuous and the entertainment outrageous, as befitted a general of Parmenion's rank. Alexander and Hephaestion shared a couch next to the king, who pointedly sat alone. Pausanias had been relegated to sharing a couch with one of Parmenion's cousins. He looked glum.

Attalus staggered across the center of the room, groping a naked sword dancer along the way and nearly making her lose her toes to a blade. Alexander eyed the general warily.

"Prince Alexander," Attalus exclaimed, as though he'd been unaware of his presence. "It's so good to see you. Some party, don't you think?"

Alexander nodded. "Yes, it is."

"Come on, Alexander," Philip called from his couch. "Let's not have any animosity this evening."

"Hear! Hear!" said Attalus. He took a step closer. "I know we've had our differences in the past, but now we're on the threshold of a great adventure and should put such nonsense behind us."

"I hold no grudge," Alexander lied. "I understand you're to command the vanguard's shield side, and may I be the first to wish you success. I'm envious."

Attalus smiled graciously. "The whole army will follow soon enough, and I'm sure your father will find a command to suit you."

"Leave a few Persian heads for us," crowed Philip. "Don't take them all yourself."

"Oh, I'm sure there'll be a few stragglers hiding among the rocks." The general turned to go, and then paused. "I am holding my own symposium tomorrow night, Alexander. Perhaps you would attend?"

"Well said, Attalus." Philip lurched to his feet. "Say yes, my boy, in the spirit of reconciliation."

"I would like to, Father, but cannot. I'm hosting the symposium for Erigyius and Laomedon tomorrow night. It would be an insult to absent myself."

Attalus shrugged. "Then how about you, Pausanias? In the spirit of reconciliation, would you like to come?"

The bodyguard glanced toward the king in surprise.

"Attalus, I'm impressed. Such magnanimity deserves reward." Philip ambled over and put an arm around the general. "If only I had more citizens like you." The two wandered out the door.

Alexander watched them leave. "Did he really think I'd accept?" he whispered to Hephaestion. "I'd rather drink hemlock than enter the house of a man who'd slandered my mother and called me a bastard."

Alexander heard the story as he and Hephaestion played dice against Leonnatus and Ptolemy in his apartment. It was proving to be a lack-luster game. They'd drunk far too heavily at the symposium for their comrades the night before, and rarely did anyone manage to snatch even a single knucklebone as they fell.

"There you are!" Iolaus stood at the open door. "Have you heard?" He was bursting with excitement and clearly praying they had not.

"Heard what?" mumbled Leonnatus, holding an arm over his aching eyes to block out the sun that streamed through the window.

"About Pausanias. You haven't, have you?" Iolaus shut the door behind him, like a child with a secret to tell.

"Go on, then." It was best to humor Iolaus.

"He went to a symposium last night. The one for Attalus."

Alexander looked up, suddenly interested. "He didn't go, did he? He must have realized Attalus was only play-acting in front of the King. In the spirit of reconciliation," he mimicked.

Iolaus grinned. "He went all right, and apparently Attalus was as surprised as you that he put in an appearance. But he welcomed him in and made him feel at ease, and plied him with drugged wine." Iolaus paused to enjoy their reaction.

"That Pausanias is a fool," muttered Alexander. "I suppose he saw making amends with Attalus as a first step to getting back into my father's bed." He drained his drinking cup. "So, what happened?"

"Listen to this." Iolaus was bursting with his news. "When Pausanias could barely stand, Attalus had him dragged out into the rear yard—and gave him to his stablemen!"

"When you say gave?" Ptolemy's eyebrows arched.

Iolaus laughed. "Put it this way. I doubt he'll be able to sit down before the next waxing of the moon!"

Alexander sat upright on his couch and shook his head despairingly. "And that man dared to accuse me of being a bastard."

"What does the King say?" asked Hephaestion. "Surely he can't let something like this pass."

"Pausanias has made an appointment to see him this afternoon, and the King must know what it's about."

"It wouldn't surprise me if he does nothing," remarked Alexander, calling a slave over for more wine. "What can he do? He's let Attalus become too strong, and it's too close to the departure of the vanguard to censure its second-in-command publicly. Would you jeopardize the invasion for a fool like Pausanias? He asked for it, if you ask me."

Pausanias came to see Alexander in his dayroom that evening. The man held his hand against bruised ribs and sat on a cushioned chair slowly, declining an invitation to lie on the couch. He had a cut on his nose and a swollen eye, and his hair was matted, with a bloody patch where whole locks had been pulled out by the roots.

"Well, what did my father say? The fact you're here tells me it can't have gone to your satisfaction."

Pausanias shook his head. His eyes were misty, making Alexander feel uncomfortable. "The King tried to laugh it off at first, then grudgingly said he'd look into the matter. He's also going to grant me extra estates in recompense when we conquer Anatolia, but I don't want that." His voice was almost a whine. "I want justice, not a bribe. I am of the Orestids, a lineage as noble as Attalus', and he deserves death for what he did to me."

"I agree, Pausanias, and not just because I have no love for Attalus either. But you know the position I'm in at court. Attalus has more influence than I do these days and my opinion counts for little."

"But you could talk to the King; you're still his son."

Alexander laughed. "Not according to Attalus." His face became serious again at Pausanias' continued hangdog expression. "I'll talk to him, but I can tell you already that it'll do no good. What you must understand is that King Philip sees this crusade against Persia as more important than any one man. Another time, perhaps, you may have had justice, but not on the eve of the invasion."

"So what should I do?"

Alexander shrugged. "Do the same as me and bide your time. I'll have my revenge on Attalus, but the time is not yet right." He grinned. "I will tell you this much, Pausanias. He may be protected now, but Attalus lives only as long as my father lives. When I become King, neither Attalus, nor any of his faction, will live long enough to regret cheering as I went into exile."

Pausanias smiled for the first time, painfully, through cracked lips. "That gives me comfort. Each time I look at him in future, I'll remember your words and know his life is dependent on another. He dies when the King dies."

Alexander laughed again. "Be careful how you say things like that. Besides, Attalus leaves for Anatolia in a few days, so I don't know you'll have much chance to look at him that often. Not that I expect you'll want to."

"That's true. When I think of him, then."

"And be assured, Pausanias. When I take my revenge on Attalus, it will be in your name as much as mine."

"Thank you, Prince Alexander. I look forward to the day."

As he had agreed, Alexander spoke with his father, but it made no difference, as he had expected. Philip was furious with the general and had already admonished him privately, but had no intention of jeopardizing the expedition by placing someone as prominent as Attalus on public trial. Besides, father and son agreed on one thing: Pausanias was a fool to have gone to the symposium.

The invasion went ahead as planned, and the news coming back from Anatolia could not be better. Parmenion was marching south virtually unopposed, the colonies throwing out their Persian rulers and coming over to him. In Ephesus, the people were even worshipping before a statue of Philip that they'd erected in the Temple of Artemis; Antipatros scowled when he heard that story.

And there was more news, this time from Babylon. The vizier had once more murdered the Great King, selected a new puppet to rule in his place, and promptly been murdered by the replacement. The empire was in confusion.

There seemed little doubt nothing could stop the Macedonians sweeping through Anatolia, or so it appeared to the satrap who ruled Caria, a southern state that lay in the path of the advancing army. Pixadorus sent his ambassador to Pella, carrying with him the offer of an alliance.

Alexander summoned his companions to his dayroom, and they didn't need to be told why he'd called them together. His father had been with the Carian ambassador for over an hour that afternoon, and both the secretary of the treasury and Arridaeus had been called in. Alexander's elder brother had emerged from the room with a smug look on his stupid face, telling all within hearing that he was getting married.

"Does my father think," began Alexander, "that he can devalue me this brazenly? It's been barely two moons since he married my cousin Amyntas to Cynane, my own half-sister, and now he deems me so unworthy that even my idiot brother is put forward for marriage to this Persian's daughter before me."

"Do you think that's what he's doing?" asked Iolaus. "Is the King really trying to disinherit you?"

"Of course. It's obvious," Leonnatus answered for Alexander. "Amyntas was once the King and could easily be again, and Arridaeus may be a retard but he's still Philip's first-born son."

"But are either of them really a threat?" asked Nearchus. "Amyntas has never shown any ambition that I've noticed, and I can't see Arridaeus becoming King. He can barely string a sentence together."

"Both are very much a threat," said Harpalus, joining the conversation. "You're not Macedonian, Nearchus, so you don't understand. The King may name an heir but he's only really suggesting who he would prefer as his successor. It's the army who make the final choice, and that is Macedonian law."

"And with the backing of the army," added Phrygius, "virtually anyone could become ruler. That's how King Philip came to the throne. His brother was the King and Amyntas the son and heir. Amyntas rightly succeeded his father when he fell in battle, but he was only a baby so Philip was appointed regent." Phrygius shrugged. "Those were troubled times and Macedonia needed an adult ruler, so the army petitioned him to assume the throne."

Harpalus took over again. "It could be argued that Amyntas has as much right to be Philip's successor as Alexander does, and allowing him to marry one of his own daughters will have reinforced that view. Even more," he added, "it could seem like the King is actually sanctioning it."

Nearchus still looked unconvinced. "But you said nothing when Amyntas married Cynane, Alexander, so why now? Arridaeus is surely not a threat."

"Arridaeus is even more dangerous than Amyntas," answered Alexander. "He may be incapable of ruling but he has the right, and that means anyone with the inclination could rule through him. At least Amyntas is a single threat, but Arridaeus opens up the whole court. So, who is the power behind the throne this week?" There was a light laugh at the joke.

"What are you going to do, Alexander?" asked Philotas.

"I don't know. I can't stop the marriage but I also can't let it go ahead. My position is too weak already to let it slip further." He looked at the faces of his companions. "That's why I've called you together, gentlemen. I want ideas."

"Kill Arridaeus?" Leonnatus always went for the simple solution.

Alexander smiled. "No, it's not my brother's fault and I have no wish to harm him."

"There is a way," said Marsyas after a moment's silence. He spoke slowly, formulating the plot in his head. "Marry this satrap's daughter yourself."

Alexander shot a glance at Hephaestion.

Ptolemy laughed. "The King would never allow it."

"Of course he wouldn't, but it would never come to that." Marsyas turned to Alexander with an eager look on his face. "You only need to offer to marry the daughter; that would be enough."

"How so?"

"Because the Carians would accept. You are, after all, a better prospect than your brother. King Philip would block it, but he could not then continue with any marriage to Arridaeus. It would be too much of an insult to say they can only marry the retard son." Marsyas grinned. "End of marriage."

"It can't work," said Callisthenes, always the voice of reason. "Alexander doesn't just need the King's permission to marry, but even to enter into negotiations."

"What if he makes the offer in secret, then tells the King. By then it would be too late." All eyes turned to Leonnatus, who blushed. A man of action, it was rare for him to use his brain.

"King Philip would be furious," said Philotas.

"Yes, but Alexander has angered his father before and I'm sure he doesn't worry about doing it again. Whatever the consequences, the main thing is that it would have achieved its objective; the marriage to Arridaeus would be wrecked."

"That's true, Leonnatus. I'm impressed." Leonnatus blushed again at Harpalus' praise.

Cassander ventured a note of caution. "You realize this could be seen as treason." They considered for a moment, his words reminding them of just what they were discussing.

Callisthenes came up with the answer. "Only if the King knows it's a deliberate ploy to sabotage his plans. If he believes Alexander truly intends marrying the Carian, then it's just his son being stupid." They all laughed, albeit nervously.

"But how does he make the offer to Pixadorus?"

"Talk to the ambassador before he leaves."

"And the ambassador would immediately want to talk to the King, who'd then make sure an unfortunate accident befell him before he had time to send a dispatch back to Caria. It can only work if someone goes and talks to Pixadorus face to face."

"None of us could go to Caria. We're all watched too closely."

"Someone who is not of our group, then, and preferably someone who is unknown to the King's spies."

"I have the man," said Alexander. They gave him a quizzical look. He smiled. "This must be my affair from now on, if you're to avoid being indicted for treason. Go now, and leave the rest to me."

Philip went hunting, pleased with himself at securing a Persian ally in the line of the army's advance. The game was plentiful and he stayed on at the villa of a Companion, not returning to the palace for nearly a week. He soon saw the code word that Philotas had left in the secret place for such things, used only when it was urgent.

Two bodyguards pounded on Alexander's door, while Philip stood behind them, shouting and cursing his son's name. The spy hole was opened, and then the door flung wide by Hephaestion, his tousled state making it obvious what had been taking place inside. Philip marched in.

"Get out." Hephaestion did as he was told.

Alexander emerged from the gloom of the bedroom, his eyes drawn to an embarrassed-looking Philotas, who had entered just behind Philip.

"Did you really think you'd get away with this? That I would allow you to marry some Persian whore?" Philip's voice was controlled but his anger evident. "Don't look at Philotas like that. You should thank him, if anything. Luckily for you, someone had the good sense to come to me before things went too far."

"What did you expect me to do?" Alexander's voice was not controlled. "I'm supposed to stand idly by while you further my idiot brother over me?"

"Marrying the daughter of some minor Persian noble is barely what I'd call furthering his career, but it was all Arridaeus was good for and it gave me a perfect ally in the right place at the right time. But no, my other idiot son has to jump to all the wrong conclusions and try to wreck it. Can you imagine what the Carians are going to think when your messenger turns up touting my named heir as a bridegroom? I'm trying to promote an image of strength, yet I cannot even control my own household."

Alexander's shoulders slumped. "Then why didn't you share your plans with me? That's all you had to do. You claim I'm your heir, but you never treat me as such."

"Is it any wonder when you go and do things like this? Sit down, boy." Philip also took a seat, his voice now business-like. "Who is your messenger? It may not be too late to catch him up before he reaches Pixadorus."

Alexander stayed silent.

"Tell me." Philip's voice raised a notch.

"If I tell you, he must not be harmed. He was only obeying my instructions."

Philip stayed silent.

Alexander sighed. "His name is Thessalus."

"The actor who took you up into the Acropolis, and has been ferrying messages to your mother for the last half-year." Philip smiled at his son's reaction. "A good king makes it his business to know everything, boy. It's a lesson you would be wise to learn."

He stood up to leave. "Pixadorus has his court in Halicarnassus, so this Thessalus is heading there?" Alexander nodded.

"Good. Well, he may have a five-day start, but there are only so many ways of reaching Halicarnassus and we hold all the land routes. We may catch him yet."

He stopped at the door. "There is one more thing. I refuse to tolerate this clique you've gathered around you any longer. I should have packed them all off to Anatolia with the vanguard when I had the chance, but I thought you'd only accuse me of some plot to isolate you. Pah!

"They're a bad influence and I know they're behind this. No, Philotas didn't tell me," he added, as that gleam came into Alexander's eyes again. "He didn't have to; he's not your only friend." Philip had long lost Harpalus' loyalty, but it did no harm to sow the seeds of doubt in his son's mind.

"You can inform your companions that they're all exiled. They have three days to leave Macedonia, after that their lives will be forfeit. Philotas can stay as he's the only one who seems to have any sense, and I will allow you to keep Hephaestion." Philip gave a dirty grin. "He might give you something else to think about besides plotting for my throne. You can also keep Cassander as your bodyguard and Iolaus as your steward; their father will vouch for them." He didn't add that he dared not expel the sons of Antipatros while allowing the son of Parmenion to stay. His moves toward deification had upset the general enough lately, and he had no wish to make an enemy of him.

Thessalus had too much of a head start and was too clever to travel openly. He reached Halicarnassus well ahead of Philip's assassins, to tell a bemused Pixadorus that he should not marry his daughter to a fool like Arridaeus but demand Alexander instead. Some pointed questioning convinced the satrap that Thessalus was conveying the prince's wishes, and a delighted Pixadorus informed his daughter that she was now to marry the heir to King Philip's empire.

He soon realized his mistake. The unexpected arrival of a diplomatic mission from Macedonia, keen to bring the wedding forward, keen to make unasked for concessions on the dowry, sidestepping any mention of Alexander, told Pixadorus he had misjudged the situation in Pella. He applied a delay to the marriage plans. He had no wish to throw in his lot with the Macedonians if a power-struggle in Philip's court was imminent.

Chapter Sixteen

A Wedding at Aegae

The marriage between Arridaeus and the daughter of Pixadorus was quietly forgotten, while Thessalus was tracked to Corinth and brought to Pella in chains. Philip spared him, not wishing to draw more attention to the farce that the affair had become, but kept him confined in the city jail. His only visitor was Alexander.

Pausanias continued to badger Philip, seeking justice against Attalus. Having already showered him with more than sufficient appeasements, the king promoted him to the command of the Royal Bodyguard and warned that any further harassment would lose him more than just the promotion. The threat ended any hope he would receive justice. He sought out Alexander.

"Joy to you, Alexander, and to you, Hephaestion."

"And joy to you, Pausanias." The two men were lazing away a long summer evening in the palace bathhouse when Pausanias found them. The building had cleared with their arrival and was now empty apart from an attendant and a couple of Companion cavalrymen who refused to be budged from the hot tub.

Pausanias lowered himself into a vacant bath, and the attendant handed him a cup of unmixed wine from the same krater that Alexander and Hephaestion were working their way through. The three men drank, their silence speaking volumes.

"Very well, Pausanias. What is it? And remember that a spoken confidence rarely remains such." Alexander inclined his head in the direction of the hovering attendant.

Pausanias did not answer until the attendant was called over to deal with the two Companions. "You remember that of which we spoke a while ago?"

Alexander nodded, and drank from his cup.

"It may come about sooner than you think. I have been corresponding with others, most known to you, some of your faction. They, and I, seek your support in bringing about that which will be of benefit to both of us."

Alexander glanced at Hephaestion, who stared into his cup. The bodyguard may have been talking in riddles, but his intent was obvious.

Alexander spoke softly. "I cannot give you my support, Pausanias, and neither do I wish to know any further details. Not necessarily because I disapprove, you understand, but because one day I must go to the army and ask for their support. They will not give it if they believe my hands to be stained."

"There is another who is involved." Pausanias paused before saying the incriminating word. "She . . . also seeks your support for what is to come."

"You've corresponded with . . . this person?"

Pausanias nodded. "Not directly, but through others."

The attendant looked as though he was about to return, so Alexander spoke quickly. "Tell this person I cannot give my support to actions detrimental to the well-being of Macedonia, but that I'm grateful for any endeavor initiated for my benefit."

"Very well. I shall pass your message on." Pausanias began to lift himself out of the bath. "Health to you, Alexander."

"And to you, Pausanias. And—we will not speak again." Alexander looked away.

"Understood," murmured Pausanias, and turned to follow the attendant into the dressing room.

"What are you going to do?" whispered Hephaestion.

Alexander shrugged. "What can I do? I cannot leave the palace without the King's permission and my every movement is watched when I do. Whatever my mother is planning, it must be without me."

With summer drawing to a close, preparations began for the rest of the army to cross the Hellespont under cover of the fall weather. Alexander would again command the Companion cavalry. He had kept himself out of trouble to his father's satisfaction and his rehabilitation was complete.

The weeks passed, and Alexander neither saw nor heard any indication of the plot he knew must be unfolding around him. He sometimes searched the faces of his few remaining friends but could find no indication they may be involved. He knew that Hephaestion was not, and it seemed unlikely that Philotas would be, given he was the son of Parmenion. Of Cassander and Iolaus, he was less certain. Their father's loyalty had been strained since the building of the Philippeum at Olympia. Antipatros considered it an act of blasphemy and had told Philip to his face.

"Yes," Alexander confided to Hephaestion. "Iolaus is rather immature and would blab too easily, but Cassander could well be involved, with or without his father's knowledge."

In time, two of Alexander's exiled companions were given permission to return. Perdiccas came home to marry the daughter of one of Philip's officers, a union that had long been arranged, and Leonnatus to spend time with a dying mother. Their arrival brought the news that the others were congregating at the palace of King Alexandros in Dodona and were there at the invitation of Olympias.

It seemed she'd been spending her time in Epirus gainfully, and now dictated policy at her brother's court. There was even talk she was working on Alexandros to launch an armed invasion of Macedonia as soon as Philip took the army into Anatolia. If Alexander knew about it, Philip must too.

"You have heard?" demanded Alexander, flouncing onto the couch. Hephaestion nodded uncomfortably.

"Will that man not leave me alone? It's one thing after another." He poured himself some wine and drank fast.

"So why do you think he's doing it?"

"Why? To put me in my place, that's why." Alexander laughed, a shrill, false laugh. "His tart, sorry, Queen Eurydice, is ready to drop another brat, but just in case she lumbers him with another girl, he sets up yet another source for an heir." He dashed down a second cup of wine and slammed the empty vessel on the table.

"So now he's going to marry my sister to my uncle." His speech was getting faster. "And any son of Alexandros and Cleopatra will be both a prince of Epirus and of Macedonia. Guess what? That's what I am! Who could be more suited to replace me?" He grimaced and poured more wine.

Hephaestion shrugged. "I think you may be reading this the wrong way. The King must have spies in Dodona who've told him that something's going on, even if they don't know the details. He's merely trying to forestall any plot. By making Alexandros his son-in-law, your father is ensuring he remains on his side. I'd wager it's all to do with reducing your mother's influence in Dodona, and you don't figure in this at all."

Alexander interrupted his drinking to consider the idea. "You know, you could be right." He laughed again, a chuckle this time. "The old bugger!"

Hephaestion smiled, the tension broken. "Can you imagine your mother's face when she heard the news?"

Alexander guffawed.

His satisfaction lasted less than a month. Queen Eurydice gave birth to her second child, and this time it was a boy. Philip named him Caranus after the ancient king who had founded the Macedonian dynasty, an honor that stung Alexander to the quick. His worst fear had finally been realized; Philip had a truly Macedonian son.

The success of the campaign in Anatolia continued, but an old face had appeared in the Persian camp. Memnon, who years before had sought refuge in Pella with Artabazus and his family, now commanded a force of Greek mercenaries in Persian pay. He knew Parmenion and he knew the Macedonians, and was proving to be a tricky enemy. Parmenion could do with some help.

But there was still one important step in the preparations before Philip could commit the army to a crossing of the Hellespont. He dispatched Aristander to Delphi, to consult the oracle on the prospects for the coming expedition. If the omens were bad . . .

The oracle gave a typically obscure reply. "Wreathed is the bull. All is done. There is also the one who will smite him."

The return journey gave Aristander time to mull the prediction, and he announced his interpretation to a beaming Philip upon his arrival at the palace.

"The bull is Persia, garlanded as for sacrifice. Its fate is fixed and nothing can stop it." He grinned. "And we all know who will smite him."

"Good. It is done." Philip rose from his throne to address the hordes of Companions thronging the Great Hall.

"My friends. We have it from the mouth of Apollo himself; our victory is assured." A wave of cheering drowned out his words. He stood, arms outstretched, acknowledging their adulation. The excitement of the moment overtook him and he made a further announcement.

"To honor our impending triumph, there can only be one setting worthy of the union between my daughter and King Alexandros. The wedding will be held in the palace at Aegae, that most ancient capital of Macedonian kings." He grinned as another roar of approval swept the hall.

Alexander heard the cheering through the open window of his apartment. He nonchalantly swung his legs off the couch and reached for more wine. "Sounds like the old fart's playing hunt the sausage with the pages again," he remarked to Hephaestion.

The wedding promised to be the most extravagant social occasion in years, and invitations were eagerly sought by the wealthy and prominent of Greece. They all received them, and were told to bring their friends.

The Macedonian court arrived in Aegae early, three full days before the wedding. The town lay to the south west of Pella on the slopes of the Pindos Mountains. It was a lush, green, sleepy place, whose abundance of temples and villas spoke of the prosperity it had once known as Macedonia's capital. The vast, ancient palace dominated the town from an upper slope, while the tombs of Macedonia's kings dotted the plain below.

Alexander's status merited a full suite, but he could only be allocated two tiny rooms in the overcrowded palace. He shared them with his bodyguards, Philotas and Cassander, while Iolaus was designated his steward and given space to lay a blanket among Philip's staff in the Hall of the Flower Maidens, named after its mosaic and one of three banqueting rooms in the palace. Hephaestion, Perdiccas and Leonnatus would pitch a tent with those of the Companion cavalry outside the walls, on a slope overlooking the royal tombs of Alexander's ancestors.

Alexander stood with Hephaestion on the broad terrace that overlooked the town.

"I did think about listing you as a bodyguard to get you into the palace," he said, "but decided against it. There are many narrow southern minds at this wedding and I fully hope to be King within the year." He smiled. "It wouldn't do to scandalize too many of my future subjects."

"Have you heard anything?" asked Hephaestion.

"Not since that day we talked to Pausanias in the bathhouse. You?"

"Nothing. I'll see what I can get out of Perdiccas and Leonnatus. They're probably under orders not to say anything in front of you, but may open up to me when we're alone."

"If they do, don't tell me."

Hephaestion gave a half-laugh. "And if I talk in my sleep, don't tell me." They both laughed. Their fingers touched and Hephaestion was gone, following Leonnatus and Perdiccas down the slope into town.

The next two days were filled with lavish entertainments, feasting in the palace, singing competitions in the theater, athletics in the stadium. Garlanded bulls and goats lined up outside Aegae's temples, waiting their turn to be sacrificed for the benefit of the meat-starved southerners, while the town filled with the sounds of carousing each evening, all at the king's expense.

Alexander spent his time hunting with his companions. His father's vulgar attempt at buying friends sickened him.

The Epirotes didn't arrive until the morning of the wedding. To everyone's surprise and Philip's fury, Olympias was among the party. As the bride's mother, he could not deny her presence, but he refused to allow her anywhere near his new wife and children. She was given quarters in a villa in the town.

The wedding went without a hitch. Olympias was allowed into the palace in time for the ceremony and took her rightful place next to Philip as the mother of the bride. They didn't look at each other once.

Philip was the guest of honor at the feast that followed, and left little doubt this was more a celebration of his greatness than his daughter's nuptials. He sat on the raised throne of his forefathers in the Painted Hall as, one after the other, heralds from the Greek cities stepped forward to present him with gold wreath crowns, and their sincerest wishes for a successful campaign.

The Athenian envoy raised his cross-pronged staff of office and recited the time-honored pledge to an ally. He ended with the words, "And vow that any who dare plot against King Philip will be denied sanctuary in Athens, and delivered up to Macedonia." Olympias, from her couch at the rear of the hall, the closest that Philip would allow her, sneered.

Alexander caught the look.

The festivities continued with a recitation by a favorite of Philip's, a tragic actor named Neoptolemos. He was there by personal invitation, and with instructions to deliver something pertaining to the coming expedition.

Neoptolemos had chosen from his repertoire carefully. He took his place in the center of the hall and began.

"Your thoughts rise higher than the sky as you cultivate your vast domain.

"You plan new palaces, vaster than lesser men have known.
"You fool! Your life is empty folly.
"For one there is who'll pursue the quick, and sudden, unseen, overtakes.
"It is a sorrow for mortal men. Its name is death."

There was silence in the hall. Even those who recognized the piece were unclear who Neoptolemos had in mind. They looked to the king for guidance.

Philip had no doubts. "Such is the fate that awaits our enemy!" he declared, jumping to his feet. "It's an omen. Didn't the oracle predict that the Great King would soon be a sacrificial victim?" He raised his cup to the actor. "Bravo! Neoptolemos." A rousing cheer swept the relieved audience.

Alexander let his eyes drift in the direction of his mother. She was examining the chicken leg she held in her hand, a faint smile on her lips.

The symposium continued into the night, though the women withdrew at a polite hour. With them gone, any pretence it was a wedding feast quickly evaporated and the serious carousing got underway. Yet again, the Greek guests were amazed at the capacity for alcohol exhibited by their northern neighbors.

Shortly before dawn, a torchlit procession of bleary-eyed guests left the palace and made their way down the slope to the theater, mingling with the hundreds that already jammed the entrances. The king was due to preside over the dedication ceremony for the games that would follow, and nobody wanted to miss what promised to be the highlight of this last day of festivities.

The performance was already beginning as the royal party arrived at the orchestra entrance. A heavy smell of incense filled the air and music accompanied the chanting of a choir, while shouts and catcalls emanated from the audience. Alexander stood with his father and new brother-in-law, observing the crowd from their vantage point in the wings.

"This is only the start," Philip told the pair. "Wait until you see what's coming next."

As if on cue, a trader's cart was trundled into the orchestra, making the spectators gasp when they saw its contents. Cart followed cart, each gilded and festooned with bunting, each laden with a brightly painted statue of a seated god. The audience roared their delight; this was the most ostentatious piece of showmanship they'd seen in years, and they loved it. Alexander gave his father a sideways glance. For all the disdain he now felt toward Philip, he had to admit there was still much to be learned from him.

The carts ringed the orchestra, the gods glaring out at the audience. Zeus and Hera, Apollo and Aphrodite; all twelve of the Olympian gods were represented. Another cart appeared, drawing the loudest reaction of all. Alexander couldn't help craning his head forward to see the thirteenth image, as Philip chortled with glee. The thirteenth god was Philip himself.

"That, my boys, is called making an entrance. And do you see? They approve. You can get away with anything if you have the balls for it." Alexander would have agreed, but for the look of thunder on the face of Antipatros. The senior members of the court were seated behind the orchestra, and it was obvious the general was less than pleased at this latest blasphemy.

Philip turned to the captain of his bodyguard. "Remember, Pausanias, that I want to enter the arena alone; I want them to see I'm no despot who lives in constant fear. But all the same, keep the lads close by," he added with a grin.

"Come, Alexander, Alexandros." He touched both of them on the shoulder. "We shall enter the arena together, the King with his son and son-in-law. Let our people see us." He urged them forward, lingering a moment to make a grander entrance a step or two behind.

Alexander was unaware that Philip wasn't beside him as he stepped out into the glare of the morning sun. He failed to see the figure run out of the shadows; he failed to hear the scuffle above the roaring of the spectators.

He saw the looks of alarm on the faces of those in the front row and heard the groan from the crowd. He spun around. His father lay in a pool of rapidly spreading blood, a short sword sticking out of his ribs.

Pausanias was already running. He grinned despite his fear. He had achieved his objective, a public execution of the man who had failed to give him justice. Now Prince Alexander would take the throne and Attalus, the real prize, would suffer the fate he deserved.

He sped through the vineyard behind the theater, aware of the shouts of pursuers. He had planned his escape well; a small gate was set into the wall ahead of him and a trusted slave waited with horses on the other side. He would be through the mountains within hours and on his way to a hero's welcome in Athens. He was going to make it.

His foot caught in a root and he sprawled flat on his face. The shock winded him and he was slow to rise. The voices were over him.

"Die, traitor!" A spear slammed into his back. His body arched and he flopped forward with a groan. He managed to raise himself up on one elbow and look at his executioners: Leonnatus and Perdiccas. They were fellow conspirators, recruited by Olympias during their exile in Epirus. He smiled a blood-flecked smile; the bitch was ensuring there could be no accusations flung in the direction of her precious son. Leonnatus finished him with a spear thrust to the throat.

Pandemonium had broken out in the theater, the hordes of spectators trampling over each other to escape before any vengeful troops went on the rampage. Alexander knelt by his father, surrounded by the bodyguard, themselves surrounded by a protective circle of Companions. He gently pulled the sword from the body and wiped it on his cloak. Now that it had happened, he felt deep remorse.

Antipatros pushed his way through the Companions, looking at the body of his king for only a moment. "No time for tears, Alexander. We must get you to safety first." He took charge, ordering the Companions to form an impromptu phalanx with Alexander and Alexandros in the middle. He then speed-marched them back to the palace and a hasty inauguration ceremony in the Painted Hall.

Alexander mounted the wooden dais and stood in front of the throne that his father had sat in only an hour before, while Antipatros and Alexandros stood either side of him. Antipatros presented him to those present, the fifty or so Companions who had escorted him from the theater.

There was silence from the Companions. They were still reeling from the death of their king and would prefer Alexander's cousin Amyntas, given the choice.

"Alexander! Hail to Alexander, King of Macedonia!" It was Alexandros of Lyncestis, the son-in-law of Antipatros. He pushed his way through the Companions with his friends a step behind, the group assembling in front of the dais and chanting Alexander's name. Slowly, reluctantly, the rest of the Companions took up the call. Alexander had the backing of Antipatros and his faction and, whatever their personal preferences, this was not the time to be seen to be hostile.

The ceremony over, Antipatros' guards hustled Alexander out of the hall and across the courtyard to the circular Tholos of Hercules. He sat uneasily in the stone throne built into its walls, as a ram was sacrificed and dedicated to the soul of Philip.

After the service, Antipatros barricaded Alexander into his apartment.

"The most important thing now is your safety," said the general as he handed a beaker of wine to Alexander to calm his nerves. "You saw the reaction of the Companions? If Alexandros had not acted, I don't know that they'd have endorsed you."

"Did you arrange that?" Alexander was rapidly regaining his composure, and grateful that Antipatros was proving to be the ally he'd hoped for.

Antipatros sat down at a high-backed chair and looked over at the youth. "No, that was of his own initiative. He may be married to my daughter, but his brothers are friends of Amyntas. He was looking to his own future." The general poured wine for himself.

"We must keep you out of harm's way," he continued. "At least until we get sufficient of the army here to officially proclaim you King. Once we have that, there'll be no doubt as to your succession. The Companions will accept whoever the army backs."

"But will the army back me? Why should they think any different to the Companions?"

Antipatros smiled. "The army's loyalty is to your father. There'll be anger at his murder, so promise to hunt down the conspirators and they will love you for it."

"I'll accuse Amyntas, and kill two birds with one stone."

"I would advise against going that far without proof; false accusations could make people wonder what you have to hide." Antipatros sipped some wine before adding, "We have the slave who held Pausanias' horses, so there will be an investigation. We'll find out if he was acting alone."

The two men looked at each other, both wondering how much the other knew.

"What do you think Amyntas is going to do?" asked Alexander.

"I have men looking for him but it looks like he's already fled. He has no option but to run."

Alexander agreed. "I would in his place. He knows I'll have to kill him, whether he's planning to challenge for the throne or not." His cousin would be the greatest threat. He was popular and had already been king once, and he was Macedonian.

"Quite so, but he's not the only danger. There's Prince Caranus for a start. He may be an infant, but he's your father's son and a Macedonian by both parents."

"Where is he now?" Alexander sat upright on the couch.

"He's here, in the palace. His mother and sister are with him and I have troops guarding them. He's not a major concern as long as he's safely in our custody and no one can get near him, but you may want to neutralize that threat before it has a chance to develop?" Antipatros gulped wine and waited for an answer.

"No, I don't think that's necessary just yet."

Antipatros smiled with relief. "There are two more you must make decisions about, Arridaeus and Parmenion."

"I will not harm Arridaeus, no matter what. I'll keep him with me and monitor his contacts; that should suffice. As for Parmenion, he's too far away to matter. I'll be King before he even learns my father is dead, and it'll be too late for him to declare against me once I have the army on my side."

"He has Attalus with him."

"I have plans for Attalus."

Antipatros said nothing in reply to that. He got up to leave. "You can do nothing until the army proclaims you King, so stay here for the rest of the day with my men to protect you. I have messengers on their way to the barracks at Dium even now, with orders for Cleitus to bring as many troops as possible, as quickly as possible. Knowing Cleitus, he will march them through the night, so they'll be here by tomorrow morning. The sooner we have you recognized by the army, the better."

Despite the frustration of being a virtual prisoner at such an important time, Alexander knew the wisdom of the general's words and stayed in his apartment. He was at his most vulnerable right now, king in no more than name until the army recognized his claim. This was the time for resentful Companions to strike; it would be too late once Cleitus arrived at the head of his phalangites.

It was a long, long, boring day, with only one break in the monotony. He was escorted back to the Painted Hall to address the representatives of the Greek cities—those who had not already fled the town.

"Gentlemen." He looked them over. Anxiety was on every face; they didn't want to be here. "I shall be brief as we have all suffered too much this day to concentrate on such things as speeches. My main purpose in gathering you here is to give you this message to take back to your cities: nothing has changed in Macedonia's relations with her allies.

"I will honor all my father's obligations and will expect you to do the same. I would remind you, gentlemen, that my father was appointed Hegemon of the Corinthian League in perpetuity. Therefore, as his successor, it is my duty to take the title upon myself, and I accept that duty. Now, does anyone wish to speak?"

There was silence.

Someone rose to his feet. "Sir, as representative of the city of Larissa, I welcome your assurance, and pledge that Larissa will honor its obligations to the league." He sat down again.

One by one, the delegates rose and declared an intention to honor their alliances. Alexander thanked each one, but knew it meant little; the armed guards in front of his throne and at every door ensured he would receive those oaths of loyalty.

Back in his apartment, he sent a rider to Pella to order the release of Thessalus from the city's jail; that he would grant the actor his liberty was always guaranteed to be among his first decrees as king. After some thought, he also summoned Philotas and dispatched him to Epirus with orders to bring the others home from exile. There was no actual urgency in recalling them, but it was an opportunity to remove the son of Parmenion from the palace without causing rancor. It was not so much that he distrusted Philotas, but it was better not to take unnecessary risks during these critical hours. Besides, he wanted to see his friends again.

He idled the remaining hours until the early evening, when Hephaestion arrived with Iolaus and Cassander, a new set of colored knucklebone dice, and a large krater of wine. They passed the time playing dice for ridiculous sums of money, their laughter easing the uncertainty.

Antipatros returned late that evening. He dismissed his sons, but allowed Hephaestion to stay at Alexander's insistence.

The general sat on the same high-backed chair he'd occupied that morning, trying to ignore how closely the two men were sitting together on the couch. "I've heard from Cleitus. He's marching two taxeis of phalangites from Dium and will have arrived by morning. We will present you as soon as he has them assembled."

"Is that enough?" asked Hephaestion, surprised. "It's barely three thousand men."

"It's enough." Antipatros gave him a disapproving look, as though it was no business of a wife to interrupt important matters. "Or would you prefer that I send to Attalus for troops?"

Alexander also had his doubts but deferred to the general's judgment. He had a more pressing problem on his mind. "What news of Amyntas?"

"He's long gone, but we've arrested his closest friends, Arrhabaeus and Heromenes. My men are questioning them now." Antipatros paused before adding, "And I believe your idea this morning could be a useful one."

"Yes, you're right," replied Alexander thoughtfully. The two men would say anything under torture, and a confession that implicated Amyntas would guarantee Alexander the support of the army.

"Arrhabaeus and Heromenes, but aren't they brothers of Alexandros of Lyncestis, and isn't he your own son-in-law?" Hephaestion gave the general a sweet smile of revenge.

Antipatros glared at the young man but said nothing. There was little he could say. His son-in-law was the brother of those he planned to accuse of Philip's murder. In the incestuous world of the Macedonian court, everyone was related to everyone else.

He got up to leave and raised his fist to knock on the door, the signal for the guard to let him out. His hand paused and he turned back to add a final thought. "There's one more thing. Stay away from your mother, at least until you've been presented to the army."

Alexander raised an eyebrow. "Why so?"

"The King's bodyguard strung the body of Pausanias from a tree for his treachery. Then your mother arrived, and had a gold wreath placed upon his head as he hung there. She also demanded the sword that had slain the King; as a souvenir, she said. It was almost as if she worried that some people might not think her involved in his murder."

"That sounds like my mother," said Alexander wryly. "And did she get the sword?"

"Yes, she is still a queen of Macedonia. But that won't go down well with the army so keep your distance for now. Let them hate her all they like, as long as they see no connection to you." He rapped on the door. "Now I will say health to you and bid you sleep well. You have a long day tomorrow."

"Health to you also, Antipatros, and thank you."

Alexander slept little that night, his mind a ferment of activity. He knew that the next few days were crucial, and just one wrong move could end his life. He reached under the pillow for the dagger that had been part of his bed linen since his days at Mieza, feeling reassured by the hard touch of the metal.

He knew he had two priorities: to find and neutralize Amyntas, and to get the support of Parmenion. They were equally dangerous. Amyntas was of royal blood and favored by the bulk of the Companions, while Parmenion had ten thousand men under arms in Anatolia and the lineage to make a claim for the throne himself.

But Amyntas was alone and in hiding, and the surest way to preclude Parmenion would be if he learned of Philip's death at the same time he learned that Alexander had already been proclaimed king by the rest of the army. Two full battalions were marching through the night to do just that in the morning. Alexander allowed himself a smile as he listened to Hephaestion's breathing, then his eyes closed and he drifted into sleep.

He was awake before Antipatros arrived the next morning. The general took his now customary place on the high-backed chair, pretending not to notice Hephaestion fumbling about in the bedroom.

"Cleitus is here, and has encamped his men on the plain. Are you ready?"

Alexander ran a hand through his hair. "Not until I've bathed, I'm not. Your men refused to open the door when I knocked this morning. Am I a prisoner?" He was relieved by the surprised look on the general's face.

"Of course you're not!" Antipatros lowered his voice and glanced in the direction of the bedroom. "Let me be frank with you, sir."

"Please do."

There was a long pause before Antipatros spoke. "I am a prominent figure in Macedonia and cannot be neutral in a situation such as this. I must choose sides, and the wrong side will cost me my life." He paused again, as if searching for the right words.

"Your father groomed you for the throne and always intended you as his heir, so I think you have the most chance of success—and that makes me your most loyal supporter." He smiled. "Besides, I have no wish to be subservient to the likes of Parmenion and that cur Attalus."

Alexander smiled back. "Thank you for your honesty, Antipatros. It's easy to fear the worst when you're confined to two rooms." He suddenly laughed. "It's good to know my mother is not the only one who has ambitions for me."

Antipatros stopped smiling.

An hour later, a small group of horsemen rode out of the palace and followed the road that led down to the north gate. Alexander was preceded by Leonnatus, flanked by Perdiccas and Cassander, and closely followed by Hephaestion and Iolaus as rearguard.

Few citizens dared venture onto the street to watch them pass, and Antipatros had positioned his own men along the route to ensure no ambush could be launched at this last minute before Alexander's inauguration. He and King Alexandros met them just inside the gate, and they dismounted to climb the steps up onto the walls.

The troops were gathered outside the gate, a grudging cheer greeting the appearance of the prince on the battlements; they had already been waiting for two hours. Cleitus' battalion of fifteen hundred phalangites was immediately below the wall, with a smaller battalion behind, hastily made up of whoever had been available when they'd marched out of the garrison town of Dium. The Companion cavalry lined the rear; over two hundred men, all mounted.

Antipatros spoke first. He consoled the men on the loss they had all suffered, before ranting with rage at the treachery and promising that the guilty would be punished. "At a time like this," he concluded, "Macedonia needs a strong leader more than ever. That man is among us."

Alexander stepped forward, suddenly aware that the parapet came up to neck height on his small frame. Leonnatus saw it too, and ducked down on all fours. With a grin, Alexander placed his feet on the wrestler's broad back.

"Gentlemen." He had to shout to make himself heard. "You know who I am, and I present myself to you as King Philip's son and his chosen heir. By ancient tradition, the choice of the new ruler of our great country is yours and yours alone, but I ask you to honor the wishes of our cruelly murdered king.

"Why should you choose me? I will tell you. The role of a king is one that does not come easily to any man, even a prince. It takes learning and years of experience, and I have had that learning and I have had that experience. From birth, I have been raised as King Philip's heir and trained in the art of kingship. As an infant, my father would sit me on his knee as he discussed strategy with his generals and economics with his ministers. When still only a child, I negotiated with Persian ambassadors when my father was away. When I reached manhood, I was trained in the warrior's way of Sparta and tutored by the foremost scholar ever to graduate from the academy of Plato. And finally, when the King was fighting in the east, he chose me to govern Macedonia as his regent."

He could see heads nodding in the ranks.

"But Macedonia also needs a king who can both defend its borders and lead the army to greater victories." He gazed out at the men. "How many of you were with me when I led the expedition to halt the Maedi raids? Do you remember how we slaughtered them on the banks of the River Strymon? And all of you remember who led the charge of the Companions at Chaeronea. My father promised you victories and plunder in Anatolia—and I shall give them to you."

Now men were shouting their approval, drawing their swords and beating the hilts against their shields. Alexander smiled with satisfaction. He was twenty-years-old, and King of Macedonia.

He sacrificed a goat to Dionysus at the Tholos of Hercules, and then called his senior staff together in an anteroom at the palace. There were few he trusted, but they had the experience and he needed them.

Wine was served and he waited for them to settle. He had positioned himself on a stool placed in the corner of the room. It gave the air of being a rudimentary throne, and guarded his back.

"Gentlemen, I think I can safely say that all of us would prefer it was my father who was sat here now." He allowed them a moment to reflect on the circumstances that had brought them here.

"But as that cannot be, it is now our task to ensure his death does not imperil the stability of the country. I want my succession to cause as little disruption as possible, so you are all to retain the posts and duties that you held under my father, and I have no doubt you will serve me as ably as you served him. That being said, if any of you feel you cannot give me your total loyalty, then you have my permission to withdraw now, without fear of retribution."

Nobody moved, although a few heads looked about, as if wishing that someone else had the courage to be the first to stand.

Alexander smiled. "And now to business. Our first duty is to give my father the funeral that a King of Macedonia deserves. Has anything been prepared yet?"

Aristander stood up. "The frieze above the entrance is still unfinished, but King Philip's tomb has otherwise been ready for sometime. He saw to that himself. It merely needs opening up and a sweep through."

The priest had suddenly taken ill as the court left for Aegae. He had stayed behind in Pella, and now he was here. Alexander gave him a long stare, and wondered just how many people his mother had recruited. Aristander's face colored and he sat down.

"What of the ceremony itself?"

"The cremation has been scheduled to take place at dawn the day after tomorrow, with the internment immediately after."

Alexander looked in the direction of the voice quizzically, prompting the master of ceremonies to jump to his feet. The informality of Philip's court was at an end.

"And what games are planned?" asked the king.

"Games?" The minister looked flustered. "I hadn't thought they'd be required." Trials of strength between comrades of the fallen were an integral part of a warrior's funeral, but the tradition had lapsed under Philip's Hellenization program.

"I'm sure we can find sufficient volunteers from the ranks of the Companions," suggested the secretary of the cavalry.

"See to it. Whether my father would have approved or not, it is only fitting he should have a warrior's burial." He turned to Antipatros. "And what of the interrogation of the suspects?"

Antipatros took his cue; it was like old times. "They have confessed, sir. As we thought, the assassination was the work of Amyntas and your death was also planned. The plot was funded by the Persians apparently, and Amyntas would have entered into an alliance with them as soon as he'd seized the throne." He paused to look around the room. "Macedonia would have become a vassal of the Great King." There was a gasp and some muttering from the assembly.

Alexander fought back a smile. Hinting at Persian involvement was his idea.

"Is there any news of the traitor, sir?" the secretary of the treasury stood up to ask. He, like everyone else, had taken note that Antipatros had addressed Alexander formally.

"He has fled to the south; Thebes, we believe. Do not fear on that account. We'll track the dog down and exact our revenge."

"What of the south, sir?" asked the secretary of the infantry. "Thebes and Athens will likely see this as an opportunity to break away from us."

"Then we'll teach them a lesson they won't forget." Alexander's smile was imperceptible. "They'll learn I'm not as forgiving as my father."

"But we'll be hard-pressed if the northern tribes also rise up. Don't forget, sir, that we have ten thousand men tied down in Anatolia."

"That's true, sir," agreed Antipatros. "It might be better not to attempt to retain control of the south if the northern tribes rebel."

"No." Alexander shook his head emphatically. "It would be seen as weakness and, more importantly, it would make the invasion of Anatolia an impossibility. My father took the south to safeguard our rear and we must keep it for the same reason. We crush rebellion wherever it appears."

There were frowns on a few foreheads, but nobody was willing to challenge the new king's decision.

There was another meeting immediately after the first, in a secluded part of the palace gardens. Alexander met with his mother for the first time since he'd left her in Epirus more than a year before. The reunion was brief, the conversation stilted and deliberately polite. It was still too soon to be seen together and the less Alexander knew, the less he could be implicated.

But the joy showed in Olympias' eyes. They parted with a kiss, and a promise that she could return to her staterooms in Pella as soon as Philip was safely interred.

Alexander smiled as he watched her climb into the carriage that would smuggle her out of the rear gate. She was still trying to make a point, refusing to wear mourning clothes and bedecked with her most ostentatious jewelry.

He attended his father's purification ceremony that evening. The body had been laid out in an antechamber to the Painted Hall, the heavy smell of incense invading Alexander's nostrils, increasing in pungency as he approached. Two of Philip's bodyguards stood either side of the doorway, coming to attention as he passed between them. They had both been assured they would continue in Alexander's bodyguard.

His father lay on a couch in the center of the room. He'd been washed and drenched in oils, and dressed in a linen shroud by his wives and daughters. Only Olympias and Eurydice were missing, the former from hate and the latter from grief.

Now the wives huddled in one corner of the room, attempting to distance themselves from the professional mourners who wailed and tore their hair to the accompaniment of a flute along the far wall. Cleopatra stepped out of the gloom and embraced her brother. Her mascara was smudged below her eyes.

Alexander stood over his father, the first time he'd seen his body since the murder. Only his face showed, framed in the shroud and with a laurel wreath crowning his forehead. Fresh flowers were strewn the length of his body.

Alexander took an obol from his purse and placed the coin under Philip's tongue. Now his father would be able to pay the ferryman on the journey that lay ahead of him.

"Noble Philip," he said, commencing the lament. "The son of King Amyntas; grandson of King Philip; great-grandson of King Alexander; of Macedonian kings for untold generations.

"When the oracle saw the bull garlanded for sacrifice, how could we know it was you, Father, of whom Apollo spoke? When Neoptolemos warned us of twisted fate, little did we know it would steal you from us at your moment of triumph. You were a blessing to this land, and it is our loss that you have been cruelly slain by evil treachery.

"Hear you this, my Father. I shall not rest until I have avenged you upon your murderers. Let the guilty fear and the Great King quake, for I will glorify your name with their blood."

Alexander stepped back, his duty done. The incense was stinging his nose and moistening his eyes. He felt a lump welling in his throat, and hurried from the room.

Philip lay-in-state throughout the next day as his army filed past to say their farewells. They were veterans who had served their king from the hills of Laconia to the shores of the Black Sea, and they also wept.

Alexander spent the morning in a planning session with Antipatros, emerging to announce that Macedonian citizens were henceforth absolved from all obligations to the state except for military service. It was a masterstroke, as cutting their taxes ensured the loyalty of his own people while he consolidated his kingdom. It would be too expensive to maintain for long, but he intended to repeal it as soon as sufficient time had passed for it to lose its usefulness.

Philotas returned from Epirus that afternoon, with the rest of his comrades in tow. It was a happy reunion. They crowded into Alexander's quarters and lost no time in getting uproariously drunk.

"Did you miss us, Alexander?" asked Phrygius.

"Well, he hasn't done too bad without us," said Nearchus with a laugh.

Alexander grinned. "Yes, I certainly have missed you, and yes, I have done rather well, haven't I?" They all laughed and drank some more.

"So tell us about Epirus. How did you pass the time?" asked Hephaestion.

There was a momentary silence; they'd spent much of their time plotting the murder of Alexander's father.

"We hunted," said Craterus. "Every single day. There isn't a stag or a bear left in the whole of Epirus, and as for the lions." More laughter.

"If I can have a moment." Alexander pulled himself upright on his couch. "I want to thank you all for your loyalty, and to reward you."

"That's not necessary," exclaimed Marsyas. Harpalus hushed him.

"I do not yet have much to offer, but all of you will get a share of the property of the traitors who killed my father. The treasury has already assigned a scribe to preparing the legal documents."

There was a guilty silence.

"What of the traitors?" asked Ptolemy.

"Arrhabaeus and Heromenes will be executed at my father's graveside; that is their only fitting punishment. Amyntas lives only until we track him down, and the Great King will see our swords soon." Alexander smiled, aware of the awkwardness of his companions. It did no harm to keep them confused about just how much he knew.

"You are all reinstated to your previous positions, but I can only make three new appointments for now. Iolaus, you are officially my cup-bearer, a duty you've been performing admirably for sometime." There was a murmur of assent from the group, and a grin from Iolaus.

"Cassander, you are to fill the vacant position in the King's bodyguard." Cassander nodded graciously at the prized appointment. "And, Philotas, will you be my chief-of-staff?"

A look of astonishment spread across Philotas' face. "Yes, of course. It would be an honor." That the promotion was an attempt to buy his father's loyalty was obvious. The others knew it as well as he, and were dutifully effusive in their congratulations.

The next morning dawned and the men of Macedonia assembled to bury their king. The bier was carried from the palace by the six surviving members of Philip's bodyguard, through streets lined by the infantrymen of his army.

A choir of hired mourners, dressed in black and singing dirges, headed the cortege. Next came Alexander and the senior members of Philip's court, walking in front of the bier. They wore gray or black and had shorn their hair, as was the custom. The women walked behind the deceased, as was their place.

They processed out of the gates and onto the plain that held the royal tombs, the men of the phalanx forming up on the slope above. Aristander stood ready to oversee the ceremonies at the funeral pyre, the sacrifice of a dozen bulls. The king's body was laid upon a gold and ivory decorated couch, within a wooden hut erected for the purpose.

Slaves lit the pyre and the Macedonians gathered around as the hut was consumed. They piled the king's everyday possessions onto the flames as offerings, his clothes, jewelry, swords and spears, his drinking cups and wine kraters, his dogs and goats. The throat of his favorite horse was slit and it, too, was dragged onto the flames.

A further sacrifice took place a short distance away, Pausanias' slave being nailed to a gibbet in sight of the funeral pyre. He would remain there to rot, his crucified body a warning to others. Two more waited their turn to die, but Arrhabaeus and Heromenes were noblemen and would have their throats cut as the king's remains were interred in his tomb.

The cremation over, slaves liberally flung wine on the pyre to quench the flames, smashing the libation jars against a tree as they were emptied. The living could not use vessels that had been used for the dead.

Other slaves hurried forward with a fair-sized chest, its golden adornments glinting in the morning sun and the Macedonian starburst emblazoned on its lid. It was a work of art, and Philip had commissioned it many years before for this purpose. They flung it open and withdrew a purple cloak, which they unfurled at the edge of the pyre and set to work at gathering the bones of the king together.

Washed in wine and wrapped in the cloak, the king's remains were deposited in the chest. Alexander stepped forward with a golden oak wreath, representing the sacred tree of Zeus, and gently placed it on top of the cloak.

He walked behind the slaves as they carried the chest down the slope and through the marble doorway that opened into the vaulted tomb. He held Philip's high-crested helmet in his hands while Alexandros followed with his parade breastplate. Antipatros came next, carrying Philip's quiver with its gold cover depicting the fall of a city, and the noblemen of Macedonia fell in behind the general, each carrying one of the king's prized hunting spears or a favorite drinking cup. There were lots of favorite drinking cups.

The tomb filled with Philip's possessions, arranged around the casket that would hold his remains for eternity. When they were done, Alexander oversaw the sealing of the inner chamber and the posting of guards at the outer doors. They couldn't be sealed until the master artist from the south had finished working on the hunting scene that would adorn the façade.

He barely glanced at the bodies of Arrhabaeus and Heromenes as he climbed the slope back up from the tomb.

He joined in the lengthy purification ceremonies that were needed to cleanse the dead from the living, but ate little at the funeral feast. His eyes were even more indistinct than usual and he barely paid attention as Philip's closest friends stood up to extol the virtues of the deceased. His mind was elsewhere; it was time he was seen by the people of his capital city.

He returned to Pella with his bodyguard and a troop of the Companion cavalry, not arriving until late in the evening. A silent city greeted him, the streets being even emptier than usual for that time of night. A change of ruler invariably heralded a spate of bloodshed, and people were being cautious.

He bathed and retired to his quarters, exhausted by the emotion of the day's events and the journey home. In the coming days, he would need to be alert to any sign of dissent as soon as it arose, but he had the chance to relax and gather his thoughts for now. He was asleep within minutes.

As he slept in Pella, a group of figures made their way past the theater in Aegae. Olympias turned into the adjacent orchard and led her slaves to the tree that the bodyguards had hung Pausanias' body from. It had been hanging since the morning of Philip's murder and crows had been at the corpse. The stink of greening flesh made the men's noses wrinkle as they cut it down and laid it on a board they had brought for the purpose.

They carried the remains down to the royal tombs, where two more slaves had gone ahead to rebuild the pyre that only that morning had consumed Philip's body. They laid the corpse of the murderer on the pyre of the victim, and lit it. Olympias stepped forward eagerly as the flames licked at the body, discarding her cloak to reveal the garb of a priestess of Dionysus. She held the short sword that Pausanias had used to pierce Philip's body.

"I am Myrtale," she said, "disciple of Dionysus." The attendant slaves glanced at each other; it was the first time they'd heard her use her maiden name.

"Gods of Olympus. Hear me as I make this sacrifice, and speed the spirit of Pausanias to the realm of Hades." She beckoned to a slave, who hurried forward with a wicker basket. Olympias plunged her hand in and pulled out a small snake, deftly slicing its head off with the sword. The spurting blood splashed over the flames of the pyre, spluttering and crackling as it was engulfed.

"This, the sword that ended my ordeal, I dedicate to Apollo, Lord of the Sun." She flung the blade into the flames and spun around to face her slaves, who'd been joined by a couple of curious townspeople and a half-dozen angry phalangites from Philip's army.

"I charge you, my followers, with the duty of gathering the ashes of this, my deliverer from injustice, and burying them in a sacred place at first light. Not a moment before, or a hex on you. I shall not have him suffer the dishonor of a burial at night."

Olympias pointed to the mound above Philip's tomb. "Bury him there, upon the bones of my tormentor." The slaves hurried forward while the others stood their ground. Olympias sneered at their defiance. "You." She pointed at a candle maker from Aegae. "You will make sacrifice yearly upon his remains or incur the wrath of Apollo." The man looked terrified; he would obey the command.

One by one, the soldiers reluctantly joined the slaves beside the pyre. They knew better than to risk being cursed by a priestess of the gods.

Chapter Seventeen

Hegemon of the League

Alexander awoke to the news that Antipatros was waiting to see him. He bathed and broke his fast, then called the general to his father's study; it was his study now.

"Joy to you, Antipatros. What news is so serious you must ride through the night to see me?"

The general sat and accepted wine from a slave, then waited until the man had gone. "A messenger arrived in Aegae last night, more than one, in fact." Alexander nodded for him to continue.

"The locals have driven out the Macedonian garrisons in both Ambracia and Thebes, and the Arcadians have indicated they don't intend to recognize your overlordship. As for Athens, when they heard of your father's death, the Assembly immediately voted a gold crown to honor the memory of Pausanias. I think it's only the beginning of a general revolt against you in the south."

"Then we march south and quell the revolt."

"Which will leave us exposed to the northern tribes. They'll certainly see your father's death as an opportunity to slip our yoke, the same as the Greeks are doing."

"Then I'll move quickly and be back before they have the chance to organize. I doubt they'll attempt anything with winter coming on, but I'll leave you behind with sufficient troops to deal with any problems that do arise. Yes, if I strike now, I would also be taking the Greeks by surprise." He looked up in satisfaction. "So I won't need the whole army anyway."

Antipatros gave the young man a stare. "It could be your father sitting there."

Alexander blushed and sipped his wine. "You said several messengers arrived. Was there other news?"

"Yes, and this is possibly as serious. It would seem Demosthenes appeared before the Assembly to announce he'd dreamed that Athens would shortly receive good news. That was several hours before the first messenger arrived in the city with word of your father's death."

Alexander smiled. "So, we are to assume that Demosthenes has suddenly acquired the gift of premonition?"

"Either that or he was expecting the news. If he was, then he must have had prior knowledge of your father's murder and you must arrest him. And that will be dangerous, as he'll certainly accuse your mother and implicate you. His dislike of you is exceeded only by the hatred he had for your father."

Alexander considered the problem. "It doesn't necessarily prove he was part of the plot. We'll take the attitude he merely received the news ahead of the official messenger. Have our man in the Assembly make a sarcastic speech to the effect that Demosthenes' spies are better than the city's."

"There's more. Two riders left his home and headed for Piraeus, where one took passage for Anatolia and the other was last seen trying to find a ship bound for Persia. We cannot discount the possibility he's attempting to enter into negotiations with both Parmenion and the Great King."

Alexander took another sip of wine while he absorbed this latest development. "Parmenion is too much of a patriot to agree to a pact that involved the Great King, so Demosthenes is going down the wrong path if that's his intention. My real concern is Attalus. He could talk Parmenion into siding with Amyntas."

"Are you still worried about Amyntas? The Greeks won't back him. They're more interested in ridding themselves of us altogether and aren't going to back one Macedonian over another. Amyntas has no support and it's only a matter of time until we pick him up."

"He may have no support in Greece, Antipatros, but, if I was him, I would be trying to reach the army in Anatolia. He knows Attalus will support any challenge to me and would give him the troops he needs. We must remove Attalus and nullify that threat."

"What of Parmenion?"

"Parmenion is unlikely to back Amyntas on his own. He'll wait to see who is winning first. It's Attalus who's the problem."

Antipatros shifted position in his chair. "You cannot replace or recall Attalus. He has his men's loyalty and a recall could precipitate a revolt."

"I will do whatever is necessary to remove a threat to my kingdom." The words were guarded, but their meaning clear.

"There is a man among my officers," said Antipatros, speaking slowly. "He could be what you are looking for. He's ambitious and clever, and could deal with the situation with a minimum of fuss."

"His name?"

"Hecataeus. He's an officer in my bodyguard."

Alexander nodded. "I know him slightly. I saw him playing dice against Perdiccas once, and agree with your choice if that was anything to go by. I'll send him to Anatolia under cover of delivering dispatches. Have him report to me this afternoon and I'll acquaint him with his mission."

Hecataeus left for Anatolia at first light the next morning. He carried routine messages for the army and proclamations from the new king. He was also armed with a letter of introduction to Parmenion and a memorized message from Alexander.

"Co-operate with Hecataeus and the rewards for your clan will be great, but distance yourself from Attalus."

Alexander marched from Pella two days later, taking the royal road south for Thebes. He rode out in front, enjoying the sensation of leading his own troops at last. The force was small and built for speed. He led a single regiment of hypaspists and the baggage train consisted of mules instead of wagons, a trick he'd learned from his father. A troop of the Companion cavalry accompanied the column; Alexander wanted to keep the nobility of Macedonia where he could see them.

Cleitus met them with the two phalangite battalions from Aegae and the remainder of the Companion cavalry, and a further day of hard marching down the coast road brought them to the Vale of Tempe, a narrow gorge cut by a free-flowing river. It was the first barrier on the road to Greece, and the Thessalians had stationed a garrison there.

The gorge was virtually impregnable, flanked on either side by the massifs of Olympus and Ossa. It would be too costly to assault, and there was no way around without sprouting wings or fins.

Nearchus was sent forward with the formal request that the Thessalians allow the force to pass through. He galloped back, his face furious. "They laughed at me, and then some fat captain demanded we pay a toll."

"How much?"

Nearchus stared at Alexander incredulously. "You're going to pay them?"

"If I have to, but I don't think it'll come to that." He started to grin and turned his head slightly.

Nearchus followed his gaze. High above their heads and out of sight of the Thessalians, a dozen phalangites were chipping steps into the storm-battered rock on the seaward side of Mount Ossa.

"Go back," said Alexander, "and ask them how much. Oh, and Nearchus, take your time."

The negotiations played out until dark, after which time the Thessalians could be heard singing an impromptu song about Macedonian fairies. The work continued on creating a path around the seaward side of the mountain, Alexander thanking the gods for the noise the Thessalians were making. By morning, the path was passable enough for a company of hypaspists to file over to the other side, at times utilizing goat tracks, at others climbing the steps carved into the more unassailable parts of the rock face.

Alexander took on the role of messenger himself this time, barely able to conceal his delight. The captain was waiting for him.

"What do you want, Macedonian? As I told your colleague last night, the toll is three thousand talents. Pay up or you cannot pass."

"Three thousand? You can hardly expect us to pay the full amount now there are fewer of us wishing to pass through." He gazed into the middle distance.

It took the Thessalian a while to turn and look. Five hundred hypaspists jammed the pass to the rear of the Thessalian positions. The captain's jaw dropped.

Alexander pitched his tent on the plains of Thessaly that afternoon, and sat impassively while the elders of that nation were ushered in. The ease with which he'd bypassed the Vale of Tempe had severely knocked the confidence from them and they sheepishly stood awaiting their fate.

"Joy to you, gentlemen. Please sit yourselves down."

Their leader remained standing to deliver his hurriedly prepared speech. "Sir, it is with regret that we learned of the terrible misunderstanding that occurred this morning. I can assure you it was never our intention to bar your way, and the fool who did so will be severely reprimanded."

"It is of no consequence." Alexander waved a hand forgivingly. His father had taught him to know when to be conciliatory, and now was such a time. The Thessalian cavalry were the best in the world, and he wanted them with him in Persia.

"I believe I share a common lineage with one of your leading families?" He continued, smiling at the man in question. "We are both descended from Hercules, are we not?" The man nodded dumbly.

"With that in mind, I would like to take this opportunity to strengthen the bonds between us. I am declaring my commitment to Thessaly by assuming the position of Archon of the Thessalian League, a title you bestowed upon my father and which he carried with pride." The men looked dumbfounded. They'd been forced to cede the leadership of their federation to Philip many years before, and now his son was making them do the same.

The leader glanced at his companions. "I'm sure the news will be greeted with joy by our people, sir," he said dryly.

"Good." Alexander smiled. He had secured the first of his father's three titles.

"As archon, I make this pledge to the people of Thessaly: there is to be no increase in taxes under my rule. You are to continue at the same rate you paid during the reign of my father." He paused before adding, "Except for Phthia. In honor of my succession and as it is the birthplace of Achilles, I exempt Phthia from all and any taxes." He was in a glib mood.

"That is very generous, sir," said the leader, and it was.

"There is one more thing. The Thessalians are renowned throughout the world for the excellence of their cavalry, and so I ask you to call for volunteers to join me in the coming crusade. Will your young men help to win back the colonies and avenge the dishonor of the King's Peace?"

Their cavalry were a source of national pride and a profusion of nodding heads answered him. "I'm sure I speak for all of Thessaly, sir, in saying that our cavalry are at your disposal."

Alexander's smile widened.

The Thessalians were not the only visitors to the Macedonian camp in the coming days. As Alexander sped south, so flustered delegates arrived from other city-states, keen to clear up any misunderstandings over their own actions and declare their loyalty to the new king.

He called a short halt to secure the pass at Thermopylae, and took the opportunity to assemble the envoys into an impromptu assembly of the Council of Delphi. With the Macedonian delegate making the proposal, they unanimously appointed him the council's guardian. He would be known as Protector of the Amphictyonic Council, the second of Philip's titles.

Then it was a night march on Thebes. The city awoke to find Alexander's troops formed up on the plain in full battle array. The Bouleterion took a hurried vote, and opened the gates.

Only Athens remained, and had no stomach to fight alone. A troop of its leading citizens hurried north to declare their loyalty to Alexander, Demosthenes among them. His courage failed him, and he turned back short of the Macedonian camp.

Alexander had subdued Greece without a blow being struck. As his father had done before him, he crossed the isthmus and convened a meeting of the League of Corinth. It was time to have his status as hegemon formally endorsed.

The league met in the theater at Corinth, Alexander siting his throne next to the altar in the center of the orchestra. His bodyguard formed a loose screen around him; he had no wish to emulate his father in that respect.

Having opened the proceedings with a speech of welcome, Alexander turned and beckoned a man forward from the front row. "This," he announced, "is Andromedes. He is a citizen of Ephesus."

Andromedes took up a pose in front of the king. "My friends," he said, the acoustics making his voice resonate around the auditorium. "I come to you, an exile from a beleaguered city. Each day that dawns, I pray for an end to the suffering of my fellow citizens. When will that day come? How much longer must we, the Greeks of Anatolia, suffer the accursed Persian yoke?

"I call on you, my countrymen, to rise and follow this young king on his quest. He promises to free the colonies and avenge the King's Peace, but cannot do it alone. Only by uniting behind him can that blessed day come, when the Greeks of Ephesus shall no longer be forced to pay homage to a Babylonian barbarian."

Andromedes turned and pointed at Alexander, as dramatically as an actor on stage. Alexander smiled. Thessalus had lost weight in jail and was unrecognizable without his beard, even to any watching Athenians.

"Gentlemen, I give you King Alexander of Macedonia; may his name be praised as our deliverer."

Amid euphoric applause, the governing council of the Corinthian League hurried forward to make the pledge. Alexander was affirmed as hegemon in King Philip's place, and appointed captain-general of the Greek force that would free the colonies. He had the third of his father's titles.

Alexander unraveled a scroll of parchment and looked about him. Then he began to read. It was a carefully prepared program of contributions for the coming crusade. Each city was listed and there were murmurings from the audience as he detailed their obligations one by one: troops from one city, gold to pay those troops from another, food to feed them from a third. A groan rose from the Athenian delegation as their city found itself the supplier of ships and chandlery to the expedition. One man rose to challenge the levy. It was Demosthenes.

"What guarantees, thir, do we have that the rethipient of our fleet will not uthe it against us?" He looked around at his companions as he had done so many times in the Assembly. They kept their heads down.

Alexander glanced up at the interruption. He'd had the Athenian brought to Corinth under armed escort, not because Demosthenes was a legal representative of one of the members of the league, but to rub his nose in it.

"None at all, thir," he said, and returned to reading from the scroll. Demosthenes stayed on his feet for a few moments, and then sat down forlornly.

There was silence when Alexander finished, each delegate pondering the burden imposed on his city. He savored the moment. He was their hegemon, and they knew it. He raised his eyes to the acropolis that towered above the city of Corinth. At its summit, a thousand priestesses staffed the temple of Aphrodite, touting sex to anyone hardy enough to manage the climb. For once, he felt the urge to avail himself of their services.

The army marched the next morning for winter quarters in Macedonia, flushed with the success of the campaign and full of praise for their new king. There was almost a party mood among the troops and little doubt he had their loyalty, if no one else's.

Alexander had requisitioned the home of a Corinthian nobleman for the meeting and was also preparing to leave, but would join the army later. He'd decided to make a detour to Delphi first. His time to invade Persia was nearing and it was important the omens were good.

He was interrupted by the news that the delegation from Megara wished to see him, the latest in a steady stream of envoys trying to negotiate easier terms for their city. He reluctantly had them shown in. Smiles were fixed to their lips as they tried to ignore the look of contempt on the face of the young man drinking wine before them.

"Sir," said the leader. "In recognition of your status as hegemon of the league and liberator of the colonies, I have great pleasure in announcing that the leaders of our city have bestowed the honor of citizenship upon you."

"Is that so," sneered Alexander. "Don't you think you're a trifle hasty with your honors? I have yet to set foot in Anatolia, let alone liberate the colonies." The delegation look suitably taken aback.

"Sir," replied the leader stuffily. "In the history of our city, only one other man has been granted this honor; Hercules, your own ancestor."

"I had no idea." Alexander stood up, the disdain wiped from his face.

"Gentlemen, it is with pride I become a citizen of Megara. And rest assured that your, no, our city will henceforth be viewed with favor as a true ally of Macedonia."

The Megaran smiles returned, broader this time. They had judged their man well.

The spring outside the entrance to Delphi was crowded and the shops at its gate doing a roaring trade, but all eyes were on Alexander and his troop of Companion cavalry as they dismounted and washed at the spring, as all pilgrims were required to do before entering the sanctuary.

It didn't take long to discover the reason for the surprisingly large crowd; the pythia had decreed that today was not a favorable day and was seeing nobody. It was she who sat above the Navel of the World, the fume-filled gully that lay deep within the temple of Apollo, and it was she who asked the questions the pilgrims paid for, and who received the answers in the form of an oracle direct from the gods. Without her consent, none could enter.

"What nonsense is this?" Alexander spun around to Marsyas. "Tell the guards their hegemon is here on important business," he barked.

Marsyas talked to the guards at the gate, returning a moment later. "They say the pythia cannot be consulted this close to the winter solstice. It is against sacred law."

Alexander fumed. He knew the law and should have realized the place would likely be closed. "I don't have time for this. Don't they realize the fate of the Greek colonies is at stake?" He made a decision. "Come, we shall enter anyway."

"Are you sure, sir? Entering without the pythia's permission could anger the gods."

"She'll give permission when she knows who I am, and make sure those guards know I'll have their heads if they dare try to stop me." His anger was directed more at his own negligence than at them.

The sanctuary was deserted as Alexander led his men up the steep slope of the Sacred Way to the temple of Apollo, the only sign of life being a few slaves working on repairing the roof of one of the treasuries. There were no lines of waiting pilgrims and the temple's huge oak doors were locked.

"Tell one of those slaves to fetch the pythia. I shall speak to her personally." It was Ptolemy's turn to be the messenger.

The slaves directed Ptolemy toward some wooden huts, where he could be seen remonstrating with someone through a shut door. Alexander's patience snapped and he marched over there himself, followed by a dozen worried-looking Companions. He was not just violating sacred law, but insulting the gods.

The door was a rickety affair and burst open with one push. Two women lay on couches inside, a krater of wine placed on a low table between them. They were the afternoon shift.

"How dare you!" slurred the senior pythia, lurching to her feet. "I don't care who you are; you can't barge in here and order us around. We're guardians of the oracle and appointed by the gods."

"Come with me, woman. You have work to do. The lives of thousands of Greek soldiers are at stake in this coming campaign, and I must know if we'll have victory or defeat."

He dragged the pythia out into the sunshine. She was beginning to feel scared now, with her arm held fast by this northern lout. "Sir," she cried. "Let me go." She looked imploringly at the Companions. "Tell your hegemon to let me go. The man is unstoppable!"

Alexander let go. He stood and stared at the Companions, who stared back aghast. "Did you hear?" he said, a grin spreading across his face. "I am unstoppable." The pythia had answered his question.

It didn't take long for fear of the sacrilege he had perpetrated to set in, and, before he left Delphi, he dedicated one hundred and fifty gold coins to its treasury. It wasn't a vast amount but was all he could afford. Despite the gold that still flowed from Mount Pangaeus, Philip's extravagances had left his heir dangerously short of funds.

His triumphal return to Pella was short-lived.

He had learned the story within an hour of setting foot in the palace, and reluctantly summoned his mother to his apartment. She found him slumped at one end of a couch, drinking cup in hand and feet resting on a table.

"Joy to you, Mother."

"And to you, my son. And may I offer my congratulations on the success of your campaign." She was beaming her pleasure. "You've shown how a war should be fought. Not a single life lost, unlike that butcher who called himself your father."

"Yes, it seems more Macedonians died here in the palace than on the battlefield." The barb in his voice wiped the smile from Olympias' face.

"I don't know what you mean," she blustered.

"Then let me enlighten you. Two infants and their mother slaughtered the minute my back is turned. Coming back to you now, is it?" He took his feet off the table and leaned forward to stare up at her. "It's bad enough you kill Caranus, Mother, but why did you also have to kill Eurydice and the girl?"

"I did it for you, my son. They were a threat." She looked around. "Aren't you going to ask me to sit down?"

Alexander exploded with rage. "They weren't a threat! Caranus was just a child, a baby!"

"Alex." She hadn't called him that since he'd been a child himself, and the hurt showed in her eyes. "Children are puppets to be manipulated by others; you know that as well as I. Caranus had to die eventually and the longer he lived, the more difficult it would have become. You've seen that with Amyntas. Your father spared him and now he threatens you."

Alexander grimaced. "Yes, I know that, Mother, and it's not so much that you killed Caranus as how you did it. You had him burned alive on a brazier, for all the gods!"

Olympias said nothing. She remained standing in front of her son, the king.

He drained his drinking cup, not taking his eyes off her. "Are you deliberately trying to turn the people against me, Mother? It seems like it. First, we had that farce in Aegae—yes, I heard about that. And now you make a mother watch as you roast her baby and strangle her daughter, and then force her to hang herself at the point of a sword. I'd have thought she'd welcome it after seeing her children die like that."

"She did," ventured Olympias, to her regret.

"I'm not surprised! Couldn't you have had the child suffocated in his sleep one night, or bribed the wet nurse to smear poison on her nipple? That's more your style and would have done the job just as well. And why kill the daughter? What threat to me was a girl?" He angrily sloshed his cup through a krater of wine and guzzled, deliberately letting the liquid dribble down his tunic.

"It was revenge, wasn't it? You wanted revenge on my father, and making his new wife watch as you tortured her children was that revenge. You did it out of spite. Well, let me tell you, Mother, that thanks to you, I've been branded a tyrant down in the agora.

The people of Pella assume I ordered it, and that the torture of innocent children was carried out in my name. Now I will have to travel back to Aegae and spend money I haven't got on a state funeral for Eurydice. Thankfully, the outer doors to my father's tomb are still unsealed, so I can lay her to rest there. Such an honor might help to appease the people."

Olympias hung her head. "I'm sorry, my son. I don't care what people think of me, but I should have realized you'd be blamed in my stead. You know that everything I do, I do for you, and you alone."

He stared at her as she stood with head bowed. She was middle-aged now, her face and body starting to sag. He was all she had. He heaved a sigh, the anger draining from him. "Yes, I know that, Mother, but try to be more discreet next time."

Two more would stain the snow with their blood in the coming weeks. Amyntas was tracked to a hut in the Pindos Mountains and died in a flurry of slashing swords. His assassins left the body for the crows, and the remarriage of his widow a few months later was taken as the announcement of his death.

Attalus did not survive him by long. A growing awareness that Parmenion was trying to keep his distance told the general his father-in-law must have done a deal, and prompted him into a desperate attempt at reconciliation with Alexander before it was too late. He turned over all the correspondence he had received from Demosthenes, as though warning the king of a plot against him. It gave Alexander and Hephaestion a good laugh as they read the letters, and then Alexander sent one of his own, telling Hecataeus to complete his mission and return home.

Attalus disappeared while hunting, apparently kidnapped by bandits. No ransom demand was received and his body was found a few days later, mutilated beyond recognition. He must have died a slow and painful death.

Chapter Eighteen

Pothos

"So, tell me about Xenocrates."

"Xenocrates?" Hephaestion's voice betrayed his confusion.

"Why is he writing to you? Did you think you could correspond with the principal of the Athenian Academy and I wouldn't hear about it?" Alexander sat up in bed. "I'm the King now, and inherited a whole network of spies and informers from my father."

Hephaestion said nothing for a moment, and then leaned on one elbow. "He writes to me occasionally, and I reply. He tells me news from Athens and I tell him about you." He laughed, a shallow laugh. "I didn't initiate it, and I can assure you there's nothing to it."

"Does Xenocrates know that? He was very taken with you that night in the Academy."

Hephaestion laughed again and rolled onto his back. "Probably not, but whatever he may have in mind, it's wishful thinking on his part. It's no different to your letters to Aristotle as far as I'm concerned."

Alexander smiled in the darkness. "That's not true. I intercepted and read your last one. We may both be writing to Athenian scholars, but your letters are more boring than mine." He nudged his lover in the ribs. "Just make sure it stays that way."

The confinement of the winter months gave Alexander the chance to become more comfortable with his new role. After two years of being out of favor, there were many new additions to the court he barely knew, but by keeping up the nightly tradition of feasting in the Great Hall, through choice as much as policy, he became acquainted with everyone who mattered.

Despite his promise that all would retain their previous positions, he managed to effect a few changes. Perdiccas and Craterus were made company commanders and each given command of a lochos of five hundred phalangites, while Nearchus was sent to join the fleet in Byzantium and learn the trade of seafaring. He also carried secret orders for the admiral.

Callisthenes, meanwhile, had quietly made a name for himself as a scholar with the publication of a text on Greek history. He and Marsyas, never comfortable as warriors, were appointed personal secretaries to the king. Harpalus, with his head for figures, became an assistant treasurer. The wands the appointees received as their badges of office provoked uproarious ridicule from their friends. The trio was glad when the novelty wore off.

Other promotions, Alexander was not so happy about. Key posts within the army were parceled out to the kinsmen of Parmenion as payment for his support. It gave the general an unwelcome position of power.

The spring thaw prompted the annual trampling of crops as the highland shepherds drove their flocks back into the mountains. The first reports of raids by Thracian war parties soon followed. It seemed the northern tribes had dismissed the success of Alexander's campaign the previous fall as beginner's luck, and were eager to emulate the sheep and trample the boy into the mud.

Alexander may have been young, but his men had few doubts as to his ability. Their new king had subjugated the southern cities by intelligence and daring, and they marched from their barracks in high spirits.

Leaving Antipatros as regent, Alexander led the army through eastern Macedonia to the Thracian border. At the sanctuary of Crestonia, he stopped to make sacrifice to Dionysus. The flame roared unusually high and a look of alarm crossed Alexander's face.

"Have no fear," announced Aristander. "Such a furnace can only be sent by the gods. It bodes well for the expedition." A relieved chuckle swept the ranks of watching Macedonians, but they may have been less heartened had they noticed the yellow stain on the priest's palm.

The army progressed through southern Thrace, picking up numbers of levies from the pacified tribes along the way. Lightly armed javelin men, these peltasts gave a cosmopolitan look to the army on the march, with their tattoos, long-handled swords and half-moon shields.

It took nine days to reach truly hostile territory, the Haemus Mountains. The highland tribes held the only pass and had drawn up a line of wagons along the rise, making a seemingly impregnable defensive position. Unlike the Vale of Tempe, there was no way around this time. A frontal assault was going to be costly, but Alexander had noticed something.

"Do you see?" he said to Philotas. "They've filled the wagons with rocks to weigh them down. They don't intend to stand behind them, but to roll them down on us as we advance." He thought quickly and called his officers to him.

"Coenus, tell your phalangites to spread themselves out into a loose formation on either flank. When the wagons roll, it will be up to each file to move aside and let them pass through. The hypaspists will take the center, in tight formation. They are to lay flat and link shields, and let the wagons roll over them."

It was an extremely unorthodox plan, drawing more than a few doubting looks.

"The men of the phalanx are the shock troops, sir. Shouldn't they be in the center?" queried Coenus. He was Parmenion's son-in-law, and one of the promotions forced on Alexander.

"Normally, yes, but the hypaspists have the larger shields. Those obols the phalangites carry would barely protect their heads." There was laughter, the comparison with the tiny coin making his point.

The phalangites advanced up the sides of the slope, their loose ranks the reverse of their usual stance. The hypaspists took the center, looking exposed and vulnerable. Jeering and catcalls floated down from the Thracians and they held high the severed heads that were their trophies. They expected a bloodbath.

A rumbling told the Macedonians the wagons were being unleashed, and they readied themselves. Although the maneuver they were about to attempt did not appear in any manual, years of experience gave them the ability to respond quickly to new situations.

The phalangites coolly opened their ranks to create an aisle for each wagon, some laughingly slapping their hands against the sides as they rattled by. The hypaspists didn't have it so easy. They flung themselves on the ground, some managing to link shields, but most flat with their shield across their back or curling into a ball beneath it. It wasn't perfect and there were a few cries as wheels crushed arms and legs, but it worked. The wagons bounced harmlessly over the prone men and clattered on down the slope to crash into trees or overturn on boulders.

The tattooed Thracians were already rushing forward, eager to deliver the killing blow in the wake of the devastation caused by the wagons. They stopped in their tracks, stunned as they saw the failure of their master plan. They weren't given the chance to recover. With a cry of "Alalalalai!" the Macedonian infantry rose up and were upon them, stabbing and slashing the lightly armored tribesmen. The Thracians had expected a bloodbath, and they got it.

The battle was over before Alexander had the chance to do more than lead the reserve up the slope. He rode on to join his men at the crest, to be greeted by rousing cheers. Hundreds of the enemy lay slaughtered and thousands more were fleeing in terror, while Macedonian losses amounted to no more than a few broken bones.

They pressed on, into the land of the Triballi. It was they who had ambushed Philip's wagon train and made off with his plunder, and the victory had made them arrogant.

A sizeable force moved in behind the Macedonians, cutting off their supply route. Alexander couldn't risk being trapped and immediately wheeled half his force around, finding the Triballians making camp in a glade. They melted into the trees upon sight of Alexander's scouts, daring the Macedonians to come in after them.

He sized up their position. His men would be forced to break formation as soon as they hit the tree line and, once inside, would be at a disadvantage in the fracas that would develop. He could imagine these woodsmen dropping down on his phalangites from the branches.

A plan formed in his brain. The favorite tactic of all the northern tribes was to blindly charge an enemy and, with a bit of coaxing, he was sure these Triballi could be flushed out into the open.

Keeping the rest of his troops hidden, he sent forward his archers with a screen of light infantry. The men took up position in the center of the clearing and began to rain down a cascade of arrows. The Triballi could only see a small force confronting them and it didn't take long for the enraged tribesmen to come bursting out of the woods, thirsting to take revenge on their tormentors.

The Macedonian trumpets blared at Alexander's command, unleashing the Companions in a headlong cavalry charge. It was another massacre.

Alexander turned again, and continued to harass the retreating Triballi as far as the banks of the Danube, the widest river the Macedonians had seen. It was the farthest north Philip had ever reached in his campaigns and Alexander's mapmakers could only provide hearsay evidence of what lay on the other side. The Triballi king had retreated to a heavily fortified village on an island in the middle of the river, but many of his men still lurked in the forest.

"Sir," said Cleitus, now a commander of the hypaspists. "We've taken hundreds of captives and thousands of horses and cattle. We should not risk them by pressing the Thracians further. We've already won two great victories. All that's needed now is to squeeze a treaty of friendship out of this Triballian king and return home with the booty." He smiled at the king, as though that would swing the argument.

Alexander smiled back, and shook his head. He looked around the tent, his father's grand pavilion. The representatives of his officers were gathered in front of him, a deputation sent to persuade him not to press his luck too far.

"The enemy may have lost a battle or two," he answered, "but they haven't been defeated. They need to be convinced of our superiority if they're to stay behind their borders once the army is in Anatolia. They have to be taught a lesson."

As if on cue, a commotion on the river interrupted him. He followed Cleitus and the others outside to watch the arrival of the Macedonian fleet, fifteen sleek war galleys filling the river from bank to bank. The officers stared in open-mouthed astonishment while troops ran along the riverbank, whooping and cheering their glee.

"You arranged for the fleet to meet us here?" queried Cleitus.

Alexander nodded, a hint of smugness on his lips. "I knew the northern tribes were bound to attack us this spring and we'd end up on this river bank at some point, so I sent Nearchus to Byzantium last winter with orders for the fleet to secure the river. Gentlemen, we will teach the Triballi they cannot escape us, even on an island."

He began to regret his confident statement over the next few days. Loading troops onto the ships wasn't a problem, but unloading them onto the island proved to be impossible. The current was too swift, the bank too steep, the stockade too high, and the Macedonian infantry were under a constant bombardment of javelins and slingshot and arrows. The attack stalled.

A new plan formed in Alexander's mind and he called his officers to his tent. "Have you seen how the Triballi on the far bank are ferrying supplies over to the island?" he asked.

"Those are not Triballi, sir. According to the Thracian levies, a tribe called the Getae occupies the other side of the river." It was Nicanor, elder brother of Philotas and another of the appointments forced on Alexander by his deal with Parmenion.

Alexander smiled. "Even more reason for what I plan, then. We must prove to these barbarians that it's not worth tangling with us, but they'll never end their raiding if they think they can escape across the river whenever we come after them." He sat on his father's portable throne, in the same tent his father had used on campaign, addressing the same officers his father had led—but he would take them farther.

"I propose leading a force across the river to drive the enemy from the far bank and cut the island off. This Triballian king will soon surrender when his people are starving, and it will prove the river is no barrier to Macedonian vengeance."

The army had never attempted a crossing of a river this wide in combat, and there were several doubtful looks. "How will we land?" asked Cleitus. "We'll have the same problems as on the island. They'll cut us down as we try to get ashore."

"But they won't be waiting for us." Alexander smiled, enjoying the confused looks on the faces of his officers; he was his father. "We'll cross at night and they'll wake to find us already in their midst. I see some of you have doubts. Well, who here has read the Anabasis?"

They all had. Xenophon's classic tale of how he'd led his army out of Persia was required reading for a Macedonian officer. A few smiles appeared as they realized what their leader was proposing.

"We won't be using our ships," continued Alexander. "They'll spend the night beached on our side of the river to mislead the enemy, while we'll emulate Xenophon and cross on rafts made from tent covers stuffed with straw. We have it easier in fact, for we've also captured a number of the enemy's canoes and can use them."

The meeting broke up without further argument and the officers went to organize their men. Their new king's audacity seemed to be growing with every new problem, but they were already learning that it paid to blindly follow his lead.

Alexander stood with Hephaestion at the entrance to his tent, watching as a group of phalangites sat in a semi-circle and pushed bundles of hay into one of the covers they used for protecting their tents on the march, and as a flysheet when encamped.

"They're not happy, are they?" he said.

"I think you can say that," answered Hephaestion, a wry smile on his face. "I heard that places on the canoes are changing hands for ridiculous sums. Nobody wants to trust their life to a piece of stuffed leather."

"Do you think I'm being foolish?"

"No, but I wonder how long our luck can last." Hephaestion considered his words before continuing. "Do we really need to cross the river? This could turn into a terrible disaster."

"I know, and I cannot explain it." Alexander's gaze turned to the far bank. "I don't know why, but I have to cross that river. I have to see what's on the other side."

Hephaestion stared at him for a long time before asking, "What do you mean?"

Alexander pursed his lips. "I mean that I cannot help myself. Think of it, Hephaestion. No Macedonian has gone beyond where we're standing today. Call it no more than a longing, a pothos, to go that one step farther, but I must set foot on that far bank." He stared into Hephaestion's eyes. "And I'm willing to risk my army to do it."

Hephaestion said nothing in reply, but would remember those words in the years to come, as Alexander's pothos led his army farther and farther into the unknown. And they would suffer for it.

The crossing was smoother than he could have hoped. They crossed upstream, at a point where the river narrowed and a field of corn on the far bank hid them from view. Within two hours, so many troops had crossed they were spilling over into the cornfield, and more were on their way. The fortunate few occupied the hollowed-out logs that passed for Thracian canoes, while the rest balanced on their makeshift rafts and paddled furiously against the current. Each canoe brought an additional passenger, a terrified horse of the Companion cavalry tethered to its stern.

The sheer mass of men on the far bank was becoming a problem and something had to be done quickly or the very success of the crossing would be the cause of its downfall. Alexander summoned Craterus to him, the man squeezing through the throng to reach the king.

"Craterus, we need to clear a path through that cornfield. Get a file of your phalangites to the front and form them into a line. I want them to advance holding their sarissae like this." He clutched his hands to his groin. "Tell them to imagine they're back in the brothels in Dium."

Craterus laughed and went to organize his men. They advanced in line with their sarissae held out obliquely in front of them, the shafts cutting a swathe through the cornfield and a column of men falling in behind.

They emerged onto an open plain as the first rays of the sun streaked the sky pink and the cockerels of the Getae greeted the new day. Spreading out, the Macedonians quickly formed into their units while Alexander mounted Bucephalus and rode out in front of his troops, as though on parade. Were it not for the Thracian peltasts in their midst, they could have been drilling on the plains of Macedonia.

A figure emerged from some far woods, spotted them, and ran back into the trees. A jeer of laughter rose from the assembled men. A mounted scout appeared within a few minutes, staring at the invaders in shocked disbelief.

More Getae appeared, first the horse archers that were their specialty, then the foot soldiers. They clumsily formed a ragged line at the edge of the wood, looking as though they'd just risen from their beds.

The phalanx advanced in the center, a screen of archers in front. A few Getae rode forward to loose off the odd arrow, but they were still too surprised for any concerted action. Alexander stood on the right at the head of the Companions. He could see more tribesmen streaming through the trees and knew that the longer he waited, the stronger and better organized they would become. He raised his lance and led his men into battle.

The Getae horse archers crumpled in the face of the Macedonian cavalry, barging each other as they frantically tried to turn their mounts. The Companions hit them head on, Alexander leading the wedge that was the cavalry's standard attack formation. A Getae back presented itself and he drove his lance in, the point jarring against the man's spine. He drew his sword and slashed the rump of an enemy pony, then hacked off the head of its owner with one stroke.

The enemy infantry could not stand alone in the face of the massed pikes of the advancing phalanx. They joined the scramble to escape, and learned the harsh lesson that any fleeing army discovered—losses were multiplied tenfold when you turned your backs to the enemy.

The slaughter continued through the wood and into the Getae encampment beyond. A few tribesmen tried to make a stand but the Companions relentlessly rode down anyone who dared to turn and fight. The Triballi lined the banks of their island and watched the massacre in stunned silence. Alexander was aware of them and urged his men on. He was making a point, not just to the Triballi, but every northern tribe. He wanted them to fear him.

The Macedonians reached a hill fort, taking it without a fight. The Getae were only interested in escape now. Those with horses fled the fort with wives clinging to their mount's cruppers; those on foot abandoned their women altogether.

Alexander finally called a halt to the chase. It would be too easy for the army to become strung out and vulnerable were he to pursue the Getae onto the steppe. It had happened to his father and he wouldn't let it happen to him.

He made his headquarters in the chieftain's hut and called his officers together.

"We're going to burn the fort," he announced, "then withdraw to the river and use the fleet to cross back to the other side." He grinned. "We'll be in full view of the Triballi, so use parade order to board your men. We want to impress, don't we?" Chuckles greeted his words.

Philotas spoke up. "Sir, our sergeants report we haven't lost a single man. I think our worst injury is a stubbed toe." He led the officers in their applause.

The army withdrew to the banks of the Danube and set up an altar. They sacrificed to Zeus, then to Hercules, and then to the spirit of the river, thanking them for the success of the operation. Dozens of Getae cattle were slaughtered and distributed to the men. They feasted facing the island, and the watching Triballi.

The return went smoothly and they were sat around their own campfires by nightfall, having looted or destroyed everything of value on the other side of the river. The Triballi were left to contemplate the plumes of smoke that rose from every field of corn and every vegetable patch, the food that would have sustained them in the coming siege.

They surrendered the next day. Their king was rowed across to the Macedonian camp on the same simple type of log canoe that had proved so successful in getting Alexander's men across the river. Far from being crucified, the Triballian was greeted at the bank by Philotas and conducted to the royal tent, where he was wined and dined by the Macedonian king. By the time he returned to his people, the two kings had sworn an oath of undying loyalty. Alexander also exacted a contribution of archers to the Persian expedition. They would be the hostages that guaranteed that undying loyalty.

As word spread of the Macedonian feat, so the Triballi proved to be only the first of a succession of Thracian chieftains to visit the camp. Barely a day went by that Alexander didn't play host to yet another tribal leader, eager to come to an understanding with this new Macedonian king. The Danube hadn't been crossed by an invader since a Persian army had spanned it in the days of Darius, and for too long the Thracians had believed it to be an impregnable barrier. Now Alexander had crossed without even the aid of a bridge. He'd scared them, and he reveled in it.

Word reached him that a new delegation had arrived, the tallest men the Macedonian sentries had seen. They proclaimed themselves to be of the Celts, from the shores of the Adriatic. Their lands lay far to the north, well beyond any threat from Macedonia. Alexander was intrigued. It seemed his fame was spreading.

The five men were ushered into Alexander's tent, greeted, and invited to sit on stools in the tribal fashion. They were indeed tall, even by Macedonian standards, and towered over Alexander. He was glad of the throne with its raised base.

He opened the proceedings. "I must say, gentlemen, that I'm rather surprised by your visit. I hadn't realized you knew of us so far north, and you have me at a disadvantage. I know nothing of your people." But he did know they were there because they'd heard of his exploits, and he was angling for a compliment.

The Celts didn't take the hook. "Your recent victory brought you to our attention, sir," explained the senior Celt, dismissively.

"Which must explain why I haven't heard of you." Alexander couldn't help himself.

The Celt smiled through his beard. "I am sure you will in time, sir. Meanwhile, we may not be neighbors, but are separated by common enemies." He spread his arms expansively. "It is my hope that our two nations can forge a treaty of friendship and mutual trust."

"That is my desire also." Alexander stood up and ordered a steward to refill the Celt's drinking cups, glad he was finally taller than them. "In Greece, gentlemen, we swear an oath to the gods and inscribe it on a tablet of marble. What is the custom in your own lands?"

The senior Celt stood and looked down at the little Macedonian. "We will swear the oath only, sir. We have little use for the written word." He glanced at his companions and said something in a guttural language; they all rose. Alexander hurriedly bid his attendant officers to get to their feet.

"In the name of our gods of the forest," said the Celt, "and of your gods of Olympus, I swear to uphold the friendship between the Celtic and Macedonian races, upon pain of eternal damnation."

"We shall keep faith," all five Celts chanted in unison, "until the sky shall fall and crush us, or the earth shall open and swallow us, or the sea shall rise and engulf us."

Alexander raised his opened palms in the sign of supplication. "I, Alexander, King of Macedonia, swear to uphold our friendship in the name of our mutual gods. Mighty Zeus, I shall keep faith until . . ." He glanced up at the Celt. "Which calamity do you fear most?"

The man smiled. "That the sky shall fall."

"Until the sky shall fall," finished Alexander. It was a most unorthodox oath, but neither side worried that much. They knew they'd never see each other again.

Alexander watched the Celts mount their ponies and join the escort that would take them as far as the Haemus Mountains. "So their worst fear is that the sky shall fall, is it?" he announced. "What braggarts, to imply they don't fear me." Phrygius exchanged a grin with Ptolemy as they followed Alexander into his tent.

The army would take the long way home. Illyrian chieftains had been conspicuous in their absence from the list of tribes swearing friendship to Alexander, and a show of strength along their borders would not go amiss.

His men had campaigned long enough, decided Alexander, so he would avoid a fight by traveling through the lands of his ally, King Langarus of the Agrianes. The Illyrian king had maintained ties since Alexander had been his guest in exile, and had even supplied a contingent of troops to the campaign against the Thracians. Alexander would now escort those troops home, and take the opportunity to reward his friend with a share of the captured Getae cattle. And if the neighboring tribes were to take note of the benefits of co-operation, then so much the better.

They had been on the march for only a few days when a messenger from Antipatros found them, urging Alexander to return the army to Macedonia as quickly as possible. It seemed the Illyrians saw his absence as a chance to seize back the lands that had been lost to Philip, and three tribes had forged an alliance. The new king was facing his greatest challenge since assuming the throne.

He would still be heading in the right general direction, so Alexander continued with his original plan to meet with King Langarus. The purpose had changed however, and no longer would it be a mere reunion with an old friend but a request for the loan of more of his fine infantrymen.

They met within the week, the Agriane king riding out from his own lands to intercept the Macedonian force. Alexander greeted him at the entrance to his tent, the partitioned pavilion he'd inherited from his father.

Langarus viewed the interior, remarking with a grin that Alexander seemed to have done well for himself. The two men sat on stools of the same height, Alexander pointedly ignoring his throne. Drinks were served, and then they got down to business.

"What can you tell me, Langarus? All I know from Antipatros is that King Cleitus has crossed the border and captured the fortress of Pelium, and now his Dardanians are encamped there in force."

"Cleitus has recruited King Glaucias and his Taulantians, and their combined force will invade Macedonia as soon as Glaucias reaches Pelium. Meanwhile, the Autaratians have agreed to block the trails and delay your advance long enough for the other two to join up. Then they will fall back to Pelium, and you will face all three tribes."

Alexander looked grim; it was worse than he thought. "The other two tribes I know, but the Autaratians are new to me. Are they fighters?"

"They're an ugly mob, but no fighters. It's Cleitus and his Dardanians who are the warriors in that alliance."

"Then how far away are the Autaratians, and in what strength? The key to this campaign is to keep the tribes apart, so I must defeat the Dardanians before the Taulantii arrive, and I will miss my chance if the Autaratians are able to delay me." He began to rise, ready to give the orders to break camp. "If it's they we must face first, then the sooner we do so, the better. A quick strike will stop any chance of them slowing my advance."

Langarus also rose. "You concentrate on getting to Pelium and leave the Autaratians to me. My men will be better at tracking them through the forest than your townies, and we'll do to them what they intended doing to you. Do you need more men? I'll give you my bodyguard regiment, if you like. I can defeat the Autaratians without them."

Alexander grinned. "If you're sure you can spare them, then I gladly take you up on your offer. Your men fight well and I'd already disbanded a number of my Thracian levies before learning of this new threat."

He took the Illyrian's arm. "It's a good friend, Langarus, who does not desert in times of trouble. I shall not forget this. Once the enemy is defeated, we'll cement our friendship by blood. My father gave me several half-sisters by his other wives and I shall send you the prettiest, Cynane." He didn't add that Cynane was newly available as the widow of Amyntas and, officially at least, still married to the missing man.

Langarus laughed and slapped him on the shoulder, misreading the reason for the surprised looks on the faces of the watching Macedonian officers. "Judging by the women I saw during my time in Pella," he announced for their benefit, "send me a donkey instead. It'll be better looking and a lot more useful." Alexander laughed too, and the assembled officers diplomatically followed his lead.

Langarus would be as good as his word, ambushing each of the Autaratian war parties as they emerged from the safety of their hill forts. But he would never add Cynane to his list of wives. Shortly after returning home, he fell ill and died.

Alexander continued on to Pelium at high speed. The booty from the Thracian campaign had long since been dispatched back to Macedonia and he continued his father's policy of using pack animals instead of wagons to keep the army mobile, even on the quagmires that passed for tracks in the forests and valleys of Paeonia.

Confident that the Autaratians were no longer a threat to his progress, he only concerned himself with defeating Cleitus and his Dardanians before the arrival of the Taulantii. He'd never had cause to visit Pelium before but knew it by repute. The fortress had defended the Macedonian borderlands for generations, and to have lost it to a Dardanian night raid was a blow.

Pelium stood at the head of a long, thin valley and commanded a major trade route into Macedonia. The fortress was surrounded on three sides by thickly wooded mountains and could only be approached from the front along a narrow path known as the Wolf's Pass. The location was a garrison commander's dream. A river meandered through the valley, forcing aggressors to first negotiate a ford and then fight their way through the pass, with the river on one side and a solid wall of rock on the other. Finally, the attackers emerged into a large tract of open ground in front of the fortress, only to find themselves ringed by the forested foothills, from where well-placed defenders could rain down missiles on them as they tried to form up after leaving the confines of the pass.

Aware of the defenses he faced, Alexander decided to stop short of Pelium and rest his army before beginning the assault on the fortress the next day. Barely had his men begun to pull their tents from the leather covers when the scouts galloped in to report that a sizeable number of Dardanian tribesmen were gathered in the open on the wrong side of the river. A quick attack now could substantially reduce the defender's strength.

He wasted no time in leading the Companion cavalry out of the camp at speed, but the Dardanians spotted them as soon as they emerged into the valley and easily fell back across the river, leaving only a few brave hearts to form a delaying skirmishing line. The Macedonians mowed them down.

Disappointed, Alexander called off any pursuit. To cross the ford and enter the pass without support would be tempting disaster. It was barely wide enough for infantry to march four abreast, let alone take cavalry down there. He would advance no farther that night.

"Cassander, ride back to camp and order up the catapults; I shall want the walls breached before I try any frontal assaults tomorrow. Then find Nicanor and tell him to ready his lochos to be first across the river in the morning. They will have the honor of leading us into Pelium." He doubted though, that a single lochos of five hundred hypaspists would be enough to carry the fortress.

A Companion cavalryman rode up to the group, a disgusted look on his face. "Come and see what we've found, sir." They followed him back down the valley to where the Dardanians had first been assembled.

The tribesmen had been disturbed in the middle of a sacrificial ceremony. Three black rams had been slaughtered and consumed, their horned skulls ritually mounted on poles. But the Macedonian's eyes were drawn to the large slab of rock that served as an altar. Around the rock lay sprawled the bodies of six children, three boys and three girls. The infants had had their throats cut, and the last must have been killed in a hurry as the priest fled the oncoming Macedonians. The boy lay with his hands raised to his throat; he'd lived long enough to know his death.

Alexander had seen human sacrifice during his time in exile with King Langarus, but this Illyrian trait was new to the rest. "Gentlemen," he proclaimed. "This is what will happen to Macedonian children if we let these vermin invade our lands." From the looks on the faces of the assembled Macedonians, the slave market in Pella would not be benefiting from this campaign.

Nicanor led his men across the ford at daybreak and found little opposition from the defenders, who resorted to no more than delaying tactics before falling back into the fortress. By midday, the whole army was across and encamped on the plain before Pelium, with the siege engines eagerly being unloaded from the mules and assembled. Alexander was ecstatic.

"The fool!" he told everyone within hearing. "This King Cleitus can have no idea about tactics. I would have had archers defending the ford, heavy infantry in the pass, and light infantry hurling down rocks from the cliff above." His arm swept the foothills surrounding them. "And these woods would be infested with anyone who could carry a bow or a spear or a sling."

The pack animals were sent back down the pass to graze in the outer valley. Supplies were becoming dangerously low, so Philotas went with them to conduct a foraging expedition. It was important that food be found soon, but there was little on offer from the few huts that dotted the valley, and the local game had been hunted to extinction over the years by the garrison at Pelium. Philotas' men were reduced to picking berries on the edge of the forest.

Suddenly the air whooshed with the flight of arrows and a fruit-picker fell, skewered through the calf. His comrades pulled him to his feet and they fled back to where the muleteers frantically tried to muster their animals. Tribesmen spilled out of the forest. The guards at the ford saw what was happening and a rider galloped back through the pass with the news. The Taulantii had arrived.

Philotas and his men were still trying to round up wayward mules and point them toward the ford as Alexander splashed across the river at the head of a rescue party of Companions. The Taulantians took one look at the heavily armed cavalrymen and faded back into the trees. They knew better than to stand against horsemen in the open.

Within the hour, the pack animals were safe within the camp, but Alexander paced his tent, a worried man. His army was cut off and their supplies almost exhausted. They could not stay, and to fight their way out would incur massive losses. Even worse, the sentries were reporting that small groups of the Taulantii were slipping across the river and disappearing into the foothills, and lights had been seen high in the mountains so more must be coming in over goat paths known only to the locals. By morning, the camp would be under a deluge of missile fire. He'd led his men into a trap.

Above all else, he felt anger at having been so easily outmaneuvered by an illiterate tribesman. He'd called King Cleitus a fool, but now he knew the Dardanian had deliberately abandoned his outer defenses to draw the Macedonians onto the plain.

"You're the fool," he said aloud. "You underestimated your enemy."

He should have realized the Dardanians were giving up their defenses too easily and questioned why. The answer would have been obvious: the Taulantians were close and Cleitus was sucking him in deeper to make the trap more complete. He laughed aloud, a mocking laugh. To think he'd spent an hour on positioning the catapults because he'd wanted to lessen the losses in the assault.

The hypaspists should have been sent against the walls of the fortress immediately.

He sat down and closed his eyes. He was outnumbered and surrounded, and his one advantage was the training and discipline of his troops against the unruliness of the enemy. How would his father have dealt with this? Or Xenophon? How would Aristotle have used his categories to solve it?

His mind drifted back to those balmy days at the sanctuary in Mieza and the tutor lisping, "All problems can be solved logically, boys, with just a few simple steps. Now what is the substance of this particular problem, Alexander?"

He smiled in remembrance, and then the smile widened into a grin.

His officers were incredulous at the plan but had none of their own, and so it was that they went from tent to tent to explain the king's strategy to their equally incredulous men. None, but Alexander, expected it to succeed.

At first light, Coenus assembled his battalion on the open ground in front of the fortress. The Dardanians, expecting imminent attack, manned the walls and readied themselves for battle. The Taulantians in the surrounding forests picked up their spears and bows, and grinned at each other. They had the Macedonians in a trap and the head count would be great.

And they waited. As the time passed, so a few taunts began to issue from the walls and the forests, but still they waited. Then Alexander appeared, riding upon Bucephalus and leading a long column of the Companion cavalry out of the camp. He rode to face the center of the phalanx while the Companions filed to either side and formed up on each wing.

The king faced Coenus' battalion of over a thousand men, drawn up in ranks one hundred and twenty men wide, while two troops of two hundred Companions stood on either flank. It was as though they were parading on the plain outside Pella, with citizens thronging the walls to view the spectacle.

Alexander nodded to Coenus, the nod traveling imperceptibly through the ranks to the file-closers in the rear. This was to be a display of Macedonian discipline, and shouted orders would spoil the performance.

Coenus raised an arm and the Macedonians came to the attention as one, the Companions raising their lances in salute and the men of the phalanx hoisting their sarissae high upon their shoulders. With one step, they advanced upon Alexander. When it seemed they would run him down, they spun to the left and marched in column. Just short of the trees, they turned again, striding down the side of the plain in line abreast. Now the phalangites were swinging their sarissae from shoulder to shoulder, a single swishing sound joining the tramping of their feet and the trotting hooves of the Companion's horses.

They turned about and marched back toward Alexander. He sat astride Bucephalus with his head facing forward, but his eyes swiveled to the side. He could see the Taulantii appearing at the edge of the forest, some even creeping into the open for a closer look at this phenomenon. As he'd hoped, for men who fought as a mob and competed with each other in acts of bravado, this display of uniformity was a sight they could not comprehend.

The Macedonians paraded across the plain. First in one direction, then another, wheeling left, then right, turning about, moving from line abreast to column and then back into line. All the time, in silence save for the steady tramp, tramp of their feet and the swishing of the sarissae. Not a man was out of step, not a horse broke into a canter, not a pike swung out of line.

Alexander kept his eye on the Taulantii. Scores were now lining the edge of the forest, some striding up and down with their spears aloft in mockery of the phalangites, others laughing and hooting derision, most standing in awed silence. Some were even beginning to sit on the grass. The time was right.

Alexander drew his sword. Instantly, a waiting trumpeter blew a single note and the Macedonian war cry screamed from a thousand throats, "Alalalalai!" It was followed by the sound of a thousand phalangites battering sarissae against shields and the Companions breaking into the gallop. The valley echoed with the noise, deafening after the silence that had preceded it, and the natives blanched with fear.

Already the Companions were thundering into the tribesmen on both wings. The phalanx charged the center, their sarissae gripped in both hands, points leveled at Taulantian stomachs. The Taulantii turned and ran, dropping spears and bows in their haste to escape the oncoming wall of death. Their only option was to climb the slope, scrambling over rocks and ripping flesh on brambles. Alone and in groups, they eventually stumbled to a halt, panting and shocked, their fear turning to shame and then rage.

They had run too far and would take too long to return, as Alexander had planned. The Macedonian camp had quietly been prepared for evacuation all through the preceding night, with pegs removed from tents, mules loaded with cooking utensils, pins loosened on catapults. Now the baggage train was already on the move. A mule entered the pass, loaded with a tent that had been hastily collapsed and thrust into its leather cover. Another followed, braying loudly as it took the weight of half a dismantled catapult on its back.

And they moved through the pass. The hypaspists led the way, clearing the few Taulantians who found themselves unfortunate enough to have run the wrong way. Coenus would provide the rearguard with his elated phalangites.

At the river, a wooded slope still harbored a number of Taulantii. Their task was to guard the ford and they were oblivious to the drama that had been played out on the other side of the pass. From their vantage point, they commanded the approach to the ford. They had to be moved if the baggage train was to cross.

Alexander led the Companions in the charge, sweeping toward the enemy with lance extended and bodyguard struggling to keep up. The Taulantii took one look at the mass of cavalry advancing toward them, and ran. Alexander held the ford.

He called Cleitus to him.

"Get your men across the ford and form them up to the left, facing the river. If necessary, be prepared to send some back over to me. It'll take at least an hour to get the mules across and that's more than enough time for the Illyrians to get their breath back." He grinned, still barely believing his ruse had worked. "I doubt they'll let us leave completely unscathed."

He scanned the heights for any sign of a counterattack. He had the Companions and Langarus' force of Agrianes with him on the hill, while a company of archers waited by the ford, some two thousand men in all. He hoped it would be enough. Coenus' phalangites were only just beginning to emerge from the pass, with reports that the Dardanians were pouring out of the fortress and the Taulantii were streaming back down the slopes. Both tribes were massing on the plain and would not stay there long.

The last of the baggage train had reached the other side and Coenus was pulling his men across the ford. Only Craterus' company now remained in the pass, but they were coming under increasing pressure from enraged and emboldened tribesmen. Alexander could see figures moving down from the higher slopes and knew he was running out of time.

"Hephaestion, tell Cleitus to set up the catapults, with orders to pick off any chieftains they see. Anything that slows the enemy down will help right now." He'd seen the crewmen on the bolt-shooters in training, and they were expert enough to hit a shield from several stadium lengths.

Hephaestion hesitated. "Cleitus is on the other side." Alexander had already turned to other matters and didn't hear him. Hephaestion stared at his back for a moment, then pulled at his horse's reins and set off for the ford.

A troop of Taulantii horsemen thundered out of the trees and charged the Macedonian position, scattering some of the Agrianes. Alexander met them head on, once more leading the Companions in the charge. A tribesman fell, clutching at the lance that protruded from his stomach, and Alexander barely drew his sword in time to parry a blow from a Taulantii spear. His bodyguards closed around him and he found himself excluded from the fighting by their horses. He could only watch as the Companions galloped past and Phrygius locked swords with a Taulantii warrior. The two men struggled face to face, and a grubby native fist reached out and grasped at Phrygius' beard, pulling him down and across the back of the tribesman's horse. The hilt of the Taulantian's sword crashed down on the nape of his neck and Alexander heard the groan.

Cassander took the tribesman with a single lunge of his lance, but too late; Phrygius was already sliding to the ground. Alexander leapt from Bucephalus and knelt down beside him. He was alive, but his neck was cricked and he was struggling to breathe. Alexander had spent enough evenings studying anatomy in Aristotle's shed to know that Phrygius had a broken neck.

They got him back to the hill and a party of Agrianes stretchered him across the river. It was the first time one of Alexander's original clique of companions had suffered a major injury, but he didn't have time to dwell on the fate of his friend. The number of Taulantii emerging from the slopes was becoming overwhelming. It was time to leave or be massacred.

He led his men down to the river and watched them splash into the ford. A "thwump" made him spin around, in time to see a Taulantian chieftain skewered by a metal bolt. He glanced across the river. The three bolt-shooters had been unloaded and partially assembled, and two of the stone-throwers were being set up. With every second, more and more men were reaching the safety of the far bank.

But the Dardanians were spilling out of the pass and joining with the Taulantii on the slopes, presenting a solid front. They had to be kept back long enough for the last of Craterus' company to reach the ford. He turned Bucephalus and splashed into the water himself, shouting at those archers who were still midway across. "Turn and fire! Turn and fire!"

They obeyed without question, standing knee-deep in the ford and loosing off arrow after arrow until their quivers were empty. Craterus' phalangites streamed past them, reaching the far side and immediately turning to form up into a phalanx.

"Get across, sir," an archer roared at Alexander. The king became aware of just how few of his men remained in the ford and did as his nameless subject commanded. The archer followed, the last man to cross.

The two armies stood and stared at each other across the river, one with grins on their faces and jeers of derision on their lips, the other realizing how deeply the dead were piled around them, and how none of the bodies seemed to be wearing Macedonian uniforms.

The catapults were repacked and the army formed into columns for the march. They left as if on a victory parade. The Companions brought up the rear, ready to turn if any Illyrian tribesman dared to step into the ford before they were out of sight.

Phrygius died during the night and was cremated the next morning, wrapped in the yellow cloak of the Companions. Alexander appeared clean-shaven at the funeral, and all but the Agriane tribesmen and a few of the most grizzled veterans had shaved off their beards by the time they broke camp to resume the march.

Hephaestion rubbed his chin ruefully. "I feel like an Athenian dandy now. Do you think the men will keep it up?"

"They will," replied Alexander, "like it or not. I'm going to include it in army orders when we get back to Pella. If it saves just one life, then it will be worth the grumbling. I shan't lose another man so needlessly."

They rode on in silence for a while, and then Hephaestion asked, "When we were at the river, why did you choose me to carry the orders to Cleitus?"

"Why not you? I had to send someone."

"Yes, but why me? Was it to get me across the river and out of danger?"

Alexander glanced around. "Of course not."

They made camp that night and stayed put for two days, foraging for food and readying themselves for battle on a field of Alexander's choosing. When the scouts could find no sign of a pursuing enemy force on the track behind them, Alexander began to suspect the Illyrians believed him to be fleeing headlong into Macedonia.

He was right. The scouts ventured all the way back to Pelium and found the two tribes still celebrating their victory. The Taulantians had taken over the vacated Macedonian campsite and a massive drinking party was taking place on the plain in front of the fortress. So confident were they that they'd seen off the enemy, they weren't even bothering to post sentries.

It was too good an opportunity to miss. Leaving Philotas to follow with the rest of the army, Alexander raced back to the valley with a scratch force of hypaspists, Agrianes and archers. The ford was unguarded, as the scouts had said.

They waited until dark and then crept down the Wolf's Pass, hearing the revelry from the Taulantian camp long before it came into view. Alexander spread his men along the edge of the forest, whispering orders to each group. The Agrianes were to move through the camp, the archers would cut down those who tried to escape, and the hypaspists were to surge through the open gates of the fortress. Meanwhile, they waited for the camp to subside.

It was a mild, moonless, summer night, with dew already forming on the ground and the hoots of owls in the trees, and Alexander unleashed the Agrianes. They slipped silently into the camp, moving from tent to campfire to tent, slitting the throats of the sleeping and the drunk, with the odd, muffled, death rattle the only trace of their presence.

Alexander waited with the hypaspists, impatient to get into action but knowing the longer the Agrianes remained undetected, the more Taulantii were already dead. Finally, a shout emanated from the camp and Alexander urged his men forward.

The hypaspists dashed through the fortress gates and began the business of slaughtering groggy-looking tribesmen as they stumbled out of the huts that made up this border town.

"King Cleitus is mine," shouted Alexander, leading his bodyguard toward the garrison commander's block and guessing, rightly, that the Dardanian king had requisitioned it as his own. But Cleitus didn't wait. He slipped quickly through a postern gate, leaving his men to their fate.

The killing continued until mid-morning, Alexander not breaking off the chase until the mountain that marked Taulantii territory came into view. The Macedonians collected themselves together and, suddenly weary, began the trek back down to the valley. Their tunics were smeared with blood and tribesmen littered the undergrowth at every step.

They were greeted with cheering as they emerged onto the plain to find Coenus leading the phalanx through the pass. Alexander accepted their accolade and permitted the building of a trophy from the discarded Taulantian weapons. He had won yet again, and the border with Illyria was secure.

Chapter Nineteen

The Lion of Macedonia

The army packed their equipment and began the march home. They'd been on campaign for almost six months and desperately needed to rest, so Alexander didn't hurry the pace. He'd already lingered in Pelium for several days, letting the men relax and negotiating the surrender of the Illyrian tribes. The terms, as always, were generous, and King Cleitus and King Glaucias arrived together to swear the now customary oath of friendship with Alexander.

Two days into the march, and a messenger from Antipatros found the army still encamped on the border. Alexander retired to the privacy of his bedchamber to read the dispatch, and it was worse than he could have feared. Demosthenes was once again busy in the Assembly, convincing his fellow citizens that Alexander's prolonged absence in the north must be because he was dead. He'd even produced a bandaged and bloodied soldier who told how he'd seen the king fall in battle with the Triballians.

Encouraged by Athens' lead, Thebes was now in open revolt. The commander of the Macedonian garrison had been killed in a carefully planned ambush and the garrison besieged. They had plentiful supplies and held the Cadmea, the ancient fortress that dominated the city, but were heavily outnumbered and could not hold out forever. Athens was promising to send troops to aid the rebels, and there was even talk of Persian gold.

Alexander's face was grim as he read the final piece of news. The Great King had reinforced Memnon's army and demanded he push the Macedonian invaders all the way back to the Hellespont.

The mercenary had succeeded too well and Parmenion now held little more than a strip of land along the coast. If he lost that too, the ten thousand men in Anatolia would be annihilated and Alexander would be reduced to fighting his way ashore when, or even if, he attempted the invasion.

He finished reading and sat for a few minutes with his head in his hands, then stood up, squared his shoulders, and walked through to the outer chamber of his pavilion. He passed the letter to Philotas to read out to the waiting officers, and watched their faces as they listened.

"Gentlemen," he said as Philotas finished. "I blame myself. I knew the dangers of spending too long in the north and I, at least, should have returned to Pella from time to time." He smiled and added, "Or ensured there were a few Athenian spies in our ranks. Had they been reporting our victories, we could have prevented all this." The customary titter of polite laughter was noticeably subdued, but he didn't let it daunt him.

"I know it sounds bad, gentlemen, but it's no worse than the position we found ourselves in upon the death of my father. And there's good news as well, if you think about it. Antipatros says Athens has promised troops to Thebes but has yet to actually dispatch any. Obviously, cooler heads in the Assembly are not convinced by the rantings of Demosthenes, and are waiting to see what happens first. They may be willing to encourage Thebes, but not to go too far themselves until they're certain I'm dead. And that's our advantage, gentlemen; I'm alive."

Only Philotas smiled dutifully.

"We can do nothing to aid Parmenion while Thebes is in revolt," continued Alexander, "so there's no doubt they are the priority. We march for Thebes, and quickly, for the longer we allow them to get away with it, the more chance Athens will commit itself to arms. We only need subdue one city to silence the other." His voice hardened. "And this time, I shall ensure that neither Thebes, nor anyone else, dares rebel against me again. I have been lenient for far too long."

Less than two weeks later, the army stood on the plain before Thebes. The march from Illyria had been far too fast and over terrain that would have exhausted the freshest of men, but there'd been no choice. Alexander had to make his presence known in the south or risk losing the whole of Greece.

As it was, he reached the plains of Boeotia before the Thebans were even aware of his coming. When the news spread, they failed to believe it, insisting it must be Antipatros marching from Pella, then that if it was an Alexander, it must be his son-in-law; Alexandros of Lyncestis must now be the king. Only when the army encamped outside their gates and they saw the fair-haired Alexander ride out on Bucephalus did they believe that their nemesis stood before them.

Alexander smiled as he stared back at the crowds lining the walls, feeling more confident now than any time since he'd received Antipatros' letter. He'd deliberately taken the inland route from Illyria, avoiding the coastal passes that could so easily be defended by a handful of men. Once in Thessaly, he'd been greeted as a hero and joined by contingents of volunteers from the cities of the Boeotian plain. He welcomed the fresh troops. They had their own scores to settle with Thebes, he knew, but legitimized his mission under the guise of the Corinthian League.

Even better, Athens had still not committed troops and would certainly now wait to see how Thebes fared. He would not have to face two enemies after all.

He reined in Bucephalus and returned to his pavilion, erected for safety within the walls of the Sacred Enclosure of Iolaus. He took a moment to enter the heroon, its hero's hall, and reflect in front of the painted statue of the legendary champion, once the charioteer to Hercules himself. It was here, he'd been told, that the lovers of the Sacred Band pledged their vows to each other. Marsyas found him there.

"You wanted to see me, sir?"

Alexander nodded. "If the Thebans agree to open their gates, I will march away without entering. They will be restored to the league with full privileges."

"And you want me to tell them?" Marsyas smiled. "Only if I can have a herald's staff."

Alexander smiled in return. "I'm sure that can be arranged."

"Why the change of heart? Your temper's certainly cooled on the march."

Alexander shrugged. "Maybe, and maybe I've had time to think. The Thebans believed I was dead. In those circumstances, the Corinthian League was dissolved and they were justified in demanding their independence. Now they know they're in error, I'll give them the chance to renew their allegiance to the league and to me as their hegemon." He shrugged again. "Besides, the men are exhausted and I want to spare them more fighting if I can."

An hour later, Marsyas, equipped with herald's staff, was escorted through the gates of Thebes to address the Bouleterion. Reading from a scroll, he delivered Alexander's message, an invitation for the Thebans to lay down their arms and rejoin the league without fear of retribution. But no sooner had he returned than the gates opened and a troop of cavalry issued forward, charging down those Macedonian pickets posted closest to the walls.

Encouraged, the Thebans followed it up with a force of light infantry, and Alexander found himself barking orders for a counterattack as his own headquarters came under threat. His Thracian levies advanced, but the Thebans had no urge to tangle with Alexander's northern tribesmen and swiftly retreated behind their walls. The danger was over, but it had been a shock.

Alexander ordered a count of the scattering of Macedonian dead that lay around him, and swore at his men as the cheering from the Theban walls rang in his ears.

"If Thebes wants blood," he raged. "Thebes will have blood."

He called his officers to his tent that evening. He sat in his raised throne, a simple model of the Theban city laid out on a low table before him. The officers gathered around, crowding the diminutive figure. Alexander stood up.

"Tomorrow morning, the whole army will move around to face the Elektra Gate. There are two reasons for this, the first being that we'll then straddle the road to the south. If the Thebans are prepared to make a fight of it, then maybe they're expecting reinforcements from Athens after all. Let's make sure that if the Athenians do come, they have to battle their way through the mass of our army to reach the city." It was sound reasoning that produced a few nodding heads.

"It's the strongest point in their defenses, sir," queried Cleitus.

"Yes, and I said there are two reasons." A chuckle ran through the gathering and Alexander let it subside before continuing. "The second is for precisely the same reason they've made it their strongest point. The walls of the Cadmea merge with the outer wall alongside the Elektra gate, so that's where we're closest to our troops inside the citadel. We only have to reach the wall for them to let us in, and that must be the Theban's greatest fear. They've put a double stockade in front to block us, but now they have to defend those stockades. The Elektra Gate is the one place where they can't hide behind their walls and slaughter us as we try to scale them. They must come out and fight, and we outnumber them three to one."

The officers considered the logic. "They'll still be fighting from behind a defensive position, sir," said Philotas.

"Wooden palisades, nothing more. The men of the phalanx should be able to carry them without too much effort."

Satisfied, the men accepted their assignments for the attack. Coenus would lead his phalangites in an assault on the right flank, with Cleitus and Philotas commanding a second force of hypaspists and Boeotian levies on the left. Alexander retained control of the reserve.

At first light, he asked Aristander to lead the army in prayers for victory, and then marched them out of camp, making a show of circling the city to their new positions. It was late August, and the morning sun was already warm on their skin and baking under their armor. Alexander gambled on one last attempt to avoid the need for battle.

Marsyas again rode forward, lifting his herald's staff high to declare his status, the sun glinting on the looped prongs at its tip. He passed through the two lines of nervous Theban troops behind their stockades, his eyes taking in details to pass back to Alexander.

"People of Thebes," he shouted at the heads lining the walls. His voice floated back to the Macedonian ranks, faint, but distinct. "King Alexander, Hegemon of the League of Corinth, sends you his greetings. He understands how you've been misled by the falsehoods and rhetoric of those in the pay of the enemies of Greece and, as I told you yesterday, wishes nothing more than to see you restore your city to its rightful place within the league."

Alexander smiled as he heard the words. Marsyas couldn't stress the League of Corinth enough. Now the Thebans knew its hegemon was still alive, continued opposition was treason against the league they had sworn allegiance to.

"Your hegemon calls upon all who truly have the interests of their city at heart, to fling open the gates and hand over the ringleaders of this treachery. Only they need fear retribution from the league."

A few minutes wait, and then a voice called, "Come back in an hour, herald. The Bouleterion will debate the issue and deliver their answer then."

"Good work, herald," said Alexander as Marsyas rode up to him. "What of their defenses?"

"Dismounted cavalrymen with short lances man the first stockade, but hoplites in full armor are massed behind the second. Judging by their clothing, most of those on the walls are ageing citizens and slaves. They'll offer little resistance when the phalanx gets that far. They're well-armed though, and my guess is their weapons originate from the cache Demosthenes is rumored to have supplied to the city."

Alexander grimaced. "And which he bought with Persian gold," he commented.

He cursed the delay. With every minute, the rising temperatures were taking a toll on his men. Ptolemy placated him with the observation that it would be having the same effect on the Theban hoplites.

But, in the event, it took much less than an hour. An anti-Macedonian faction had returned from exile to instigate the rebellion, and they dominated the Theban Bouleterion. They could expect little mercy from Alexander, and knew their best chance lay in resistance and the slim hope of victory. There was talk, after all, that a column of troops was hurrying to their relief from the city of Arcadia.

A figure appeared above the gate, clutching a herald's staff. "Men of Macedonia," he yelled. "Come and join the people of Thebes in overthrowing this tyrant who seeks to choke all Greece in his grasp. We'll fling open the gates so you can deliver up the criminal in your midst."

It was a mimic of Marsyas' speech, designed to infuriate Alexander, and it did. He rode to the front of the Macedonian line, his cheeks a bright red and his lips snarling curses at the Theban walls.

The Macedonian siege engines opened the assault, battering the wooden stakes of the stockade. A few breaches appeared here and there, but the Thebans were quick to plug the gaps, using the very boulders the Macedonians were firing at them. Alexander lost patience and ordered the assault.

A trumpet blared a double note, and the massed ranks of the phalanx leveled their spears and stepped forward as one. Their roar, "Alalalalai!" was matched by the Theban battle cry. They were going to make a fight of it.

The men of Macedonia broke into a trot, and then a charge that smashed against the first stockade. It had borne the brunt of the artillery barrage and buckled under the onslaught. The Theban cavalrymen put up a fierce fight but were soon overwhelmed by the numbers of phalangites pouring through the gaps. They fell back toward the second line, the Macedonian charge running down most. The phalanx slammed into the second stockade, but it had suffered less punishment and the hoplites on the other side were armed with pikes of their own.

Alexander watched the attack falter. The rear ranks were brought to a standstill while those in front were crushed by the weight of those behind. The stockade wall and the determination of the Theban hoplites negated the power of the sarissa.

The heat inside the phalanx rose steadily. Men groaned and fought for breath as sweat stung their eyes and ran down their bodies in rivulets. Some died silently, others calling for parents and lovers. Many remained standing as though performing their duty even in death, the crush of those around keeping their bodies upright. All the time, the Theban hoplites stood behind their stockade and chose their targets at will. A jab here, another there, seeking out exposed faces and gaps in armor.

Alexander did the only thing he could and pulled back the rearmost ranks to allow those in front to withdraw. He ordered a second wave to advance in their place, hoping the lighter armored and more nimble levies that made up the bulk of his reserve troops would have more luck against the stockade.

"Do you see that, sir?" Ptolemy pointed toward the walls. "Just to the right of the Elektra Gate is a postern, and it's open."

Alexander followed the extended finger, and Ptolemy was right. The Thebans were using a small postern gate to communicate with the men on the stockade and to ferry wounded back into the city. A wicker palisade and a dozen spearmen provided an outer defense, but the gate was being left open when not in use. Alexander immediately saw an opportunity to break the stalemate at the stockade.

"Perdiccas, ready your lochos to charge that postern gate, but circle around first so you take them by surprise. That's important, as they must not have time to shut it before you get there. Seize the gate and get your men inside, and then line them up along the walls." He held Perdiccas by the shoulder and stared into his face. "I don't want you to enter the city, just to have your men hold that stretch of wall and raise a Macedonian cheer." He made him nod his understanding before he let go of the shoulder.

A few minutes later, Perdiccas led his company of five hundred phalangites out of the ranks of the reserve. They disappeared around the corner of the wall as though on some new assault against the eastern gate. Alexander breathed a prayer for their success. The carnage at the stockade was continuing, the levies from Boeotia having no more success than the phalangites. If Perdiccas failed, nothing was going to shift the Thebans from their entrenched position.

Philotas galloped over from his post on the left wing. "The Thebans are breaking out," he shouted, his face panicked. "We pushed them from the stockade and into a sunken road, and then they turned and began fighting like cornered boars. The archers are gone and the Phokian levies are giving way. Sir, you must reinforce the left!"

Alexander removed his helmet and rubbed an arm across his forehead. It came away sopping wet. "I can give you a lochos of hypaspists and all the levies from Plataea, but that's all. I'm saving the rest for a third assault." He looked toward the city in anger. "Where's Perdiccas?"

As he spoke, he caught sight of a running figure at the corner of the wall. It was Perdiccas. His phalangites followed, hugging the wall and losing men to spears and arrows from above.

"Go on, Perdiccas!" roared Alexander, his voice adopting its customary high pitch when excited. Perdiccas himself cut down two of the Thebans guarding the gate, and then fell to an arrow shot from the walls. Alexander gasped with shock, then groaned in dismay as he saw Theban spearmen surround the prostrate figure. Then his view was obstructed as the leading phalangites swarmed around the postern.

An anxious minute passed, and then a trumpeter blared the infantry's rally-on-me signal from above the postern, followed by a resounding "Alalalalai!" from a hundred throats. They had forced the gate.

The sound of a Macedonian war cry on the city walls alerted the Theban hoplites to the enemy in their rear. Their defense crumbled almost immediately. Assuming the enemy must have broken through elsewhere, they deserted the stockade and surged toward the Elektra Gate. Their concern now was to get back inside the city as fast as they could, while the old men assigned to guarding the gate were panicked into opening it to let their fellow citizens in.

Several thousand hoplites squeezed through the gate at what became a shuffling pace, and those who noticed there was a grinning Macedonian pressed up next to them could do little more than shout an unheeded alarm. Hundreds of Alexander's troops were mingling with the retreating army and passing into the city unchallenged.

A commotion broke out beside one of the two towers that guarded the entrance; it must now be in Macedonian hands. In the center, Cleitus' men were scaling the section of wall that abutted the Cadmea, helped up by ropes thrown over by the besieged garrison. The sound of fighting could be heard from within the city.

Alexander reached the postern gate to find a prostrate Perdiccas surrounded by a gaggle of his men. The shaft of an arrow protruded from his neck and blood stained his tunic from a spear thrust to the groin. There was a further gash on his forearm and another above the knee. A sergeant was attempting to pull out the arrow while others constructed a stretcher from the wooden palisade.

"Leave the arrow in his neck," shouted Alexander as he leapt from Bucephalus and knelt by his friend. "If you snap it, we'll never get the tip out." Perdiccas was unconscious and the lifting of an eyelid confirmed he was near death. Alexander tore strips from the clothing of a dead Theban and applied tourniquets to the wounds on the limbs, and then instructed a phalangite to press a wad of cloth to the groin wound.

"Take him to my physician," he told the men. "He will save him if anyone can." He had retained the services of Philip of Acarnania, his father's doctor.

Perdiccas' men gingerly lifted him onto the makeshift stretcher and set off toward the camp, a small group of horsemen standing aside to let them pass. They wore the yellow cloaks of the Companion cavalry.

"May Athena watch over him," murmured Hephaestion, as the former members of the Pig-Stickers stood in salute to another fallen comrade.

Alexander entered Thebes through the postern gate and climbed a stairway onto the wall. A pall of smoke hung over the city and the screams of women mingled with the clashing steel of warfare. His gaze settled on the huge mound of Amphion hill, where Theban hoplites were making a last desperate stand atop an ancient tumulus rumored to contain the bones of their legendary king. They were dying by the hundred.

"I shall make my headquarters in the agora," Alexander announced grimly.

Such was the crush of men in the narrow streets, it took him nearly an hour to reach the open space that was the Theban marketplace. He assembled his senior officers for reports.

"The city is ours, sir," Philotas told him. "Some enemy cavalry managed to escape through a north gate, but otherwise the defenders are either slain on the Amphion or captive. No further fighting is being reported from anywhere within the city."

Even as he spoke, the officers pricked their ears at the sounds around them. They glanced at each other uneasily; Alexander caught the looks.

"Let the men celebrate their victory a while longer," he said. "I want Thebes to learn the consequences of treason."

"This is a Greek city, sir," reminded Cleitus.

"I haven't forgotten that, and this lesson is for the rest of Greece as much as for Thebes."

The officers were silent at that, and careful not to look around them as their victorious army ran rampage through the city. Not a Theban was safe. Fathers were put to the sword, mothers raped, their sons and daughters violated. Those who sought sanctuary in the temples were dragged out and slaughtered on the steps. The city burned from end to end.

A troop of soldiers pushed their way through the throng of booty-laden phalangites gathering in the agora. The men were Thracian peltasts, dragging a Theban woman by the wrist. A bodyguard stopped them at the edge of the group around Alexander and asked their business. They demanded to see the king.

The officers parted in front of Alexander and he surveyed the scene. The woman's dress was torn and she had a black eye, but he could tell she was an aristocrat from her clothing and demeanor, even with a Thracian arm clamped around her neck. He indicated to the infantryman to let her go and the woman buckled for a moment, then recovered herself and rose back up. She stared Alexander in the face, a look of disdain on her lips.

"She murdered our captain, sir," the Thracian sergeant said. "The men would have killed her outright, but she says she's from a noble family so I told them we should get your permission first. We killed everyone else in the house though." He grinned and added, "Even her dogs."

"What's your name?" Alexander asked the woman.

She pulled her shoulders back and announced, "My name is Timoclea. I am of noble birth and marriage, and sister of the famed Theagenes, who fell leading the Sacred Band on the field of Chaeronea. And what is your name, sir?"

Alexander smiled, despite the gravity of the moment. He knew when he faced true nobility. "So, what happened?" he asked, looking at the Thracian sergeant.

"The captain knew she must have treasure somewhere, sir, and she told him she'd hidden it in a well in the garden. We realized he was missing a while later, and one of the men discovered his body at the bottom of the well. He was under a pile of rocks, sir. She must have pushed him in and thrown them down on top of him."

"Where were you while she was doing all this?"

"It was a big house, sir, and full of females." The Thracian grinned again. "We were busy, but the captain had already finished with her. He always was more interested in gold."

Alexander turned back to Timoclea. "What do you say, madam?"

She smiled haughtily. "That barbarian will rape no more Greek women."

A smell of charred flesh wrinkled Alexander's nostrils and the sound of a wailing child could be heard from one of the body-strewn alleyways. It was time to stop the killing.

"She is free to go," he said to the sergeant. "She's under my protection and is not to be harmed." He smiled at the look of dismay on the Thracian faces. "She was only defending her home, after all," he added by way of explanation. "Your captain should have been more careful."

He addressed the officers. "Get your men under control and encamped back outside the walls. They may keep whatever booty they already have on them, but there's to be no more killing or looting. Philotas, I want guards placed to ensure it. Put them on the gates, at the temples, and outside the homes of all Theban men of note."

It took the rest of the day to subdue the rampage. The Macedonian and northern troops, content with their treasure, readily obeyed the order to return to camp, but Alexander's local allies had generations of scores to settle with their neighbor. The guards were needed, as bands of Boeotian peltasts continued to roam the narrow streets in search of Theban blood.

Alexander retired to his tent within the Enclosure of Iolaus, but soon knew that sleep would come to him even slower than normal that night. He rose and entered the heroon, telling the two duty bodyguards to wait on the portico outside. He needed to be alone awhile. The white eyes of the statue of Iolaus stared at him in the darkness.

A sound made him start; it was Hephaestion.

"I woke up and found you gone. What troubles you?"

Alexander gave a slight laugh. "King Cadmus founded Thebes a thousand years before Achilles sailed for Troy. It's the birthplace of Dionysus, the city of Oedipus, of Zethus and Amphion, of

Hercules and Iolaus. It has spawned Pindar, and countless other poets and actors and philosophers. And tomorrow I intend to destroy it. Amphion played his golden lyre here and the walls built themselves, and tomorrow I will tear those walls down. And you ask what troubles me?"

Hephaestion shrugged. "Do you have to? You were generous enough in Thrace and Illyria, so why not now? These are Greeks, after all."

Alexander spun around. "And that's why I must destroy them. I'm about to take my army to Anatolia, but I dare not as long as there's even a spark of defiance in Greece. A revolt by the northern tribes would likely amount to nothing more than a few skirmishes along the border, but the southern cities could sweep Macedonia away. I must make an example of Thebes to cow the rest."

"You'll be hated for it." Hephaestion leaned against the wall of the heroon with his arms folded, discussing the fate of a city as though it were the topic for debate in the schoolroom at Mieza. "It's a bad king who rules through fear. Aristotle told you that."

Alexander made that hollow laugh again. "And he taught me well. Which is why I won't be blamed for Thebes' destruction, but merely for carrying out the orders of the Greek people." He couldn't see Hephaestion arch his eyebrows in the darkness.

"How so?"

"Thebes is not only guilty of treason against me as their hegemon, but of breaking the common peace of the League of Corinth. Therefore, I have called for a meeting of the league to debate their punishment and scheduled it for first light tomorrow morning. So, who will attend?"

Hephaestion shook his head. "Nobody will. You have to give them time to get here first."

"You're wrong, Hephaestion. There will be delegates tomorrow morning. They're already here, in fact, as part of my army. The commanders of the Boeotian contingents are all members of the governing councils of their cities and, as such, are legally able to represent them at a meeting of the league."

Hephaestion snorted. "But the Boeotians hate Thebes." The realization of what Alexander was planning finally dawned on him. "You sly bastard. They're going to order the destruction of Thebes for you."

Alexander smiled in the darkness. "And it will be my duty as hegemon to carry out the orders of the league."

"Well, make sacrifice to Dionysus, then. It's his city you're leveling."

"I know that only too well, Hephaestion." Alexander walked over to touch his companion on the arm and lead him out into the moonlight. "And you wondered why I couldn't sleep?"

Dawn came at last, and Alexander re-entered the city. Buildings still burned and the slain lay where they had been butchered. The stench of death made him feel dirty. Groups of Thebans moved through the streets collecting bodies for disposal, civilians for cremation on a huge funeral pyre in the agora, soldiers in a military grave being prepared outside the Elektra Gate. Six thousand had died, and thirty thousand more awaited their fate within the walls of a city that had become their prison.

Alexander convened the meeting in the Great Hall within the Cadmea. The room was full but the three invited Thebans sat alone. Their leader stood up to plead for mercy for his city, and was ignored. Then it was the turn of the Boeotians.

One after the other, they launched into a tirade of accusations against the city that had dominated the Boeotian plain for generations. Wasn't it true that Thebes had betrayed Greece and fought for the Persians in the time of Xerxes? Hadn't they inflicted massacres of their own on the Orchomenians and Thespians? Hadn't they left Plataea in ruins?

Alexander listened in silence. He knew one sign from him would be enough to turn the direction of the delegate's speeches, but he said nothing. His continued silence was taken for what it was, an indication that the Boeotians were free to inflict their revenge. The vote could have only one result: Thebes was to be leveled and its people sold into slavery.

He waited for the cheering and catcalls to subside before standing. When he did rise, his face was grim.

"Gentlemen, I am your hegemon. My duty is to carry out all and any orders passed down by the league. It can be a difficult responsibility at times, and this is such a time. It is with a heavy heart that I accept my duty." He sighed for effect.

"As instructed by the league, I swear to oversee the leveling of the city of Thebes and the bondage of its people. I propose that monies raised from the sale should be used to pay the costs, with any surplus going to Macedonia in recompense for expenses incurred defending the league. In addition, I declare that the Boeotian League should be dissolved, and Theban lands be shared between the former members of that league."

The hall erupted in applause at the demise of the hated league. The Boeotian League had been a Theban invention, created for the same reasons that Philip had created the League of Corinth, and used in the same way. The delegates tactfully failed to notice any similarity.

Now that Alexander had achieved his aims, he could be magnanimous. "I have some requests to make of you, the representatives of the Corinthian League. In deference to the gods, I suggest that all priests be exempted and temples spared. It is also my wish that dispensation be granted to anyone who has shown friendship to Macedonia in the past, or who can prove they attempted to dissuade their fellow citizens from revolt." He smiled. "Also, the home of the poet Pindar is not to be razed."

There being no objections, the meeting was adjourned. Alexander watched the dejected faces of the three Thebans and imagined their thoughts as they filed out of the hall and into slavery. His classical education cried out against the destruction of a city with such a heritage, but it had to be done. The calamity he was inflicting on the Thebans would ensure the rest of Greece kept thoughts of revolt to itself.

The leveling of Thebes took the best part of a month and the sale of the slaves even longer. Traders flocked to the city and auctions took place twice daily, swelling the coffers of Alexander's treasury with badly needed talents. And it seemed that not only the Boeotians took delight in owning a highborn Theban, for prices remained high despite the glut of slaves on the market.

Slave traders weren't the only visitors to the Macedonian camp. In a repeat of the charade on the banks of the Danube, emissaries arrived daily from all corners of Greece, each congratulating Alexander on his victory and offering a gold crown or citizenship of their city.

Alexander accepted them all but demanded more of Athens. They had been the instigators of the rebellion in the first place, had failed to support their ally, and now he found their effusive plaudits at the destruction he had meted out particularly irritating. He demanded that the city surrender Demosthenes and several more of the ringleaders.

But Demosthenes and his cronies controlled the Assembly and were not about to deliver themselves up to hemlock or crucifixion. They had the measure of Alexander now and surmised he needed Athenian goodwill (and their fleet) more than he wanted a few heads. Remembering how Demades had accompanied Alexander to Athens after Chaeronea, they bribed the orator to go to him and plead for clemency. The wily old fox took their gold and headed for Thebes, and then spent a productive hour drinking wine in the king's tent. The discussion was frank and open, as should be when acquaintances meet to discuss business.

"Let me put it this way, sir," concluded Demades, reaching for more wine. "We both know you won't besiege Athens for the sake of revenge on Demosthenes, and we both know the need for King Alexander to be seen in a favorable light by the Athenians. Need I say more?"

Demades returned to Athens with pardons for the conspirators, and a fat fee from Alexander to be his eyes in the city.

And then the deed was done and the garrison in the Cadmea looked out over a wasteland of rubble and foundation stones. It was finally time to return to Pella and prepare for the coming crusade.

It was a triumphant return to Macedonia, though Alexander had to suffer a bout of ranting from his mother for destroying the home city of Dionysus. He placated both her and, he hoped, the god by promising he would grant special privileges to Thebans he met in future. Dionysus forgave him only after he'd sworn an oath to that effect over the blood of a freshly slaughtered snake, in front of Olympias' private shrine to her patron god. Having a priestess as a mother sometimes had its advantages.

Not only that, he was flush with the gold raised through the sale of the slaves. The debts he had inherited from his father, and added to during the loss-making campaign in the north, had been paid off with a tidy profit remaining. Prudent was what he paid his treasury secretary to be, so he joined his army at their winter quarters in Dium and presided over the Festival of the Muses.

Legend had it that here, on the plain before Mount Olympus, the nine goddesses of the arts and sciences had chosen to make their home. And here they were celebrated in turn, one per day for nine days.

Alexander turned it into a celebration of his victories and a thank you to his men, and the festivities were lavish. Wine flowed freely and sacrificial animals were distributed to the troops, and a huge drinking pavilion with room for a hundred couches was hired and erected on high ground to the north of the marshes that covered the region.

On the second day, Alexander sacrificed at the nearby sanctuary of Zeus Olympus, and then led his entourage through the marsh to take their places on the slope that overlooked the theater. The performance was in honor of Clio, the muse of heroic poetry, and they all sported her attribute of a parchment scroll on the terracotta trinkets they bought daily from the many peddlers.

With such a guest in the audience, the performers could not but include extracts from the Iliad, and Alexander felt his eyes moisten as the orators recounted the death of Patroclus.

A buzz of conversation in the crowd snapped him from his reverie. "See what that is," he snapped at a bodyguard, annoyed at the interruption. It was a few minutes before the man returned, but by then the audience was a sea of craning heads, all staring at the royal enclosure.

"They say the statue of Orpheus is sweating, sir," said the bodyguard. "It started not long after we, you, stopped to look at it during the hunt yesterday."

Now Alexander understood the reason for the crowd's attention and turned to Aristander for an explanation. The priest sat open-mouthed. So close to the crusade, such a phenomenon must surely be a bad omen.

His face suddenly brightened. "Of course the statue is sweating, sir. As the bards of his time struggled to compose tributes worthy of his music, so bards today will struggle when composing tributes worthy of your accomplishments." The priest rose to his feet to emphasize the point. "The spirit of Orpheus must have taken one look as you passed his statue, and felt pity for those who will write epic verses of your exploits. He was sweating in sympathy for the sweat that will flow from their brows. Don't forget, sir," he added with a flourish, "that Orpheus was also a poet and knows better than most what tribulations they face."

Alexander pondered the answer for a moment, and it made sense. "Go down to the stage and announce that to the audience, Aristander. I don't want them to worry unduly."

Had he been there, Aristotle might have offered a more scientific explanation; that condensing moisture caused the appearance of sweating on the sculpture, and was a relatively common occurrence in statues made from Cypress wood.

The talents raised from the sale of the Theban slaves were quickly evaporating, but Alexander put it from his mind. Perdiccas had arrived from Pella, the rapid recovery from his wounds an added cause for celebration. Alexander gave him a tour of the new pavilion, and was so impressed with it himself that he determined to buy it for the coming campaign.

"After all," he said, placating the secretary of the treasury. "I'll be expected to entertain the citizens of the colonies as I liberate them."

The festival dragged on for another week, but Alexander's treasury was empty long before that. Nevertheless, he returned to Pella satisfied. His men were content for now and the promise of Persian plunder would silence their gripes when they realized he could no longer afford to pay them. He knew though, that he couldn't wait any longer. Either he launched the invasion soon or cut costs by disbanding his army.

And with Greece finally secure and the winter lull upon them, the time for invasion was right. Parmenion was recalled to Pella for a series of planning meetings, but the news he brought from Anatolia was not promising.

"It seems this new Persian king is more capable than his predecessors," said Parmenion, gazing at the scene painted on his drinking cup. "He's alert to the danger you pose and is reinforcing the armies of all his loyal satraps in the Troad. We also have proof that his gold armed the rebels in Thebes." He looked up. "Why didn't you kill Demosthenes when you had the chance?"

"I also wondered that," added Antipatros. He and Parmenion were alone with Alexander in his study; this was a meeting of only the most senior of his generals.

"It was expedient to leave Demosthenes where he was," answered Alexander uncomfortably. With hindsight, he now questioned his own judgment on that matter and changed the subject quickly. "What of the landing site?"

"The coastal strip earmarked for the landing is still secure, but you must cross in strength because Memnon will attack as soon as he knows you've landed. Your head is worth money to him and I think that may be the only reason he hasn't attempted to destroy us already. He's waiting for you to arrive."

"Then the landing site is hardly what I'd call secure."

Parmenion looked annoyed. "Don't forget, sir, that my army has been in the field for nearly two years now. Many units are badly below strength and the men are jaded. They're ready to come home, not embark on a new campaign."

Alexander took the point. "Very well, we should cross as soon as possible to relieve them."

"Not in winter, sir," said Antipatros. "One bad storm and our transport ships will be lost. And your men need a rest as much as Parmenion's. They've been campaigning since the spring."

"I am aware of that," snapped Alexander. He, too, was getting annoyed—at their patronizing attitude. "I would remind you, gentlemen, that I do have some experience in commanding troops." The two generals said nothing.

"They won't be expecting us in the winter," Alexander persisted, "so the earlier we cross the greater the surprise. We'll go as soon as the weather is stable enough to give us a few clear days to get across the Hellespont. That's still a few weeks away yet, so the men will have their rest." He spoke with an air of finality.

"Yes, that sounds to be a good plan," Parmenion said grudgingly. He had no wish to make an enemy of the young king.

"Crossing earlier will also increase the chance of bad weather afterwards," added Antipatros. "That will prevent their fleet from interfering with our supply ships. It's a good plan." He'd been around Alexander longer.

"Good," said Alexander and began to rise. "Is there anything else?"

"Erm, there is one matter that needs to be addressed." Parmenion spluttered as he spoke; he'd been caught out by the sudden end to the meeting and had a mouthful of wine.

"And what is that?" Alexander sat back down.

"You don't yet have an heir and you can't leave the kingdom without one. What if you were to fall in this campaign?"

"Parmenion is right, sir. You must have an heir."

Alexander stared at the two men. "It may have escaped your notice, gentlemen, but I'm unmarried."

"Then get married, sir." Parmenion's voice had a note of urgency. "It really doesn't matter who, just as long as you do."

"And impregnate her with a son, of course," added Antipatros.

He'd been expecting this for some time and still it took Alexander by surprise. He knew they were right and he would have to produce an heir eventually, but the mechanics of it were not something he relished. He also had the feeling the two generals were coercing him for their own ends. They both had eligible daughters and whoever became his father-in-law would be in a very powerful position indeed. He wouldn't put it past them to have discussed this beforehand.

"I haven't come this far to sit at home celebrating a marriage and awaiting the birth of an heir." Alexander leaned forward to impress the point he was making. "How old need an heir be before it's safe to leave him in the hands of others? What if the first child is a girl? It could take years before I'm able to launch this invasion. My father kept delaying and I refuse to do the same. Do you realize I've been King for over a year already?"

Antipatros opened his mouth as if to say something, then thought better of it.

"No, gentlemen." Alexander stood up again, and this time headed for the door. "I appreciate your concern, but I've been charged by the Corinthian League to recover the colonies and that's what I'm going to do. There'll be time for raising heirs when I return from Anatolia."

Alexander would not return, and his reluctance to produce an heir would see his empire die with him.

His last weeks in Macedonia passed uneventfully, save for the arrest and disposal of the last of Attalus' relatives on spurious charges. There would be no coup while he was away.

And then the candles burned late in the planning room as the details took shape, and the noblemen of Macedonia eagerly awaited their assignments. Many were to be disappointed.

Alexander announced he would be leaving Antipatros behind as regent, which was not unexpected as the general was now advancing in years. The surprise was that a full half of the army would also remain behind, and those who found themselves relegated to garrisoning the homeland sneered at this display of Alexander's faith in his supposed allies, but never in his presence.

The situation was more precarious than they knew. Out of an expeditionary force of thirty thousand men, less than a third would be coming from outside Macedonia, while reports from the south spoke of shiploads of disgruntled young men booking passage to Anatolia; Memnon would soon have whole regiments of Greek mercenaries under his command. The image of Alexander leading a Hellenic crusade against the barbarian was looking increasingly suspect. It was rapidly turning into a Macedonian treasure hunt.

The nobles assembled in the Great Hall of the palace. They'd been called at Alexander's orders and the rumor was strong he'd be announcing the date of their departure. The hall hummed with excited chatter, though a few asked why the king had bothered to summon officers who would be staying behind, and where were the commanders of the foreign contingents?

Alexander entered through the door behind the throne. The secretary of the treasury accompanied him, and Harpalus and three scribes followed with bundles of clay tablets. The presence of the civil servants prompted a murmur of disappointment. Maybe this wasn't a military meeting after all.

Alexander sat and hushed his audience. "Gentlemen, let me explain the reason for this gathering." He looked around the hall, uncomfortable at what he was about to say.

"As most of you know, my father left me many debts. It's been a struggle to pay them." He could see the expressions on their faces changing. "But it's done! My father's debts have been cleared." Faces were blank.

"However." An audible groan rose from the rear of the hall. "War is an expensive business and keeping a standing army a continual drain on the economy. Both are an extravagance Macedonia cannot afford, even with the gold from Mount Pangaeus. Happily, gentlemen, there is gold aplenty waiting for us in the Troad. Persian gold, compliments of the Great King."

Now he had them completely confused; was he after their money or not?

Alexander turned to look at the secretary of the treasury. The man stepped forward. "I have informed the King that the treasury is empty. We cannot pay the troops." He stepped back, his part played.

"Do you see my problem, gentlemen? The gold is there, enough for all of us, but we can't get to it unless I can first pay my troops and provide them with the supplies they need. The treasury, however, has come up with an answer."

There was a general murmuring coming from the men in the hall. So much so, that Parmenion stepped up onto the dais and raised his arms to quiet the crowd.

"Thank you, Parmenion. Now I may not have coins in the treasury, but what I do have is property. There are the buildings around the agora and two gymnasiums in Pella alone, not to mention this palace itself. Then there's land; the wheat fields outside Methone, for instance. I am, it seems, quite wealthy." He smiled at the treasurer, who bowed his head in assent.

"So I have drawn up a list. All of you are on that list and will receive a deed of land or property, or maybe it will be shares in a concession. They are my gift to you, gentlemen, and I ask for nothing in return, other than you demonstrate your loyalty to your country and your faith in the cause on which we are about to embark." He fell silent and gazed at some point above their heads.

Harpalus shuffled forward on cue; the assistant treasurer. He began to recite the names written on the first of the clay tablets. One after the other, the nobility of Macedonia were ceded crown property; a villa to a rich baron, a herd of goats to a lowly second son, an orchard here, twenty slaves there, a farm, a franchise. And it went on, and all those present knew these were not gifts. The king was selling his assets to raise the ready cash needed to take the army to Anatolia.

And the gesture was not lost on them. Voices shouted out the amounts, fifty drachmas, a hundred, make that gold coins. They vied with each other as the scribes scribbled their pledges down and the king smiled serenely.

"But, sir, you're giving everything away. What are you keeping for yourself?" It was Perdiccas, pushing his way through the crowd to stand in front of the dais, still limping from his wounds.

Alexander blinked as though woken from a dream. "Myself? What am I keeping for myself?" He said nothing more for a moment and then replied, "My hopes, Perdiccas. They are what I'm keeping for myself."

Perdiccas stepped up onto the dais. "I need no bribe to share in that, sir. I shall give you all I have to fund this expedition and ask for nothing in return, other than the chance to follow you." He looked out across the hall and raised his voice for the benefit of those at the back. "To the ends of the earth, if that is where you take me."

His speech inspired the rest and they fell over themselves to give back their gifts, pledging even larger donations as they did so. Alexander had his war chest.

He stood up. "Gentlemen, Perdiccas said he would follow me to the ends of the earth." He smiled a moment. "Well, I don't ask for that, at least, not yet." It produced a laugh. "But I do ask that you follow me to the Hellespont and join me in the crusade to liberate our countrymen from the Persian yoke." A cheer greeted those words and grins were on every face.

"But when?" shouted a voice from their midst.

"When? I will tell you when. Return to your homes and tell your butlers to prepare your farewell symposiums. We march against Persia in ten days."

The hall erupted. Men stamped their feet or beat the hilts of their swords against the walls, anything to make a rhythmic noise.

And then the cheering turned into a chant, "Alexander! Alexander! Alexander!"

One man watched silently from his place in the crowd. With his king framed in the beam of light shining through the highest windows, Hephaestion could finally see the resemblance he'd heard others speak of. Alexander, with his mane of fair hair, bulging forehead and white-toothed grin, truly looked like the lions that prowled the mountains of the interior. He was a lion, a lion of Macedonia.

The end